Burn Slowly

by Fabio Casto

translated into English by Sarah Jane Webb

Copyright © 2013 Fabio Casto

All rights reserved

ISBN-13: 978-1502987662

PROLOGUE

Lusaka. Zambia. Remote suburbs. The sort of place that makes one long for air-conditioning.

The sheet metal of the interior appeared as precariously assembled as a house of cards, and resembled anything other than a medium-sized business enterprise. Apart from the orderly desk (with very little to keep in order), an old zinc-plated filing cabinet and, piled on the floor, cardboard boxes held together with adhesive tape (and barely containing the mass of papers), it could have been a prison cell. The neon tube, hanging low from the ceiling and pervading the room with a bluish light, probably came from someone's aquarium, though how it ever got there was not worth pursuing. Even Christ, whose crucifix was secured to the wall panel with wire (as if nails were insufficient) seemed to be sweating. Which was hardly surprising, given the fug of humid heat in there.

"Sign here, please," said Pac, handing over a contract with hard-cover binding, open at the last – blank – page.

The hand reaching across was pitch black: a skin colour only generated in that corner of central-southern Africa; the frizzy hair thinning on top, and the more abundant moustache on the face of Mr. Malembu, proprietor of

Tractors&Pulleys Inc., were somehow reassuring. Before stooping to sign, he shot Pac one last glance, seeking not so much a contractual but a personal go-ahead. Pac complied with the nod and half-smile he'd learned years ago while studying for his Master's degree in Business Administration. Only then was Malembu able to take the pen proffered and put an end to his agonising indecision. Grasping it tightly, he proceeded with a laborious circular movement – not something he'd done frequently in his life; and possibly, only with supervision. Then he looked up, his black eyes meeting the watchful chestnut-brown gaze of the man opposite him, who sat counting the seconds separating him from his release.

His mission completed, the contract replaced in his crocodile briefcase, Pac, with genuine satisfaction, shook the man's rough and calloused hand; a hand immediately joined by its twin, enfolding his own in a vice-like grip, while pumping it up and down for what felt like an eternity.

"I can't find words to express my joy and that of my employees." The deep voice resonated like a saxophone. "Please accept my invitation to lunch, I would be honoured. This loan deserves a toast!"

His smile revealed perfect white teeth which barely competed with the sparkle in his eyes. "Honestly, thank you. You've no idea how important this loan is for all of us."

Pac tried unsuccessfully to return the smile, secretly

disturbed by all that enthusiasm. He was obliged to put up with this for a while longer – the time established for the usual courtesies of the occasion – far too long for his liking.

Although virtually suffocating from the heat and humidity, he politely waited for Malembu to make the first move towards opening that tin can of an office.

The man stood up, noisily pushing back his chair, and said "I was so lucky to come across your company." Then, bowing slightly, he accompanied Pac to the 'door': a thin sheet of metal which opened with a juddering sound like the death rattle of a zebra savaged by lions.

The light outside was dazzling, and Pac shaded his eyes while adapting to its intensity. At last he could fill his lungs with clean air.

He made his apologies to Malembu. "I'm sorry not to be able to accept your invitation, believe me, but there's a car waiting for me." After another, hurried handshake he walked off at a fast pace towards the gate, without looking back. Loosening his tie and undoing the top two buttons of his shirt he suddenly realised he'd sweated even more than he'd thought. Rivulets of sweat were coursing down his legs and into his socks which – either because no longer able to absorb a single drop, or through the pressure of his walking – released moisture into his loafers as he squelched away from the building.

The ceaseless noise from the works – cutters, drills,

hammers – and the stench of grease and solder diminished as he made his way towards the gate of the compound.

A hired car, an old Mercedes, awaited him outside the entrance. The driver started up the engine, and within minutes Pac was leaving it all behind.

He slumped into the back seat with a sigh, waiting for his heartbeat to return to normal, well aware that this anxiety was not imputable to the heat alone: there was far more besides.

The driver reached out his hand to switch the radio on.

"Don't even think of it: leave it off," barked Pac.

The man eyed him in the rear-view mirror, muttering indistinctly.

What a relief to be finally delivered from both heat and noise.

In a few days' time, a bank manager would travel the few miles that separated him from that village to visit a certain gentleman (what the hell was his name?) for more signatures, shortly before the latter became aware of a sharp and inexplicable pain in his stomach, of increased salivation and a bitter taste in his mouth. But by then Pac would be safely flying home – his one source of comfort, as the car drove on, mile after mile, skirting round potholes in the scorching surface of the road.

If truth be told, there might be something else that could lighten his burden: something that would alleviate the burgeoning angst he felt within him. The remedy was there, within reach, in the belly of the totemic animal he carried with him, and whose skin he was now stroking – not the animal itself, of course, but an evocative symbol.

No, he mustn't: he had set himself some rules, and couldn't afford to break them at the slightest excuse. Although...

He opened his briefcase slowly, keeping his gaze fixed on the window whose view offered nothing sufficiently engaging to distract him from growing temptation: abandoned sheds; cars, stripped and burnt on the edge of the road; sparse and shrivelled vegetation – nothing animated this landscape, except for the odd van occasionally crossed along the way.

Was this The End, then? Or merely an impression induced by his mood?

Meanwhile, having lingered caressingly on the textured crocodile skin, his hand had slid furtively inside the briefcase, recognising the company tablet, documents, sheets of paper, pens, etc., then halting on a thin plastic wrapper, causing it to utter a subdued, almost startled rustle.

Grasped, slipped out, placed on his lap. "Don't be silly," – he told himself – "you can look at it now: just a peep." The small apricot turnover was the colour of ripe wheat, evoking memories of festive Sundays.

He absolutely *must not*.

One last look and he put it back, proud of his self-discipline, redirecting his attention to the couple of phone calls he should be making on his satellite phone.

"Could you open that damned window all the way? It's stifling in here!", he said to the driver, who nodded.

First he should call the office to communicate the successful outcome of the operation. Within an acceptable period of time, a certain small company that had done so much for the local economy – in terms of employment, progress, improved lifestyle – would be swamped in unsustainable debts deriving from the 'harmless' and much sought-after microloan generally relied on by everyone to boost their sales. One of the first side-effects would be an increase in the local trade of incense and votive candles, and the resorting to tribal witchcraft – but who cared, anyway.

Pac made the call, ticking the first item off his list.

Meanwhile the Mercedes was racing across seemingly unvarying landscape.

Next, he would call Samuel and order a pulse-Doppler navigation radar, a multi-function display, a laser telemeter, and some software currently in use in the aerospace and defence industries. Within four weeks the goods would be delivered to the usual Middle-Eastern address.

The deal would afford him additional funds and some time off, which he would use to focus on something that had obsessed mankind since the days of Icarus. What's more, he must hurry. For all he knew, The End was near –

nearer than expected.

Through the windscreen, the aircraft hangars of Lusaka International Airport loomed in the distance. An airplane was coming in to land. Once again he'd made it.

For how much longer could he resist?

"Well..." he thought, "as I've done such a good job, I deserve a treat." Leaning his head against the backrest, "Shit! To hell with it!", he muttered, grabbing the consolatory confection from his briefcase and tearing it from its wrapping so noisily that the driver glanced up at him through the rear-view mirror.

He could only see a stuffed mouth gobbling; a pair of eyes goofily half-closed; the head tilted back in a pose of gratified bliss. He speeded up, disgusted.

Oscar wore a chain round his neck. He lived in a cave – yes, really! – a remote, damp, rocky cavern in wind-swept heights in an area to the south of Lebanon's mountain range, near the Israeli border. From there, with suitable equipment and in the right sort of weather, you could see as far as Mount Megiddo, about 50 kilometres as the crow flies. The air up there was always fresh, the oxygen pure as though polished with some non-abrasive finishing product. To the imposing trunks, verdant treetops and lush shrubs; to the veins of the leaves; to the rocks emerging from the ground as if by a fairy's incantation – to whatever caught your eye, the brilliant sunlight reserved a balanced role of magnificence. A luminosity highlighting the texture of bark, smooth or grooved, which formed paths and highways for ants returning from their construction sites. A radiance that induced insects to stay under cover, keeping undetected their airborne communication and their gossip. It was just as well that these places be hidden from human eyes: the very thought made one's skin crawl!

But Oscar was a tolerated exception, having quietly adjusted over the years, blended in with the local idioms, and making no more noise than the other creatures. Perhaps even less, considering what he mainly did – or, rather, didn't do – inside that cave, day in, day out.

On taking his leave after one of his infrequent calls, his only visitor felt like Pac-Man after swallowing a flashing Power Pill: ready to maul ghosts to pieces, complete a level, and move on to the next one. Which is another reason for being renamed Pac: his rechristening, celebrated in stark and solemn solitude many years and lots of hair ago, was meaningful none the less – whatever some people may say, disparaging the term 'rechristening' as a useless neologism.

Studying the signs of the approaching End had caused Pac to identify intimately with the apocalyptic philosophy of the early Christians, who had roamed these parched regions two thousand years ago warning humanity that the game would soon be over, and urging it to change its evil ways while there was still time. Pac felt united to these early Christians by a shared sensitivity and by clear, unchallengeable vision – barring, in his case, the involvement of a Redeemer, or a messianic-astrological wait for any king-priest character.

Could a non-believer be apocalyptic? It would certainly be harder for a believer to be non-apocalyptic, he mused. He'd never given the matter serious consideration, however, having other priorities on his mind – or rather, a single, crude and vital priority. Because Pac was, above all, obsessively fond of his life, and certainly not in a hurry to die. Call it romanticism, if you like, or the habit of almost forty years, or selfishness, but he seriously loved his present existence. And nothing on Earth could induce him to part with it. Why should he? He'd had no part in sullying the admirable promises punctually paraded and acclaimed at election campaigns. Or at least he'd had nothing to do with the economic policies that had caused such havoc. Nor with policies of society, of alimentation, energy, environment, health or the military. He didn't belong to the Bilderberg Group, to the Trilateral, to the Council on Foreign Relations. He didn't possess a Central Bank, nor had he been consulted for the approval of pre-packaged economic booms and crises; he didn't even subscribe to any political movement. He didn't own newspapers or televisions to launch alarms, to air analyses, to influence the so-called masses; and possibly no-one would have listened anyway. So why should he die through no fault of his own? He'd never waged war on anyone, let alone his home planet. He was the result of millions of years of evolution made possible by the existence of the necessary preconditions – a biological line that had witnessed wars and famines and plagues. As had its progeny. Survival. Even if merely a matter of chance, it was nevertheless *his* chance, and therefore of existential relevance, to be defended – to be safeguarded at all costs. Having been engendered by centuries, millenniums of history, why should his current life be sacrificed through the fault of others? Why shouldn't he take action to save his own life, to perpetuate his bloodline, under improved and renewed conditions that he himself had planned?

It was certainly no mystery that the third millennium of the Gregorian calendar had initiated under the worst possible auspices. Turbo-capitalism and neo-liberal doctrines: the middle finger of the economy, that Pac contributed to market, swallowed up resources – natural, human and moral – transforming man into the automated moron that so much science fiction had depicted as a menace, albeit without the aid of robotic technology: the economy's stock character, an insane creature who identifies with his job, role, or absence thereof. With such unassailable pretexts as the economic crisis, the military-industrial complex, multinational companies, terrorism, and the media – and on the strength of intelligent propaganda –

the New World Order and its vassals were gleefully approaching the realisation of their objective: the dominion of the world – 'dominion' being intended in the broadest sense of the term.

After all, hadn't this been mankind's ultimate goal since the dawn of time? As a slave of the overlords who would be back sooner or later, he had always tried to emulate these gods, taking advantage of their absence to assume the role of master.

Now was the time to realise that traditional religions, especially those of biblical origin, had betrayed their mandate. Like so many lotteries, those same religions promised rich awards to those who – but for rare exceptions – could never hope to win anything in their life. The game was rigged: the rules, the price of tickets; the hand that drew the number out of the ballot box; the jury, the advertisements, and even the jackpot – they were all a hoax.

Institutions set up by man had failed. The quality of life hadn't changed: it had simply adapted to the times. Yet man's stupidity had remained unaltered.

Like a solitary string of pearls round the throat of our existence, the exceptions referred to above were introspective disciplines which – refuted by cutting-edge physics and biology – could not be deemed capable of acting on a wide scale, even less of managing to oppose ruling mainstream logics.

The signs were clear to Pac. Whether they were clear to others didn't matter at all.

He couldn't predict the exact hour or date: all he knew was that when the time was right – when it was too late to change the course of events – the righteous would inherit the Earth, provided they safely boarded a *vimana*, a flying machine placed in a geostationary orbit.

And he knew the time was terrifyingly near.

Launching a small spaceship powered by liquid propellant, however, was out of the question. It's not as if you could rent Cape Canaveral! In order to have lift-off, manoeuvre the vimana, get it to reach the speed of eight kilometres per second to enter a low orbit round the Earth, conclude re-entry operations and, above all, remain alive during each of these phases, what was needed was a powerful, accessible and inconspicuous propulsion system.

Clearly, if similar technology existed (and Pac strongly suspected it did), it wasn't available on the market; and the chances of stealing it were nil.

The more complex the matter, the less competent he felt, aero-spatial studies having about as much in common with his schooling as canon law did. The Internet was useful, of course, and so were his efforts at self-teaching and his sporadic gathering of expert advice; but something vital was always missing: no book from the vast collection lining his living-room walls, no manual, or well-worn specialised magazine – of the many scattered around the house – was able to fill the void. More than an unresolved question, this was *the question*, and not merely of a technical nature.

What the literature was unable to transmit was confidence, empirical experience, a guarantee that the banger wouldn't go off in his hand. His admission of ineptitude had, however, found comfort in the testimony of those who had studied the matter in great depth, had described and recorded it down to the finest detail.

If the future was out of bounds, and the present posed inexplicable bars on man's urge to observe the planet from afar, the past was all that was left. And this, it turned out, was the fissure through which one could snatch glimpses of an unofficial world, an ancient reality deliberately concealed and manipulated over the centuries, full of historical information surrounding myths, legends and cults which we had been taught to look upon as primitive animist beliefs, wild metaphorical interpretations of natural phenomena. After contributing generously to the profits of a well-known online book store, Pac had taken a few hesitant steps towards the theories of Paleoastronautics and its fascinating and plausible notions, which told of artefacts such as the Baghdad battery, dating back to the second century BC and capable of generating electricity; of the celestial maps of Mesopotamia, where the only astronomical observation instrument was the Ziggurat; or, again, of pre-Columbian finds identical in every way to what would now be called an airplane. These notions had thrilled him to the point that he was left dumbfounded, by revealing knowledge unheard of by academic ears, and anachronistic to uninitiated eyes; by imposing a new interpretation of ancient historical dynamics; and, above all, by suggesting a term which would soon become as insidious and seductive as a promise of carnal submission: vimana.

Vimana: A word that disinterred wonders encrusted with antiquity, that evoked deities of otherworldly powers, air battles and nuclear explosions; a word that provided humanity with the proof that it belonged to a cosmos vibrant with life and with brotherhood.

Doing business in micro-economics wasn't such a big deal: small beer, socioeconomic realities irrelevant in the eyes of most scholars, especially in the broader scheme of things. Nothing worth investigating, at least not on the surface.

For the Law of Chaos, and for those who had been concerned with applying its effects on economic systems, decades earlier – operating from headquarters that now paid him a fat salary and generous bonuses for goals achieved – each innovation in the economy-environment-society triangle created an even more insidious adaptogenic mutation than a large development model, inasmuch as it was more difficult to detect, easier to transfer and – mainly because of its veneer of presumed harmlessness – decidedly easy to reproduce.

This formed part of the conclusions reached by a team of pioneers, engineers and sociologists, hired all those years ago to analyse every possible form of human development – and its antidote. Not long after that, Pac's office had been set up. The economy's traditional hit men, engaged in promoting the Empire on a wide scale, in announcing the good news of globalisation to poor countries, submerging them in debt and enslaving them to reserved interests – using every antidemocratic and criminal means at their disposal – would now have to be flanked by a sizeable army of small-scale economy 'weed-killers', working topically, like disinfectants.

The difference between hit men and weed-killers lay wholly in the size of the target: the former was destined for national economic systems; the latter for single, well-defined realities. For instance, let's consider, on the one hand, a *coup d'état* in the Middle East, aiming at the removal of a representative of the people stubbornly committed to promoting social policies; or, again, the under-selling of a Latin-American oil field through a contract tailored to meet an oil company's demands. And, on the other hand, the subtle, relentless sinking of a family-run guesthouse in a tropical bay, or the takeover of an Indonesian carpenter's shop. The difference should be obvious enough.

Throughout the so-called Third World, enterprises as yet unexposed to sick, corrupt bureaucracy would be visited by the likes of Pac, alerted by an increasingly capillary network of informers and monitoring-analysing systems. We've all heard of ingenious inventions, simple and revolutionary, renewable and eco-friendly: good news, in fact. Finding these was the work of the boffins in certain departments at Central Office, connected to the databanks of patent offices.

The method worked when they succeeded in arresting the element heading the line – removing an innovative system, a small and seemingly insignificant initiative – before it spread and influenced developments, triggering a domino effect, toppling the other pieces in the same direction with the force of new questions and evolutions. An email, with a dossier attached, would cause people like Pac to come into action.

Weed-killer tools were as numerous as they were imaginative: insurance policies which, owing to incomprehensible clauses, turned out to be fraudulent and predatory; attractive financial contributions that effectively delivered the control of the business into the lender's munificent hands; false NGOs, offering their noxious support. Swindles, skilfully masked, and often given a legal veneer by banks and investment companies – and defended by obliging lawyers and judges, difficult to contrast effectively in the absence of adequate time and money.

Emerging countries posed fewer difficulties, and at the beginning of his career Pac pursued incentives as mosquitos do a pale, plump calf, heedless of the risk of transmitting a VHF. Somehow his objectives were always achieved, and determination distinguished Pac from the start: driven by devouring ambition, he worked hard, exploiting the prestige of a post-graduate Master's in Business Administration that he'd paid for himself. Having indoctrinated his conscience, and adjusted his ethics to the new parameters, it was just a matter of getting on with it; and having a good time – which he could afford – once operations were concluded.

But when signs of The End began to manifest themselves, his innermost biological instinct of survival surfaced, exposing questions previously submerged by other concerns. Something wasn't quite right: that beautiful world revealed festering stigmata that begged for first aid – and lamented, unheeded, the denial of sympathetic protection.

In a brief space of time, about as long as it took his mental pen to join together the dots of a neural network and reveal a pattern, Pac had radically rearranged the priorities on his agenda. Even management, though unaware of the actual reasons for the decline in his performance, had noticed his on-going inner turmoil; for lack of a better alternative they opted for a treatment consisting, quite simply, of isolation. On top of that already entailed by Pac's lifestyle.

Which is why, within an unusually short time after his previous mission, Pac now found himself on a flight heading for the sumptuous, shimmering mountains of Nepal.

There, Pac would be met by a shaggy bovine, bearing round its neck a gift (the desperately-needed solution for the Star Pac's antigravity issue); and by the brutally cold climate.

Signs of The End of Time?

A production system so integrated and interdependent as to be vulnerable: to the point that any isolated natural event, such as the eruption of a volcano, or social upheaval, such as a general strike, anywhere in the world, posed a serious threat to its survival: how much longer could it last?

The fact was that the entire concept of modernity had been shaped by a single matrix, based on assumptions such as the theoretical growth of the GDP, and a virtually unlimited availability of natural resources (idiotic delusions now clearly showing signs of collapse, and equally clearly lacking an emergency plan): wasn't this the preliminary step towards an imminent disaster? And what could happen next, if not an armed conflict?

Our civilisation had lost control of the meaning of words, and therefore of relative thoughts. We had lost our familiarity with the sky, with our contemplation of its blue infinity: so much so that a grid of chemtrails overhead provoked neither alarm nor curiosity; we still delegated representatives of astronomic allegories, calling them ministers; we let ourselves be influenced by fears, superstitions and antiquated traditions. Mankind had lost its moral capacity to be indignant about that which they hypocritically claimed to represent and protect: hospitality, human rights, brotherhood, respect for others, non-violence. We considered ourselves 'Developed' while, if Development upheld these principles, reality evinced the contrary. We accumulated instead of sharing; raced instead of strolling; despaired instead of smiling; a growing number of apparently normal people fell prey to fits of homicidal mania.

Our civilisation watched as the total control of our everyday lives was concentrated in the hands of a select few, determining even so-called Free Choice: from a civil uprising in an Eastern-European country, through our route around the aisles of a supermarket, to the harmful products cynically made available to content the uninformed consumer.

What could be the destiny of such a civilisation, how soon? And what else?

Against the eventuality of what catastrophic event were underground military bases around half the world – from the United States to Europe, from Australia to Western

China – stashing away food supplies and consumer staples? Why had a Noah's Ark for vegetables been built – a frozen Garden of Eden, a strong-room excavated in the permafrost of Spitsbergen Island, in the Norwegian archipelago of Svalbard, in the Sea of Barents – inside which millions of seeds of various plants originating from over two hundred countries were stored, safely guarded against explosions, earthquakes, or terrorist attacks?

A genetic bank for a new era? Weren't there enough of them already, all over the world? Or were these species known to be exposed to a calamity that would soon destroy them? Was someone aware of an imminent event that would devastate mankind, for which they'd been preparing for years? Was it a coincidence that, as well as by the world's leading governments, this project was also sponsored by the Gates Foundation, by Monsanto, and by the Rockefellers, one of the most powerful and influential families on the planet and one that has always been accused of placing science in the service of eugenics?

Why was the SDI (Strategic Defence Initiative, a.k.a. Global Shield or Star Wars), so strongly sought-after by American administrations, also designed to be pointed spaceward and conceived as an anti-UFO device, as even suggested by former Canadian Minister of Defence Paul Hellyer? As far as we knew, the scientific community was still busy theorising possible exobiological microbial life, which it considered harmless. Where we preparing for interplanetary warfare?

This, and others, were indicators that something was in the air – as well as being signs that any sane individual should be able to read of their own accord, had they but gone to the trouble of investigating.

But the point of non-return had already been reached, and Pac was not prepared to wait for humanity to redeem itself, or to be brusquely woken from sleep-walking.

ONE

Kathmandu: one of the few places in the world capable of evoking promises with its sensual phonetics: correctly pronounced, the name sounds seductive and soporific at the same time. Like poetry recalled by the light of dawn, this was the capital of a country where the mountains above hailed the world down below; where animals were protected by the manifestation of the God Shiva – in the semblance of Pashupati – although being terrified by the blood-thirsty manifestations of his wife, the goddess Parvati.

Nepal: the stairway for replacing lamps in the celestial vault, this was also the nation of Kumari Devi, where pre-pubescent girls were elected and worshipped as living goddesses until the arrival of their first menstrual cycle. Said to be home to the gods – for their fondness of winter sports, perhaps? – this was the land that gave birth to Siddhartha Gautama, the Buddha, no more a Buddhist than Christ was a Christian. Nepal: a serene version of India, where Hinduism and Buddhism walked arm in arm, changing sides from time to time. Nepal: a collective hypnosis whose pendulum oscillated between past and present, creating a temporal deception; and still today the favoured destination of those in search of a diamond to cut through the illusion, while wading through the dust and the litter, dodging the ubiquitous livestock, praying in temples which invited the soul to partake of a cup of tea, while luxuriating on a star-stuffed sofa.

So, back to Kathmandu, the last leg of the hippy trail through the Orient, when that word still had a meaning, and the term 'unforeseen' wasn't restricted to losing your luggage at the airport. A marzipan city, built on the ruins of an earthquake; a place where you'd stand on a street corner admiring mediaeval architecture and envisaging, as if just completed, the coronation ceremony of the king; then, turning into another street, you'd realise that the latest technology was struggling to impose its own concepts of good taste, of habits and customs, on a society that might well not feel the need for change.

To Pac, this was one of the capitals with the most polluted air and water in the world, the valley of Kathmandu being a basin surrounded by towering snow-topped guardians indifferent to the fate of a dramatically increasing population. Above all it was bitterly cold, although in daytime the toxic, humid fumes of the pullulating traffic took the edge off the chill air.

To be sent to a country eighty-percent covered in mountains among the tallest in the world had struck Pac as an affront – a squalid, gratuitous provocation. One of the clauses in his contract clearly stated that his area of competence was comprised of territories whose thermometers never fell below eighteen degrees centigrade, the 'temperature of consent' which guaranteed his operative efficiency. His initial objection, however, had fallen on deaf ears, and in view of the times of crisis (which he reckoned he could read very well), he'd had no choice. As if that weren't enough, through rapid investigation he'd learned that the local cuisine relied on – and even prided in – its generous use of hot chili powder. Which was totally unacceptable... Alas, one always had to be ruled by someone, in this world!

The guide he'd chosen at the airport was driving to a recommended hotel, while Pac sat comfortably in the back of an ancient mouthwash-green vehicle manufactured in India, whose registration certificate might have been disinterred in an earthenware jar.

Kimley (the guide) seemed perfectly at ease driving in traffic ruled entirely by Darwinian laws: the largest and the smartest, those who best adapted to these intricate street dynamics, would have the upper hand. What seemed to make the difference, here, were attributes such as survival instinct, adventurous spirit, recklessness, and a devout fatalism – the absence of which was manifested by the victims of a natural selection, along the pedestrian margins of every street: human or other wreckage; buildings of varying sizes, revealing seriously decrepit inner structural components; stray animals; pedestrians who, wistful and envious, observed the passing traffic, regretting they didn't even have a coin or two to ride those bumper-cars.

Like miniature models on an electric circuit subject to frequent blackouts, the cars proceeded in stops and starts along the few asphalted roads through the all-pervading dust. They would accelerate as much as possible, convinced they gained time, only to break suddenly, the drivers babbling angrily, banging their fists on the steering wheel, or honking their horns loudly in frustration. This urban hysteria was vented in the shadow of crude buildings, some inhabited, others abandoned; and of grimy posters: the one overlooking the road hung in tatters, the misleading slogan sliced in half; makeshift stores elbowed spanking-clean houses with immaculate, ornate windows; gardens like a scattering of chopped parsley on rancid mash potatoes.

Pac observed that chaotic, scuttling misery, unable to turn his eyes away and feeling the warm embrace of stupor. This sort of scene was certainly not new to him: in fact, after years and years of wandering, the places he visited all looked pretty much the same. Shoddy standards induced similar results everywhere: the same rutty streets, crumbling to dust; the same waste piling up on their sides; the cubic huts of sweated lime and mud that would soon collapse, making way for new hardship: more building space for new, invigorated hopes. Lack of imagination produced the same stagnation, that stale greyness so dear to his organisation's top management, enamoured of colour to the point of draining it from the entire world.

Dust was always dust, everywhere – and the eradication of joy produced the same fields of salt, everywhere.

Nevertheless, the filthy car window could not conceal the impression of fatalistic acceptance: the strange variant of adaptation that could be read on the tired faces of those people. A word buzzed inside Pac's head, 'serenity', which he immediately caught and splattered against the inner walls of his cranium. It wasn't that – and even if it were, he couldn't accept it. The face of an old woman, with her wrinkles and colourful garb, strolling along with the assured gait of one at peace with her destiny, even though the basket born on her head seemed heavier than herself. The hint of a smile launched in Pac's direction induced a shudder, as though the car's passenger compartment were no longer able to protect him.

But protect him from what?

The impression branded on him as he entered the city – while the anonymous Charon in front of them pushed ahead, pounding the steering wheel with his fist and intermittently punching the horn (first long, then short, then again very long) – was that of entering the gates of an enchanted oxymoron, peopled by men and women in the service of an entity he would never know; engaged in what didn't concern him; and illuminated and warmed by a sun which, in that valley and at that altitude, had an entirely different effect.

Not better or worse, mind you. Different.

The full light of day, reviving that scene with glowing colours lit by a phosphorescent patina, seemed capable of moving all those human walk-on players in a mysterious and unexpected manner, their number burgeoning as – young or old, ragged and smiling – they approached the window to peer at him as if he were some dish visible through the glass door of an oven. And that light, which would soon be quenching its thirst behind the mountains, caressed his skin with a gentleness hitherto unknown to him.

And this, he realised, was driving him berserk.

As the car turned into a secluded driveway, its tires scrunched and scattered the gravel as might a kangaroo in a field of popcorn, while the windows finally afforded the reassuring view of a lush garden, where moist shrubs and brightly-coloured flowers conversed politely, and great trees bowed their trunks, offering oases of restful shade to those kind enough to recognise their beauty.

Not a soul around – not a sound. This enabled Pac to open the car door, somewhat disdainfully, paying attention not to dislodge the handle, and to vacate that mechanical dinosaur with renewed vigour. Tall, fair complexion, broad face; what hair still resisted loyally was worn short, rarely subjected to combing or lotions, and left free to go its own way; the surplus flesh fondly embracing his waist, as well as the roguish twinkle in his chestnut-brown eyes, immediately endeared him to strangers, who saw him as someone they could trust. Though not strictly handsome, he *embodied* (not just a figure of speech) the sort of jovial empathy that could render him attractive in some situations. Too bad he was actually a bastard, which brings us back to the reason for his visit, and to the crunch of gravel underfoot as he made his way to the entrance.

The Grand Hotel Manang was a new accommodation complex in the heart of Thamel, the part of town frequented by tourists. As spacious as its owners were affluent (it belonged to Indian entrepreneurs with a passion for Five-Star hotels), its decor was embellished with pink and gold stucco; columns painted with geometric motifs; a light-blue ceiling dotted with recessed lights that bathed the ceramic floors in light; floor-length yellow curtains. Though luxurious by local standards, the place was rather kitsch, if truth be told (no distinctive character, nothing to remind guests of which country in the world they were visiting) and, apart from the basic colour scheme, distinctly lacked the feminine touch in the details and the aesthetics.

The mere act of leaning against the dark, solid wooden desk, uncluttered by leaflets that usually fill receptions; of placing his elbows on that smooth counter – where one could easily have played a game of skelly – was enough to make Pac breathe more easily, and smile (although this last was exclusively for his own edification).

Suddenly materialising through the back door, the receptionist regaled him with the full benefit of his own broad smile. He was a skinny youngster, proud of his uniform and white shirt, whose thick black hair – combed back and groomed with an overgenerous amount of gel – made him resemble a Mars bar dipped in trout slobber.

"Good morning, Suh", he said, with characteristic lack of vibrant alveolar consonants. "May I help you?"

Of course he could. "I have a booking. The name is Moon."

"Moon?"

"Yes. Keith Moon," Pac repeated wearily (assuming the sort of intense expression that no hotel employee would dare argue with), but without talking to him directly; that was something he had yet to achieve.

Being able to choose their undercover names was one of the many advantages that the agency offered its 'travelling salesmen', and over the years Pac had learned to make the most of it. If anyone dared show the least sign of doubt, even before saying a single word he would wave under their nose his valid passport, complete with electronic chip, just as he was doing now.

The passport named for Milton Friedman had expired – the irony of this being wasted, under the circumstances – and he'd lost the one named for Peter Sellers. But this passport was brand-new: one of those he kept for special occasions.

And what could better represent a special occasion than being sent to such heights and temperatures?

"I'll check immediately, Suh," said the boy quickly, diving into the massive register – filled in by hand, with pen and ruler – that occupied a large part of the counter. He passed his finger slowly down the page until his sticky, gel-caked hairdo oscillated horizontally. "Yessah, suah, Mistah Moon..." he smiled, before turning around and unhooking one of the many keys from the large key-rack behind him.

"Please, Mistah Moon," he said again, crossing the counter and taking the trolley that Kimley – still waiting in the garden for instructions – had unloaded as soon as he'd turned the engine off.

Partially opening the zip of his thick Sahara-coloured pullover, Pac yawned noisily while picking up his crocodile briefcase and letting himself be guided inside the hotel's gleaming belly.

A broad staircase of light-coloured stone; a few floral paintings of questionable merit on the landings; that antique-pink everywhere, on all the walls and corridors – enough pink to nauseate even the most effeminate of taste. Up and up, flight after flight, to the third floor, Pac finally surrendered to the sensation of being swallowed by a salmon.

After checking that the central heating worked, and

turning all the lights on and off in the bedroom and bathroom (knowing that a seemingly blown light bulb in a hotel was irrefutable evidence of being spied upon by a hidden TV camera); after haggling over the price and being conceded a fifteen percent discount; and after obtaining that his final invoice indicate an inflated price – compensated by a small tip which the lad hastily pocketed – he was finally able to leave the room without deigning to give it a second glance: he'd seen more than enough; the room was like any of the others with which he was all too familiar: same bed, same bedside table, same set of towels, and so on.

He ran down the stairs, almost in fear that all that pink might detach itself from the walls and splatter his face and his thinning hair. He wasn't even curious that the concessions he'd requested had been agreed upon by a junior hotel clerk: the one who continued to call out his thanks, which he hadn't even bothered to acknowledge.

Pac went outside through the glass doors and breathed in the fresh air among the surrounding vegetation: it was cooler than he'd expected, but the treetops, the shrubs and the many leafy plants served as springboards for the oversized insects. And he knew that the oncoming dusk augured hostilities to his skin.

Kimley immediately greeted him with a nod. Fortyish, he was a mastodon of a man, unusually tall, belonging to the Gurung, a Tibeto-Birman ethnic group. He wore scuffed boots, combat trousers and a brown leather jacket, his mass of thick, unruly hair contained beneath a baseball cap which he never took off; occasionally he would lift it a fraction, briefly, to let in a little air – the minimum of oxygen requirement for his hair. Sparse English vocabulary, unkempt beard, small eyes. His face was lit by a broad, benign grin that rendered affable his every utterance, every unsolicited comment regarding his country and its attributes.

But the main reason for singling out Kimley at the airport was an accessory that he consulted continuously like an oracle, which had belonged to the realm of Pac's hidden dreams since his late teens: a Casio watch with calculator. Of questionable utility, it had a futuristic digital display that, since the Seventies, had been an object of adoration and dreams: for its interplay of lights, functions, bleeps, it became an icon of revolutionary aesthetics and algebraic feats, unprecedented skills and recreational features, bridging the gap between the land of discipline and the launch pad of eccentricity: one that rode above the morass of insipid normality.

So much for that. Pac returned the nod. It was still daytime, and his business meeting wasn't until the following morning: what could be better than a stroll to stretch one's legs?

Kimley led the way, legs astride as if in some way

padded (maybe just full of himself); he seemed happy to be doing what he was paid to do. They left the gravelled driveway. Then, suddenly, all was chaos. They found themselves in the crowded neighbourhood of Thamel, said to be the tourists' favourite part of town; a quick glance around, however, convinced Pac that, among the small groups of day-trippers in search of a memorable experience, and the solitary spoiled brats – false-bohemians, genuine junkies – no-one deserved a mention in his precious list of elected posterity.

To start with, Pac's nostrils filled with the rancid stench of an open sewer, flowing dangerously near the new trekking boots he'd bought for the trip. Leaping across the stinking rivulet he was almost knocked over by a cart drawn by an old man with a grimace, whose fatigue lightened the day for the couple of merry American tourists aboard.

As Pac stood there, undecided whether he really wanted to venture further on, he felt Kimley's large hand pat his shoulder to attract his attention.

"Shall we go on?", he said, his nut-brown face breaking into an engaging smile of even, pearly white teeth.

"OK. Sure, let's go," said Pac, not in the least bit convinced. Before his eyes, much too close for his liking, was a plethora of individuals engrossed in all sorts of activities, a dense, turbulent flow, confused and confusing, which he wasn't at all sure he wanted to join. All in all, he would have preferred to put forward his business meeting, or plunge straight back into his pink five-star nightmare. For a moment he rummaged inside his memory-chest of seedy experiences, seeking to draw strength from the last time he'd been exposed to so many people, to such utter chaos. But he could find nothing of the sort.

While inhaling spicy dust and fried incense, and watching his step to avoid being run over by a scooter; while dodging crippled beggars; peddlers; storekeepers and restaurant owners who loitered outside the front door to their shops and – as if endowed with a photocell device – mechanically broke into action as he went by, uttering their best greetings and even putting their hands, steepled as in prayer, to their forehead. While the notes of *Om Mani Padme Hum* resonated in twelve different musical versions (from Gospel, to Pop, to Indian, and through to traditional Nepalese) from equidistant loudspeakers, full blast, in waves that overlapped and created an echo effect, possibly contrived to induce visitors to buy. While being offered all sorts of hand-crafted items: from carpets to statues of Hanuman or Vishnu; from traditional paintings of ceremonial themes; to garments and scarves of pashmina wool (genuine and imitation); to masks; to musical instruments; and through to fabrics stacked ceiling-high. While all this pandemonium all but reduced Pac to an epileptic fit, Kimley strolled along beside him, bestowing his brilliant smile on all and sundry, and promising his customer that they'd soon reach ancient Durbar Square. Under the protection of Unesco, the square – dating back to the seventeenth century – still preserved its architectural heritage.

In less than twenty minutes, Pac felt totally drained, no longer able to discern, appreciate or reject anything, or take in another single drop of that human brew.

His guide, unperturbed, consulted his watch, nodding his large head as though agreeing with himself.

"Here we are. There is ticket office. This way, please," he announced cheerfully in his raucous voice.

The pokey office selling tickets to Durbar Square, providing access to the royal palace, was flanked by two extremely thin policemen, busy chatting with half a dozen tourist guides – some authorised, some not – all with carefully groomed hair, waiting for customers.

Sitting behind a grubby window, a ruddy-cheeked clerk in a white shirt briefly interrupted his animated discussion with a colleague and, without bothering to look up, tore from a new book two pale-green tickets, in such a rough and careless manner that he almost ripped them in half.

Pac fished out from his pocket a banknote so faded that its colours might have been scraped off by some penniless pavement-artist; he handed the note over to the clerk, who gave it a fleeting sidelong glance before stuffing it into a drawer he'd opened against his swollen belly, which an overstretched shirt failed to conceal; he then resumed his conversation where it had been left off.

Holding his tickets (or what remained of them) and with Kimley at his side, Pac sensed the armed truce that awaited him just ahead. Only a few more steps, four or five at most, separated him from the archaeological area: reserved, protected and paid for, and therefore cleansed of all the rancid human secretions left behind.

The two gaunt policemen, who could have shed their crumpled uniforms simply by jumping up and down where they stood, remained immobile, staring at the twin scraps of pale-green paper the size of a celebratory stamp, which they knew had only just been torn off – yet something was apparently amiss. They consulted each other in undertones with an air of diligence and concern, then examined Pac closely, their nostrils dilating, as if they smelled something edible; they inclined and overturned the scraps of paper, X-raying every detail, weighing up with untiring prerogative a pending suit that involved the very nature of their jurisdiction. Then the verdict: the tickets seemed to be ok, but in this state they could just as easily be old, recycled; the date was torn in half, the year was missing. Supposing they were last year's? Supposing someone else checked them again: how would that reflect on them?

"What's wrong, Kimley?", asked Pac irritably. He'd been in that country less than an afternoon and his blood was already turning sour. "Nothing. I speak with them," half-muttered his guide. Straightening his cap he addressed the two, who nodded, turned back to the ticket office and pointed to the tickets, nodding again. One of them kept a watchful eye all around, making sure that no busybody approached them or interfered with their work.

Meanwhile an ancient, ragged gentleman made his way towards Pac, dragging himself along the dusty ground by the sole force of incredibly thin but surprisingly strong arms. His legs had been amputated at the thighbone a long time ago.

Having his back turned, Pac hadn't noticed the old beggar, and might not have seen that bag of bones at his feet even if he'd turned around. While Pac tried to get the gist of what Kimley and the two public officials were debating (the former engaging in a theatrical dissertation, the latter two displaying unvarying passivity), the little man tugged at the calf of his trouser leg. At first Pac thought it might be a dog but, on turning around, to his increasing irritation he was confronted with yet another snotty-nosed scrounger: having first looked about two meters from his new boots – where all he'd seen was the tail end of a track that must have been left by something at closer range: something that was still tugging at him, more insistently now, at his knee – he finally lowered his eyes and met the beggar's gaze. He felt obliged to back away in alarm: from there below, a pair of cloudy, impenetrable eyes – like clots of tar set in a face entirely covered in bristly beard – were staring up at him. The old man didn't need to say anything (or perhaps he couldn't speak at all), but the whole scene was so eloquent that words failed Pac. He was, quite simply, unable to respond. Inhabited by an incredibly ancient, wrinkled being, his resolute expression anything other than imploring (almost as if he no longer needed to ask, but merely expected to obtain), that bundle of ragged clothes barely covered his shoes yet was able to emanate such vitality, such a compelling demand for respect for his proud existence, that Pac's cerebral functions were struck dumb.

For a moment he stood undecided. Then, quickly recovering his composure, he faced the man with an equally inflexible expression and, sure of his ground, returned a mirror reflection of that which had been intended to subjugate him. From below and from above, the silent, riveting exchange became more penetrating. Then was interrupted by a voice.

"Come!", Kimley called out. Pac jumped to, and turning on his heel without a parting nod to the pauper, he quickly strode across to join his guide at the entrance to Durbar Square feeling, in the depth of his being, even more exhausted. He didn't tip, he ignored beggars, he didn't give presents, or donate to charities. He didn't go in for that sort of thing: it didn't make him feel any better. His conscience – or what remained of it – grazed on other pastures. He had no need for benedictions, gratitude, or karmic credit cards. "Therefore, my dear cripple, your application is rejected. If you really want to improve your life," he thought, "trust in your god to save you from the Apocalypse. Or else think how well you'll fare in your afterlife. But don't involve me in your dramas. They're no concern of mine."

Although he hadn't caught the man's response, it had sufficed to catch the look in those eyes, that had stared at him unblinkingly, to imagine the insults hurled at his back. As if he cared!

"All sorted?", asked Pac, curious to learn the result of Kimley's negotiations. Smiling, the guide put him in the picture.

The agreement reached by Kimley, he learned, provided for the date and the hour to be stamped on the reverse side of the tickets: an operation requiring the intervention of the ticket-office clerk, reluctant to comply with such an unusual and unauthorised procedure, for which he and the pudgy cheeks had refused to assume the least responsibility. Supposing, during a possible subsequent control, someone happened to query such an extraordinary measure: how would this reflect on him? No, he was sorry but those tickets would have to be invalidated, and new ones purchased, he'd stipulated. It was just as well that Pac hadn't been paying attention. Finally, with an ostentatious gesture of benevolence, the policemen had intimated to the clerk that he accept the solution without further objections, as people were queuing to buy tickets and there was no time to waste; the two officers had then parted from the guide with a complacent nod – not reciprocated.

On hearing of that bureaucratic "procedure", proudly conveyed by Kimley between gestures, grunts and pidgin English, Pac was filled with his usual disgust for humanity and for its superstructures, its multifaceted character and the sickening, unpredictable peculiarities inherent in each individual. That which many considered the innate biodiversity of *homo sapiens sapiens* – the maximum expression of our evolution – Pac had long believed to be the cause of degradation, that festering possessiveness and fear of oneself and of others that always informed the worst misdeeds. Too many people, too many heads – but, sadly, not enough brains to go round. Stupidity wasn't universal, of course, but the occasional spark of genius was promptly stifled among the ashes of social structures – snuffed out by the fat finger of social, religious, political, cultural indoctrination: severed heads, walking bodies.

Fortunately he was momentarily disinclined to brood over such thoughts, and managed to dismiss them.

Inside the archaeological zone the atmosphere was different, and not only because of the absence of motor cars – which of course helped reduce the surrounding smog. Apart from a few tourists, and a handful of stalls selling fresh drinks, they were surrounded by royal palaces which, in the glorious past, by those standards, would have been considered sumptuous, but which now – as they plodded along the dilapidated stone paving – were merely tall brown ruins, decorated with regular, brightly-coloured motifs. All of them symbolic, no doubt, though Kimley hadn't bothered to explain. Whether out of ignorance or scant sense of duty, Pac didn't care: this was just a sensible escape from the electrified jungle of which he'd felt the voltage.

Narrow, tortuous streets, crossroads amid which stood abandoned temples, steps and statues – a stone virtuosity that somehow reassured, transmitting a sense of the labour undertaken, of historical decline. Nevertheless, names like Kasthamandap, Maju Deval, or Nasal Chowk failed to interest Pac as much as the thought of getting to his dinner, the time for which – according to the futuristic watch on Kimley's caramel-coloured wrist – was still a long way away.

From those tall, imposing buildings, whose open windows revealed glimpses of furniture beyond the long red curtains, and from the pointed temple spires, the sunlight cast long shadows and bathed the streets and walls in sepia. Human figures seemed to materialise around corners, bowed and rapt in contemplation of a divinity, and veiled in faded colours. And the substance of that silence somehow mingled with the air and ended up in your lungs.

Pac settled on a step at the foot of a temple, despite suspecting this might not be permitted. Kimley remained standing, looked around, greeted a colleague, put his hands in his pockets. From where he sat, Pac realised what a perfectly fit and well-proportioned physique the man had. His initial interest already spent, like the free phone calls in a special offer, Pac felt the urge to leave: it was time to see if his guide was worth the agreed fee.

Kimley expressed regret for Pac's scarce interest in those historical wonders, especially after all his efforts to obtain entry. He tried offering other morsels, including the Pashupatinath, the most important Hindu temple in that country, as well as the sub-continent's primary place for the worship of Shiva, in this case in his benign role as shepherd of men and beasts – a conception common to many religions, and which induced Pac to remark that, if they saw themselves as a flock of sheep, they deserved their condition, which still reduced them to walking in single file.

Initially reluctant, convinced that to contemplate those ancient stones – mainly small blocks of a subordinate votive nature – was tantamount to declaring an obvious mental deficiency, Pac eventually agreed to go, provided Kimley kept him away from the swarms of pilgrims and beggars, and above all from cremation ceremonies, frequently celebrated along the river. He had no desire to dwell on concepts such as mortality, the inconsistency of perceived reality, or impermanence; to tell the truth, his aim was the opposite: the harvest of life, and its protection from imminent global threat.

"Easy!" exclaimed Kimley with renewed enthusiasm,

gesticulating with his large hands. "You not see that. That is for Hindu. You not Hindu," he said, twirling the ring that held the car keys.

Pac was pleased. In fact, he was very pleased not to be anything, not only Hindu. He was willing to forfeit all caste-related privileges, as long as he could get out of there.

His wishes would be satisfied, but they'd have to go back and retrieve the car, said Kimley. After immersing themselves once again in the kaleidoscopic legion of souls they reached a shortcut, and proceeded along a dirt track so damp their boots kept slipping, with their eyes fixed to the ground to avoid the urban refuse. Finally they came to a stop.

Pac waited in front of a food stall. He could have bought a packet of crisps, a bottle of water, some home-made biscuits. He would certainly have liked to: he'd had no lunch and all that exercise needed refuelling. He might have been tempted, but for the grubby nails of the peddler who dished out the food, and the nonchalance with which he spat on the ground; or the two urchins on the corner who kept their eyes on him just as he'd put his hand in his pocket to feel for some change: all this – along with the need to ensure that he attend a business meeting that guaranteed a fast escape at a pre-arranged time – dissuaded him, leaving a sense of frustration which he knew would be hard to dispel.

A short ride in the car (with Pac wondering if the motor

would even start up), in traffic which he'd decided to ignore; an unlicensed car park; another entrance ticket, bought without too much hassle this time.

The Pashupatinath was an impressively large complex, affording a view of temple tops in every direction as far as the eye could see. Maybe the edifices on the horizon didn't belong, and the complex was much smaller, but it seemed enormous: a city within the city. Again, stone, solidity, durability, like the faith it was intended to represent.

Walking towards the *gaths*, Pac felt as if he was about to be swallowed by the temple's soaring verticality; its cells; the flights of stairs leading up to the buildings, square or pointed; or to ample flat spaces far up above his head – and which might suddenly have tipped, closing in like a dome, or collapsed on top of him, burying him alive. He had to climb further up, breathe deeper, get more light, to overcome those sensations. And, while he strained his legs in this impromptu exercise, he felt distinctly as if he'd walked into one of those unfinished constructions of toy building bricks he used to make all alone as a child. In view of the elaborate oaths and snorting emitted by Pac as first he slipped, then stumbled, banging his knee, this stone construction must have been in urgent need of some refurbishing.

But the view from up there was undeniably better, offering a quadrangular perspective of the whole structure;

and the sun poured down, warming the skin caressingly. Pac's breathing was slowly recovering a more regular rhythm, especially after he'd decided to sit down on a stone bench and observe. Observe.

Hands stuffed inside the pockets of his padded jacket, Pac – not in the least enthralled by the sight of ash-covered sadhus engrossed in their ablutions along the banks of the sacred river Bagmati (a murky brew in which only radioactive fish could have survived) – refused to make the effort of interpreting the various representations of Shiva that decorated the scattering of minute temples across the terraced slope, but succeeded in resisting an imaginary game of paper aeroplanes. And calmed down.

Once Kimley – with his inimitable slow caution – had finally settled down on a stone, Pac watched his guide as the features on his wood-coloured face relaxed while he surrendered, sighing, to the enchantment, heedless of Pac and of his needs. And there he stayed.

At that point Pac could only shrug, and let Kimley enjoy whatever it was that those present, particularly down there below, perceived and assimilated – something that was alien to Pac, but whose atmosphere could do him good.

After all, he thought, allowing one's senses to take over – albeit pacifically – was one of the best ways to feed one's existential piggy-bank. Especially after the recently-escaped chaos. From where they stood, the confusion animating the opposite river bank seemed more under control. The air was cooling, and the sultry glow was fading, veiled by the thin mist spread across the sky.

In the distance, the mountains, the roofs of houses, an airplane. Moving around below with slow, heavy steps, these souls seemed to have left their thoughts and words, their problems and their pain outside those gates: those gates which were able to enclose and isolate that which for others it was unimaginable to withhold. Women in long robes of simple, measured elegance bowed and gathered. Men in dark clothes sat immobile, their hands steepled. Immersed in their nourishing, softening spiritual balm, these people often brought a smile to Pac's face, as he watched them, intrigued by what their expressions transmitted. It may or may not have been an illusion, but those men and women appeared to be, and possibly were, at peace. And from that height it struck him that they were anything other than consumers. At least in the common, materialistic sense of the term. Crazy thoughts, he mused. Truth be told, he was growing tired. He was there on business, and in idle moments such as these he soon got bored. What with the things he still had to do; and the little time (just how little?); and the parts he had yet to order; and the unresolved matters. And everything else…

"What do you think of it?" asked Kimley, removing his cap and fanning his face, exposing a thatch as thick, unkempt and brittle as a meadow of aged pubic hair.

"I appreciate the atmosphere," replied Pac, without

turning around.

So Kimley, his eyes half closed, breathed in and started praying, a faint aura of well-being pervading his face.

A couple of well-dressed Westerners were taking photos nearby, and commenting on the cremation ceremony that was about to take place in the near distance – and from which there was no escape. A sparse gathering of relations occupied one of the six Gaths dedicated to this function, surrounding the pyre which was devouring its meal of human flesh and of cheap firewood, the deceased having belonged to an underprivileged cast. The acrid grey smoke, billowing skywards, resembled a post-mortem initiation path, tracing the journey towards another dimension where that conscious exhalation would soon be met and judged, its karma deleted, before returning to this material delusion, to this conventional appearance, but incarnated in a happier, more prosperous existence, perhaps a few steps higher in the amphitheatre reaching up to Nirvana. This is what the women's eyes suggested, while the murmur of their prayers rose and spread all around. High in the sky, crows and vultures flew among the branches and spires, emitting funereal cries as if to warn the pilgrims or whomever else happened to be in need.

If asking to be exempted from witnessing those farewells had been of no use; and if the place itself – though undoubtedly fascinating – could not shield him from the fumes of corpses, or from the theatrical performance of that company (who seemed to confuse stage acting with real life), then inevitably he had to make the move.

Which he did, and fast. He'd had enough.

The acid-green car seemed much closer now than when they'd left it, among beaten-up, decrepit, dust-covered vehicles, nevertheless retaining an integrity and dignity the likes of which she couldn't begin to achieve, lacking bumpers, mud flaps or wheel rims; her treads worn out; her exhaust pipe riddled with rust and holes, a piece of wire saving it from the indignity of dragging along on the ground.

Distracted from his intimate and finely-tuned channel of conversation, Kimley at that point opted for something different, and less tragic.

"You must see Bouddhanath," he said peremptorily, as they climbed into their means of transport, though 'mean' would have been more fitting, both inside and out!

"Another cheerful gathering of old buddies in a swinging fashionable joint?"

If Kimley saw the joke he certainly didn't show it: he touched his cap, managed to turn the key without breaking it, and kept his eyes fixed on the traffic. So much the better.

Here I am again, sitting in the back seat of a car and looking out the window, thought Pac. Strangely enough, that seemed to be his ideal place. Or rather, the only one – he corrected himself – enabling him to spy on the world in suitable peace and perspective.

A cow with a garland of flowers round its neck rested in the shade of a large tree. The painted gate of a temple spewed out groups of men with pensive faces. Dust rose from the street as a woman, crouching, picked up the pieces of a broken pot, rebuked by a young man who waved an admonishing finger.

Pac raised his eyes, misting up the already-grimy window with a heavy sigh. He was in the concave depths of a wooden spoon, bits attached to its rim as if just drawn from the boiling brew of an earthenware pot. And from above, an evanescent vapour of miniscule bubbles, specks of dust and gas, whirling together in microscopic orbits, had begun their slow descent, eclipsing the sun and the fading sky like a breaded contact lens, sinking towards that tired land, far away from the beaches.

Pac was brusquely aroused by the sudden braking of the car. In the rear-view mirror, Kimley shot him a quick glance, seemingly to check that everything was alright. Without saying a word, he took advantage of the pause to raise a hand from the steering wheel and stroke the peak of his cap. Then he returned the attention of his roast-chestnut face to the road.

Meanwhile, Pac passed his hand over his forehead, and up across the top of his once-bushy head, where now desertification progressed relentlessly, day after day.

The cold was not a problem yet –Sun had just stepped out of her knickers – but it would be, by the time she had finished preparing for the penetrating solemnity of Night. Only then would the bells start ringing, and Pac would get out of his tourist's clothes and remain safely secluded in his heated hotel room, like some cryophobic Dracula.

In the meantime, inside the car, he could easily stand a repetition of the show outside. He'd always been prepared to visit, get to know and explore – in any country, including those already infected – the kaleidoscope of human activities, past and present; the expressive forms and sounds, cultures, artefacts and traditions of the natives. All this would soon survive in his memory alone, to be evoked, in the near future, with inevitable nostalgia. Possibly while crouching near a fire that he himself had lit, on one of his first nights as a survivor, having just returned to the earthly atmosphere, and being as yet unaccustomed to the unavoidable destruction underfoot. These were his thoughts, as he carefully kept his forehead away from the window.

Although he had evaluated numberless possibilities, he had no idea what to expect on that final date: the Armageddon. A terrible explosion, single or multiple; a second Flood. A slow and progressive war, ending with total nuclear destruction. Or the advent of a new messiah, on a chariot of thunderbolts; or the clash between angels and demons. The landing of impressive spaceships in strategic points on the planet. An invasion of cosmic locusts; or of invincible robots, emerging from the depths of the oceans and from the planet's crust after being hidden, millennia ago, by the Lords of the Earth, before they'd gone off on holiday on Sirius. Or maybe an announcement, aired worldwide, saying something like: "Ladies and Gentlemen of the Earth: this is it. If you have any weapons, use them. And may the best side win!" The simultaneous eruption of all the volcanic pimples on the face of the Earth. Or, better still, a holographic vision of an Annunciation – by the Virgin Mary for Christians, by Buddha for Buddhists, by Mohammed, Jehovah, Brahma, Zoroaster, Amaterasu, John Lennon, Yoda, Martin Luther King, Laozi – artificially induced by HAARP, inciting the final battle by accusing one another of humanity's deplorable degeneration and of the miserable number of fans acquired over all that time.

He honestly didn't know what to expect, any more than a golf ball knows the reason for being so violently abused. But there was no point in racking one's brain: he was sure that, when the time was right, he would understand.

The point was, how long now before the blind date? Months? Years? Weeks? From data at his disposal even this was hard to establish, but he was sure there wasn't much time left. Hopefully, enough to build a vimana and escape to safety.

A sign of The End of Time?

Not now. They'd arrived.

The gigantic Bouddhanath stupa was by far the largest in

the world. Situated inside a perfect ring of tall brick walls, it was home to gompas and monks, cultural associations and paintings, ritual mandalas, scholars, the fragrance of incense, prayer wheels and photographs of the Dalai Lama in his youth. It was a miniature replica of a Tibetan town, the synthesis of a community, the epitome of an ancient civilisation in serious danger, like a grenade thrown by an invisible hand from the other side of the mountain range, to land there, in the middle, its austere beauty transmitting at once a severe warning and an implicit promise. This centre of worship for Tibetan refugees – small people with muscular legs, expanded lungs and sand-blasted souls, escaped from the blood-thirsty genocidal Chinese repression – was the beating heart of the circular village, whose perimeter was a succession of craft shops and stalls, and whose centre hosted the stupa, the object of constant veneration, especially by those who were preparing to cross the Himalayas or had just returned; and constantly teaming with people: the curious, the devout – and the natives, though the term was not strictly appropriate as they were mainly refugees.

From the terraced base rose the *kumbha*, an imposing white semi-circular dome, dozens of metres in height. This was surmounted by a perfectly square plinth, decorated on each side with the eye of the Buddha, and embellished with the motif of the third eye above, and with the Nepalese sign for the number one slightly below, symbolising the union of all living beings; contemplating the cardinal points; representing enlightened omniscience; and conferring to this Unesco world heritage site an air of pacific, tolerant magnificence, which induced pilgrims and visitors to walk around in small, meditative steps.

A place of hope, peace and hospitality, visibly loved and protected by all those who appreciated its symmetrical rules, dictated by order and severity, by methodical continuity; by those who, within the walls of the complex, worked for its material and spiritual safeguarding; by others who were unable to repress a smile as, deeply moved and happy, they looked up at the ornamental strings branching off from the stupa in all directions, hung with hundreds of colourful little flags painted with prayers that fluttered in the wind.

With small steps, Kimley and Pac walked inside the stupa, where they were engulfed by semi-darkness and a sense of claustrophobia. Here, some were lighting incense, others were participating in the on-going service, others still were reciting a hushed prayer which flowed into the soft sing-song of speaking, whispering, commenting voices that permeated the atmosphere. Sacred images, meditation, introspection, lateral glances; the twinkling expanse of candles like a loving sea, sizzling soundlessly, reflecting off the white walls and off the extremely, unexpectedly low ceiling; nostrils invaded by the fumes of fragrant incense; the flame of a candle burning low, evoking the hip-swaying movement of a belly-dancer.

Pac observed and savoured the scene: surrounded by drowsy monks; an overtly enthusiastic tourist, bundled up in colourful, locally-crafted clothes, stared all around with moist eyes; clicking cameras; repressed protests on reading the signs that banned the use of flashes; the shove of someone who, on entering, had recognised his as a desirable position. Nothing would stop Pac from escaping that cavernous hole, as he accelerated and overtook a capless Kimley, who must have drawn substantial nourishment from such a spiritual banquet.

Air, light.

If the Pushipatinath had rendered Pac nauseous and anxious, in this overgrown carbuncle he'd felt under the constant scrutiny of a spying eye, which annoyed him. No, this wasn't his scene, he told himself impatiently.

Even before he could recite the customary brief prayer, Kimley had followed outside, glowering long and darkly at Pac, wondering deep down whether anything could ever instil any passion into this dried-up atheist, with his apathetic inclination towards rational disbelief. Yet it was he who paid his salary and expenses, so Kimley gave up making any further suggestions and said he'd be happy to drive his client back to his hotel, in nearby Thamel.

It would soon be dark, and Pac seemed anxious to respect the temperature curfew.

Kimley hazarded one last attempt at organising a good,

healthy walk before sunrise, to salute the sun from atop the temple of Swayambhunath, also known as the Monkey Temple, whose views would induce sighs of beatification and ethereal optimism, laced with delight at the prancing playfulness of the charming, mischievous little beasts. But to no avail.

"Listen, don't take this personally but, for all I know, there's a monkey temple on every bump in Asia," replied Pac, "and the idea of watching the condensation of smog drifting up from the valley, refracted by the early rays of the sun, only to re-descend and cheerfully breathe it in, doesn't exactly thrill me."

This time the drive was short, delayed only by the prolonged tantrums of the starter. It took some convincing to get it going again: time, a thunderous thump on the dashboard, and a brief mumbling by the irked driver, which didn't reach the back seat. It was comforting to realise that his instinctive suspicion, aroused at first glance, had eventually been proven right. The luxury of dependability, thought Pac as he waited, could not dwell in this ancient Indian automobile. At least, not always. Fair enough.

A relaxed if not exactly smooth journey, during which Pac – tired of looking out of the windows – started to examine himself: in particular, he started to caress his stomach, that flabby, overflowing deposit of biogas and frequently renewable combustible fat. And suddenly an all-engulfing appetite materialised out of some dark and hidden recess, while an angry figure in a mask costume flew towards him, grabbing him and holding him fast, enveloping him in his cloak: the speaker of *Radio75*.

"Stop here!" Pac shouted, not realising that Kimley would obey him literally, bang in the middle of thick traffic, so that all around them the din of horns would rise like the trumpets of Jerico.

"Oh shit, not in the middle of the road!" Pac spluttered, inadvertently launching a squirt of saliva that stuck to the feet of the miniature model of a saint swinging from the rear-view mirror. Fortunately Kimley didn't notice. Having parked to the side, leaving the flow of traffic free to jam elsewhere as it pleased, Pac dashed out and ran to a faded wooden food stall, and to the startled lad standing behind it.

"Hi," he said, rummaging in his pockets, "give me two of those bananas, a packet of pistachios, one of almonds, and two bottles of water. Without gas, please."

Swamped in an oversize grey sweater, the boy responded with a dignified smile and a nod. He hadn't understood.

Pac repeated slowly, indicating the bananas first, and the number two, then the pistachios and almonds that hung from an iron hook; he picked up the bottles of water, checking the virginity of the thin plastic strips round their caps.

That would be dinner: like it or lump it. After all, he could do a lot worse, and this was the low-calorie regime he had freely decided to follow. It was a matter of being consistent: it made sense. If Pac really intended to board the Star Pac and circumnavigate the planet, he'd have to show up for the appointment in good shape, perfectly fit and free of surplus weight. Being too lazy for physical exercise, he had worked out a correct, well-balanced diet. Which he always forced himself to respect. Almost always. Besides, he only needed to see himself in the mirror, bloated and pigeon-shaped, or to stroke his navel to find renewed motivation. This was his directive, his categorical imperative, his supreme commandment (when in the right frame of mind), and nothing, no-one could lead him astray.

Pac paid the boy his due: four nimble fingers protruding from the cuff of his sleeve swiftly collected the money and returned the change, which proved to be correct. Pac suddenly feared that those faded and almost transparent banknotes, so tattered as to be almost impalpable, could disintegrate in his pockets before he even left the country. Close inspection confirmed: the possibility was far from unlikely.

Plastic bag in hand, and with his appetite increasing, Pac climbed back into the car, where Kimley shot him a glance of deep disgust, an undercurrent of keen disapproval which the guide reluctantly redirected towards the windscreen. The message was perfectly clear. There hadn't been the slightest mention of dinner, of local restaurants and specialities. And now, all this hurry to get back with that miserable fare to the hotel; you'd have thought he was setting off to feed the animals at the zoo. Dinner was clearly not contemplated in his plans – at least not in his company. It was always the same with these businessmen: no tips, no consideration. Nothing. They could go back where they came from, for all he cared.

Having entered the gravel driveway of the Grand Hotel Manang at high speed, the car swung round, skidded briefly on its rear wheels and came to a halt.

Climbing out of the car, Pac couldn't but appreciate the perfect timing: the sun was down and there wasn't a star in sight – the batteries of the overhead projector had gone dead. All around, black shadows, dull reflections, rustling noises from the trees and shrubs. Darkness had descended: only the lights of the hotel illuminated the clearing outside the entrance.

The air had turned bitterly cold, though not quite as bad as he'd expected.

He thanked Kimley for their afternoon tour – discerning what looked like acute disappointment on the man's face – and summarised details for the morning's meeting. It was time to consult St. John's oracle on his computer, to check whether his hyper-critical eyes could spot new signs.

Just before closing the car door, very gently to avoid further damage, Pac asked Kimley one last question: one which – judging by Pac's expression, suddenly wide-awake and exerting numerous facial muscles – must have originated from a well-lit compartment in his brain.

"D'you know anything about vimanas?" he asked, while Kimley adjusted his baseball cap. "Is there a temple, an inscription, anything around here that represents one?"

Kimley looked as if he'd fallen out of the sky on a clear day, his gaze completely vacuous. He evaded the question by lifting his wrist and pushing a lateral button on the plastic case of his watch, which lit up with an oily green brightness and emitted a mechanical beep, as if to answer in his place.

"It's ok, it doesn't matter," said Pac, heading for the hall.

But when the car started off, scattering gravel all around, he thought he heard unintelligible words dispersing in the darkness. Meanwhile the ancient uniformed porter threw open for him the gates of that warm, welcoming womb: the place all sentient mammals dream of re-entering.

Composed of the prefix 'Vi' ('bird', or 'to fly'), and of the suffix 'mana' ('inhabited man-made place'), the Sanskrit term 'vimana' is cited in ancient Indian texts such as the *Vedas* and the *Samarangana Sutradhara*, where these flying machines are described as powered by liquid mercury, and also sound-propelled

The *Drona Parva*, in the *Mahabharata*, recites: "The Mind became the soil supporting that vimana; the Word became the tracks along which it wished to travel." And again: "When it moved, its thunder filled all the points of the compass."

In 1875 a manuscript of the fourth century BC was discovered: the *Vymaanika Shastra* (Aeronautical Science), giving details of how vimanas were powered by heated mercury; of their flying characteristics and their operation with vortex mechanics; and on the specific materials to be used for their manufacture. Based on their different functions, these were catalogued into four main models, complete with detailed technical drawings of veritable spaceships. The text provided the following definition: "That which flies from one place to another is a vimana. Experts state that what can fly in the air, from one island to another island, from one world to another world, is a vimana."

This thesis also referred specifically to the pilots' diet, contained instructions as to their equipment, as well as listing thirty-two secrets which pilots had to abide by, such as the transfer of latent spiritual powers from man to actual spaceship. Among the functions described there was that of making oneself invisible; of modifying one's form; of using radars; of creating virtual images to confuse one's enemies; there were descriptions of ultrasonic and other weapons, and much more.

Vedas, the most ancient religious texts in the world – presumed to have been written as from 1800 BC, though some speculate that they could be dated much earlier – also repeatedly mention these magnificent devices, sub-dividing them on the basis of certain characteristics: those able to navigate in the air and in water; or on land and in water; those with two or more motors, just to mention a few.

Vimanas are also mentioned in the epic poems *Mahabharata* and *Ramayana*, where they are deployed for military purposes in terrible and ferocious battles. The former describes the launch of blazing bullets; weapons capable of manipulating the weather; ultrasonic missiles. Technology owned by the gods, before whom man, whether involved in their personal warfare or not, was totally powerless: a victim and a prostrate witness to fantastic marvels; a submissive and faithful servant; a happy and ecstatic apprentice of life and of the cosmos, of its rules and dimensions which those celestial travellers, those remote creators of events, dispensed on this newly-born civilisation.

To these supernatural celestial ships and to their occupants, sculptures with aerodynamic forms pointing skyward were dedicated and consecrated as representing the itinerant temple of god; the latter, in periodic contact with the current mortal monarch, watched from his vimana the sacrifices, praises and ceremonies made in his honour. And if by 'mortal' one intended a biological cycle much shorter than that of the above-mentioned divinities, the temporal parameters of many sacred texts regarding inordinate ages, dates and events otherwise incomprehensible would finally assume a realistic collocation.

According to the records, the Buddhist emperor Ashoka (304-232 BC) – mindful, for the good of humanity, of the need to conceal the celestial routes from the profane – ordered that contemporary science be catalogued in nine books, including the *Secrets of Gravitation*; and for fear that the knowledge derived from Hindo-Arian texts be used for belligerent purposes, he ordered that the nine books be kept in remote Asian localities.

One of these may have been today's Lhasa, in Tibet, where ancient Sanskrit documents have recently been discovered dealing with the presence in man of an anti-gravity energy capable of causing objects to levitate through the development of a centrifugal force. This capacity is also well described in traditional Tibetan texts regarding the *durakhapalam*: a cube-shaped metal device powered by prayer and by particular psychic energy, said to enable dimensional, physical and interplanetary travel. Again, these texts dwell on concepts such as invisibility; energy made entirely of antiparticles; space-time deviation; the faculty to "become as heavy as a mountain of lead". Documents which Pac knew to have been taken seriously by the Chinese government during research that went into their space programme. Presumably, another of these remote localities might be Turkestan, or the Gobi desert where, inside some caves, Russian scientists discovered some strange semi-spherical objects which they defined as "ancient instruments for cosmic navigation", made of glass or porcelain, with a conical extremity containing mercury.

Now, the following information could easily form a chapter which could be entitled "The effects on our planet of wars among the gods", where we could examine strong scientific evidence of how atomic explosions in remote epochs were not merely the result of excessive transcendental meditation and mystical revelation. We could refer to Harappa; and to Mohenjo-Daro in Pakistan, believed to be one of the seven Rishi cities of the Rama empire, where skeletons were discovered whose conditions seemed to indicate sudden death following a nuclear explosion; where objects of everyday use were found to be vitrified and exposed to abnormal levels of uranium and plutonium radiation; and where there are no craters or other signs of meteor activity. Where science meets mythology, as in the vast area in Rajasthan, India, covered by a heavy layer of radioactive ash, where a significant rate of foetal malformations and tumours, and prohibitive levels of radiation have been registered. We could quote the passage in the *Mahabharata* that describes a catastrophic explosion as clearly as we would today: "A single shell, loaded with the power of the universe; an incandescent column of flames and smoke, as luminous as a thousand suns; a vertical explosion; the cloud of smoke rising after the first detonation and blossoming out in circular waves like giant umbrellas; an unknown weapon; burnt corpses; loss of hair and nails; all food products contaminated. To escape from the fire, soldiers diving into the streams to wash themselves and their equipment." Around the city, archaeologists dug up skeletons fifty times more radioactive than normal, some of them immortalised while shaking hands in the middle of the road, as in a freeze-frame. Bodies from thousands of years ago, lying there, unburied.

We could go into all this, yes, but it's somewhat off-topic. All we need to add is that ancient chronicles abound with reports on flying machines. And not only from Indo-Aryan regions, but from North, Central and South America, from Africa, Europe, the Middle East. The Babylonian set of laws *Halkatha* recites: "Knowledge of flying is most ancient: a gift from the gods of old for saving lives."

Even earlier, the highly esteemed and incomparable Sumerians were a source of staggering knowledge, of inexplicable innovations, that seemingly materialised out of nowhere and are still in use.

But we'll stop here.

The fact is that so-called official science, from the height of its podium, simply dismissed these intriguing quotations as figments of an overactive imagination or, at worst, as ill-interpreted natural phenomena (which in part could be the case); that it swiftly swept what it could not or would not explain under the ever-skimpier dogmatic carpet of the academic élite, incapable of covering up the swelling, rolling sand dunes that shouted the truth. The fact is that admitting these and other theories before the council of the wizened sages would mean opening wide Pandora's box: it would result in an overturning of truths presumed to be well-founded – and of the related historical-scientific curriculum hitherto enforced on the masses – and it would shake that podium. To Pac, all this looked highly promising. An idea had started to buzz inside his head: an intuition that behind the symbolism of those myths was an essence of truths; of events that had actually taken place; of tangible facts, codified and ritualised to be transmitted more easily to future generations, and to ensure they resisted the progressive distractions that time always hurls at memories. The disdain with which these stories were received by the Establishment had been enough to prompt closer investigation; also, this was the only vein he could tap to procure the necessary propulsion for the Star Pac.

Had they been reports on events incomprehensible to the layman, narrated through elementary parallels with the natural world surrounding us, one may have been inclined to draw equally elementary conclusions. However, in view of the use of specific vocabulary, comparable to that used currently and indicative of competence and knowledge – and given the technical details and accurate descriptions of devices powered by unknown forms of energy – the matter assumed totally different relevance.

But what was Samuel's role in Pac's attempt to bring together long-lost millenary technology and modern spacecraft?

For all Pac knew, Samuel was the only discreet and dependable supplier of the devices, equipment and technical advice he so badly needed – and which were so difficult to find.

He had never investigated the provenance of what he ordered and paid for, lavishly.

Maybe Samuel worked for an aerospace corporation, and didn't mind making a bit on the side; or else he belonged to some obscure criminal organisation that smuggled low-quality Soviet technology. He hadn't the faintest idea. Which was just as well.

Even his name, Samuel, sounded false; it had to be. And the fact that he should choose a name which in ancient Hebrew meant 'his name is God', Shemu'el, had somehow intrigued him.

A telephone number, a safe, encrypted satellite system, and an educated voice from which he had inferred that the man was no longer in his prime. That was all. But what mattered was that everything he ordered should be supplied punctually, and always by the same person.

On one occasion only, not so long ago, their conversation had lasted a few minutes longer than usual, when his insomniac compulsion was in full swing. This was Pac's obsession, his fixation: the only variable in the

Star Pac's fundamental functions that he couldn't resolve and that had deprived him of his sleep for time immemorial; the key to his survival and to that of the few fortunate founders of the new civilisation – of the new world.

"Listen, do you have something in stock capable of reaching eight kilometres per second, without attracting attention?", he had asked while lying on his sofa, an aromatic cloud of smoke hovering above his head. "Antimatter, plasma or mercury-powered engines. Anything."

The voice at the other end had remained silent, and Pac hadn't paid attention to the distant buzz perceived in the background. Then the rasping response, as if from a larynx lined with fiberglass: "Sorry, my friend. Try again in twenty years' time."

A voice slightly altered: obviously camouflaged.

Although not new to that corner of the globe, Pac still hadn't got used to a typical local custom, hard to ignore: the constant spitting on the ground, preceded by an impassioned upward scraping – requiring, he'd learned, studious and intense practice – whereby blobs of organic goo were drawn from the oropharynx by a reflux induced by skilful contractions; these were savoured before being noisily ejected alongside the offender's shoes – if he had any. A distinctive trait of maturity, sought-after and emulated since pre-school age and exhibited with feigned nonchalance to the day of one's cremation.

At first the sound effects had alarmed him. Strolling along the yellow dirt tracks of the noisy bazaar filled with traders, travellers and pilgrims, he'd felt as if he was being followed first by one or more persons, and soon by everyone. He'd tried turning around suddenly, but it hadn't worked; and calling out "olly, olly, oxen-free" was no longer an option. It was only after stopping to examine the situation that he'd realised he wasn't actually being followed, but was the victim of resonance: by constantly moving among numerous males old enough to indulge in the above-mentioned practice he was exposed to a continuous cacophony, mainly behind him, but occasionally ahead – which was possible, by the law of large numbers.

Nevertheless, comprehension had by no means led to acceptance: even less to adaptation. Pac kept his hands deep inside his padded pockets, so that his head was the only part of his anatomy exposed to the air, saturated with electrons in an advanced state of decomposition. His broad, freshly-shaven face deliberately maintained an expression of regretful discomfort, with occasional lapses into downright disgust.

Kimley, who intermittently dispensed greetings to friends and colleagues, seemed to be exonerated from any such form of social inclusion; to the point that elderly strangers frequently pointed to him, visibly annoyed by the prevailing lack of devotion to ancient traditions, forsaken by young people in their haste to acquire an absurd and degenerate modernity.

It was morning, and Pac's appetite could be measured in astronomical units.

The lanes leading up to a Café recommended as one of the best in town (and who was he to argue?) were far cleaner and tidier than expected. The area, explained Kimley while walking ahead of him at a fast pace, belonged to a more tranquil and affluent part of Thamel. Here, Italian, Japanese, French and local restaurants and small bars welcomed anyone who wished to sit at the small, characteristic outdoor tables, especially in such sunny and unusually warm weather.

A fresh and pleasant morning, Pac conceded.

The light that pervaded the streets and the narrow multi-coloured shops; and shone on the busy people with their carrier bags and carts, on their curious glances, on their amusement at the tourists; that light that poured down from a clear and lustrous sky and scattered, refracted by the empty glasses as if by tinfoil; the light that picked out the goods piled up at the entrance of the stores: that light was possessed of a candour, an intimate transparency that, considering the smog, was simply extraordinary.

Pac could no longer think. He was overcome at that precise moment by the sensation of having donned a pair of spectacles, as if in play, convinced he didn't need them; only to discover, embarrassed and amazed, that in reality the material outline of every object and form was entirely different: less approximate; much clearer, richer in minute details and nuances which, now in focus, beckoned to him joyfully.

A super-refraction of pure light.

At the entrance of the Northfield Café – flanking an elegant book store which he would like to visit sooner or later, he told himself – the tables were laid out in a horseshoe arrangement, occupying a good half of the lane and leaving a passageway barely sufficient for one pedestrian at a time.

There were few clients around, not much shouting and little pressure: this enabled Pac to unwind while consulting the menu brought to him by the waiter. A waiter who, in another continent and at that time of day, would be sitting at his desk in school, learning something other than the burden of making ends meet.

Light-headed, and with a lingering craving from the night before, he felt his belly beneath the table, then pinched it hard, observing that it hadn't diminished at all. This, he'd learned, was the only trick that effectively helped him tune in to the frequency of *Radio75*, whose number indicated his objective.

"Fruit salad with low-fat yogurt and muesli; no sugar. And some green tea," he said to the waiter, who made notes

– mental notes.

Kimley, on the other hand, spoke to him at length in Nepalese, miming a few gestures and concluding with one of his broad grins, which he sustained unvaried while turning his head away from the retreating waiter towards Pac. The latter found himself exposed to an eloquent display of teeth, trespassing beyond the boundary of his privacy for an interminable passage of seconds, until retiring behind the gradual closure of Kimley's mouth; Pac was left to wonder whether the long-limbed fellow – still dressed in yesterday's clothes, cap included – might suffer from latent ailments that his watch-cum-calculator were unable to relieve; or whether he should be worrying about something else.

He didn't wait long for an answer: the waiter had asked for his father's help: not because the boy had been the object of indecent advances, but because he needed assistance in carrying the trays of food, easily distinguishable between those ordered in English and those in Nepalese.

The table was soon opulently decked out with carbohydrates stuffed with fat and dairy products, saccharoids and yeasts, some still-warm delicacies and some fresh and creamy ones. A calorie funfair, where the only attraction that Pac could afford – like the fifth of six children of a factory-worker whose factory had exploded – consisted in putting his hand into a glass jar and drawing a number on a strip of paper rolled inside a macaroni. A losing number.

After consulting his watch, Kimley started the mopping-up operation, demolishing – with an almost savage voracity – sweet and savoury pastries, buttered toast spread with jam, scrambled eggs and sausages, washing it all down with long draughts of warm chocolate-flavoured milk and with fruit juice. Then pausing open-mouthed to release a loud belch, he checked his elaborate Casio again, exhibiting a beatific expression and announcing that he was ready to leave – without divulging the length of their breakfast break.

At that point Pac's cereal bowl had long been wiped clean and set aside. He'd watched, impotent, the injustice being perpetrated before his eyes. Yes, something important wasn't going as it should have. Quite apart from the obvious disproportion just witnessed, which – he told himself – should teach him a thing or two, the fact was that some people (and this robust gentleman who took advantage of his magnanimity was a glaring example), were graced with the faculty of stuffing themselves with every possible treat and gastronomic delight, blithely ignoring the rules of correct food combinations, and assimilating nothing other than cheerfulness. While for others, not even manhandling the weighing scales would influence the verdict of the display screen – despite their having endured months and even years of dieting, sacrifices, rigour and discipline. Whether it was a question of metabolism or genetics no longer mattered: it was an unspeakable form of discrimination, all the more biased, insidious and despicable for punishing defenceless people like himself, who certainly didn't lack self-control, determination or wisdom. While possibly favouring the most ignorant and self-destructive, the most prone to degradation and perdition. Perhaps this was the worst, the most detestable and humiliating injustice of all. Which is why it would have to be abrogated. In the new world – the one he was designing – the criteria of beauty, health and harmony would be modelled on his person: certainly slim and attractive at the beginning of the undertaking, when the foundations of civilisation had to be re-laid on the wasteland which his vimana would find on landing. But he wouldn't exclude the possibility of putting on a few kilos later, what with all the stress from that arduous venture, and with human need for gratification. In such an event, the others also, the few survivors, could – indeed must – put on weight as he'd done, if not more. All equal before the mirror. Now *this* is what he called freedom, community, a sense of brotherhood extended to physical form.

One standard for all!

The bill, which had ended up in his hands without his noticing, brought him back to the present like a slap across the face. A faded, harmless-looking scrap of paper, but bearing – impressed in blue ink – the price of his excessive kindness.

Kimley was looking elsewhere, as if at a passing friend, a hint of a smile almost surfacing but immediately repressed.

Pac was relieved to find he still had some banknotes in his pocket. Had a few dematerialised during the night – he mused – only to reappear in a new dimension, brand-new, colourful, smelling of metallic ink, and worth far more than the current exchange? Pac used some to pay for what he hadn't eaten, and decided not to give too much importance to what had just happened. He must rise above such things; and anyway he had work to do – which would prove to be even more insidious than that breakfast.

Obviously, and as usual, tipping was out of the question. He would leave that to the customers who were slowly filling the place, those Western tourists who loved to wear oriental trinkets, necklaces and rings and brightly-coloured scarves.

This was the right time to make a move.

The non-governmental agency which handsomely paid for his services, reimbursing 80 percent of his expense reports (which he did his best to inflate disproportionately), had asked him to meet a certain Balaram Bhasal, head of a community called *Future's Haven*, whose mission was to provide shelter to children who lived on the streets, give them regular meals twice a day, and an education up to their school-leaving diploma. This, in exchange for simple domestic duties, such as producing hand-made incense – whose sale was one of the community's main sources of income – subject to the authorisation of the children's parents, in the few cases where these were alive and known.

This place clearly threatened the interests that the agency aimed to represent: food, employment and certified education in the elusive dynamics of that micro-economic set-up were seen as bacteria that had to be sterilised.

Kimley drove several miles out of town to get to their destination. Leaving the confusion and torpor of Kathmandu behind, they passed the small town of Bhaktapur, traversed districts where street-paving was optional, and where large, brightly-coloured houses and impeccable temples alternated with hovels made of mud and stone, wood and sweat, dust and hunger, with their to-ing and fro-ing of women and toddlers, the former carrying things, the latter running and shouting with the muffled ebullience of their eggshell minds.

The greenest of mountains made way for soil of brown; for sensations of yellow evoked by forsaken landscapes, hunched like overlapping breasts. A muddy, ascending road, a bend, the snowy peaks of mountains that delimited the view with their constant, inescapable presence: stunning, admonishing. A short downhill stretch, a pothole, and the car that Pac had given up as a bad job came to a halt.

From there, he would proceed on foot. Alone.

"I shan't be long," he said, triggering Kimley's automatic watch-consulting reflex. Whether gloating over his toy, timing each daily activity, or covering up a far more serious tic, Pac couldn't decide; and while unable to look away from the rocky mass looming ahead, which fortunately he was not setting out to conquer, he was struck by the thought that his life would have been very different, if only his childhood wishes had been granted, even occasionally.

But this wasn't the time to dwell on such thoughts.

As he pulled out his crocodile briefcase, he glanced quickly at his figure reflected on the outside of the car window: his white shirt and navy-blue pullover were alright, apart from the bulge. Beneath the reach of his mirrored image he wore pressed trousers and clean ankle boots. That would do.

He covered a short distance uphill along a (fortunately dry) path, away from prying eyes, although there was only Kimley, already intent on adjusting his car-seat to reclining position. There was nothing else but sky-grazing mountain tops, the bitterly cold, dry air, and a haphazard scattering of unadorned dwellings.

A couple of steps ahead lay a low, flat rock that was sure to suit his needs: a scrap of mineral dropped by the mountains that must have plunged and rolled down the grassy slopes to the valley below with a thunderous din. Seated on the rock, he gazed around him. Silence was everywhere: a silence that seemed imposed, definitive, though for the moment he had no time to absorb it. Closing his eyes, he breathed in slowly until he felt a slight constriction. A brief, intense moment of orthodox preparation. Oblivion, visualisation: he knew what he might be in for, especially on such hostile, forbidding terrain. He knew the doubts and weaknesses that might assail him. Focus, Everything was alright. Empty; black; void. Breathe out. Passively Indifferent mode: ON.

He re-emerged to the light: he was ready. He stood up and started walking, silently, following the path traced on a map that he'd printed, visualising his next target. The weed-killer was in action.

The path that led him to the community shelter traversed fields of wheat, skirting gravel, shrubs, the flower-filled garden of a house whose plump, smiling owner waved at him from her window. Already tiring, he plodded slowly up an acid green, grassy hill, through the brittle, rough growth, rolling in slow waves chased erratically by gusts from the mountains above. Late morning at the end of April; quiet abandonment to the peace, to the absence of sound except for his own footsteps. But the unfamiliar pastoral scent disturbed his nostrils, distracting attention from his laborious, contemplative ascent. Soon his nostrils decided that they'd inhaled enough, far more than they were used to; and his lungs, ever their staunch allies, were in full agreement. So, out of breath and feeling vaguely dizzy, Pac leaned against a rock, and once again surrendered to the contemplation of those supreme mountainous overlords and undisputed progenitors whose dominion – comprising both the sky and the earth – delimited our view, forcing us to look up in wonder.

That's what he called authority: sired by the molten core of the planet, the sharp fangs of those mountain tops could capture the viewer and enslave him, reducing him to a tiny particle of the Himalayas. There they towered, venerable and venerated, observing the inane activities beneath them. Whether they were really the gods' abode he had no way of telling, but definitely an inspired and obvious choice. By his usual process of association he was struck by the thought that, with all those places of worship and houses of God already scattered across continents, and many others constantly in construction, these divinities were more like speculative builders than like burning torches in the dark forest of our existence; and he couldn't but conclude that, given an entire celestial body in which to elect his lofty mansion, he personally would have opted for a tropical island. A matter of taste.

He had digressed again. Was it laziness? If not, what was it?

Better not investigate, leave everything as it was: he had more than enough on his mind. He stood up once more, and increased his pace.

The community was nearby: he recognised the building as it had been described: the size of a hay loft, with a roof of red tiles, and a second building, higher up, starkly unfinished, like a tree pruned by a sadistic gardener. Nothing else, apart from the odd solitary goat. Any lingering doubts would be dispelled instantly by the vibrant echo of children shouting in the distance. All he had to do was to follow their call, so to speak.

As Pac roamed around the garden of the mountain orphanage, he was welcomed by a tall, gaunt gentleman with penetrating eyes, hollow cheeks and a dark complexion. The man walked towards him with such a wide grin that Pac found it hard to reciprocate: his cheeks couldn't stretch to the task. The striking thing about that smile was a superb gap between his front teeth: a gap wide enough for a mollusc to escape through; or for a forked-tongue snake to suddenly leap from, towards the over-curious onlooker; or through which to spit at one's desk-mate during a history lesson.

Wearing a high-neck sweater and a burned-orange woollen cap, Pac's host welcomed him enthusiastically, and took him on a guided tour of the promising activities of *Future's Haven*.

"We're happy to meet you, at last," breathed Mr Balaram Bhasal barely audibly. He must have had a cold or something, because out of his mouth came a mere whisper of a weak, tired voice.

They shook hands, which made Pac aware of how sweaty his own were. Strange, this had never happened before.

"My pleasure, Mr. Bhasal. This place is charming. Yours is a moving, not to say exemplary enterprise," he said, underscoring his words with a slow nod and a rapt expression. That would do, he mustn't exaggerate.

"Please, Mr. Moon, follow me," murmured Balaram, with perceptible accent.

They set off at a slow pace, paying the necessary attention to where they trod – in view of the strong smell of manure permeating the valley – especially now that the sun was doing what it could to warm the air.

At the rear, where the valley dropped steeply without terracing, Balaram stopped. "You see... those two wells," he said, indicating the lids of two large man-made cesspits. "That's where organic waste, human and animal, ends up. Bodily functions, you understand."

Pac understood.

"Ours, and of the community cows and sheep. Through fermentation, through pressure and heat... these biomasses are transformed into gas, which we use for cooking." His speech reflected the typical rising intonation of the Indian subcontinent, the musicality of his words ascending in vertical swirls. "In addition, with milk from our cows we make cheese that we sell in town. These constitute our sustenance."

And here they were, the flocks of little girls and boys: small crowds the age of which could be counted on the fingers of a single hand; some of them barely weaned. They ran all over the place, observed curiously, commenting in whispers among themselves. Clean and, in their way, well-mannered and dignified, respectful of the important personage whom they'd been told not to disturb.

It was nearly lunchtime, and soon they would be joined by the older school children who occupied the other edifice, the one with no windows, whose second and third floor were more in the builders' mind, rather than the actual building.

"That's what those funds are for," said Mr. Balaram, straining to put as much voice as he could in that sentence, which highlighted the official reason for Pac's visit. "When it rains, in winter, teaching here is complicated and the children fall ill." Some of these could be heard shouting and laughing nearby. "And if we managed to complete the remaining two floors we could accommodate more children, guaranteeing an elementary education and a certificate… and with that they could further their studies and find work. Have a future," he concluded, one hand gesticulating while the other held firmly a toddler who had squirmed towards them like an inquisitive lizard.

Pac nodded, smiled, saying how impressed he was with

everything. While congratulating Mr. Balaram Bhasal, he seemed to share the enthusiasm that the man exuded, especially when he gazed at him with those large, dark, docile eyes, that seemed to protrude from their orbits, lightening his face with benevolence. Eyes that, on closer examination, revealed a fighting spirit that had been sorely tried, a well-defined personality, but not invincible.

"These are our resources," he continued, his face moving closer, his sincerely preoccupied expression trying to compensate for the inadequacy of his voice. "We are self-sufficient as far as possible... we have solar panels to heat water; we produce and sell incense of excellent quality... natural, organic. Come, Mr. Moon, follow me, I'll show you!"

Pac wasn't at all sorry to put some distance between himself and that ever too-close and disturbing tooth gap, evoking a registered letter from the tax office; although now, as they entered the community shelter and educational centre, he was bothered by the clamour around his legs: each one of his steps was surrounded by other, smaller and more fragile steps of the little ones, who often crossed his, forcing him to stop so as not to tread on them. Their feet were tiny, but their joyful excitement was considerable, though all he could see of them from above was their dense, dishevelled mops of hair. Hair which, sooner or later, would also fall away.

Already feeling distressed, he tried to control as best he

could that too-familiar agitation, that sense of bitter uneasiness he'd worked on in all those years: that voice on his shoulder, that drop of blood oozing out of a heart pricked by a wreath of horns; his hands were sweating again. This, perhaps, was the only test for a job like his. Relatively easy when it involved getting people to sign papers; but more complicated when the moral and psychological implications had to be faced.

A moment of absorbing, conscious inspiration, of purity – which passed quickly.

Under a large porch of sheet metal were gathered all of the community's members, guests and operators; two of these – two thin women of firm yet kindly manner – were trying to keep the children's excitement in check.

Sitting next to his host on a decrepit wooden bench, Pac observed with feigned interest as two embarrassed little boys took sticks of bamboo; these they rolled zealously but gently, modelling around them a dense, brown mixture taken from an aluminium saucepan where it had been mixed with water from a pitcher. During the entire operation, the warmth and glory was all for the two little workers.

"This is a composite of sandalwood and of the excrements of our cows, what we don't use as fuel," explained Mr. Bhasal, taking a stick from the hands of one of the children who, sitting cross-legged on the floor, observed his masterpiece proudly, surrounded by the small crowd watching this demonstration: the satisfied matrons, and the small guests, attentive and curious in their hats and simple, make-shift clothes, which Pac deemed unsuitable for the harsh climate. The small, milk chocolate-coloured craftsman seemed uncomfortable in the face of so much attention, especially that of the wealthy, well-dressed Western visitor. Equally uncomfortable were the expressions and grimaces on the faces of his school mates; with their ruddy cheeks, some of them looked exactly like those dolls; the toys played with by children in more prosperous latitudes, while waiting for their next whim to be satisfied.

Up there, among those enormous mountains, fostered by that rustic routine, was concentrated a nucleus of laborious promise which that particular child, cold and intimidated, exuded with such singular force; with those burning eyes that fixed Pac, as only the flame from such a source could do. They stared, insistently, binding him with the ties of insidious humility. From those pupils shone the purity, the wings of a life as it should have been and always should be; the reflection of a wild, leaping cosmos; the combustion of stars. In those eyes Pac saw something: he felt as if he'd been reached, caressed, traversed by something which he perceived as elementary and universal, innate and intelligent: something that made him shiver, causing him to feel suspended for a prolonged instant, arresting and maintaining him in a state of wondering anxiety. He tried in vain to read in the depths of those eyes, sinking, then suddenly it all vanished and there he was, gulping, crossing his legs and readjusting his posture.

That gaze, however, was still fixed on him, back-lit by a benign, immaculate spark: the core of compressed time. How much longer would his own eyes resist, in the face of such a trial?

Finally, the child's attention was distracted by a friend; he turned away, ready to join him, but before he could make his escape he was promptly immobilised by the embrace of his putative father. Captive, he was forced to remain in front of the man to whom they were explaining things that didn't interest him.

"This stick of incense is as natural as it is unobtainable on the market," said Balaram smiling, almost moved. "No chemical compound for its combustion, no additive for the aroma. Isn't that wonderful?"

"A miracle of simplicity," commented Pac, turning it over in his hands while the little ones watched attentively, impatient to roll sticks themselves for the joy of this droll foreigner.

"The fact is that food is expensive...". Emitted through his gapped incisors, Balaram's voice seemed to be on the verge of failing, but nonetheless he persisted. "This year the cost of wheat and rice has doubled; as has that of teachers and school supplies; clothes and basic necessities; my fund-raising trips; the new school. Year after year, prices go up." Words that opened a lacuna, a velvet-lined space in which a designated container should be deposited.

There was no need to say more: the conversation had reached its objective.

Pac got up, took his briefcase, and Mr. Bhasal realised that it was time to continue the conversation in private; to take the step that – with all the necessary common sense and pragmatism – would make that day somehow historical: the beginning of a long dreamed-of serenity, embodied by that polite and elegant guest, whose sincere and transparent gaze had reassured him from the start.

Leaving the children to play in the field and the women to their chores, they went into the house. Not surprisingly, this too was clean and frugal; though permeated by the same mix of odours as those outside: the manure and incense used to produce a fragrance that was both raw material and end product.

Balaram's office was adjacent to the kitchen. As he followed the spare gentleman, Pac couldn't help savouring odours of an entirely different nature, emanating from that room like a billowing, swirling cloud of candy floss. The scent of genuine, spicy food, lovingly prepared as only women (most women, at least) can do when cooking for small children, the act of nourishing being the loftiest, most irrepressible and moving expression of femininity, biological urge, unparalleled tenderness. He recognised curry, and certainly something oven-baked: the aroma of soaring sugar-levels: that fragrance of sizzling carbohydrates was unmistakable, causing his sensitive stomach, inundated by gastric juices, to rumble.

Why was it so easy to be distracted?

Now the door of that pokey office had been closed, Pac was all set to play his usual part: this time as the legal representative of an Anglo-Indian philanthropist, whose profile had been conjured up by Pac's employers at no great cost: a website, some documents and contacts. A cover-up that would shortly change the fate of this community.

Apart from its noble purposes and the altruism dispensed, that community really did represent a threat – as should be clear, by now, even to the unobservant. To the Church of the Potentate, this near-total energy self-sufficiency was an oath, punishable by flaying; it was a blow to their gains, not only economic, but also command and attitude-related: an attack on the drowsy absent-mindedness of citizenships tamed at the cost of great sacrifice: an affront whose avenge could only be eternal damnation. And if this applied in the so-called Western world, it did all the more in Nepal, one of the poorest countries in the world. In the epoch of globalisation, the concept of auto-sufficiency had been banned. Although this might elude many people's comprehension, the meaning of globalisation was control, dependency (energetic, cultural, economic and health-related, of the media etc.) from a single source, a single mind, a single apparatus that decided for everyone. Without too much fuss and lamentation.

One hand resting on the briefcase in his lap, Pac explained that the figure he represented was keen to preserve confidentiality, that he wanted to be kept up-to-date on the actual use of the generous sum that he was about to donate – provided Balaram, according to foregoing agreements, was prepared to give up an insignificant share of *Future's Haven*, purely in order to sponsor their project with suitable emphasis, also at the international level. This was sure to entail an increase in visibility, and consequently the possibility of obtaining greater contributions; media support that could help amend the sad situation afflicting the entire country by aiming to develop and promote such invaluable enterprises. It was to be hoped that politicians would soon adopt serious measures against the deplorable state of affairs that robbed its most precious resources of their very future, while tormenting his conscience and everyone else's, calling them to action. He was also keen to stress that the ancient benefactor whom he was honoured to represent would have done everything in his power, in the near future, to free himself of his oppressive business commitments and visit this splendid garden of refuge, and to shake Balaram's hand in person.

Balaram sighed, nodding slowly, his cheeks taught and hollow, his eyes half-closed in a gentle expression. He was moved, grateful. And the short ensuing silence seemed to enhance the sensation of such manifest pleasure.

Pac drew some papers from his briefcase, while banishing from the temple of his mind the recent memory of the eyes of a little boy holding an incense stick, which seemed to interfere with his concentration.

Just then somebody knocked. That same little boy. Summoned by himself? Was this some sort of punishment?

The child couldn't have been more than five years old, with short hair hidden under the hood of the large padded jacket he wore (he was one of the few who had one), over simple, dignified clothes. And those eyes...

He ran to Balaram, who welcomed him with a warm embrace and a kiss on the forehead.

"Sorry. Ram is always at my side, he doesn't like to leave me. Do you, little one?"

The little head nodded, while the boy embraced Balaram tightly.

This didn't help, thought Pac. But he'd manage. It took more than that.

Two pairs of eyes observed him attentively, as one watches a trained nurse dress one's wound: with trusting optimism.

The management of this shelter and education community, which included the two thin women as well as Balaran, had already pondered the offer, and after a long and passionate discussion had voted in favour.

Which is why Pac didn't have to wait long to replace the papers, duly signed, inside the scaly briefcase, leave the office, shake hands again, and find himself surrounded once more by little orphans (now more numerous as classes were over), who stared, hid, came closer to touch him, laughed, hopped around like fruit flies on a fermented bilberry.

And just when he thought he'd made it, when he'd already pictured his hasty retreat to the car, seen himself speeding off, then getting on the first plane and leaving behind him that concentrate of laborious vitality – that futile project for a morrow that would never come, if not to reset the meter of stupidity and of belated good intentions; just when he'd considered the possibility of opting out and devoting all his energies to his escape plan, viewing this as a considerable acceleration of The End of Time; just then, the trap that brought him down and buggered any chance of departure closed in on him.

"Why don't you stay to lunch? We've prepared a special menu for your visit!" exclaimed one of the women, with a radiant smile.

In the bat of an eyelid the entire community of former street urchins exploded in a joyous, uncontrolled choir, which echoed all around the valley, cheering to a proposal which Pac, aghast, immediately turned down.

"I... I can't..." he mumbled. "Thank you, but you see... there's a car waiting for me, and much as I'd like to, I really..." he tried to say, as yet unaware of the formidable power that unbridled, recently reincarnated white dwarfs were capable of deploying to obtain their objective. And he stood no chance of opposing them, with his rational, hollow-sounding justifications.

Which is why he found himself in a large cafeteria in the company of those well-mannered and excited imps, unaccustomed to novelties (especially if fair-skinned and with anomalous features), eating gurr, tama and tserel, which roughly translates as potato pancakes with cheese, soup of dried bamboo shoots and vegetable rissoles. All of this cooked by the two youthful-looking, patient women who helped themselves cheerfully, while also filling up Pac's plate. And the more his plate was piled with steaming food, the more his stomach clenched in a ball so tightly and sorely that it burned like the fire from a pile of dried leaves. More food for him: less for them.

Somewhere, from the mouldy dungeons of his soul, rose a voice – melodious, graceful, admonishing – a voice he'd always believed he could ignore; a voice that would never meddle with his affairs. But which, in a flash, like the tentacle of an infected octopus, had insinuated itself in his mind, reminding him of what he was about to do: the wickedness and benediction, condemnation and salvation, the sacredness and blasphemy concealed in that food, and in the act he was about to commit. While they were all stuffing their mouths, laughing and savouring that feast, chewing and swallowing and sipping, Pac observed the food before him, which should have been a cheerful, reckless exception to his diet. Even *Radio75* refused to air the songs and comments that the masked speaker normally broadcasted, especially at meal times.

He'd never sunk so low. The sabotages, bankruptcies, expropriations he'd dealt with so far had always belonged to the aseptic sphere of book-keeping; to studied and targeted missions, like those of a bomber pilot releasing "Intelligent Weapons" from above (Jesus Christ, words had really forfeited their meaning, and people must be out of their mind to allow this oxymoron to exist and proliferate); a pilot who nevertheless would have time to get back to base and enjoy a cold beer without even seeing the flash of the deflagration.

That had been, and should be, his job.

However now, for some incomprehensible reason, he was witnessing an event directly, he could read the future – he could feel it in his bones. The food in front of him – which he knew he didn't deserve – the food on that stainless steel tray behaved oddly: those pancakes and rissoles seemed to spit their oil in his face; in his soup bowl, vegetables had joined up on the surface to form a frowning emoticon, so belligerent that Pac was obliged to scramble it with his spoon, to drown it for fear that others might notice it; or, more likely, to save himself from growing even more distressed.

As if that weren't bad enough, he was having to fill his mouth with delicacies possessed by a demon that he himself had instilled, and for which no exorcism seemed to work; he was having to chew and savour them, assuming a rapt expression before these people's eyes, their questions, their pleasant conversation: all this was torture, he told himself. It was putting him to the test as no sergeant major could ever impose in times of peace.

Only the thought of this challenge helped him hold his ground, gave him the strength not to give up, not to betray himself in conversation. He knew he could come out of this invigorated – or devastated.

So he listened to Balaram's stories of a lifetime's experiences – of spiritual retreats in an ashram in Aurobindo, whose teachings inspired this oasis of rectitude – while remaining the constant object of amused and covert comments; of giggles bursting forth here and there; of the penetrating gaze of his host; of the continuous hospitable attentions of those who experienced his visit, his presence at their table, as a celebration of the creative process; as an occasion to show the children how, through committed consistency, one could build the present, and pave the way for the future. And that festive atmosphere was indeed even more indigestible than the food that now writhed in his stomach.

When he finally managed to escape from their grip, the sun had already reclined behind the mountains; the air was assuming cooler tones, as he ran downhill – fast and resolutely – to avert a sense of tearful defeat. He would not allow that exceedingly constructive, serene image – the portrait of a party that he knew to be a funeral – to inhabit him. Everything would be terminated, destroyed, swept away.

Soon.

So what was this malaise, this sadness that now clouded his vision? This dizziness, this nausea? Why had they all been so kind to him? Why? They shouldn't have, they shouldn't dare. He was aware of sweating as he ran, perceiving his belly as a sack of worm-shaped bacteria about to multiply and devour him.

Which perhaps served him right. Or maybe not.

The car was there, with the same stains in the same places, excoriated by the same rust.

Kimley was asleep, and the sight of him placidly immersed in a state so different from his own pissed him off even more. Pac took a running jump and kicked the car-door violently, causing Kimley to jump up equally brusquely, looking around him bleary-eyed, his fist clenched at the ready. He checked his watch, but one look at his employer's face was enough to make him realise that it was best to start up the engine immediately, drive off fast and keep quiet – and hope for the best.

The return road became opaque, of a sooty grey that the dim lights of the car couldn't alleviate. Through the car windows they could barely make out the signs of neglect, of resignation; in the flickering torch light, the eyes of dirty, defeated men, the robes of exhausted women whose tomorrow would be unchanged, illuminated by the same sun, governed by the same gods.

Images that would once again be dimmed, that would soon be set aside.

Pac snorted, then cleared his voice as if to say something. He rummaged inside his briefcase, stroked the rough paper of a packet of sandalwood incense, which he lifted to his nose: it smelled of something too good for that particular moment: something, he thought, that maybe one day he would appreciate.

He slumped against the padded back-rest and pulled out his satellite phone.

"General Markets, can I help you?" chimed a ladybird-voice the other end.

He knew that voice: it belonged to a certain Megan. Pleasant, no longer young, her long honey-coloured hair tumbling down in tight ringlets, which she often ruffled with nervous fingers.

"It's me, sweetheart," murmured Pac in an undertone.

"Sorry?" asked the voice, suddenly growing cold.

"Pass me the warehouse, Megan."

"Oh, it's you, hi. Give me the code."

"..."

"Hello?"

"Yes, sorry. BF616CZ."

A tinkering sound, a click, another sigh.

Kimley glanced at him in the rear-view mirror, stroking his cap and frowning. And continued to hope for the best.

Outside, the night was drawing in fast, the street was already dark. Shadows of valleys and mountain tops, few lights along the rough-surfaced sides of the street. Houses, hovels, wreckage, stooping figures, caught in the car's headlights. A silence polluted by exhaust emissions.

He wouldn't call Samuel, this time. A quick hot shower, and he'd fly home as soon as possible.

By the time his office replied he'd retrieved enough breath to report; the community's fate was none of his business – he didn't want to know. But those eyes...

A shiver; a thought: banished. He started to dictate, his voice shaking, and Kimley would soon damn him, on an empty stomach.

***

At that point a visit to Oscar was urgently called for. Oscar, the name that the child Pac would have given to his kitten, if only he'd been allowed to keep one. A name that he'd found a use for, anyway.

Placed at the southernmost end of the land of cedars, Lebanon's mountain range rose like teeth – perfectly healthy, rotten or gaping – in a crooked jaw. Forbidding, luxuriant places, animated by creatures who sang and hunted in the moonlight, exuding hormones, growling, devouring one another and hopping among long, narrow leaves, slippery petals and sturdy branches; drunk with pollen and gastric juices; with grasping antennae, skewering beaks.

But there was nothing much in daytime. At least, not that Pac could see, committed to one of those treks initially hailed as healthy and invigorating, only to be damned later as a masochistic sham. He was still halfway there, in the phase where his outing resembled an inane metaphor of life such as are still being palmed off as exotic and original in novels; in the phase where the thought of turning back and getting into his car had already evaporated, along with the awareness that it would cost him a greater effort than doing the opposite. Surprising himself, he had blessed and invoked this vehicle with sheer abandonment: something otherwise improbable, but for distance and necessity; just as the paint on the coachwork, once blue as the varicose vein on grandma's ankle, would certainly have testified, had it been redeemed of the geological strata of mud, dust and offensive neglect.

Space. Physical and mental space, expanding at every step on that soil begging for water. An emotional fissure was clamouring for air, to set up a hotbed of resentment and repressed bitterness.

The ascent was steep, etched on the side of the mountain like a tortuous vein on the ear of a calf; the ensuing flat stretch gave one's lungs a break, bequeathing to others the onus of hacking through the scrub and brambles that hindered one's progress; while the rays of the sun filtered through the vegetation like luminous rain, scattered by a gentle, precious breeze. The air was freshened with the wild fragrance of uncontaminated flora after weeks of dry weather: a mixture of sweet and acrid, an aroma of fermented sucrose, of pungent evaporated resin, of boiled lymph; unlike his own body-odour, reeking of rotting onions. His bulky form was still a considerable distance from his destination: about two hours on foot, he reckoned; three, if he counted his lunch break; and the air was getting hot in the merciless sun which, as soon as it broke through the clouds, beat down on the clumsy biped, who puffed like a young ogre at his puberty initiation rite.

During a second reflective halt, immersed in landscape that allowed his gaze to roam freely among boundless rolling expanses, he was usually close to giving vent to the above-mentioned oaths, experiencing what experts called aversion for the cause undertaken; marinating in a brew of bitterness against all humanity: a bitterness by which (as should be clear by now) Pac was afflicted.

However, Oscar was the single, unmatched exception.

Very soon his damp emotions evaporated, and all he felt was weariness. Shouldering his small trekking backpack,

Pac tackled the last leg of his pilgrimage: climbing up a tree-covered face he was obliged to hang on to branches, rocks and tree trunks, making the most of his quads and milking from his strained muscles enough lactic acid to supply those same bakers and confectioners responsible for his weight and fatigue. Left hand on root, right leg on rock, and heave; right hand on parched soil, rivulet of sweat like spurting artery; legs pushing, arms pulling, grabbing; belly-fat dragging; gravel underfoot; and so on, upwards.

When he finally reached the small meadow adjacent to the opening in the mountain, a secret refuge unknown to maps, he removed his backpack with a quick movement and collapsed, exhausted, passively welcomed by the dry, warm earth.

The sensation was incomparable.

A light breeze was blowing, caressing with impartial softness blades of grass and sweaty skin, mineral surfaces and insects' antennae, leaves – and his thoughts. That same breeze helped Pac regain control over his breathing, now calmer. That same breeze had traversed valleys and planes, oceans and villages; inflated sails and hindered butterflies, driven windmills, blown bridal veils, transported pollen, lifted kites and skirts, enlivened torpid contemplation – and diffused culinary fragrances, delighting domestic mice and causing bears to prick up their ears.

Pac rolled on his side, his mind savouring joy. He got up and walked towards the narrow entrance of the cavern. It was semi-dark and cool inside, with tall walls; a drawing on one of them, done by himself, years earlier. There was something reassuring in those rocks, a sense of comfort and protection, a womb that could cosset and embrace in its mineral walls of dark grey, streaked here and there with rough veins of a lighter grey.

Oscar was there, exactly where he'd left him on his previous visit. Poised and smiling, protected in that cool, damp, natural cavity, decked with scented moss and with a scattering of gravel and small stones like pieces of a tabletop game suspended for unforeseen and pressing reasons. About to take its leave of those present, the waning afternoon sun bathed in a jaundice-yellow light the wiry figure sitting on his heels, his trunk erect, his arms laying on his legs, hands clasped in front of him. Hardly any light reflected off the orange tunic that scrupulously covered every inch of his emaciated body, so intent who knows where, and in whose company. Certainly of the kind we'd all like to have at our birthday party, judging by the perpetual hint of a smile that enlightened his face; and notwithstanding a beard longer than Pac remembered, like a prickly bush, entangled luxuriantly over the fertile domain of a face where grooming had been banished as subversive.

A sturdy-looking golden lock joined two links of a silver chain that adorned his scrawny neck with obscure functionality, and suited him perfectly.

Without averting his eyes from the holy man, and careful not to make a noise or utter a syllable, Pac retrieved his backpack, from which he drew what he needed and arranged it with practiced precision on the imaginary X chalked by the Rational Order of Things. Then he backed away slowly, until he was once more in the open air.

Time was slowing down at last, and so was his breathing, aided by the unruffled silence, soothing his aural sensibilities, so harshly jangled outside this ambience.

He sat on a flat, dusty hummock, exuding contentment and drying off the last rivulets of sweat that crowned the success of his enterprise. From his special-guest armchair he could now enjoy the spectacle, in itself bewitching enough to justify all that hassle. The sun and the moon exchanged greetings from their respective celestial sidewalks, like old school friends in a suburban town bumping into each other by chance: shouting pleasantries across the road, slowing down without stopping, laughing heartily, then proceeding their separate ways, with the usual promise of organising soon a cosmic class reunion to celebrate the good old days when the universe was born. With the changing intensity of the landscape's colours; with the woods and mountains preparing to welcome the night; and the rising of a gentle breeze patrolling the territory with its enlivening presence: with that same pace, Pac turned down his internal volume-control and opened his escape valves, enabling his compressed, fermented emotions to run off and disperse, thus favouring the natural decline of radioactivity described in Chapter III of the "Guidelines for the Prevention of Accidents in our Nuclear Power Station." He let himself float, unwind, while his features relaxed, even into the trace of a smile.

Only when the god Apollo was about to clock out did he decide to leave his armchair and retrieve from his backpack the bars of chocolate, apricot turnovers and crisps, fruit juice and organic-cheese sandwiches that made up his dinner on that eve. The eve of a ritual, of a celebration that would cleanse him of impurities, whereby he would restore (albeit momentarily) a connection with his inner self, switching off the aerials inside his head; cutting off the low-voltage wiring that powered the ordinary; setting the stars ablaze with his vital spark. Needless to say, in that specific circumstance alone, *Radio75* would be disabled: not a word would be spoken of feelings of guilt. This was the single famous exception: everything was under control. Truth be told, he would certainly need a lot of calories. Savouring and devouring this meal with the delicious kick one got from bending the rules, with the voracity of real appetite and the sensation of recovering from his fatigue: all this took no time at all, and left no trace other than the fragments of bread and cheese caught between his teeth – to be enjoyed by bacteria first, and by his dentist later.

Finally it was time to return inside: he had work to do.

He lit the wick of the small kerosene lamp, and suddenly the walls of the cave were awash with amber-coloured light; it was like lighting the Christmas tree for the first time ever – for those who have such memories. Or, for those who don't, it was like a child setting fire to a screwed-up piece of newspaper, and carefully inserting it among the sticks and twigs of his first campfire, under the strict supervision of an adult – if you've ever had this experience. Condolences to those who haven't.

Thus illuminated, Oscar was even more stunning, more authoritative. The faint, vibrant yellow light reached his spiky brown beard, highlighted the long wavy hair that fell to his shoulders, the closed eyelids that might open at any moment; the orange robe that seemed to come alive, transforming him into an anthropomorphic torch waiting for its castle, into an attic totem. The priest of any so-called primitive civilisation would have hired him in the pantheon of his divinities. His immobility was power, his existence was the food of divine banquets, his closed eyes and his unfathomable mind were the hope, the prophecy, the software connecting microcosm and macrocosm, the sharp curved borderline between yin and yang. His absence was his kindest gift to civilisation; that hint of a smile was the space halberd in the fratricide war that man had been forced into. God of the word of peace. God of that part of mankind that distinguished itself from its animal brothers through placid presence. God of the Mesopotamic beard.

God indicating a backward path towards inner ecstasy. Et cetera.

On a full stomach, Pac drew from his backpack a small canvas bag and some bottles of water. The bag contained a tube of Paracetamol tablets, the bottom of which concealed a not-yet flashing, not-yet stroboscopic vegetal pill; which, in turn, contained a synthetic compound: methamphetamine!

With the slow, deliberate movements of a priest with a host, Pac swallowed this pill, washing it down with a long draught of mineral water, low in sodium and dry residue content.

And became Pac Man.

Rummaging in his backpack again he fished out some alkaline batteries and a black zip-up CD case. He leafed through this at length, undecided, until he'd short-listed *Goa Trance Volume 7*, *In Drums We Trust no.2* and *House Journey remix*.

He chose the first. He lightly touched the display of his portable stereo, which lit up. He oriented the two loudspeakers towards Oscar and towards the cave's chamber, trying for the best sound; as attentive to acoustics as were the architects of Greek amphitheatres; or of those temples aligned with the Earth's axis, built on the intersections of the planet's magnetic grid, to exploit its energy. Sound equals energy. It all made sense.

Lastly, before pressing 'play', he made sure that a stick

of incense burned on either side of the entrance, near the red candles.

Now he could proceed.

When the ceremony started, and throughout the twelve hours that it took to complete it, a rhythmic pulsing of sound waves – first at medium volume, then pumping as loudly as the stereo could manage – was perceived by the variegated surrounding fauna with increasing perplexity – and at considerable range, by their standards. Some of them came nearer, others moved away, disturbed. But only Pac Man let himself go with such growing enthusiasm, with enough ardour and rapture to pasteurise his egotistical mix.

While Oscar continued to smile impassively.

Signs of the imminent End of Time?

A civilisation that had lost touch with the food with which it nourished itself, allowing a handful of people to take over the entire food-production chain, transforming plants and animals into goods, maximising their gains by altering their biological course; who industrialised the existence of sentient beings through mass breeding, zootechnics and automated slaughter houses; and created pathological prerequisites to boost the pharmaceutical industry. They commercialised every aspect of our existence, from the emotional, to the sexual, to the spiritual sphere. They behaved like a virus which, a moment before dying together with its hosting organism, wonders what had gone wrong. A society such as this could not but collapse, implode in a bacteriological detonation. And not only was the timer on that bomb impossible to de-activate: it was scarily close to zero.

Religious fanaticism; the apparent clash between armies of Eastern and Western civilisations. Natural calamities, increasing both in number and intensity; the decline of suitable conditions for life to proliferate and flourish; nuclear threats, real or assumed; and the progressive limitation of individual freedom by the hand of controlling technologies, accepted in the name of a studiedly manipulated perception of security. Wasn't there a meaning behind all this?

Failed attempts to "build towers that scraped the sky", or the presumed inability to develop space exploration effectively, especially considering how speedy and impressive its progress had been, over a short number of years, decades earlier, and how rapid its decline in recent years. Were these warning signs, preludes to a modern punishment on the part of controllers unobserved by common eyes?

The cradle of civilisation, the Middle East, was still a theatre for events capable of influencing the fate of humanity as a whole, just as it had been in the past. Was Jerusalem still the navel of the world from which the final war would break out, as indicated by some of the prophecies, including the Essene ones? And the recent events in those countries, the orthodox, expansionist, hair-shirt policies adopted: were they a clear step in that direction? Was it true that the Third Temple of Jerusalem was secretly being restored? And was this intended, perhaps, to house the Kabod of Yahweh: God's *celestial vehicle*, if one replaced the classic translation, 'glory', with the original Sumerian 'heavy object', and considered the description given by the prophet Ezekiel, who used words such as "...luminous and radiant vehicle, equipped with wheels within other wheels"?

The actuation of false-flag operations, i.e. of terrorist operations manipulated by intelligence services and designed to appear to be conducted by others, for the purpose of unloading responsibilities, affect interests and create conditions to destabilise enemy countries: was it part of this rush towards global degeneration? Could it be that the wars in Iraq (ancient Babylon), and in Iran (ancient Persia), were the realisation of biblical prophesies to which Pac attributed a particular historical meaning?

If our knowledge of the past could enable us to foresee the future, if the two coincided, the former and the latter, Alpha and Omega, the beginning and the end; if the calculation of time was to be considered cyclic, and not linear; and if a cycle, orbit or circuit was not strictly mathematical, but astronomical, and therefore subject to gravitational interference: then perhaps we should pay attention to the ages of the zodiac, the ancient calendar in which the sky was divided into twelve houses of thirty degrees each, and the passage from one era to the next was calculated to take place approximately every 2160 years, 'approximately' being an embarrassingly appropriate term. The same eras whose beginning and end, as it happened, coincided with epoch-making events, with sudden turns in the course of human history.

The era of Leo, approximately twelve thousand years ago, as reported by the most ancient civilisations: Adapa was created and assigned to tending the Eden, the terrain in which the earliest cereals (barley and wheat) were cultivated, and where the first domesticated animals (sheep and wolves) were bred. These evolution leaps occurred roughly every two thousand years, a fraction of the time actually necessary for normal natural selection. The earliest settlements of primitive workers were established, and here slave farmers toiled for their overlords, seeing to their food-related requirements. Long enough to learn that the Flood swept away our species.

A lack of records prevents us from knowing what happened during the subsequent Cancer and Gemini eras, but chronicles resumed during the Taurus epoch: some people survived, and their descendants continued to work for the gods of Mesopotamia, of the Indus valley, of early Egypt, earning themselves the opportunity of taking some important steps forward. This was the start of urban civilisation, where mankind was later granted sovereignty, religious and secular powers. This period saw the invention of the Nippur calendar, still in use; the flourishing of the Sumer civilisation (with its arts, writing, education, astronomy), then of Babylon and Akkad; it saw the priest-king become the intermediary between the people and the local divinity. It witnessed tauromachy, female divinities. Until the radioactive effect of a war among the quarrelling gods, the constantly fighting overlords, destroyed this great civilisation: an episode later reinterpreted as punishment for Sodom and Gomorrah, four thousand years ago.

And we reach the Aries epoch, which shifts the hegemonic axis, replacing previous symbolism with a new and updated iconography, from the Exodus to the advent of Christianity. There were new laws, new customs and a new religion; the Mosaic ram horn (already a symbol of Vedic and Egyptian priestly power); or the anger against the Golden Calf, whose celestial and earthly domain had come to an end. The vindictive Lord of Hosts: virile omnipotence – as opposed to matriarchal. Shiva as head of the human flocks, the symbol of destructive, purifying fire.

The current epoch should be easier to interpret, despite the considerable shortcomings of scholastic systems. And wasn't this the end of the age of Pisces, with all its Christian symbolism? What would become of the Lamb of God, transformed into the acrostic *ictus*, fish? Widespread monotheism: the Fish God, baptism – from incinerating fire, to water that washes away all sins. Yehoshua Ben

Yosef, the Jewish innovator; the mystic who travelled to India and returned with a far broader and clearer outlook on things, owing to Buddhist and Hindu influences; the man whose figure inspired the founding of that earthly cult, Christianity (whose analysis is superfluous), superimposed to the far more ancient allegory of the Sol Invictus. Would the perceptible decline of the Church, no longer capable of proposing a credible and functional vision of the world and of Truth in a manner equally suitable to that of the foregoing two millennia, induce the heads of its multi-tiered hierarchy to give up its symbols of power spontaneously? Or would it resist tenaciously, mobilising its consolidated armed phalanxes, and inciting the conscience of its remaining unshakable followers to defend Christianity and Tradition, the loss of which would instate terror and social instability? Would the passage to a new zodiacal house subvert social organisation again? Would it impose a new religion, new symbols, defeat empires? Or would it really be the beginning of an epoch emancipated from the past and from slavery: an epoch built from scratch, on burnt wasteland in which to plant new seeds?

Would this be the era of Pac the Great? Would he manage to organise the world according to criteria he himself had established?

Above all, would he be the protagonist of those future events?

To find out, all he had to do was survive.

TWO

He must hurry and finish the Star Pac quickly. On the screen of his tablet he observed the constant unfurling of the flowers of evil: the signs of an inevitable collapse. Whether overtly or covertly, the mass media and publications specialised in geopolitics and economics did nothing but add grains of coloured sand to the sophisticated and irreversible mandala that was taking form. Israel threatened Lebanon and Syria – already unstable because of artfully orchestrated riots – accusing them of funding and protecting Hezbollah; the accused responded with anti-Zionist proclamations.

North Korea was blamed of attacking a South-Korean submarine. The European Union was in the throes of increasing nationalist uprisings; continuous protests; clashes between workers and police forces in riot gear; student demonstrations against 'social butchery' policies adopted by governments to counteract damages they themselves had caused; or brought about by measures imposed on them by various Central Banks.

African soil, villages and homes were soaked in blood. Why? Rivalry between different ethnic groups or religions, retaliations for ancient conflicts, any other reason? No-one mentioned corruption, control of mineral resources, diamonds, oil, gold. And, as usual, no-one paid much attention.

The Caucasus powder keg was throbbing once more: Georgia, Russia, Chechnya, and now Russia again. China dictated the rules: what with its holdings of U.S. securities and control over the American national debt, it still had Uncle Sam by the balls. Another solar storm had wreaked havoc with telecommunication satellites; an Indonesian volcano was awakening after centuries, disturbing – through the osmosis of magma – the slumber of its Japanese neighbours and of the entire Ring of Fire. A lethal virus, manipulated by a well-known pharmaceutical industry, had got out of control before it was ready to hit the market (Pac had been alerted by email!). If there was a devil, he must be sharpening his horns right now, sniffing his armpits, jacking off, doing push-ups to tone up his pecs; or preparing his backpack for a long one-way journey.

Where to? Guess!

And there was Pac, still racking his brain trying to find a solution to fly his ark to salvation.

It was a late-Spring afternoon when a perplexed-looking Pac suddenly stood up from his sofa and started walking barefoot around the living-room floor of bleached oak, skirting open periodicals, approaching the tall bookcase that reached up to the false ceiling: a whole wall of books, essays, manuals – and a few classy porn magazines, well hidden behind novels – arranged in a seemingly random order of which he knew the logic.

Pac took a book with a red cover and leafed through it

quickly in search of an answer. Then closed it again and put it back in its place, with a preoccupied frown. It was still afternoon, and through the closed window panes all he could see was gently-stirring branches and rustling leaves. The wind was blowing, bringing nearer the large, heavy, rumbling grey clouds that had quickly obscured the sun; the sun whose cheerful rays, early that morning, had had no need to force their way through double glazing but had poured in freely, each photon welcomed after its tiring journey of eight point thirty-three minutes. Now, with the sky growing sombre and all colours and reflections muted, the air was loaded with electricity, threatening to discharge its stormy fury on the earth.

The absence of Fernanda, his domestic help, was like a massage to his brow with warm essential oil; the green, well-tended lawn surrounding his house, the luxuriant wood surrounding the lawn and the tall hills in full bloom encircling the wood all sang tuneful praises of their splendid existence; the nearest human being was, reassuringly, miles away as the crow flies; and the nearest village was a few miles further. Advantages of his profession, necessity, choice. Isolation was somehow a direct expression of Pac's vitality, of his perception, of his philosophy.

Living on his own was good: he had more time for himself, for studying and thinking. Solitude was intimacy, invulnerability, distance from the meanness of the world. A world that he knew all too well and that he was obliged to deal with, in any case; even if to make it worse: or rather, to accelerate its scrapping, its decomposing, and then revert to keeping a safe distance.

Storm or no storm, the stink of rot never penetrated the vegetation surrounding that villa. Nor did any other unpleasant smell, image, fear or noise. And the agency had nothing to object to his location, despite additional complications and expenses when he travelled. In that elaborate bubble of clean air, in that fabric embellished with tiny Rajastan mirrors, he could devote all the time and concentration he needed to think about the Star Pac, to get his former life out of his system, and find joy and comfort in the closely surrounding natural landscape; the latter, he felt sure, instilled in his home and in his very being an influence, a biological emanation, a magnetic vegetal perspiration – the lymph of life as it should be: pure and luxuriant, balanced and caressing. Simple, yet complex. This was the sense, the direction.

It was already dinner time when Pac, wearing only his boxer shorts, traversed his ample open-space living room, threw a glance at the fuchsia leaflet of a new pizza house specialising in "ultrafast deliveries" that glared at him from atop a scattering of mail on the table. Ready to satisfy his, by now, keen appetite, he reached the kitchen where, on opening the fridge, he found it filled, as usual, with the sort of spicy food he detested. Pre-cooked and hotly spicy.

Some limp celery, two radishes and a maimed pear. Where the hell were his soya burghers, his tofu? And his heads of lettuce, greens, seitan? One jar of yogurt, not a single fucking soya pudding; no unsweetened muesli, nor an egg, or a packet of dried fruit. Nothing there at all. Empty, neglected and depressed, like his stomach. Apart from that disgusting spicy stuff which he would gladly have thrown into the rubbish bin – if he hadn't paid for it.

Fernanda, the buxom Arab-Hispanic maid who was supposed to look after the house (and therefore, indirectly, himself) for three whole days a week, including meals, was well on her way to getting the sack – though theirs was mostly a verbal agreement. Pretending to cater for Pac's personal appetite, to oblige and comply with her moral duty, she filled the larder and the refrigerator with food that only she appreciated; and close to its sell-by date, to justify its premature disappearance. Causing her to put on a conspicuous amount of weight, if one compared her current waistline with that of the now-remote first year of her services. Plus he had to reimburse her for her shopping. He had protested, instructed, and sometimes, when really hungry, he had even shouted at her, but to no avail. While not exactly a healthy and friendly relationship, it offered intermittent advantages to both of them.

It was up to him now, he thought, while stamping his feet and waving his fists, which made his layers of fat shake like ionised gelatine: it was time to deal with this once and for all, he noted on a virtual reminder.

He had started to stroke his soft, swollen stomach, causing two immediate and parallel effects: an abundant production of saliva at the thought of what, alas, he would be forced to eat: an exception to which, despite himself and his manifest good intentions, and in the absence of the slightest alternative, he could oppose no resistance. And the sudden lighting up of the red *On Air* sign at *Radio75*'s studios; from which the warm and sensuous voice of the masked speaker – backed by the Jackson Sisters' undoubtedly effective *I believe in miracles* – admonished and consoled, like a Baptist preacher, inciting him not to forsake the path of righteousness.

The reverent speaker was right, of course; the road to Aesthetic Harmony was long and difficult, and paved with *chili con carne*; and Pac's delusion of being affected by body dysmorphic disorder had been swept away by his latest online consultation with a shrink.

But he was hungry, for Chrissake!

It's a spinning wheel – he thought – and the puce-coloured leaflet which he already held in his hand seemed somehow pleased with the role it had attained, expressing the satisfaction you would expect of coated paper of electric magenta ("Fuchsia Fashion" for the hypoglycemic stylist; or "Hollywood Cherry", for the real sophisticates).

The interval elapsing between the end of his phone call and the arrival of his tepid pizza was patiently dedicated to an empirical analysis of the term "ultrafast": low-quality commercial or brilliant example of free competition in a free market?

Meanwhile the light outside had almost completely dimmed, suffocated by battalions of condensed vapour preparing to unsheathe their swords: howling wind, to frighten the leaves; thunder, to send moles scuttling to their dens; causing couples of birds to huddle together; and ants, crickets and boars to run for refuge.

The young delivery boy who rang at the gate and showed up on his doorstep was lathered in sweat, almost as if he'd run there, instead of riding an overheated moped. He removed his crash-helmet, releasing a lock of blondish hair that hung lankly on the cheek of an unremarkable face.

Neither of them bothered to open his mouth; a wordless nod was good enough.

All things considered, he'd got there quite fast, thought Pac, paying the bill. But not fast enough to deserve a tip. Which he wouldn't necessarily have accepted, from a guy who'd met him at the door wearing rather revealing pale-blue boxer shorts: revolting sight. He'd heard it said around town that the fellow was eccentric, but hadn't realised he was as bad as that. No, from the boy's speedy departure and lingering expression of disgust one could deduce that he'd never have accepted a tip.

Back indoors and feeling optimistic, Pac dove into his faux-leather sofa and opened the warm take-away box with the enthusiasm of a grave-robber forcing the freshly-retrieved casket of a king. *Radio75* could raise its volume in a last desperate appeal as much as it liked!

The appearance of the so-called cheese reminded him fearfully of semi-congealed white candle wax; as did its taste. The tomato was ketchup, and the dough was sweetish. An aborted attempt at a new pizza-dessert? Without a doubt he was chewing on something that evoked the unknown. At the end of the second slice his survival instinct, placated, was replaced by the vain quest for a lost flavour. At the end of the fourth, something worthy of note happened: while the mush descended his oblivious oesophagus (the undoubted advantage of that dairy concoction being that it didn't need chewing), from the depths of his digestive system his liver – whose colour matched that of the leaflet (this could have inspired some subtle retroactive speculation) – exclaimed loudly, "What the fuck was that?", thus voicing the indignation of the apparatus which it felt it represented.

The starting notes of a guitar tune (the ringtone of his phone, which he'd left on a wicker chair) made him jump from the sofa, interrupting his accusing inner voices.

Since we're feeling so anesthetised...

The multi-touch display refused to reveal the caller's identity: bad sign!

In our comfort zone...

It was a safe device, updated by the agency with the

latest technology to protect its operative agents from any threat or claim; as for friends or family, he simply didn't have any. He eyed the phone in his hand, as it continued to play the Placebo tune at length; whoever was calling was keen to hear his answering voice.

See you at the bitter end...

He decided to answer, and the first thing he heard the other end was a background noise of fluctuating intensity: an old Chinese fry shop where an excited turkey was pecking at the receiver from a third end of the line, while from a fourth a macaque replied with handfuls of sand and guttural sounds.

"Hello?"

"Crrr... ssshhh..." the voice sounded, as if from beyond the tomb. Pac couldn't understand a word.

Yet he instinctively recognised the voice as vaguely familiar. "Yes?"

"Hello! It's Samuel! Can you hear me?" Now the voice was shouting. Samuel? How the hell was that possible? What did he want from him?

"Can you hear me?!" repeated the voice, shouting even louder, enough to be audible above the background noise. Now unfiltered, Samuel's voice was different from what Pac had imagined over the years: it made him think of a mature man exuding unusual vigour. His tone was that of someone irked by unforeseen circumstances that interfered with a very important operation. Like any other outside business etiquette, the voice merited no *a priori* courtesy.

"What... what the hell do you want?" asked Pac, one hand on his hip.

"Listen to me. Listen to me carefully."

"I'm listening... though I can scarcely hear you!"

Pac didn't like this at all. Perhaps he should hang up: this wasn't what they'd agreed. Only he was the one supposed to make the calls, to place orders. And that line was anything other than safe or encrypted. And this exposed him to risks that he had neither the time nor the inclination to take.

"That's why I'm telling you to listen, damn it!" exclaimed Samuel the other end, his agitation catching Pac off guard.

Decide he must, and did. "Ok, I'm listening."

Perhaps Samuel had found an antimatter engine, one never knew.

He waited but – gobbling turkey and gibbering macaque apart – there was no sound: no trace of Samuel's booming voice.

"Hello?" he said faintly after a few seconds. Then they were cut off.

If he needs me he'll call again, thought Pac. And in fact, just before he bit into his last slice of pseudo pizza, his mobile rang again, while Pac's pancreas breathed a sigh of insulin-induced relief.

Samuel again, of course. This time Pac didn't say a

word, didn't interrupt him, he merely registered the quieter presence of the two disrupting agents.

"I'm in Nepal."

"What?!" exclaimed Pac, before letting him proceed.

"Yes... and I need... Listen," continued Samuel "you couldn't come over, could you?"

If this was a joke, it was in very poor taste. He'd had enough of Nepal, for a series of reasons; the mere mention of the place annoyed him.

"Sure, why not?! I'll hop on the first plane. No! No way. Are you drunk, or what?" He needed to talk, and paced the living room aimlessly, which helped dispel his growing annoyance.

"Of course I'm not. I've never been more sober. The fact is..."

The line suddenly went dead, replaced by a monotonous crackling; then returned, more distinct: agitated turkey and hurtling macaque seemed to be exchanging some interesting comments.

"I didn't hear a thing!" shouted Pac, holding the phone in front of his mouth. "What the hell's happened to you?" he blurted, surprised at his own question. As if he cared. He didn't even know what the guy looked like, let alone his real name.

"I've been kidnapped! On Machapuchare. Maoists... I think...it's... ransom," was what Pac thought he discerned through that sand storm.

Pac collapsed against the padded backrest of his sofa, exhaling loudly.

"Did you hear me?!"

"Of course I heard," Pac thought. But he was too tired to pull himself together and…

"But what am I supposed to do? What exactly do you need?" he asked with a note of ill-concealed disapproval, hoping his might remain a polite question, asked for the sake of it. Although this clearly wouldn't be the case. "Would you like me to call your embassy?", whichever that may be.

"No! Absolutely not. Don't even think of it!"

The less the two had to say, the clearer the conversation became.

"So what do you want?" insisted Pac, reluctantly predicting what Samuel was about to ask. "Some consolation? Keep your cool, don't let things get on top of you, and everything will be all right," he said, lowering the tone of his voice.

In the ensuing few seconds of silence he almost hoped they'd been cut off.

Then Samuel answered. "Thanks, very kind of you. Actually – ahem –the gun at the nape of my neck suggests that I should ask you to come here. And fast."

"You must be mad!" Pac exclaimed. "I wouldn't dream of it. And to do what?" He had other things on his mind, and he'd had enough of that damned hole among the mountains.

From the other end came excited, unintelligible voices, seemingly to lend authenticity to the situation: shouted orders, rebukes addressed to that same recipient.

"I'm the prisoner of an armed militia, in a cold country. Please. I have no alternatives. Believe me, there's no-one else I can ask for help. These people will kill me!"

"Precisely, the mere fact that it's cold there suggests that I should leave you where you are, to preserve well," said Pac. "Listen," he added, pressing a hand to his forehead. "I'm really sorry... I'm in Cairo on important business, and I shan't be able to move for a while. If there's anything I can do from here I will, gladly, but..." He let the sentence roll like a ball launched on a frozen mile-long pool table, curious to see how far it would get before it came to a halt.

A sigh, some slow, heavy breathing.

"I'm not joking. You're the only person I trust," came the reply.

"That's too bad, then. When it comes to us, the word 'trust' only applies to the sale of goods. Call me when you find a second-hand shuttle!"

Suddenly Pac was struck by ball-lightening: shit, this man was his only supplier; and, much as he was sorry to admit, most of his planned escape from Earth depended on him. Which meant that if he lost his one supplier...

"Jesus Christ!" he swore.

"That's something else I was calling about," resumed

Samuel, almost as if he'd perceived the glare of that thunderbolt. "If I remember correctly, some time ago you asked me for a propulsion system capable of ferrying a vehicle into the atmosphere, right?"

A freeze-frame of Pac's face would have shown him wearing the lively look of someone who'd found his wife in bed with an unknown female in a g-string.

Had he heard correctly? Or had the turkey caught up with the Indian blackbird in the race to vocal evolution?

"I have just the thing for you. Something fantastic, unobtainable, totally innovative," said Samuel, knowing he'd struck the right chord, the nodal one in fact.

"What is it?" asked Pac, biting his lip and knowing that he'd soon regret that question.

"Sorry. You'll have to come here, pay these rude fellows the ransom, and trust me."

Too much to ask, thought Pac. It wasn't so much the cost, nor that he'd have to go back where he'd just concluded a mission (though, incidentally, this would be contrary to the agency's strong recommendations. But with a brand-new ID and some precautions it could be done); it was a question of trust. Should he trust an anonymous smuggler with a cultivated voice? Supposing this was a trap? Some sort of revenge?

He scratched his head, to no avail.

"So?" – a distant croak, like a mechanical cougar sharpening its claws on a dissection slab – "These natives are impatient."

"Shit," he thought, "what do I do now?" He looked straight ahead, towards the French windows, beyond which lay a scenario of extremely low pressure; there wasn't a sound, apart from his own breathing. The pendulum of decision seemed to stop exactly where his doubts and fears awaited expectantly. The End of Time was near, while an operative Star Pac was still remote. Propulsion was the greatest obstacle, and here was someone offering him springy boots.

A coincidence?

"When roast fumes reach the pen, ducks grow quiet," as the newly-minted saying goes. And Pac decided that the only possible solution was to learn to jump over fences, a bagful of abuse at the ready.

Which is why very soon (sooner than he'd hoped) he found himself seated in a winged refrigerator, observing how devoid of sentiment the expression 'air corridor' was, and how much more exciting it would have been to think of himself as surfing the polychrome crest of a celestial wave made of sparkling stratospheric pollen. Tour operators would certainly have benefited considerably, as would have the soporific life of those passengers.

Take the one at his side, for example: he must be a hyperactive businessman, of today's generation *nouveau riche* Indians, proud of the smart suit that defined him. He kept scratching his neck, pausing briefly to glower at anything that would distract him from that itch – almost as if his thyroid were producing some particular irritant.

But maybe this was just a false impression.

Civilities were disposed of with the same speed as the snacks just served; snacks which had left the slight feeling of anticipation induced by mere starters to a palate desirous of a proper meal.

"What do you do?" asked Pac in an undertone.

"Consultant. And you?"

"Financial advisor."

They looked into each other's eyes inquisitively, just long enough to realise that neither of them was talking up-front.

"D'you know that eighty percent of what we say we've already said at least once before? That means we keep on saying the same things... mostly bullshit. That's how we live, how we use our brain," said one of the two – no matter which.

"I believe that secularism is one of the most ingenious tricks ever played on man or history, to the advantage of its advocates. Not because it wasn't a logical step in evolution, but because it didn't judge and punish what had been committed previously, in the name of allegedly unquestionable truth. But that's nothing new."

Some turbulence, and the "fasten seatbelts" sign went on.

"Just think that the female koala, after six months' breast feeding, weans her offspring on her droppings. Ever asked yourself why those animals look like traumatised teddy bears? In my opinion, and I don't think I'm mistaken, their diet is eucalyptus only, for a lifetime, to remove the memory of that taste from their mouth and from their little heads. A sublimation of sorts."

"What do you believe in?" asked the Indian.

In 'theogamy': the physical union between god and man. But I'm still a virgin. And you?" The man was scratching his throat again.

"In the banal polarity of the physical world, and in the absence of dualism in the one we'll reach, sooner or later. When there will be few of us; when sadhus will come out of their hermitages, and pilgrims will return... when all saintly men will descend the Himalayas to meet in Varanasi, and they'll all hold hands... My friend, when all this happens, the lips of Maha maya reality will open wide, enfolding the fullness of our erect essence in warmth: we'll perceive it all around, enveloping, and releasing; immersing us in moist solstices and withdrawing in dry equinoxes, alternating, lifting us to reunited ecstasy, to converging sensual pleasure. And we'll ejaculate our essence of light from the top of our seventh chakra, squirting out like llama's spit towards and through the oesophagus of the universe, to inseminate the stars."

"This guy has just earned himself window-seat number

12B on the Star Pac", thought Pac.

On Sandy Beach, on the island of Barbados, there was a palm tree.

There were lots of them, in fact, but this one was special. It had yet to reach vegetal senility, which meant it was still sturdy, yet flexible enough to be used as a catapult by the fingers of a golem high on hash cookies. Its long frayed leaves formed a cocktail-umbrella that was just the thing for the guests of this exclusive resort, whose property stretched well beyond the long sandy creek lapped by the docile waves of the sea. Slightly taller than her surrounding sisters, the palm tree reached skyward, inclining her trunk respectfully in homage to the caresses exchanged by land and water on a shore inset with fossil gems. An outpouring of marine embraces, rewarded with voluptuous abandon.

The dense vegetation beyond the beach was constantly groomed by gardeners, and what flora grew spontaneously from the sandy soil was mainly large-leafed green weeds. Prevented by their reduced height from admiring those rites governed by lunar phases, this lowlier flora was not only beset by envy, but also constantly bothered by lizards hunting for insects; by insects hunting for spores.

Like a precariously-balanced ice-cream stick planted in a small mound of shaving foam, our coconut palm tree felt she was special: she was the custodian of a secret. A secret she wore with nonchalance, quite oblivious of its purpose –

but this was part of the scheme; evidently whoever had devised this enigma knew his palm trees too. Painted at eye level on the side of the trunk that was never warmed by the sun was some writing – or rather, a message. Emblematic, ambiguous, if anyone ever managed to read it. Not that the guests of this luxury resort weren't capable of it. On the contrary: their wealth was implicit in their very presence, and they certainly weren't backward, if the promiscuous copulating, hard night-partying and morning hangovers were anything to go by.

But for the message on the palm tree to be manifest the right key was needed, and it wasn't in a buried treasure chest, nor in the hands of a human being. The numerical combination, if we can call it that, belonged to the Moon alone: only she could make the writing on the trunk visible, illuminating it with a glow similar to that of a vampire squid in the abysses of the ocean; only the reflected light of the Moon could cause that chemical shutter to open, revealing a message written with a magic marker. And when this happened, cyclically, it was she, the Moon, who attracted attention, inspired wonder, while land and water also benefited from increased intimacy and renewed lunar exuberance.

But there's no secret without someone in the know. Excluding its creator, of whom we shall hear later, we could hint at coincidences, sometimes banal – as in beggar holding bowl meets rich man with hand in pocket, facilitating passage from one to the other – but that would be monotonous.

What would be unrepeatable, on the other hand, would be the sight of Pac wandering along the beach at night, slowly swaying as if trying to disperse the fumes of alcohol (heaven knows how delicious the local piña colada was); and that intimate feeling of uncleanliness of which he was unable to rid himself.

In those days, bonus trips were a generous incentive given by the agency to its most talented weed-killers whose performance, in turn, guaranteed a bonus to those above them, and so on, up and up as far as one could conceive the summit; or to those who showed signs of anxiety, lack of confidence or, even worse, remorse for their doings. Incentive trips, therefore, were the miracle all-inclusive cure: from massage to condom, from courtesy cocktail to swallowing; by her, one understands.

That night, Pac conformed to both of the aforementioned categories: brilliant performance, dark mood. The Star Pac idea still hadn't dawned on him, but all the premises were there: he'd been noticing and weighing up the signs of The End of Time; an itchy sense of exoplanetary self-preservation had begun to surface as the possible (though not yet the only) way to go. The emotional desert forced on him by his work, which deep down had always attracted him, was transforming itself into vacuous solipsism. Moreover – and let it be quite clear that this will not be dwelled on any further – Esther had gone off recently: tired of living like a recluse; worn out by his long absences, which had induced a severe form of depression that not even her continuous two-timing could relieve. This latest, perhaps Pac's only truly involving emotional relationship had finally broken up, deepening the silence that already oppressed him.

Esther had left, and rightly so. He too should take his leave – one way or another.

But for now he was wondering along the beach, his feet sinking in the sand: a glittering marble sand which, that night, received the weight of his heavy body – clad only in an orange sarong tied around his waist and reaching down to his knees – caressed his state of mind gently; inducing him to breathe in the moonlight, to savour the shadows projected along the beach, right there in front of him. That frosty, translucent light incubated and evoked spirits which he felt coiling tightly around his skin, his cheeks, his neck, dancing to the drum-beat of his heart; spirits that stomped their feet, shouted and grimaced, sneered and turned cartwheels, tapped with their fingernail on the glass pane that separated them from freedom, inclining their heads the better to see their reflected image; what magic was that: one's own image as a spirit, reflected on the boundaries of inhabitable space?!

It was too chaotic indoors: the peaceful outdoors was what he sought. From a distance, the resort was a mass of haphazardly arranged lights, a degenerate party to which he felt uninvited, despite being the guest of honour. Echoes of loud voices, of drunken escorts, the humming of insects, salt breeze on his skin.

This was the third time he'd found himself on that beach in less than four years, yet he'd never seen it so naked, so generous. If it hadn't been for the full Moon – a bright stamp on that picture-postcard – there would have been nothing but darkness. The same darkness, he observed, glancing behind him, that seemed to protect his presence: a darkness so close that he could have reached out to stroke it, feel its texture, savour it; perhaps (who knows) even play with it.

What was behind that blackness, so black that it seemed to engulf you? He could try to imagine it, straining his eyes more and more, with every new wave breaking nearby.

And then he saw it.

Blurred at first, uncertain, sensed rather than grasped. What was it, a lost firefly, a reflection? He moved closer, it was right in front of him, but on the dark side of a group of trees. He paid no attention to the ground, which changed from sand to a rustling carpet of leaves, dried twigs and shells. A palm tree like many others, close to others, with six, seven fallen coconuts at its feet, some rotting, others desiccated. The luminescence was in front of his eyes, and if it hadn't been for the wind that stirred the large leaves overhead, letting the moonlight filter that far down, perhaps the picture wouldn't have manifested itself that evening.

Pac smiled, frowned, took a step backwards and almost tripped over a coconut. He glanced around: no-one in sight. He re-approached that vision, reached towards it with lightly-stroking fingertips, feeling only rough bark; then moving vertically, touching the trunk lengthways, its undulating scars like wrinkled wounds. Man-made! And suddenly he felt part of a game to which he'd been enlisted: a magic trick studied by a joker who might be dead by now. Maybe, he thought, some bored wandering student; a decidedly eccentric escort; or some deviant fellowship that communicated by such means. He smiled again, feeling relieved, comforted by this riddle. Which he learned by heart so he could write it down later.

"For those who dream and those who fly, for those who escape and those who hope, the stars are awaiting. Samuel."

A phone number followed: and this was precisely what enabled Pac to start building his stairway to heaven.

And now, in our own time, he was preparing to meet that number and that voice.

Skyrocketing, drawing circles around the planet, dining with peanuts and lemonade. Or coast-cruising windward of the sun, sailing on the waters of interplanetary space.

What would he do between saying farewell to the Earth's atmosphere and coming back to it? What would he see?

What inexplicable emotions would his heart release, once he'd thrown open the door to the safe where they were locked away? How many stars would be count? Without the annoying haze of the atmosphere, the cosmos from up there would be revealed in all its staggering magnificence, in its absolute dimension and absence of anchoring coordinates, except for fabulous gratification, dizzy bewilderment.

Total darkness would no longer be fearful, but sweetly seductive; emptiness, an invisible pattern of ionised gas filaments; bunches of stars hanging from eternal galactic vines, each incandescent grape teaming with deserted or populated planetary midgets. Spiralling clouds, implosions and explosions that blossomed light-years ago. The Moon never so close; Mars, the Sun, Venus, Jupiter. What would he feel? Union, detachment? Belonging, desertion?

"I'll land on the Moon," he thought. "I want to feel like he who sings the glory of the new day in the forest, when the night is still occupied in its dominions. Like a new-born Adam at his first thought, when dawning, dazzling, idyllic consciousness overstepped sentience; pristine, cradled in the arms of the goddess of procreation, amazed at being able to understand and think; beatifically lost. The re-birth of the renewed man, before touching down and founding a fresh civilisation. "I'll turn my eyes away," he thought, "so as not to witness the destruction of the foregoing, the current expression of barbarous mediocrity to which I myself contributed, to drown it as soon as possible in order to avoid further and worse suffering. Amen.

The Himalayas had this effect on him.

Sitting on the right aisle of one of the most modern airplanes he'd ever flown in, he was on the receiving end of dreams and visions evoked by spectacular views of the Land of Eternal Snows: stories of obstinate mountaineers and of devoted souls in prayer, of ultra-terrestrial hermits and of orange, luminescent peaks, set aflame by dawns and sunsets. Lakes stretching as far as the sky; and human – only human – boundaries.

Shortly before take-off, in Kathmandu, he had limited himself to a few hours' stopover, and to stamp his passport: no strange names this time: suspended between academic truth and fiction, 'Adam Smith' had seemed to him both balanced and anonymous, as well as being the first ID he'd laid his hands on. Along the sides of the only runway, lit by the sun already high above, hefty women soldiers had watched the to-ing and fro-ing, hands locked behind their backs, swaying right and left for no apparent reason. A *Cosmic Air* flight took off with a deafening roar, startling even those who were reading or leaving the toilet.

Meanwhile, the plump (and visibly moustached) air hostess of the *Yeti Airlines* AY-133 flight to Pokhara had distributed cotton-wool ear plugs and sweets, delight and displeasure, implying that careful consideration had been paid by top management to consistency between company name and physical appearance of the flight attendants. A matter of credibility.

On that twin-engine propeller plane, two rows ahead of Pac, a gentleman with moustache and tie was sitting pensively, munching pumpkin seeds. Pac watched him turn around, scanning the entire row of passengers as if to check that none of them was doing anything inappropriate, then settling down again. In the same area, a bald Japanese with huge spectacles was snoring away contentedly.

All this Pac found very boring but, in a way, useful: it distracted him from budding tension as touchdown neared.

Here he was again, in that freezing-cold dump. Alone, without the protection and formidable powers that his agency could always be relied upon to provide. In civvies, so to speak, on an unofficial mission for which he couldn't even signal his position and possible movements; furthermore, after accurate calculations during which he'd repeatedly got lost, he'd thought it wiser to disable the GPS on every electronic device he had with him.

Certainly solitude was great, provided you had comfort and protection.

And all this to venture into some stinking hole filled with who-knows-what kind of famished monsters, to seize and abduct a perfect stranger, guilty of being Pac's only supplier; and manage to leg it fast... and intact. And always providing that it was all true: that this wasn't some kind of trap or ambush or revenge. Who knows? There were those in this world who'd gladly have given him a good thrashing; torn his nails from his hands and feet, one by one, with rusty pincers; some would have loved to lubricate his eyes with super-glue instead of eye drops; or to embroider his whole body with thin razor-blade cuts, then throw him into a small pool of adult piranhas on an enforced starvation diet.

Plenty of people out there would thus rejoice, in many different languages and dialects. Another good reason for his solitude.

Whatever condiment was now oiling the workings of his brain, it was too late now for second thoughts. They'd landed, and he hadn't even noticed. The pilot had deposited the twin-engine plane on the landing strip of the tiny airport with the meticulous care of a bomb-disposal expert with a stutter: conscious of his limits, of the intrinsic unpredictability of nature, and of being in the dark as to the content of lessons he's skipped during his training course.

Situated at an altitude of almost nine hundred metres, the town of Pokhara was the second most-frequented Nepalese resort. Set on the shore of lake Phawa Tal, at the foot of the Annapurna mountain range, it was a destination much favoured by energetic trekkers, attracted by the views of those mineral giants. Pokhara was cleaner, more disciplined and charming than Kathmandu.

This was Pac's first impression as he waited for his luggage to be retrieved.

Kimley was waiting for him outside, smiling. And for good reasons. Black leather jacket, beard a little longer than the time before; scuffed boots replaced by better-made footwear. Leaning against the bonnet of his inseparable automobile, he distracted his attention from his Casio watch to welcome Pac with a vigorous handshake.

Pac was also happy to find him there: having had to pay him in advance, via bank transfer, it was good to see him. The thought that Kimley had arrived on board that Indian jalopy didn't even occur to him, uptight as he was about the purpose of their reunion.

As for Kimley, he'd been told this was an unforeseen business opportunity – in that same area, as it happened.

Not even the biting and treacherous cold seemed to concern Pac, or prevent him from asking himself what he was doing there when he had so much else to do, when anything would be better than finding himself with a wad of banknotes strapped to his body, knowing that he was about to face some purported kidnappers in order to ransom a certain Samuel, while getting himself into who-knows-what, and how much, trouble.

And what for?

"Jesus Christ, why does it have to be so difficult to satisfy the perfectly human and innocent desire to mind one's own business, and not depend on anyone?" he thought, while the car's padded back seat, under his weight, exhaled the memory of his previous visit.

Having enquired as to their destination, the robust Kimley adjusted his baseball cap as if that ritual somehow encouraged the starter. And that might even be true, judging by all the little saints and necklaces that dangled from the rear-view mirror. But the car started off, and after consulting his watch again his guide insinuated the car into the calm urban traffic, where the number of pedestrians exceeded that of the vehicles, and that of the cows and goats the number of pedestrians, within an undoubtedly harmonious and variegated order: tourists, obsequious pedlars, farmers, and breeders whose herds grazed anywhere and everywhere. A few monks, Tibetan women in traditional robes seeking buyers for their knick-knacks, children, overloaded rickety carts drawn by humans of burden; a snake charmer, performing with quiet concentration on the roadside.

Perhaps it was the ubiquitous mountains, whose peaks literally encircled the town, tickled the feet of the sky, or impeded the path of passing clouds; peaks mostly snow-capped, milk-stained, like pilasters supporting the fate of reality. Or maybe it was the great lake, now visible through the car window: the seemingly endless expanse of water, as if scooped out of an integral whole by a titanic spoon in ancient times; water of liquid emerald, mirror for the mountains' vanity, a reflecting surface decorated with small rowing boats that transported naïve dreamers inside that meek incantation, inviting them to dive into that upside-down image of the many-pointed grey and white massif, to love and to float in it. It may even have been this unexpectedly welcoming landscape that calmed Pac's inner turmoil, provoking the sudden, unmotivated smile he saw, and studied briefly, reflected from the close by window.

Yes, that was his smile all right. Those were his teeth, his cheeks: how strange it looked. How long was it since he'd last seen it? And why there, at that precise moment?

"We are arrived. Here is Hotel, but full maybe," said Kimley in his poor English, watching him in the rear-view mirror, pointing towards the gate of the Hungry Eye Hotel.

The crafty devil probably wanted to take him where he'd get a commission, but Pac took no notice. This one should do, as far as he'd been able to make out on the Internet. It was in a far lower category than he was used to, but this time there would be no reimbursement for his expenses, no inflated invoices. This time he was here as an ordinary tourist, he kept repeating to himself, as if this could be of some comfort; and having checked online that the place had central heating (a rare luxury in those parts) he'd adapt to the rest – assuming, of course, that their website was truthful.

Pac got out of the car and took his trolley from the boot, while a small group of elderly tourists on mountain bikes went slowly by: skinny legs, flashy gear and crash-helmets, faces flushed and sweaty, strange grimaces of pain with which they tackled their adventure. After a quick briefing, during which he informed Kimley that he needed to be driven the following morning at a certain hour to such-and-such a place for an important business meeting that he absolutely must conclude; that he would act as Pac's interpreter; that perhaps it was better to hire a jeep; and that he shouldn't worry, it wouldn't take long, Kimley was dismissed. And from the way he shook his head he must have been very sorry not to have managed to extort a few perks out of such a loyal client; not to mention dinner. As he left, however, his scowl relaxed into a more serene expression: presumably he'd devised some way of skimming money off the hired jeep and the petrol fill-up; his next assignments (whose costs would be covered by Pac's banknotes gripped in his hand); or what place to suggest for breakfast, which he was already looking forward to.

But we weren't to know this.

Pac walked towards reception, hoping the hotel wouldn't be full. He'd decided not to book in advance, to avoid the risk of leaving a trace, but to take a chance. Judging by the warmth with which he was welcomed he'd done the right thing.

After negotiating resolutely with the manager, some Shanghara Kulu, he opted for a 'superior' room with view of the lake, before discovering that the substantial difference with a standard room was the size of the lock. The lights were ok: they all worked, including that of the bathroom. This took a little longer to get going, causing some initial alarm, dispelled as soon as it lit up with a faint sizzling noise, to the joy of the manager who participated in the inspection. The room was small, clean, its walls unadorned: perfect for his needs. Two heavy woollen blankets would warm his dreams. There was even toilet paper. And radiators, those gems of technology, white up to where the rust started.

He'd received clear and simple instructions for paying the ransom, yet the intensifying palpitations throbbing throughout his body suggested that he was experiencing a certain anxiety; or – as he put it himself – that he was scared shitless.

OK, – he said, looking out from the balcony as if the gentle waters of the lake could somehow lend an ear – a fringe of Maoists refusing to integrate and recycle itself within the political system recently veneered with democracy was skimming money from trekking. Nothing new. And money was all they wanted.

Of course, the fact that this was about Machapuchare – a massif of almost seven thousand metres, forbidden to climbers and considered sacred by the locals – could be considered aggravating circumstances; but this clashed with the group's proclamation that they were Maoists, and therefore commies, atheists. For all he knew, the sacred and profane had never opened diplomatic offices in their respective territories. An as-yet virgin mountain must have had strong appeal for some. He smelled a rat from under the reassuring cover of reason: a dense, sickening and troublesome effusion. But look: the suspicion that bugged him suddenly dived like an uncloaked superhero into the midst of this miasma, and emerged strangely invigorated, fresh as a rose. Then off it flew.

Meanwhile the stench expanded. In homeopathic doses, even an unpleasant odour could, in time, appeal – to one prepared to bend over, to be seduced by the blandishments of a possible experience. Because this was it: an experience which promised to make his vimana fly.

Pac drew the rough, dusty curtains, made sure that all the locks were closed, then sat cross-legged on his bed. Thinking, and trying not to; dismantling, oiling and reassembling his invincible weapon, Determination: charging it with all the energy he could. And, like every self-respecting warrior monk, cultivating the hope that he wouldn't have to unsheathe it and cause unnecessary wounds – although indications suggested the contrary.

When everything was ready he decided to lie down, observing the thought of dinner drift close above his head, and letting it pass without a murmur. This in itself was highly unusual.

It was evening by now, and there was no light for the curtains to obstruct. Before going to sleep, bundled under the heavy tobacco-coloured blankets, he took an oath: at the first sign of danger he'd put his own safety before anything else: Samuel or no Samuel.

And while he was at it, he added another resolution, something he called a 'health incentive': as soon as possible, he would spend part of the content of the money-belt – kept strapped to his waist – on some playful, irrational and deplorable activity.

At first, the fructose granules cuddled up closely together, embracing, hoping for a collective salvation; then, exchanging a last farewell, they realised this was the definitive parting before a long and complicated adventure; they started to sink one by one: some fighting, some resigned. Yes, this was the end: there was nothing more they could do. The boiling liquid would soon dissolve them for ever. But there were other frightening aspects: how long would they agonise before dissolving, before passing away? Would they find something the other side, if there was another side? Would they meet again? Above all, what was beyond that murky dark surface? Was there light, or more darkness? None of them would be lucky enough to tell the story. Not one granule had chanced to fall into the saucer; dipped into the cup, a shiny spoon had accelerated their passage from solid to liquid state, tracing a vortex, turning and turning. And it was all over.

Pac had observed the scene from above, absorbed in different thoughts. Those fructose granules in his coffee had looked to him like tiny stars, a sugary constellation swallowed up very slowly by a black hole; extinguished, before his very eyes. A corner of the universe had caved in. Which is why he'd picked up the coffee spoon and had put an end to that misery.

Seated in front of him, Kimley was still eating. Pac found him almost repulsive.

His own bowl of fruit, yogurt and muesli was empty; he'd struggled to finish it. Strange as it may seem, eating was the last thing on his mind.

That deserted, anonymous diner, with its tall, mouldy walls and cracked plastic tables, was dominated by the giant figure of a divinity, posed benevolently – with its four arms and surrounding animals and objects – from the height of the wall, overseeing everything. In that place, Pac told himself, they were consuming their 'last breakfast'. Whatever the outcome of this expedition, the following morning he would be elsewhere. If he was still alive he'd be out of that country (you bet!); if not… too bad…

Which is why he didn't really mind Kimley stuffing himself at his expense. In a sense, this helped counteract the vague sense of guilt that might oppress him in the near future. A sort of insurance policy.

Although, on close examination, Kimley's seemed more than simple appetite. His voracity, and the looks he gave him, seemed to reveal something else: something more – resentful, so to speak.

Eat up, dear boy, eat up.

Which Kimley did, and how!

Pac lifted his cup to slowly sip his coffee, imagining that he was investing his body with an allowance of crumbling, dissolved galaxy, still partially charged with energy. Enough for his needs.

There was Pac; and there was Kimley who, when searched, had manifested his annoyance and had promptly been told to shut up, in the local idiom, by an armed man wearing a mask. The search had been light enough, even superficial, judging by the timid, uncertain hands that had briefly skimmed over arms, trunk and legs, down to their ankles; almost as if the man had completed his training by watching Bollywood adaptations of American whodunit B-movies. A quick feel, and off you go.

There was a young specimen of brown yak with a splash of white on his muzzle, a small pouch of fiery red and an old-fashioned jingle bell around his neck, lying on his side snoozing.

And there were two other individuals, as well as the one mentioned above: one was short and squat, like a demijohn, with dark, rough hands; the other was taller but basically similar. They were dressed (and smelled) like shepherds; but for the sake of anonymity, and in order to enhance their image, they wore black balaclavas from which, through twin holes, peered two dark spots floating in yellowish puddles which, before their livers disintegrated, must have been off-white.

Anxious eyes striving to remain impassive and, like the rest of their body, with obvious difficulty.

The three criminals – these ferocious mountain bandits – started at the slightest sound, rocking the little square table around which they were all sitting.

The tallest and most robust among them breathed angst through the small aperture in his balaclava revealing his dry lips. He snorted, drumming vigorously with knotty fingers, producing a dull, rhythmic sound, as if waiting for his turn to exercise a tribal right: the right to vote in a commission for an armistice between nomadic Mongolian warriors and non-migratory Caucasian farmers – between patriarchal monotheists and matriarchal polytheists – in which his drumming acquired dignified meaning. In the surrounding silence.

Pac had been moved to that shack of rotten wood – which doubled as a cattle shed where, among those present, only the yak was at ease – after reaching their meeting point near Baglung, a hilly district sixty kilometres west of Pokhara. From what he'd learned in the few preceding hours, the area was home to the Magars, a Tibeto-Burman ethnic group fairly representative of that country and consisting mainly of farmers. This may not have meant much, but the fact that this tribe was known to be a hotbed of soldiers, including the brave Gurkhas, had sounded an alarm in Pac's head, increasing a concern for his precious safety that had influenced his mood for days. Pac was possibly just feeding his paranoia in circumstances of which he knew but minor details, but along the entire bumpy journey in a military jeep (the best that Kimley could find, Pac had been assured), thoughts of some incident, metaphorical or otherwise, of some trap or revenge or other misadventure that his Determination wouldn't be able to control, had bothered him as much as his chauffer's atrocious driving.

The meeting, we were saying, had been set in the barren suburbs of the small town of Baglung, in a certain dusty dirt track, where only a few ruminating wild beasts and a sleeping dog were prepared to attend as witnesses totally unrelated to the events. Moreover, despite the sunny weather, the cold that morning was downright indecent.

After a long and predictable wait, during which neither of them had opened his mouth, they'd been flanked by one of the bandits. Brusque manner and a lean physique, he was emboldened by the aforementioned balaclava that masked his face, lending him a grim confidence. Without saying a word, but exhibiting characteristic mastery of body language, he'd hooded them to resemble sacrificial victims, tied their wrists behind their backs with rough rope, and pushed them into the back of a van. Since time immemorial this vehicle had been administered alternative remedies in place of allopathic mechanics, judging by what Pac had experienced along the journey: jolted at every pothole, thrown about every time the driver slowed, using the handbrake only; and muttering heathen prayers as he felt the van skidding dangerously up the steep incline, and round the narrow hairpin bends of a slippery track that most would describe as impassable; but enough to say it was inimical to any vehicular manoeuvre.

Not being able to see a thing had had its advantages for our travellers, and the description of this trip should have been in the plural, Kimley having the same rights as Pac, if not more. At least the latter knew what lay ahead. Pac, however, had been too busy looking after number one – avoiding brusque movements and safeguarding his joints inside that wheeled cocktail shaker – to worry about Kimley. Shortly before the bandit's arrival he'd simply warned his guide that the business men with whom he was concluding a certain operation would probably take some precautions; but having no idea what to say or what to expect he'd kept it vague, and had faked a reassuring smile, implying: don't worry, we'll make it quick, and then I'll take you out to lunch!

And Kimley had nodded. Or so Pac though.

Time seemed to drag inside that van, as did the jolting and bruising; despite his heavy sweaters, Pac felt the cold become sharper and more insidious, and his feet freeze inside his trekking boots. By now they must have reached quite an altitude; he hadn't been able to rub his hands to warm them; or to scratch himself; or even to make out how many people were in that van, apart from the two of them. Angular sheet metal. Cold feet.

Was there anything else?

There certainly could be. Growing apprehension, for example, mixed with a sense of intrepid insolence induced by that hood, which made him feel like an executioner, an unfailingly cold-blooded killer. And this thought-process had lent him strength: had transformed his anxiety into something which, he knew, could unleash an overpowering fury. The greater his fear, the greater his courage: that was the way to go!

And all this because of Samuel: to free him from his Maoist kidnappers.

"To free": resonant words. But why kidnap Samuel? Who the hell was he, anyway? Apart from being a peddler of aeronautical equipment, a consultant and the man who bragged that he could get his airborne lifeboat to lift off the ground…

And these Maoists? The Maoist movement which he's soon have the pleasure to meet resembled that of the few remaining South-American guerrillas. Apart from the similarities in their modus operandi, certainly inspired by the area's topography, Pac was intrigued by their tenacity in fighting for ideals such as freedom, democracy, justice. Noble, humane values, unfortunately and inevitably destined to be diluted, amputated or sacrificed, if victory were ever secured. It was a matter of time: as always, time would demonstrate that ideology, and religion too, were containers for what we believed was right – containers which sooner or later would transform themselves into energy vectors, empowering something completely different. It wasn't ideology that failed: it was mankind. Rebellious victims had always transformed themselves from winners into organised executioners. History repeated itself: it was cyclic, as the Indians rightly said. Technology, in this sense, merely acted as a multiplier of potential, because it didn't oppress human dignity. Anglo-American settlers who'd fought the British Empire had in turn become imperialists, inebriated by such delusions as 'manifest destiny'. Revolutions in Asia – from the Red Khmers in Cambodia to the people of Burma – in South America and Russia. Repressive, vicious Israeli politics; the pseudo-independence of African nations. Revolutions and self-determination had failed, imploded: they'd been absorbed; together with any attempt to elevate society, to liberate it of power games – the games of potentates.

The dial had to be reset, and this is exactly what was about to happen.

The reason for such human dynamics was anything other than clear; possibly an innate propensity for revenge, for compensating wrongdoings. Hence adult human psychology had never risen noticeably above petty infantile psychology. Which is why history had been, and still was, a stage within a playground managed by elegantly-dressed pimps.

This, too, was a reason why monarchy was the only form of government meriting consideration. A single leader, no intermediaries: one accountable, be-headable person, supported by the dogma of civil conscience, within a context of absolute spiritual, practical and speculative freedom, and of scientific evolution.

There were oxymora he still needed to work on, but Pac was sure that on his return, and above all while he was in orbit in the Star Pac, he would fine-tune these concepts.

Needless to say, the monarch in question could be no other than himself: King Pac I. And shortly before imagining the coronation ceremony, held inside a bungalow and broadcast worldwide (civilisation as we knew it would soon be destroyed; but communication satellites, and much of technology, possibly not) – shortly before a young survivor, a girl clad in the few remaining hopes, had placed on his head the royal crown of thorns – the van stopped; and Pac was suddenly back in the semi-darkness, obliged to re-evoke the figure of the hooded executioner, with accompanying persuasive power. Magic of the mind. At first he'd thought the van had broken down: but all things considered it was in far better shape than he was.

Anyway, here they were.

Once their hoods had been removed and their wrists untied, they were led – stunned by blinding sunlight – up a steep ascending path towards a shack on a promontory, several hundred metres higher. Pac registered all around an ample, arid, rocky valley, beyond which the imposing snow-capped peaks were visible. As always.

No noise, cry or voice disturbed that spectacle. The sun was high; the gods' air conditioning whipped his damp hot face, his stiff hands.

Ideal place for a barbeque with friends, this; or for an unauthorised building, or even an execution, he thought.

Kimley wore a permanent, dazed frown: he'd immediately checked his watch, and continued to do so with increasing frequency; he'd kept his chin pressed down on his chest against the flashing sunlight, as if afraid of appearing in the evening news, and had had to be pushed uphill by the driver. The difference in bulk, ethnic group and mood between the two was evident: Kimley could easily have got the better of him, if he'd wanted to. Gurung versus Magar, on Weird Channel, tonight only.

Pac had apologised to Kimley as well as he could, but he couldn't have done without a witness and an interpreter; and a guide, to be on the safe side. And Kimley was all three, for the price of one. In a moment of recklessness he might feel safer if he involved someone else – especially a native – along with Samuel, whose fate he ignored at the moment: he might even be dead, for all he knew.

In those long moments, their walk up that precipitous unstable track – which had caused a stunned sensation in their ears – had had a beneficial, warming effect. Pac had tried to reassure Kimley with looks, gestures – and shrugs, as if to say: it can't be helped! That's the way they are! Well aware that, by then, his guide was prepared for the worst, Pac also proceeded at a forced pace, limiting his breathing and ribcage movements to the bare minimum; and was careful not to lock eyes with any of the others, while keeping his own skinned and ready to register any threats – which, at that point, were more than likely.

Once they'd reached the top, somewhat breathlessly, they could have spent unparalleled moments contemplating that enchanting, timeless panorama. Lofty, divine, enveloping, serenading them with strains of age-old sweetness: valleys and mountains; and clouds; constantly drawing nearer, and brushing together, in a perennial intimate encounter; an undulating mountainous ocean, blue, green, softening to the grey of maturity. But the barrel of a gun had broken the spell, recalling their attention to the small wooden shack whose open door seemed to suggest more than one meaning.

Pac had entered after Kimley, and before the firearm.

The other two kidnappers, the tall and the short one, also wearing balaclavas, were sitting, motionless.

If Kimley felt any hatred or resentment towards Pac, it didn't show; however, on close inspection, he appeared to be not unfamiliar with this kind of situation: cautious, he'd quickly scanned every corner, registering details; he hadn't said a word, though he could easily have exploited the 'derby' situation, communicating with these men if he wanted to, clarifying any misunderstandings. Was he merely afraid, or what?

They'd sat down. No sign of a pale-skinned Westerner.

At least, that's the way Pac had always imagined Samuel, though he had no elements to build the identikit of someone he'd never seen, with a false name, whose voice on the phone was often scrambled. Samuel might not even be a Westerner, but he certainly wasn't at that table.

When the largest of the bucolic trio, presumably the boss, stopped drumming his thick fingers on the table and demanded loudly to see the dough, he betrayed the nervousness of a wannabe-pusher at his first important deal.

Suspicious, Pac turned to his watchful interpreter.

"You can tell your fellow countrymen that first I want to see the great absentee," he said defiantly, his eyes fixed on the threesome. He didn't intend to betray any fear, to give them any satisfaction. Quite the contrary. His fear – a continuous surge that caused his leg to tremble and accelerated his heartbeat – had to be kept under control, to be distilled into drops of defiant stoicism. It certainly wasn't the first time he'd had to deal with people of this sort: he had a wealth of experience to put to good use. They'd soon find out.

Kimley frowned as he laboriously translated Pac's English into his own Gurung, which he then had to adapt to the Magar idiom: not exactly his forte. A fine and elaborate intellectual exercise, performed by his guide with the same meticulous care of a yogi trying to awaken the kundalini serpent by beating it with a stick.

By the kidnappers' reaction to his request, Pac gathered that something in their great scheme was beginning to falter, indicating that their feigned professionalism (meriting respect, like any other form of honed skill) was being replaced by disconcerting inexperience.

The three started to argue and gesticulate fretfully, like Arabian traders on a full-moon night, awakening the brown yak, who stood up shaking his head. This caused the bell around his neck to ring, resounding like a call to order in a court room where a legal dispute was being decided on. The first warning went unheeded; but at the second, much more vigorous shake – when small black creatures became dislodged from the yak's fur and were propelled towards the unknown; and the yak almost freed himself of the small red pouch hanging from his neck – the trio fell silent, glanced briefly at the animal and conceded a little calm, although subdued less by the noise of the bell than by the nauseating bovine stench.

Resuming his composure, the boss of the villains – the one with eyes more Mongol than Tibetan – made an attempt to intimidate, so pathetic that even he seemed unconvinced: shaking his fist at Pac, and shouting a word that filled the entire shack, he insisted that the ransom be coughed up unconditionally, while his colleagues, arms folded, nodded in agreement.

Returning the same response, an inexpressive Pac thought that he knew nothing about these people and that, under such dodgy circumstances, it was better not to give in to their requests.

In fact, after exchanging long indecipherable glances through the small openings of their balaclavas, the bandits capitulated. With a nod, the Nepalese version of Subcomandante Marcos ordered that the prisoner be brought before him; the third bandit at the door immediately ran out, while those present were left staring at each other.

No-one dared take their eyes off their presumed enemy, not even when, from outside, they heard the screech of latch chains and the crash of wooden planks; or when the yak – whose roaming around the room was putting Pac's nerves on edge – emitted a cryptic sneeze.

When the masked shepherd returned he was preceded by the figure of a warmly-clad elderly gentleman with light-blue eyes. He was tall, taller than anyone else in the room, and very thin: Pac noticed this immediately. His white hair was all dishevelled on the one side; his eyes alert and scared. Despite the circumstances, he retained a distinguished air, that of an urbane, avuncular gentleman with manicured hands who played chess and would always ask permission before rising from the table. A benign face, weary but gentle; one who must have conquered many hearts in his day. His presence immediately posed the question of what a man like this was doing there. By logical exclusion, he picked out Pac and launched himself headlong in his direction in an attempted embrace – rendered impossible with his hands tied behind him – but the sentiment wasn't lost on the others.

He was dirty, emaciated (he must have lost weight); pale and emotionally tried, as his red-rimmed eyes bore witness; and he was shaking so, once untied, he was allowed to sit down beside his liberator.

Pac thought this sensitivity, and the refinement of his clothing, must have encouraged the Maoist rebels to think they had precious goods on their hands.

But were they really Maoist rebels?

Harbouring some doubt, Pac was immediately distracted by the angry shouting of the threesome who, as Kimley explained, now demanded their tribute; more decisively this time, adding for emphasis a gun, which their presumed leader was banging on the table so violently that even the yak glowered. His finger on the trigger, the man firmly held a large short-barrelled revolver with a faded wooden butt, which must once have known soft cloths and lubricating oils, but which now conferred a grotesquely ambiguous look to its holder and to those who saw it as a means for making easy money. But when a thick thumb lifted its hammer and arched it backwards, it became clear that the weapon was still able to do its duty.

It was pointed unhesitatingly at Samuel.

Frightened at first, the latter bent forward towards Pac's ear: "See that yak? The pouch it's got round its neck?" – the whisper was so resolute as to sound like a threat. Or was it an order? – "It mustn't leave this room except in my (possibly living) hands." Then, lowering his gaze, he resumed his pitiful countenance.

Confused, aware of the tension churning inside himself, Pac hesitated, surprised at that statement from Samuel, whom he'd believed to be frightened. Now he had to think fast: to find a way to get out of there alive. He knew there was no time to lose.

What was the connection between the flame-red pouch tied to the yak's neck and the gun aimed at Samuel? And what did Samuel expect him to do?

Truth be told, he understood less and less, but under the circumstances he could only play along; if only to satisfy a reckless curiosity – of the kind that killed the cat. And if this was a game, he might as well play hard.

"You shan't get a cent out of us," he said, turning to Kimley who seemed reluctant to translate, for obvious reasons. Then Pac added: "Thank Hanuman that all went well and that you didn't hurt a hair on my friend's head!"

The translation, whispered hesitantly, was followed by

sullen silence.

"We have Ganesh on our side," continued Pac. "And pitting yourself against the god who removes obstacles will do nothing other than worsen your already critical situation," he declared with such a fierce frown that even the yak – under the unexpected scrutiny of the two – lay down on the floor, careful not to produce a sound from the bell round his neck.

The moment had come for Pac's trump card, his metaphysical sprint: for the prodigious phrase that would dispel friction. He hadn't intended to go so far, but he had no choice. With narrowed eyes, Pac breathed in oxygen through his nostrils and edged gradually away from the table: the weapon of his Determination admitted no obstacles.

And when Kimley had finished translating – slowly, very slowly –delivering his final words with a feline tension of all the muscles that might be called on to save his life; when Pac had had all the time to do the same and seemed on the verge of exploding; and when two enormous tears streamed from Samuel's eyes as from overflowing bathtubs; it was then that the rapid sequence of events degenerated like a tangled audio tape, limbs ready to spring into action, until from an undefined corner of the shack resonated words that no human being had ever heard at that altitude.

"Borrowing the Power of the Sun... the deadly Sun

Attack!"

This was a quotation from a famous Japanese cartoon of the Mecha genre, created by Yoshiyuki Tomino. Together with Go Nagai and other *mangaka* of that florid period, the knights of rebirth, he had devoted his art to imposing – beneath the threshold of consciousness and ready to surface into awareness – a sophisticated subliminal imprinting aimed to shape and prepare a generation for extra-terrestrial contact and for its implications. He achieved this by using archetypes and mystical symbolism of Oriental derivation, and by staging conflicts and battles in which the real weapons were actually psychic, in order to influence the existential course awaiting those televiewing minds, now poised between infantile disillusion and the hormonal tsunami of puberty.

Pac had got this idea while observing a Burmese monk in a prison in Rangoon, a few years earlier. Pac had been arrested by the local authorities, whose suspicions had been aroused by the movements of the overweight young foreigner, and by the questions he went around asking on the refining and transportation of heroin. They had discovered his real identity; and, worse still, that of his employers, who weren't exactly on friendly terms with the local military dictatorship.

He was a novice, they couldn't *not* arrest him. And they were glad to do so.

While diplomatic negotiations for his release were underway (the Burmese government seemed to be in no hurry), he'd been thrown in jail.

Crossing the threshold of a prison, one is normally most frightened of the inmates themselves: the mouldy, incorrigibly violent dregs of society, whose lustiest dream, after that of being set free, was to watch – with upraised arms, like a host of children – the arrival of a novice, hoping to be the lucky one to have him as a present. Which is why these days people tend to see warders and the prison itself as their refuge, as the manifestation of their inalienable rights: law and order that protects, like a pair of pig-iron underpants, what we most value at times like these.

But in there it was exactly the opposite. Affected by the incorrigible fault of being totalitarian and inflexible, dictatorships usually found indigestible any form of constructive criticism, verbal or otherwise, and proposals for improvements and social equity, even when proffered cost- and tax-free. Hence the prison was full of monks and of ordinary people: dangerous dissidents; plotters and enemies of the homeland; in the worst cases, pacifists. The pokey, muddy, cramped cells within those decaying walls probably contained the essence of Burma, a true representation of a people subjected to starvation and to forced labour for the enrichment of an élite, as paranoid as only a paranoid élite in power could be.

Pac overcame his initial human fear, therefore, thanks to unexpected courtesy, to a curiosity filled with hope, to gazes of good-natured resignation. The men were few, mainly elderly; the younger ones elsewhere. He found it hard to believe that this space could contain such an exorbitant crowd of hearts and souls.

Wrapped in a shabby red tunic, Ashin was one of them: more experienced than he seemed, his face lined with scars on a still-smooth skin, his head shaven, his body marked with even more tell-tale signs. Pac's cell contained five people, a bucket of water, a hole in a corner of the dirt floor, and no window for launching dreams. The other four figures seemed close to death, dried up and curled in on themselves like baked parchment. Even if they'd wanted to, they wouldn't have known how to communicate with Pac, who stood out among them like Sissy the bitch, who came third in the national dog-beauty pageant.

Ashin, on the other hand, knew a little English owing to his correspondence with a few groups of supporters formed in the North of Thailand by more or less clandestine refugees – which is why he was here. Although formally monks were not supposed to be involved (at least those who hadn't been bought by the junta in power), some were secretly authorised to maintain contacts, to promote changes and to spread awareness with anyone who might be of help. Despite precautions, some were punctually identified and arrested.

During the weeks he spent in the can, the equally young Pac had decided that the best way to while away the hours was to do as Ashin did, i.e. nothing: he just sat there all day – yet was evidently very busy, in his own way. Pac decided this was an opportunity to mould his character, knowing that to be the master of your own destiny you need Determination: in thought and, obviously, in action. Dithering over decisions, playing for time, were symptoms of fear; and in his profession, in his life, this could lead to serious consequences, as his current predicament clearly demonstrated. Had he been more resolute at some earlier stage, perhaps by now he would be running his finger down the first-class menu on a flag-carrier flight. He had a lot to learn, he'd told himself – as he sat on the floor next to the young monk, who didn't so much as deign him of a glance – and he certainly wasn't short of time.

What he proposed to do was to train his mind to concentrate; induce it to create a void that would come to his aid at times of need. A void into which he could channelize strength, willpower. It didn't really matter whether this originated from fear in a specific situation or from another rush of emotion: the sense lay in convincing himself, in committing to remain uninvolved in whatever might weaken him. This, and only this, was the purpose of the sentence "Borrowing the Power of the Sun... the deadly Sun Attack!". So simple, yet so allusive: a metaphor he'd chosen as his starting code, as his Power button – nothing exceptional, simply *Power*. But this had proved more complicated than he'd hoped.

The first week of his mental training saw him engaged in greeting his university friends; reorganising the shelves in his garage; asking himself how much longer he'd have to wait before his release: in other words, identifying and rooting out anything that could distract him from mental relaxation, the precondition for a meditative state. During the second week the two of them were immersed in perpetual silence, as if actually inside a temple; although in Pac's case this was merely a sinister side-effect of fear, he had gradually managed to turn down his inner volume, contain his mental haemorrhage of images to single photo-stills; and then to halt, come into possession of the remote control and learn its basic use. In the course of the third week – during which Pac, too, had had his head shaven in respect of local customs and of basic rules of hygiene imposed by their surroundings – Ashin, moved to pity, had decided to speak to him.

"Our mind," he'd said, "is a nub of light, a knob of dough. If made to levitate and conducted along the path of awareness... if fed devotion and rectitude, our mind can help us build our own reality, conduct us towards self-realisation."

"What we think," the young monk still wearily reiterated, "is what we are. What we are is what we do. What we do, finally, is what we obtain. This attitude helps us accept, understand and overcome what happens to us. The same attitude helps us shape what we consciously choose as our life."

"It doesn't seem to work very well for you. Perhaps you should put more effort into it," Pac had commented.

"What you see is what happens – what we experience – when fear takes charge. What you can't see or know is how much freedom and peace dwells in the minds of the upright. Alas, they are not the majority," Ashin had admitted.

Perhaps political and philosophical discussions were better avoided, especially if these could cause further aggravation to someone who – with his naked humanity, simple beauty, abused benevolence – was offered no friendly hand though he reached out his own, dispensing comforting truths, recipes of a humble cuisine for an inattentive palate. After this they'd both resumed their inner occupations.

This had been the start of a process that had transformed an echo, a candid relic of childhood, into a psychic device: this, while dismissed with scorn as heresy by most of his brain, was to save his arse on more than one future occasion.

Towards the end of his detention he would even have been able to divert the path of an ant with the power of his mind, if he'd tried. But he never found out.

He'd decided instead to help Ashin in the only way that

could be of use: by conversing with him so that he could practice his English, an indispensable tool for managing his secret correspondence with refugees; an activity that incarceration could never weaken, just as the entire process of Passive Resistance to the authoritarian rule could not be arrested.

"I'm inwardly convinced that one day my Burma will be free, liberated," he'd told Pac one day, not long before sunrise, when the earliest stirrings had suggested that an inchoate something was in the air, even inside that cell.

Pac had watched as Ashin assayed an awkward semblance of a smile, his brow knitting as in an effort to preserve a confidential plan for which he'd give his life. And Pac had listened with the utmost attention.

"Soon," he'd continued "and without your help, on which we no longer count, my country will smile again – hope, work, build and dream." Then he'd stopped, leaning back against a wall mouldy with humidity and stained with blood. Sighing slowly, he'd placed a hand firmly on Pac's shoulder. "We'll weep with joy, jump around like grasshoppers in a field, confused like fireflies mirrored in a pool of water. We'll progress, bless and meditate."

Suddenly, Pac had shifted his position to brusquely shrug that friendly hand from his shoulder; from a nearby corner, a guard had been observing them silhouetted against the light. Ashin, smothering that hint of a smile – one of defiance that seemed on the verge of breaking out uncontrollably – had isolated himself in prolonged silence, as if searching his dictionary for other words and checking his grammar before he could continue. And when he did – the guard appearing to be absorbed elsewhere, and Ashin's whispered words covered by the moans and lamentations of other prisoners – he'd seemed pleased to have expressed his thoughts.

"I won't be there that day," he'd said.

Whether induced by pessimism or political far-sightedness it was impossible to tell, but in the half-light his resolute tone had resonated darkly with lurking possibilities.

Remaining in his half-lotus posture, Pac had hazarded a question: "Will you forgive your torturers, those who have condemned you to this misery? Or will you simply take their place, as the foregoing local revolutions did?"

Ashin had scrutinised his face attentively, while seemingly formulating a response in Burmese and then engaging in the pleasant and stimulating effort of translating it into English.

"You Westerners...," he'd replied, "ever ready to judge, to offer unsolicited advice, then hide in the shadows of diplomacy rather than get your hands dirty!"

Pac had nodded, as if he didn't consider himself among the accused.

"The salvation – whether physical or spiritual – of every single pawn in this tyranny doesn't concern me. On the contrary..."

Ashin's unfinished phrase had roused Pac's curiosity. "I detect a shade of aversion in your words." Actually, for the sake of comprehension 'aversion' had become 'hate', though not rendering faithfully what Pac had really intended.

"I don't think your words are compatible with that coloured sheet you wear," he'd continued, close to the young monk's ear; and then, drawing back to ensure that he was seen, he'd winked at Ashin, with the hint of a smile. The earliest lights of dawn had started to pick out the outline of objects hitherto obscured in darkness, and the air had resonated with the incomparable gift of birdsong.

The monk had then returned the smile, the veins clearly visible all over his shaven head.

"I'm not a damned bodhisattva. I have already broadened the salvation front from my own to that of my entire country, including the good people who belong there. As for the evil ones, I hope they burn in your Western Hell," he'd declared, with evident conviction.

As the first movements, sounds and steps resounded from nearby cells and from far-away rooms, they'd put an end to such conversations which, easily overheard, could have caused them unwarranted trouble.

The next morning, much to his surprise, Pac had been released without being able to say farewell to his friend. But that was only the first of his regrets.

Ashin simply wasn't there: he couldn't be found.

Persuaded by the looks he got from the warders, Pac had soon come to terms with this and had started to savour the scent of freedom. He was walking, escorted, towards the gates of the prison, and already perceived traffic in the street beyond, when a voice behind him had suddenly called out his name.

It was Ashin. Standing with his back to a wall.

Pac would never forget how he felt as the guards' hands had blocked his arms to prevent any action on his part. And possibly – as he reflected later – to oblige him to watch.

He'd seen young Ashin, in his red tunic, smile in the distance and repeat his name, calmly now, as their gazes met. He'd watched as an old man in uniform had shouted something, first in his direction and then to a prison guard; he'd watched as the latter, tense and awkward, had pushed the monk against the wall and drawn a gun.

In those brief instants Pac had been unable to breathe, understand or move. All he'd felt was a paralysing buzz, a numbing dismay that would have caused him to pass out, had the guards let go.

A shot, and the monk had collapsed to the ground, leaving blood and brains splattered on the wall behind.

Without a moment's hesitation, Pac had been dragged away to the gate and thrown out, where a car was waiting to expel him from the country.

A triple message: to his employers, to himself, to

prisoners and hostages inside and out.

That was one of the occasions when he'd felt a visit to Oscar was indispensable.

Kimley drove the van back down the same steep track which he was now trying to remember by heart, hindered by pitch darkness that the one operating headlight couldn't even begin to penetrate. He was moving away from three corpses studiedly arranged on the bare ground, pending the arrival of hyenas, jackals, Himalayan griffons, and any other scavengers who – enticed by so much exposed meat and blood – might contribute to cancelling those traces. He must speed away, his foot firmly down on the accelerator.

The path became a flat dirt track, occasionally occupied by nocturnal figures which appeared suddenly, like wandering ghosts, and were avoided by swerving abruptly, at speed, while praying that they remain still or innocuous. Beggars attracted by the van's headlight, animals, occasional overcrowded rickshaws without so much as a hind light. And the loud roar of the engine protesting its abuse against the darkness.

With a severely injured body on board, Pokhara hospital was still too far away.

Despite returning by the same route, the road seemed less bumpy, almost as if the vehicle were trying to smooth over the ground's asperities out of a sense of responsibility in an emergency; or maybe the passengers' minds were simply focused on other things.

As hard to restrain as urgent urination, blood spurted out copiously from the wound into layers of sodden cloth pressed against the stomach of a body lying on a metal floor. Apparently unconscious. Deep wound, haemorrhage, damaged internal organs. Weak but regular breathing.

And talking about breathing, what their nostrils were unable to filter was a bovine stench – rancid, ruthless, almost gamy – which, to all intents and purposes, acted like a stupefying biochemical supplement in the interior of the van.

That night the darkness, so thick you could savour it by the spoon, so caressingly enveloping, with luminous freckles scattered across the face of the sky, conceded a vague and intuitive view of the mountains, whose snow-capped peaks evoked misty lighthouses on Mediterranean headlands.

It was cold, atrociously cold for the tattered relics of garments they wore and, despite their speeding along, time seemed to flow too slowly: the town couldn't possibly still be so far away.

Kimley, the chronograph expert, had stopped checking the time ever since – after a brief convulsion of liquid crystals – such information had disappeared off the digital display of his watch. And from that moment on, deprived of rhythm, everything was different.

But here, at last, after a narrow gravelly bend in the road, were the first sparse lights of the small town, some of them reflected on the lake. Weak lights outlining an easily accessible geographic and temporal horizon, steeped in monsoon fog that made the place resemble a convincing high-altitude mirage. The connection inspired the same hope for rescue.

Dirty, and seriously concerned about that now corpse-like being, Pac was more bewildered than shaken while awaiting an unsettling number of explanations. He felt bombarded by a friendly fire of emotions, incapable of choosing what to focus on – disgusted, or guilty. Despite the icy cold, a trembling formation of corrosive beads of sweat emerged from his bowed forehead and streamed down his temples in thin rivulets. Satisfied, though pissed off – and surprised, despite himself. Pressing down on the wound, his hands smeared with warm blood, soiling his fingers, his wrists, his soul. Although he tried not to look, he could feel that slimy liquid: the more he turned his head away, the more the tactile sensation became keen, clear, until that blood was somehow accepted and absorbed as his own, and he perceived the importance of his hands stanching, of his palms sinking, of those two lives joined in a temporary bond of mutual assistance, of complementarity to which he had to and wanted to adhere. He was tired, terribly agitated and – this he recognised, despite everything – determined.

Kimley, on the other hand, was relieved, face sneering,

hands tightly gripping the steering wheel. He knew that single hitch would be solved, one way or another: he just needed to reach the hospital as soon as possible, and was sure to find affiliates to help him sort things out. Everything had gone smoothly, exactly as he'd wanted, exactly according to the master plan.

Samuel, wounded, was putting up a fight while losing blood and energy. Eventually he passed out, although one could almost swear that he exuded something like contentment, from his lips down to the hand clutching an apparently very ordinary flame-red bundle.

I almost forgot to mention: alongside the moribund Samuel lay a young specimen of domestic *Bos grunniens*, in reasonably good shape, albeit momentarily knocked out by an excess of adrenaline. It was Pac who'd insisted on taking him along so a vet could examine him (and the gods can bear witness to how much he'd had to insist and beg for the necessary help to load him onto the van); concerned about the stress to which the yak had been subjected, he truly wished to remove him from the bad company he kept. This, he knew, could only get him into trouble – such as becoming involved in a case of attempted murder.

Reconstruction of what happened in that hilltop shack can only adhere to what actually occurred, which is so confusing that the actual chronological order of the events is unclear: that's the sum of it.

Kimley was holding back and leaving the last words untranslated in order to engage the limited mental faculties of the three shepherd-bandits, in the hope of gaining time and creating the necessary conditions to wreak havoc.

They all sat with their hands on the crude table, its rough wooden surface snarled with splinters.

Pac stared at the leader of the three, charging his gaze with all the strength and daring he could muster: eyes half closed, jaw set. He was scowling with contained fury: he longed to bash in those eyes (black and yellow, like the flag of a losing team) peering through that stupid balaclava that scared nobody. He stood immobile, ready.

Kimley whispered something; chest thrust forward, fists clenched, breathing restrained; he glared unwaveringly at one of the two hooded villains.

Samuel was ignored by everyone, but in fact was trying his best to conceal his gulping and trembling.

The other two masked robbers sat, filthy hands on the table; one of them – whose distress was betrayed by an accelerated heaving of the chest – didn't dare move a muscle. Silence. Bated breath. Samuel's light-blue eyes. The yellow eyes of the boss. A drop of sweat on Kimley's brow. The ancient pistol on the table. Balaclavas. The yak's furry ears. Heat, breathed through Pac's nostrils. And again, the pistol. The silence, the yellow of the shack, the clenched fists.

Like a bedevilled snake, Kimley had sprung suddenly

towards the three Maoists, who'd immediately scattered: one had flung himself onto Samuel; the second had dashed towards the door; the third had hopped onto an electric sledge which his neural launching-pad would propel into a void: the void in which floated a memory of gripping a somewhat ancient gun. But he was too slow for Pac, who'd rendered him inoffensive with a hefty right-handed blow on the temple, making him crash to the floor along with his gun. Adding to the recommended daily intake an extra dose of surprise, Kimley had turned out to be a fierce fighter, managing with insolent dexterity to land a kick in the stomach of the bandit about to open the door and make his escape; and, with a fourth-dan judoka throw, to floor and knock out the man who had attacked Samuel; the latter, who had taken a savage beating, had been trying helplessly to protect himself with his hands – like a child faced with a salutary smacking from his father, knowing full well that it was useless – and ending up grovelling and blubbing "No, no, stop," even after his squat kidnapper had already passed out on the floor; and Kimley had moved away, to finish with the bandit at the door, still doubled over from the kick but not yet silenced. All this was done with a speed that would have put to shame a premature ejaculator. Pac had time to aim and deliver the finishing blow, and take stock of the fact that the party was over.

Then a loud bang: inside an ancient cylinder chamber, a trigger had liberated an incandescent metal suppository which had soared – like a shuttle saying farewell to the world; or like a human cannonball breathing in the rarefied air and wondering how much higher he could rise – only to stop, or rather to crash unexpectedly into a soft obstacle.

The shooter was the yak.

Accustomed to contemplating entirely different scenes, he'd jumped to his feet at the earliest signs of fighting and, anxious to make himself useful in some way, had started to stamp his hooves where he stood, in an orderly manner – front right and rear left –until a tall man with a bleeding lip had staggered and limped towards him and, staring at him with insincere benevolence, had clearly made for his flamered bundle. At which point the bovine had got into yak-reverse and with a single step had trod on the gun that had fallen on the ground, firing a bullet that could hardly believe it's luck. So happy was it to be released from the barrel of the weapon, that it ricocheted off some unspecified surface, presumably a beam on the ceiling, to finish in Samuel's stomach; Samuel had managed to snatch the object of his desire from that woolly neck before crashing, without a single lament, onto the old wooden floor boards. Followed by the actual perpetrator, whom the noise of the shot and the excessive stress had caused to pass out on top of his victim.

The rest had happened, on that hilltop, after loading Samuel onto the van that had driven them there, and after Pac had insisted on taking the yak as well; on that hilltop, where Pac alone had tried to stanch those wounds; had felt the warm slimy blood colouring his fingers; while Kimley, seemingly out of his mind, had ran to and fro like a bat out of hell, gripping an automatic firearm which he'd drawn from who-knows-where, on which he'd fitted a silencer (useless, in their current whereabouts), which he'd also dug up from a hiding place undetected by the bandits' naïve search.

From the van's window, Pac had then watched as he'd rushed into the shack and carried out bodily the three half-unconscious wretches, one by one. Kimley had arranged them with arms and legs wide apart, like sacrificial victims, removed their balaclavas, crouched beside them and briefly examined their features; then he'd straightened up, taken a few steps backward and aimed his gun: the bodies had jerked as the first mortal bullet exploded with a dull hiss. They'd ceased to move when the rest of the ammunition (probably the whole magazine, thought Pac) had pierced those already mangled corpses.

Only when Kimley – with a sinister expression on his face, and his gun still smoking – had approached the van, did his pace slow down and, as the dwindling sun faded his shadow, had directed an unfathomable glance at Pac. Then they'd driven off at great speed.

Kimley owed him an explanation: his role in the story was anything but clear.

What's more, Pac felt exploited and made a fool of, although he couldn't quite define the sensation.

Samuel had been rushed to hospital, opened up even more than he already was, and operated on by a medical team trained in the best Indian centres, in the best hospital available at that moment – i.e. the only one. He was in a comatose state of the kind accessible with a mere transit visa, like those stop-over countries which – while mercifully looked down upon by mass tourism – people like to say they've visited in passing: it sounds so cool. It was just a matter of waiting: waiting for him to board the right connection and have a good journey back.

The severe-looking gentleman heading the aforementioned medical team had expressed a cautious pessimism, bordering on the fatalistic (if Samuel had survived the first two nights), before disappearing, followed by a procession of white coats.

And during that interval, that long and tiresome wait, Pac had felt prickly shivers down his spine: rushes of tension that had helped him rationalise what had happened. That episode had seriously threatened what looked increasingly like his sole chance of completing his vimana before the Apocalypse; furthermore it had caused the collapse of a poor animal at the mercy of events, and finally – although of marginal importance to his plot – it had wiped three supporting actors off the scene.

He had a gut feeling that he too had risked his life, and it wasn't what you'd call a pleasant sensation.

So there he was, sitting and thinking, on a wooden stool in a hall outside the ward, at the crossroads of three different corridors; potted large-leafed plants eyed each other, while a gigantic poster of Himalayan peaks at sunset, photographed in the 80s, emanated a blend of authentic confidence and charm, inducing one's eyes to bask in the blue of the sky, the white of the mountain tops, and the assorted greens of the valleys.

A place like that was certainly of some comfort.

Pac sat and thought, leaning against a boiling radiator to which his back had formed an attachment. And couldn't shake off an awkward feeling of guilt, which shouldn't even have begun to bother him.

After all, he'd been dragged into this, and he'd involved Kimley who – I'll repeat, in order to dispel any doubt – owed him a comprehensive explanation: including a clarification on the presumed randomness of his being hired as a guide.

He hadn't known about the yak until the last moment, and this was another distressing factor. Once he'd left Samuel in the bowels of a hospital (which had seemed, that night, like a flickering candle in a cathedral closed for restoration); once he'd obtained some reassurance, however vague and inadequate, he'd immediately climbed back into the van and rushed to whom Kimley – before disappearing – had defined as the best vet in the area, as well as a personal friend; the man who, according to his guide, would cast a magic cloak against any possible local curiosity.

Woken in the middle of the night, Dr. Raju had immediately set to work. However, the glance that the short, bald vet – a qualified surgeon – had given his patient certainly wasn't very promising. Initially he thought the yak was dead, and the large tongue hanging out of its drooling mouth had rendered credible this dreadful supposition. The doctor later confessed that he'd never seen an unconscious yak, and that this had hindered the establishment of that fundamental relationship of trust and collaboration between doctor and patient. But after auscultating the yak's heart and lungs he'd hazarded a reassuring prognosis.

"You no worry," he'd said, leaning a hand on Pac's shoulder, "everything be all right. Yak no die."

And for some unknown reason Pac had believed him.

Dr. Raju had insisted that he remain alone, once the malodorous shaggy bovine had been lifted onto the disinfected autopsy table. In view of the animal's weight and bulk, this operation had drained Pac of what little energy he had left.

Finally, when he'd seen the doctor put on disposable latex gloves and close the door in his face, Pac had stood there frozen, incapable of pulling himself together. An onlooker might have noticed tears beginning to well in his eyes, had it not been for a surreptitious wipe with the back of his hand, and the forced smile with which he'd turned towards Kimley.

"Sure," the latter had repeated softly. "He'll make it... he's young!" And suddenly he'd dashed off, straightening his cap.

Pac never discovered the reason for Kimley's unsolicited support, which had caused Pac a certain amount of embarrassment, despite proving important, even vital. The man saw himself as a guide, yet he'd cold-bloodedly killed three shady individuals: probably riffraff, the dregs of the old Maoist movement, unable to find a new life for themselves. A fanatic schizo? How dangerous and unstable was he? Did he owe him his life, in a sense? After taking him and Samuel to the hospital he could have left, and yet he'd driven him all the way there.

This other wait had been equally exhausting – unbearable. So much so that, once he'd entrusted the poor yak to the care of the vet, Pac had decided to leave.

A taxi, the comfort of a new face, the still-young night in that small town with no street lights; and he'd found himself sitting on that wooden stool, embracing a radiator; embraced in turn by an intact and unused money-belt, encircling his waistline with pecuniary affection.

Pac could have returned to his hotel room, showered,

eaten something. In this exact order. Or he could have experimented alternative solutions.

He could have, but didn't.

The next morning he woke up with a start, as if he'd been slapped full in the face – as sometimes happens. Sitting on that same stool, his boiling, sweaty back leaning against the radiator; his throat dry. It was daytime: a beautiful day. And he felt like shit.

At the crossroads of three corridors, in that small lay-by for elves on pedal-cars, one witnessed the cautious to-ing and fro-ing of relations – pacing slowly, heads bowed – some waiting, some disappointed; some, more rarely, smiling. From their number, one could infer, in proportion, that the patients in the hospital can't have been very many.

But this is mere speculation.

When Pac opened his eyes he was immediately struck by the intensity of the light that pierced the four large and somewhat grimy windows, illuminating the room and reflecting off the white tiles of the floor, so that everything seemed to have an evanescent contour; by studiously narrowing and bending his bleary-eyed gaze, he could see the white coats sail and stroll on shimmering milk, enveloped in candid auras, sponsored by the only manufacturer of battery-powered halos.

The optical diversion was short-lived, though: just long enough to feel the onslaught of a severe headache, and to witness a vocal gaggle of nurses rush by with a defibrillator, almost tripping over their own feet. Remembering how and why he'd found himself inside that hospital, he'd had a flashback of the foregoing episodes, while becoming aware of the acute discomfort of his backside – and of a sense of desolation, of alienation, of futility (was his presence really necessary? Couldn't he have gone home?). The grumbling of his empty stomach; and, last but not least, of Kimley sitting at his side, watching him. He's mistaken his shadow for that of some anxiously waiting relative.

"Why the fuck are you still here?", rasped Pac, his vocal chords slowly warming up, one by one, but as yet unable to guarantee full efficiency: this took time. "What do you want?", he croaked, before clearing his voice completely. He absolutely must get himself some water, among other things. Or rather, get breakfast.

Wearing dark clothes, Kimley had donned a light-coloured shirt under a brand-new pullover, marginally more elegant than the one he'd worn up to that moment. The too-long sleeves of his padded jacket prevented Pac from verifying whether he'd replaced his Casio watch.

"Lovely day, isn't it?" asked Kimley.

Pac rubbed his eyes, passed his hand across his brow, then scratched his head, asking himself what the man had in store for him. Whatever it was, he didn't need it. Not at that moment.

"Sure," he huffed, "splendid. Now, will you tell me what the hell you want, or would you rather I asked the questions? I happen to have about twenty ready and waiting."

"When things go as planned..." said Kimley with a smile, leaving the sentence unfinished. As he sat next to Pac, gazing fixedly at the Himalayan poster, his voice had the quiet tedious tone of an inattentive priest in a confessional too cramped for his other needs. Even his English was different, more refined and articulate than when Pac had first met him: more gentrified, like his hair which now, without a cap, appeared oiled and groomed, of a brilliant jet-black.

Pac was torn between the need to get up and stretch his legs, as far away as possible, and trying to obtain responses to all his questions, still hanging from the ceiling like so many happy little spiders spinning round one another.

Nearby, an elderly couple dressed in simple clothes and heavy concern strolled hand in hand, whispering in each other's ears and exchanging slow nods. Then they disappeared, swallowed in the depths of the corridor leading to the west wing.

"I'm protecting my country," said Kimley suddenly, knowing exactly what Pac wanted to hear, and the effect that his words would have on him.

That phrase was enough in itself to shed light onto many recent events. It was clear that he was dealing with a spy, an agent of the Nepalese Intelligence Service. One piece of the puzzle was in place, and explained Kimley's flat accent, so unusual in that part of the world.

Pressed by Pac's gaze, Kimley continued: "Thanks to my cover as a guide I can obtain information on extremist fringes that have failed to align with the new political panorama, which saw their victory in the destitution of the Gyanendra monarchy."

As he listened, Pac had to recognise Kimley's bravura, and was unable to restrain a certain regret.

"There are too many hot-heads in this country, and we're always on high alert. Over internal and external matters."

He seemed in the mood for talking, for opening up after what, for him, must have been a successful mission; and the desolate, dignified atmosphere of that hospital lent itself to unwinding, to conceding confidences to someone you assumed you'd never meet again. Kimley explained that sources of potential concerns were mainly geographic. Southern India, on which his country largely depended for any form of transport, goods, labour, services and energy, was ever a red-hot front for trafficking in firearms and counterfeit currency. On the opposite side, Communist China: not an agreeable presence, as Tibet's history testified. If Chinese policy was to lay its hands on Tibet's mineral and water resources, the same threat was potentially valid for neighbouring Nepal, which had witnessed an enormous increase in its territory of Chinese agents, official or otherwise. Not to mention insidious atheist propaganda.

"Caught between two fires, two giants," said Kimley with a sigh, biting his lip and staring blankly at the skirting board opposite. "What's more, I imagine you know what often lurks behind revolutions..."

Then, for the first time since they'd started talking, he turned to gaze at Pac, narrowing his eyes slightly. He had the superior look of someone who knows and observes you, aware that you're in the dark – as you should be – and will remain in the dark. His air was vaguely affected, as if he was hiding rather than manifesting, and favouring an attitude to avoid another. Pac had this sensation as he glanced at two hazelnuts set in a face of bleached ebony, spoiled by a thin, uniform scar visible along the curve of his cheek; and a cunning expression that did nothing for his appearance, and which caused Pac to feel a momentary chill.

They remained immobile for a long while, immersed in this unilateral, non-verbal communication – which was neither physical nor emotional – so crudely credible yet so byzantine, that Pac had to avert his eyes, lest he learn that Kimley could also fathom his sexual preferences.

It was obvious that, thanks to his position, before accepting his post as the guide whom Pac believed he'd chosen freely, Kimley had certainly glanced through all the information Big Brother had on him. Fortunately it wasn't all the truth and nothing but the truth, otherwise he'd probably be dead by now. Pac, too, started to stare at the mountains.

"Top management is always corruptible" proceeded Kimley, stretching. "And here we have too many interests at play". His tone had grown more serious, bordering on the intimidating. Though, to be honest, Pac couldn't imagine why.

"Do you consider me a threat?" he asked. Better clear any doubts, now the cards were on the table.

"You and your friend have enabled us to acquire some interesting information," replied Kimley, stretching out his legs, in heavy trousers – black, as were his boots. Whether Kimley's preference for an all-black look was merely a matter of taste, a way to hide stains and save on the laundry, or a trick to acquire an air of greater severity Pac didn't know, but the result was undoubtedly to make him look like an aspiring actor aping his favourite screen idol. "Those three were as much Maoist rebels as we are. You did notice, I trust," said Kimley, somewhat defiantly.

Pac nodded. His hunch had been correct. "So who were they?" he asked.

"Ordinary criminals who regularly extorted money from tourists. Would-be blackmailers masquerading as something else, in the hopes of acquiring a capacity to intimidate. Miserable outcasts. Scum, godless people in the wrong place."

Pac considered this for a moment before asking: "But if they really were common rabble, why did you agree to come along when I called you? If you already knew what this was all about, why dirty your hands and waste your time on a thing like that?"

"I've just told you," retorted Kimley, while a nurse clunked speedily down one of the corridors in her sanitary clogs. "Atheists in the wrong place. Machapuchare is sacred, and concerns only us guardians of the temple. No busybody, yokel or – worse still – infidel may dare violate it. On pain of death, as you saw for yourself. As your friend found out, too, though that wasn't my decision."

Pac said nothing.

"It was the will of the gods. A sign which, for me and for all of us, must prove the importance of our mission," said Kimley, frowning. "And, to answer your question, Machapuchare isn't merely our concern, or that of infidels who shouldn't dare violate it. I wanted to verify in person that everything went smoothly, that nothing was overlooked; to carry out an on-the-spot inspection and get rid of a busybody. Your friend could get into deep trouble for going where he shouldn't have gone."

Wait a minute, thought Pac. Guardians of the temple, infidels, gods? What was this all about? It was all too allusive: he wanted to know more. But a small inner voice told him to keep quiet.

"And finally," concluded Kimley folding his legs and

placing his buttocks squarely on the wooden chair, "to make sure that the content of that pouch didn't end up in the wrong hands."

This was too much, Pac could no longer hold his tongue.

"And what was in that pouch that was so special?"

For the record, Kimley had got hold of it as soon as they'd crossed the hospital threshold, and up until that moment Pac hadn't given it a thought. Suddenly he felt a real dickhead: his concern for the two patients had made him lose sight of his objective. And this wasn't like him at all. In hindsight, if Samuel had gone as far as calling; if he'd asked for his help, despite their being strangers, but knowing of his interest; finally, if he'd shown himself so determined to retrieve that pouch that he'd got a bullet for his pains, then there must be some truth in all this. And having lost sight of it represented a significant shortcoming on his part. However, he consoled himself, Samuel's life was instrumental to his purposes. Ok, he wasn't such a dickhead after all.

"And what are you hiding, on that mountain?", he continued in a lazy voice, trying (and failing) to appear uninterested.

"The pouch has been stored away safely; what it contains isn't important. The mountain is sacred. Every stone, blade of grass, clod of earth, flower, mineral... all that regards that mountain is inviolable, off limits. And we make sure that it stays that way," said Kimley, maintaining a severe countenance. "You won't understand: you couldn't."

Cool it, thought Pac, don't react, let him talk.

"You two are here under our protection: the Police won't bother you. Just as they didn't interfere with what happened to your friend, as you may have noticed."

That was true, come to think of it. But he still didn't get it.

"And you'll leave as soon as your friend has recovered," said Kimley, blocking the next question in line. At that moment their glances met again, Kimley half-smiling, Pac with mixed feelings. "And you're not to come back, ever. On pain of immediate arrest."

Kimley made to stand up, and Pac had to choose a question quickly.

"Let me get this right. So you – and whoever the hell you represent – are not Intelligence agents?"

Kimley nodded.

"So what are you? A sect? A bunch of town-hall gardeners for the maintenance of that stupid mountain? Or what?", he said, immediately regretting the word 'stupid'; no point in exacerbating the dissent.

His ex-guide shot him an admonishing glance, immediately dissimulated. "Just think that the genuine essence of my people – the hidden soul of the Nepalese – is far more devoted than is apparent, without any distinction whatsoever. And this is our strength. What this sacred land of mine lacks in terms of real economy is amply compensated by a religious economy, able to achieve marvels, and to procure miracles from the gods. This is a protected land," whispered Kimley, close to his ear. "protected by our Lords of the Thousand Incarnations. And it is our duty to defend its secrets and protect its assets and heritage until They…" – raising his gaze skywards, with the hint of a smile – "until They return. As we've always done, from time immemorial, and we always will!"

Fanatics, thought Pac, orthodox pulpiteers: blockheads, like the rest of them.

He knew the type: the worst! And any doubts would have been dispelled at the thought of the three poor wretches on that hilltop; there can't have been much left of them by now.

"Congratulations!", he replied. "Excellent work – and well paid to boot," he remarked, with a note of sarcasm he wasn't prepared to omit. He felt vaguely moronic, as if he'd walked into a surreal comedy, thinking it was a documentary. That tourist guide had been taking the piss from the start: he'd even managed to make him believe (though he couldn't imagine how) that he'd chosen him at the airport; and that was annoying enough – without the breakfasts, the jeep, and everything else...

"Shit", thought Pac. "And here I am with a moribund supplier, the Star Pac at a standstill, and The End of Time inexorably approaching!"

He was tired; he could have tried to assert his rights, at

least in part, yet he raised no objection to Kimley's orders. It would have been of no use at that moment. After all, disappearing as soon as possible was his own uppermost priority: he didn't need to be told, especially not by Kimley. He wanted to get out of there, get away from that reek of poverty, from the cold, and the dust that had stuck to his skin ever since his first visit.

The sooner the better, he repeated to himself.

He watched as the "bishop" (ex-guide, custodian, or whatever the hell he was) stood up, slowly fastening his jacket; he then extended his hand, to crush Pac's forcefully, for a few seconds longer than necessary.

Pac knew he had no choice; all things considered, his curiosity wasn't so important. He'd survived and his plan wasn't compromised, it would still go ahead.

"Good bye," said Kimley.

"Good bye," echoed Pac.

He observed Kimley moving down the corridor towards the stairs, looking more shabby and miserable than he ever had before assuming the label of puppet.

As Pac also rose to his feet (the stool had devastated his back), a pain shot down to his ankles. It was a relief to be able to stretch his legs.

The corridors teamed with the usual bustle of anxiety and trolleys: the lunch trolley – its plastic wheels in need of oiling – with its boiling, enticing cargo of food, instantly generated an electro-chemical reaction causing Pac's *On*

Air sign to blink red.

In designing the hospital, the architect hadn't included a canteen for non-patients. Only a café where, on explicit request, he might get a snack. Hopefully.

The snack bar had been converted from the former labour room, after someone had realised that the locals weren't ready to forsake the good old habit of delivering their babies at home. Of course, the lack of infrastructures, of decently-kept roads, of ambulances; the fact that most of the patients were tourists, and that the small town of Pokhara was mostly a mountain outpost for Himalayan trekking: all this hadn't done much to influence the choices of those who speculated, corrupted and economised! The bar had four small tables, a large number of chairs and, suspended in a corner, a colour TV of Indian manufacture, tuned into a reality show set in a zoo in Mumbai. The windows overlooked a new wing under construction: practically a building site from which resonated the shouts of workers trying to make themselves heard over the alternate din of a pneumatic drill and a cement mixer. For the joy of the in-patients.

To be honest with himself, Pac could afford to switch off that warning sign. Strangely enough, considering the time elapsed since his last meal, he didn't have a huge appetite. A twinge, the mere need for nourishment. He was making progress, he thought, caressing his stomach: it was certainly flatter. And even if it wasn't, he decided, it didn't matter.

The waitress had her back to him when Pac leaned against the dark, sugar-sprinkled counter. He was the only customer, accompanied by the sonorous presence of the TV, on whose screen flowed depressing pictures of grimy youths and enchained elephants. A blackboard hanging high up on the wall displayed in red, yellow and green the menu of the day.

Two scrambled eggs on toast, no cheese, he decided. But when the waitress turned around and noticed him, he felt his blood turn to liquid nitrogen, his breathing come to a stop: he couldn't take his eyes off her.

The girl couldn't have known more than twenty full orbits of the planet round the Sun, including Springs whose blossom lingered on her skin. On this, the colour of roasted chestnuts, of quality milk-chocolate prepared by a maître chocolatier, Pac's gaze hovered and ranged freely. That skin had to be silky-smooth over those sinuous, gentle and well-proportioned features. Her eyes – green and transparent as a tropical bay – held a naivety that could disarm and enchant; her cheeks, plump as ripe apricots; a pert little nose inviting a nibble; moist, voluptuous lips, magically designed, delicate and harmonious. The hint of a smile constantly suggesting that she was about to dispense pearls of involuntary kindness. This natural inclination, this facial expression that she couldn't control, this ability to grace her surroundings with such a magnetic aura: all this deeply embarrassed Pac.

"Yes Sir?" she said, her smile a myriad of tiny rotating stars. One of these landed on Pac's cheek, disintegrating in a thousand colours.

Beauty, Pac managed to think. Was Beauty our only salvation, the only purpose and means of our existence, the asset to be increased, distributed and protected? Shouldn't natural selection endow those who were capable of respecting it, to the exclusion of those who weren't? Wouldn't this principle be more logical and comforting, as an alternative to banal oppression, to the destructive potential of impending effects? And could that girl be the answer, a warning, a street sign in the dilapidated suburbs of our existence, as was this historic period of humanity? Could he learn from her? And what was his role? Or was that merely her smile of resignation, of defeat? Had Beauty – along with its incalculable power – already capitulated?

He realised that he'd been lost in thought too long: the girl was already serving another customer, a tall gentleman with a well-groomed moustache who had also – Pac noted with a quick glance – remained ensnared in the net unwittingly cast by the young maiden.

Enough – he told himself – that will do. He had to break free of that spell, which would only tire and depress him.

"Eggs and toast, without cheese. And a bottle of water. Take away."

Pac rummaged in his pockets, to find money (and a hard-on): something else he could brood over endlessly. He lowered his eyes to the counter, but this reflected the girl's movements; he turned and glanced at the reality show broadcast live on TV, then scrutinized the man now sitting at a table, trying to come up with some amusing banter.

But in the end, before leaving, he couldn't help throwing one last glance at such a wellspring... it happened so rarely.

Smiling at her, he gripped the warm package and swallowed something whose nature he daren't investigate – and left. He'd eat in the taxi on his way to seeing the other patient.

The term 'veterinary clinic' evokes the smell of disinfectant, cleanliness, white tiles, and on the wall, a calendar with pictures of happy, healthy animals.

The place Pac walked into was precisely nominated veterinary clinic, or 'Private Clinic of Dr Raju – Veterinary Physician and Qualified Surgeon'. As testified by the plaque (with faithfully reproduced capital letters) on the wall outside the house; this, however, was the sort of dump where only an anaesthetised yak could feel at ease.

Doctor Raju opened the front door. From his diminutive stature – which enabled one to count the few hairs still attached to his scalp – he'd seemed pleased at the visit, being at a loose end due to lack of business. They descended the few steps leading down to the basement that served as a surgery.

On the night of the accident everything had happened so quickly as to seem at a point of no return. Panic – expertly-managed, but panic nevertheless – had prevented Pac from registering the outlines of spaces; from evaluating details – such as whether he was doing the best thing. In Samuel's case he hadn't had the time, and that was the only hospital. For the yak he'd had to trust Kimley, and the very thought induced a singularly allergic reaction. Judging by the half-whitewashed walls, whose upper half was peeling and mouldy; the dust on the shelves filled with slumbering boxes of medicines possibly past their sell-by dates; the intermittent neon light, when the light of day, outside, was glorious; the stench of mangy dog; and the sense of general neglect that the ample room transmitted, he might have found something better.

The yak was still lying on the steel table, and on seeing him thus stretched out Pac assumed the worse. The animal covered the entire surface of that work counter, like a big brown cuddly toy: the first-prize at a funfair stall. His gentle eyes were half-closed, and his left-side rear leg was bandaged, making him look like a hero in a propaganda film; his face wore a mysterious expression that might easily be interpreted as a smile.

"Is better," said the doctor in a kind little voice. "Only sedated."

"Why? What's the matter? Is it serious?", asked Pac,

placing his hand on the rough, shaggy pelt covering the head of the young bovine, without thinking that the same hand would continue to reek of rotten musk for several days: a pungent, bitter essence that no detergent could possibly eliminate.

"Nothing, nothing. Pain in leg: maybe he fall. Maybe," said Dr Raju, while smiling and nodding. "Better he no walk for some days. Leg get better, animal happy. I think. I put little medicine in food and he rest."

A few days, thought Pac, observing the bovine's dazed expression. Who knows what sedatives they used in Nepal: morphine, cannabis, or other; he must be having one helluva trip. Pac rubbed his hand at length on the animal's head and stroked him once or twice; then – gazing into dark eyes which seemed to beg for attention and for a little freedom – he smiled and said goodbye; and (imagining for a moment that this was possible) he telepathically apologised. Although he knew he wasn't directly responsible for what had happened, he felt someone ought to apologise to the yak, so he decided to act as a spokesman. In fact, sooner or later every human being should apologise to all sentient beings – but this was another matter.

What we need to know is that Pac departed feeling at peace: despite the place being far from aseptic, the oversize furry critter was well, and the doctor seemed to have done a good job.

He also said goodbye to the doctor, shaking his hand vigorously for longer than necessary, in the hope of passing on at least part of the stink from stroking the yak.

But to no avail.

"Thanks for the visit," said Dr Raju still nodding, almost as if he had a spring in the nape of his neck. "I hope to see you soon," he added, rubbing his hand repeatedly on his coat.

He was clearly referring to the bill, but Pac always paid at the end: no down-payments – you never know. Which is why he parted from the doctor reassuring him that he'd be back soon, very soon.

Outside, the sun was still high above the mountains, the air warm enough to induce him to take an invigorating stroll.

He wasn't far from the centre. Scarcely a soul would be around at that time of day in the small town, and everything seemed close at hand. And, apropos of hands, on sniffing his own from a safe distance he became aware, without a trace of embarrassment, that it could do with some serious washing. This reminded him that the hand wasn't the only malodorous part of his body and – in the blink of an eye – justified this lack of hygiene as a consequence of *force majeure* events.

He walked through anonymous and desolate suburbs, a succession of humble, rough, and often dilapidated dwellings, up and down dirt roads; crossing occasional groups of mountain-bikers; passing by stalls and carts; skirting around urban waste, and beggars clothed in tattered rags; reaching the main, paved road, busy with traffic; assaulted by the odours of fried food, engine oil and incense; observing the bustle of people bowed with fatigue yet ready to greet him with a smile. He took a lakeside walk that stretched for miles, offering a view of snow-capped mountains reflected in the placid waters of the lake; mingling shades of green and pale-blue, the sky, mountain peaks, and the expanse of water; savouring all this while avoiding personal involvement for which he felt no inclination, he entered the *Hungry Eye Hotel* and got down to business.

This included fetching some food that wouldn't trigger feelings of guilt, from the choice of valid options offered by stalls and small restaurants.

It also included evaluating whether to spend another night at Samuel's hospital bedside, and establishing a maximum time limit before returning home to deal with pending matters. Clearly there wasn't much he could do with someone in a coma.

In the end he opted for taking a taxi, going to the hospital and administering his inestimable kindness, though the thought of his clean, comfortable hotel bed stayed with him all along. Even when he found himself in the unsupervised intensive care unit, wondering whether his presence there made any sense. Artificial bluish lights projecting grey shadows; the occasional nurse walking along the corridors; apart from these there was no sound, no sign of life. Everything was suspended, at a forced standstill, like the souls lying in those hospital beds. One could almost expect to see a brand-new ghost wander by.

The night had just started, the silence was oppressive. Pac was about to collapse. He slipped into an empty room, closed the door and chose a bed. The one near the radiator would do fine.

Just as he was clarifying the tricky matter of how to perform the Star Pac's flight tests without being intercepted by radars, satellites or spy planes; after establishing at last, in the pre-rem phase, what psychometric tests to use in the selection of his future Eve hostesses, the queens who would contribute the feminine element dominant in the New World – after seeing the disasters caused by the opposite sex to a civilisation that, any time now, would self-destroy; from the recesses of that psychedelic dream – as we were saying – he was awakened by a young man with an incipient moustache and a white coat two sizes too large who, in a politely hushed and heavily accented voice, was trying to communicate something.

"Sir... awake!"

A few seconds to surface, and he was able to answer: "Yes... awake."

He watched bleary-eyed as the man insisted, shaking his

arm more and more vigorously. Although still smiling, he was raising his voice. His brow knitted, furrowed, lines deepening, in a grimace Pac couldn't quite decipher. Pac conceded that he'd been a pleasant sight to wake up to: olive skin, on which were sketched gentle features and a hint of a well-groomed moustache; dark, reassuring eyes; regular white teeth, now on show, set in a face nodding slowly and convincingly as if to convey something extraordinary.

Delight: that was what the man transmitted.

Pac looked at him, batting his eyelids to reduce lacrimation.

"Yes," he rasped, gulping to moisten his palate. "I'm awake, thank you."

"No!" insisted the male nurse, almost reproachfully. "Your friend. He awake."

The yak, he thought! But as soon as he realised he was in a hospital he knew that it could be none other than Samuel.

Taking advantage of such enthusiasm, Pac accepted the help of an extra pair of arms to pull himself up, and ambled unhurriedly towards the other room, realising that it was morning. As well as with daylight, which freely distributed natural optimism throughout the entire edifice, the place teamed with bustling doctors and nurses like an aseptically reassuring milky way: testimonials of sanitary candour, as in a hymn to life sung by a choir of white corpuscles. Shaking hands, distributing smiles like scattered gifts of candy, delighting their fortunate and deserving recipients.

The first thing Pac noticed as he walked into Samuel's room was that two beds were now occupied; but the other in-patient, being a well-mannered old man in black polka-dotted pyjamas, didn't have to be asked for privacy: and, still able to walk, he went off on his own two feet, in small shuffled steps, his eyes fixed on the floor; the hint of a polite smile wrinkling his face, he pointed to his companion with his hand (a gesture whose obscure meaning was accompanied by a muttered comment), then using the same hand to stroke his gonads.

On seeing Samuel, Pac was pervaded by an unfathomable sensation: that elderly gentleman was both a stranger and a voice that was somehow familiar, and the two aspects had always inhabited separate quarters. Their coming together, especially under such singular circumstances, generated an awkwardness and a need for politeness that slowed down his pace. The sparse hair, combed to one side, was of the ceramic white of those who had long used up their reserve of melanin. The lines on his fair and reddish complexion lent him an air of respectability earned on the field, so that he looked like a general wounded in battle. He still had thin tubes going in and out of his body, through natural orifices and those created through medical necessity (Pac didn't care to think which); but those eyes were open, and this was enough. They were crystal blue and bright, totally out of tune with their context.

Samuel gave him the hint of a smile. Tired and strained, but a smile nevertheless, an expression that only someone who'd been through such circumstances could really understand.

The sickly, stale smell of sleepless nights and bad breath was recycled by what little sun and air penetrated the half-opened window which Pac closed against the draft. He pulled up a stool, with (given the circumstances) an unseemly screech. Then he sat down.

Samuel's eyes were red, his face gaunt: he smelled of hospital, that characteristic aroma – of armpits, stewed apples, and the distinctive aroma of cheap disinfectant procured via some fiddled contract. On seeing him clad in the white pyjamas kindly provided by the hospital management, Pac remembered that he himself was still in the same abused clothes that he'd worn when he got off the plane days earlier: padded beige trousers, boots, and two sweaters under a light-blue down jacket, now also in need of a good wash. And those blood stains which he tried occasionally to hide from view could only have gone unnoticed if he'd enlisted for the casting of a commercial on domestic accidents. He was in no position to object to other people's odours.

He touched Samuel's hand lightly: it was lukewarm. His breathing was still laboured, but he seemed to be over the worst of it.

"You owe me one," he said.

"I'm fine, thanks. Glad to see you too," replied Samuel with little more than a hoarse whisper.

They eyed each other wordlessly, with an ill-concealed awkwardness that only they could fully understand, studying one another like strangers in a blocked lift.

"Listen to me," blurted Pac, meaning to clarify a few important matters. "You've got to get well fast. We need to get out of the country as soon as possible," moving closer after glancing around quickly to make sure no-one was around. "We've received an ultimatum, and I want no more trouble!"

Samuel, who hadn't understood, wanted first of all to be told what had happened. Above all he insisted on ascertaining that the precious flame-red bundle was still safely in Pac's possession.

"This isn't the moment," replied Pac lightly, although this was the cause of the whole incident. "Lots of things have happened, you aren't the only one who was hurt. Some very weird people are involved – too weird and dangerous for my liking. I still don't know what the hell you were doing on that fucking mountain," he said, searching Samuel's face for an answer – and not finding one. He blew out his cheeks and added: "Forget about the bundle... it's lost. You'd better concentrate on recovering, or we'll end up in jail. I don't know about you, but yours truly has no coverage at the moment to save him from getting arrested. So make sure you recover quickly."

Samuel had got stuck at a certain detail, a turn in the middle of the sentence. Pac hadn't noticed but, owing to the thread that ties material body to immaterial mind, he'd blown like a gale on the card-tower of Samuel's precarious physical data, including his blood pressure: so much so that some of the devices to which he was attached had stopped chattering among themselves and had dutifully paid him their electronic attention.

An unscheduled beep had immediately caused an orderly of pensionable age to look in, glance from the monitor to the patient and back and – as soon as the beep had reverted to normal – glared for a few seconds at Pac, before leaving as abruptly as he'd appeared.

"Say it again, please. The bundle: you have it, right? Please tell me you have it," Samuel seemed to implore, lifting his trunk with noticeable difficulty, judging by his expression and his colouring.

"Apart from the fact that you still haven't told me what the hell's in it," replied Pac, playing for time before conceding that he was short of decoys. "Anyway, no, I no longer have it. Kimley took it. Sorry. Mission failed – whatever it was. "And now let's have it: what was in the pouch that was so important?"

Samuel exhaled, casting up his eyes, and remained quiet for several minutes, his arms stretched out. He seemed battered and broken in the face of an option that he'd rather

211

avoid, but which was there in that room and had to be dealt with at that precise moment, with a sort of stranger. It was time to let fall the mask, and he decided to talk.

"At this point," he said, eyeing Pac with a mixture of politeness and resignation, "we might as well skip the formalities."

Whether this was a sign of candour or of esteem, it made no difference to Pac, who had other things on his mind.

"It's a stone," grumbled Samuel testily, keeping his eye on the door: no sounds, no passers-by. "A mineral, a crystal, I wouldn't know how to classify it."

Pac was about to interrupt, but refrained; it was better to wait.

"Dear man, I must inform you that that mountain was full of them, once upon a time. There are rumours that two small fragments have actually been discovered in recent years. Which is why I was there," he said, trying to control his laborious breathing. "They have the regular geometric form of crystals, with inserts of a particular and totally unknown metal. Apparently they're not of Earthly origin, they're immune from degenerative phenomena and, chemically speaking, present no defects of any sort. Extraordinary... in the real sense of the word. Some believe them to be the mythical Chintamani Stones; others identify them as equally mythical stones having magical powers, of which legends abound; but I prefer to embrace a different theory. I believe that, when they searched me, those bandits mistook them for common gems, and decided to kidnap me to obtain a ransom. Oh yes... they must have considered me an excellent deal!"

Samuel paused for breath, and to check that Pac's level of attention was worthy of the vital information he was dispensing. That young gentleman with the receding hairline seemed to be lacking the means to understand, if his expression was anything to go by, thought Samuel. Nevertheless, now he'd started, he decided to continue: after all, he owed it to him.

"My country's military Intelligence have been studying them since the Fifties. I've had access to documents that prove how these small, shiny, egg-shaped objects covered in reddish spots are capable of developing powerful energy, if exposed to certain high-frequency electromagnetic fields. Impressive energy, believe me..." he said, before moderating his words with the gesture of a hand. "Believe me. The military have been studying them to develop experimental weapons, quantum instruments of which we know little or nothing, and, above all, new forms of spacecraft propulsion. Technology that would instantly humble and render obsolete the mechanical systems currently in use," he said, trying – and failing – to click his fingers for added emphasis.

But there was no need: Pac's head was already inaugurating neural runs in which phosphorescent synapses opened and closed as each electrical impulse skied along happily. A few words had been enough to capture his attention.

"Propulsion, did you say?", he asked, raising his index finger to make sure he'd understood correctly.

"Yes, research has been on-going for years. And let me tell you, it seems to work. Apparently these stones are not difficult to operate: the problem is controlling the impulses they emit, channelizing the energy produced so that it may be used. But information on this is not fool-proof, and neither are the sources," said Samuel leaning back against the pillows, pleased that he'd elicited attention.

"But what are we talking about? Where do these stones come from?"

Samuel said nothing: he was far more tired than he cared to admit, and his body was still too weak. He asked for a glass of water, which Pac handed over distractedly.

When he'd finished drinking, Samuel checked the clock on the wall to make sure he still had enough time before the doctor's rounds, and said he was ready to continue.

"This is a point of no return, straddling myth and reality."

"I consider myself an open-minded fellow: go right ahead, this is the point that interests me," interrupted Pac.

"I know. That's why we're here," replied Samuel, his satisfaction evident in those blue eyes. "It seems that in remote – very remote – times, a spaceship crashed into that mountain."

"Spaceship?!"

"Spaceship."

"Spaceship," whispered Pac, taut with concentration. If a small mirror had been inserted into his mind, the beam from its reflection would have roasted any unfortunate insect that happened to intercept it.

"This is where the myth of the Sacred Mountain comes from. You know: the gods, Hinduism. The *Ramayana*, the *Mahabharata*, and many other epic Indian texts talk about battles among gods using highly sophisticated weapons and flying chariots, spacecraft on which they flew and fought. Later these memories were absorbed by religious tradition and survived through time..."

At the very mention of vimanas Pac almost gave a start, undecided whether to feel satisfied and excited at being told what he already knew (what potential for his plan in the words that he was hearing!); or to adopt a vaguely sceptical, unperturbed attitude in the face of such vacuity, of the scientific inconsistency of statements overflowing with unknown variables.

"Today we'd call it – how shall I say – a close encounter, or UFO crash," was all he said, curious to listen to Samuel's explanations, while at the same time hearing his own critical inner voices which, for the moment, he tried to keep from spoiling this fiesta of the absurd.

"In a sense...". Samuel's tone was that of someone truly informed. In attempting to smooth his hair with a slow gesture of his hand he succeeded in dishevelling it further, which might have lent him a certain air of authority during a TV show – some added value in the eyes of the spectators.

"At the time it was the crash of a warring god," he continued. "And, my dear fellow, what was retrieved remains a mystery. The fact that it was recognised as the Sacred Mountain – a witness of events mentioned in Vedas texts – kept away the curious and is believed to have preserved those few remaining relics, buried in time."

"So the stones were their source of energy and propulsion? But how is it possible that they were found after… millennia?"

Samuel was showing unusual vigour for someone who'd just woken from a coma – albeit medically induced – and, as he added more details to the theory he was propounding, Pac asked himself where the old man got all that energy.

"Today's Nepal is in a seismic zone. In its dramatic force, the earthquake of 1934 brought to light and made available extraordinary finds, immediately veiled in silence. And from then on, official and alternative archaeology started searching for the Stones and for finds believed to be impossible. This was the long-awaited signal to resume research expeditions. Considering this area the cradle of Arian civilisation, esoteric Nazism was one of the first actors on the scene; later replaced by military projects and by other secret esoteric societies – the ones that are still in control. They weren't merely looking for knowledge, but rather for goods manufactured in epochs disregarded by history books. The current glacial meltdown, climate changes, and mutations in the morphological characteristics of rock faces are accelerating the prospects of this research in a remarkable manner."

"Military projects?" asked Pac, helping himself to water from a bottle on the bed-side table.

"Exactly as I said, friend to whom I owe my life. The summit of that high command – where certain Intelligence divisions are interwoven with special military units – participate in this race. But even they have had, and continue to have, a fair amount of difficulties… because, you see, this is still forbidden territory, and even if they obtain (or, should I say, buy) a permit from the authorities, the sensitivity of the devotees is ever on alert. No-one is accepted, let alone an infidel Westerner. Complicated routes must be taken, or new ones traced. Of course, today's satellites help."

Pac remembered what he'd heard from Kimley, or whatever his real name was, and noticed some interesting consistency.

"But how can one trace such small objects on a mountain?", he asked, randomly selecting one of the multiple questions filed in his mind.

Having succeeded in capturing Pac's attention, Samuel remained unperturbed. Before responding, however, he became aware once more of how tired he felt. His body was sending him signals, and they were far from pleasant. Especially his wound, that throbbed and burned, rendering his breathing even more laboured.

Repressing a grimace of pain, and determined to proceed, he replied: "You're right. That's why research is difficult... it's tough work... but the people we're talking about dispose of unlimited means and funds that I don't believe would feature on official balance sheets. And unlimited time, I may add."

He paused again, and Pac realised that their conversation had lasted well beyond the capacities of a sick man. He reflected briefly on the mass of information – on that story, as absurd as it was enthralling; on the questions accumulating in his mind – when Samuel started to speak again. This time, Pac told himself, he'd stop him before he could add anything, before assisting in any worsening of his condition.

"Also, they're radioactive. Not very, but a Geiger counter can detect them."

"Do you mean they're dangerous? That in that shack we were all exposed to radiation? And what about that poor yak, who carried them around his neck?", exclaimed an anxious Pac, grabbing his forearm.

Noting his expression, and the hand that gripped his arm more and more forcibly until it hurt, Samuel made to reassure him.

"Don't worry... the level of radiation is minimal, and has negligible effects," he stressed with a nod. And was relieved that Pac had loosened his grip.

Of course, Pac could have objected to the concept of negligible, which implied limits interpreted subjectively and therefore not well defined – especially when referring to matters of health. But he didn't bother, deciding not to think about it and revert instead to the subject that had so many prospects to offer.

"And where do you come into all this?", he asked impulsively. "At this point you can tell me."

Samuel wasn't ready for that question. Not then, and not in that manner. His expression was pervaded by an irrepressible embarrassment: a sign of hesitation that, under the circumstances, was not conducive to victory; so he cast down his eyes and glanced towards the window overlooking the garden, knowing there was no escape. He also looked towards the door for assurance of privacy, then raised a hand to beckon Pac to draw closer, to receive a secret reserved for his ears only.

And owing to that gesture, to that movement of his arm, the sleeve of his pyjama withdrew like a curtain, revealing his wrist. A wrist on which, inadvertently and by pure chance, Pac caught a glimpse of a marked, precise, horizontal line; a line drawn by a firm hand with a sharp blade. Without a doubt it belonged to a time remote enough for the scar to have become discoloured, yet sufficiently evident and expressive. For a moment Pac was distracted by the story that simple line could tell, but he recovered quickly and pretended nothing had happened, concentrating on what the elderly gentleman was saying.

"I've always been strongly attracted to these topics, these much-opposed and discredited theories. This interest dates from my earliest memories. Only after retirement was I able to start serious research," said Samuel in little more than a whisper. His tone suggested that part of those statements were addressed to himself, and that many more were queuing up in an orderly line to be taken into consideration; his averted eyes and taut facial expression were of someone who had many ghosts from the past to contend with. So much so that for a moment Pac wondered if he wasn't intruding.

"Now I know. It's all much clearer," he resumed his whispering, while Pac glanced surreptitiously at his other wrist. Just as he thought: another cut, crooked, less accurate, was in full view. Was he dealing with a manic depressive, with an unstable lunatic? Or someone disturbed but harmless? As well as posing questions which he'd gladly have done without, this business lit a new spotlight on the stage, so blinding as to dazzle the actors, distract from the plot, and incinerate gnats.

Samuel had been too absorbed in his confessions to notice his listener's puzzlement and revulsion. Before he had turned his scrutinising gaze on him, Pac had regained his composure, and resumed listening.

"I was always motivated by ambition, never knowing the real reason for my quest. But something happened, when I wasn't here. Something sublime. And now, at last, I know the truth!"

Samuel's brilliant gaze, his decisive tone captured Pac's attention, dissolving the few centimetres that separated them, as if those words were capable of bypassing his hearing and going straight to his mind.

"Those stones are mine," said Samuel at last.

Pac didn't understand, as was clear from his expression.

"That spaceship was mine. The guy that was shot down in that battle. The god, that god, was I!"

After briefly unravelling this, Pac understood… and for safety's sake slowly recoiled a little from that face, continuing to look at him while striving to conceal any reaction. Which proved harder than he imagined.

He'd heard of people who'd come out of a coma describing lights, journeys outside their own bodies, mystical visions. But this beat them all, by far. This was clearly one of many easily diagnosable post-traumatic ailments, some psychic condition caused by auto-suggestion, some collateral damage. He'd certainly not heed any sentence starting with 'while', 'however', 'although'. If Samuel's account bore the least shade of credibility, those two scars on his wrists had wiped it away, as with a sponge and detergent, leaving Pac's intellect

221

clean and fragrant.

The matter was closed, that particular matter was closed, so much so that he didn't pay it the least attention. While the other, the more interesting matter, was most definitely open.

"Sure, it's all much clearer," he said, nodding and smiling that psychiatric-nurse smile. "Try to rest now. You really need to, I think."

The occupant of the other bed came shuffling back into the room, with his polka-dotted woollen pyjamas and haggard face; on seeing Samuel he gave his balls another gentle squeeze, while screwing up his eyes.

Pac made to get up from that excruciatingly uncomfortable metal stool when Samuel seized his arm – if you can call 'seize' the light touch that was the most his weakened condition allowed.

"You don't believe me, do you?"

Pac took a long, deep breath, to keep his inner turmoil in check. "What I believe is irrelevant at the moment," he said, looking Samuel firmly in the eye. "But I agree with you entirely." He moved closer, without looking away. "I think that flame-red bundle must be retrieved. And the sooner the better."

Samuel hesitated a moment, seemingly savouring Pac's last words, then leaned back and sank into his pillow with the abandon reflected by the hint of a smile. And conceded that he was ready for some well-deserved rest.

Judging by the meditative pace with which he departed, Pac appeared to be under the influence of some elixir he'd never tried before: delighted by its immediate effect but with some foreboding as to the inevitable hang-over.

This was the achievement of a fragile compromise between, on the one hand, the stone's theoretical scientific potential and his spirit of self-preservation in the face of the impending finale; and, on the other, the delusory exaltation of a fantasy spiced with suicidal mania. And as the word 'suicidal' came to mind, he could not but think how his plan could be seen as a variety of premature death. Ever preferable to extinction induced by others, of course, but an epilogue nevertheless.

This compromise, he told himself, was as wobbly as a fartist dizzied on his own effusions of gas.

Where would it take him? As far as the stars?

According to a recent survey, five people in seven prefer to have full sexual intercourse before going to sleep, rather than after. This alarming data was quoted during an on-going court trial involving a famous pharmaceutical company, manufacturer of some equally famous sleeping pills, accused of insufficiently proven side effects such as sleep-walking, mucus accompanied by diarrhea, and unwanted pregnancies. Incidentally, one wonders whether those two excess surveyees mightn't risk invalidating the statistic; and whether the world might not be teaming with individuals congregating everywhere, and insufficiently inclined to mind their own business.

That said, Pac's priority was to verify the condition of the pious ox, but since it was Kimley who'd introduced him to Dr Raju he could easily combine his two objectives.

However, what seemed simple and practicable in theory wasn't always so straightforward when one got down to details. As far as the yak's health was concerned, he managed to do everything over the phone: the bovine was recovering, although still full of painkillers, the same that added up to the items on his bill and – he imagined – wreaked havoc with the animal's perceptions.

How did a stoned bovine feel? Was he enjoying himself? Was he knocking his hoof on the door of perception? Alas, this was not the right time to indulge in such digressions, however interesting. Pac had to choose which strategy to use with Kimley, without wasting the one pretext at his disposal. He'd spent the day in the comfort of his hotel, but even there he hadn't come up with anything serious or acceptable.

That evening, at the *Lhasa Tibetan Restaurant* on the lakeside, while Pac was eating a plate of momos (traditional dumplings made with barley flour and stuffed with vegetables, served in broth) – to a background of jazz broadcast by *Radio 75*, which he listened to with small rhythmic movements of his head and shoulders, drumming his fingers on the table – he made his acquaintance with a choice of local beers, the *Tiger* and the *Everest*; and being a matter of balanced taste, quality and calories, the radio speaker raised no objections.

It was a small, neat, family-run joint, hung with sacred images, red curtains, mandalas, Tibetan flags, hymns and prayers of liberation from the invaders, and the ubiquitous photograph of the Dalai Lama. A décor of yellow and orange stripes warmed and softened the atmosphere.

He was sitting right next to a monumental fireplace of light-coloured stone, which dominated the room and warmed his table more than any other, enveloping him in a cocoon of warmth from which his neighbours were inevitably excluded; this drew disappointed looks; sidelong glances of envy and interest for that young man, as well as curiosity and some sexual awareness on the part of the few women, attracted by the pensive expression of that lone wolf, probably extremely important and respectable.

As he was a future civilising monarch, who could blame them? Was it true that our instinctive feelings often originated in a multidimensional, timeless border zone, and were therefore highly plausible? It wasn't so absurd to think of ourselves as beings whose purpose was to experiment and dare, in order to remember what our innermost, secret and unmentionable essence already knew, because it was already there. Hadn't everything already been said, done, thought, beyond time and space? Don't we try, in order to re-learn, to re-experience, within the cycle?

And wasn't action preceded by theory, which in turn was born of being: the flame that ignited the detonator fuse; the reagent that triggered the chain reaction; the crashing of clouds whose drops quenched the thirst of pastures grazed by the cow whose milk would become peach yoghurt savoured by Pac's greedy palate?

Then why didn't he act? Why didn't he put his plans into practice?

Maybe because it was late, and he'd have to wait until morning to call Kimley, and: a) propose some sort of exchange; b) propose a deal that would change his life; c) entrap him, and disappear while he was still in time; d) ask to be driven to Dr Raju's, hoping that a better idea might come to mind. Or maybe because the alcohol molecules bouncing up and down on the trampoline of his grey matter procured him far more pleasure than the vague options mentioned above.

Truth was that he hadn't the slightest idea what to do: and the more he thought the more bored he became; and the more bored he was the more he desired distraction, although local stimuli were few and depressingly uninspiring.

A tourist couple two tables away from his own were intent on fiddling around with their colourful, luminous, latest-generation mobile phones; each absorbed in his miniature screen, a meagre smile launched like an absent-minded hand-out. She, petite, blondish, Chinese baubles dangling from her earlobes; face frowning, thin lips like disused border crossings. He, younger, hairline sufficiently receding to predict the metamorphosis that would mark him in a few years' time; impatiently tapping and dragging on his touch-screen; sighing, in that world of his, behind glasses framed according to the latest rage (possibly convinced that he'd even chosen them) which made him feel at ease – as his serious, superior eyes suggested on the rare occasions when he glanced around without the slightest movement of his bowed head. They'd already consumed their meal, their tableware stacked in a corner of the stone table waiting to be cleared; and all the while (not much, if truth be told) that Pac observed them sidelong, not a single joke, comment or kiss was thrown across to bridge the distance; not a glance except to check briefly that the other hadn't moved, hadn't been sucked into their display; the reflection of the young man's was projected onto the lenses of his spectacles. Their silence, their absence, expanded until it enclosed them, protecting them – or maybe not.

Depressing, thought Pac, excessively predictable. There it was, right before the eyes of the observant: the West, losing the ethic of caring: for one's partner, one's relatives, for affections, children; and for life in general. Consumerism – of devices, of jobs, of relations. Torn, threadbare relationships; inverted roles, now useless; hurdles with no finishing line.

Now she's asking something: he replies without interrupting himself, without even glancing up at her face; they get up and leave.

Not that Pac had much to teach. On the contrary, with his parents divorced, a fate that he'd replicated and experienced in first person: whether the two things were somehow psychologically and fatally connected didn't really matter. At least, it no longer did, and hadn't for some time.

Right, he told himself, he'd had his diversion, now he could go straight back to prison. And by that he didn't mean the cage with velvet-lined bars that the girl with the swaying hips and ample bosom (concealed yet easily imagined) was tracing all around his libido as she walked by, fragrant; slowing down, in his imagination, in the exact moment that she was close to him, only to escape – intimidated by such a hormonal storm – to take refuge in the bathroom and recover her breathing, dabbing at her perspiration with a silk handkerchief.

Nice trip. But enough of that.

What means could render corruptible a member of a sect of fanatics, an agent of the mineral police, or of whatever wonky confraternity Kimley belonged to? This was the point. To be trusting him or take rash initiatives was risky by definition, if not ridiculous: like a meal dug up for starved gluttons. How could he be sure of making his escape once the transaction – whatever that involved – was concluded?

Furthermore it was clear that those stones – those cosmic hand grenades – were valuable goods for their current holder, too. Was Nepalese military Intelligence also carrying out experiments on the matter, as Samuel had suggested? Implausible, considering the country's economic condition.

More likely, Kimley had reached some agreement with the competition, or kept the stones in a safe as an emergency fund. But these thoughts were no more helpful to his reasoning than the hypothesis that this was all a waste of time; that the theories of a madman with slit wrists – one who proclaimed to be a god – served other purposes. Possible, he conceded, quite probable, in fact. He wasn't inclined to give credit to bullshit or to bullshitters: but Samuel happened to be his supplier and – come to think of it – had shown an uncommon level of trustworthiness and confidentiality since before all this trouble started. And the reason for all this – the propulsion of the Star Pac at the dawn of a new era – was hardly a minor detail.

He had to be trusting, there were hardly any alternatives. At this, he was back at square one: how to retrieve that flame-red bundle, no longer hanging from the woolly neck of that hoofed cuddly toy, whose state of health he'd been guilty of forgetting?

Granting Kimley a lift on the Star Pac was out of the question. Pac might have given it a thought when he'd saved the life of all three, but any inspiration was lost once his real identity had revealed itself. No double-crossing, spying intruders: it was also thanks to the likes of Kimley that humanity had sunk to its current state.

And so?

The idea – simple and crazy as only improvised gimmicks can be, and therefore spiced with epic adventure – came to him when he'd finally managed to expel all the beer that his body no longer considered of interest. He'd crossed the manager of the *Lhasa Tibetan Restaurant*, hands steepled against his forehead, as with a *namaste* he thanked the couple who'd just honoured their dinner bill. That traditional Hindu greeting, in that particular situation, was somehow captivating – like the term "adjuvant" on the package of a slimming cream: innocuous but decisive.

Having reluctantly vacated his place near the fire and paid his bill in turn – proud to leave the waiter a small but symbolically relevant tip (so excited was he at what was going on in his mind) – Pac strode swiftly towards the *Hungry Eye Hotel* along a road shrouded in darkness, illuminated solely by the neon lights of the few little shops that were still open.

On his right slumbered the Phewa Tal, or Phewa Lake, in pitch darkness that rendered it impossible to make out any single form or sound coming from that direction. The lake snored with a slow, regular rhythm, its breath caressing the slimy shore. There, small colourful doongas waited to be boarded by tourists who, with a single paddle, would row them to open waters, away from any noise. Towards the thick Rani Ban, the Queen's Forest, which painted the tranquil waters an asparagus green, emanating the fragrance of resin and bark; towards flowers and shadows and chestnut trees and ropy creepers; red ants and macaques; ferns and orchids; travellers and carriers along the traders' street; among laughing white herons that flew over the solemn peaks mirrored on the liquid surface; towards the World Peace Pagoda, the Buddhist stupa on the ridge; towards whatever spectacle would cleanse them of that mud, and free them of those moorings, to float on waters suspended among the mountains, among overlapping corrugated peaks, along hazy horizons that melted into cotton-wool clouds. Not a sound to disturb the rippling water, at that time of night, not a lighthouse to reveal its secrets.

While, on the other side of the road, sleepy youths wearing leather jackets, pashmina blankets or threadbare pullovers closed the stores, spat on the ground, turned off shop signs, or sold the last bottle of water for that day.

In a silken tranquillity that would have seemed alarming in a metropolitan context, Pac found himself thinking how pleasant the temperature was, how relaxing this solitary stroll. And it wasn't this thought that surprised him, nor was it the fact that he was going back to his hotel so late. Rather, it was the sudden retching that made him double over and be copiously sick, followed by a deep rumbling from the depth of his bowels as they conveyed a flatulent discharge towards liberation, along with the clear sensation that he was in for a long night in the company of an unknown toilet. A night of cursing and swearing, cleaning and rinsing, of feeling hate and disgust, and recapitulating his latest meals to plan his revenge: retaliations which at that moment – as he quickly made for privacy – had yet to take shape, but which he swore would be inevitable and never sufficiently cathartic to cleanse the bitter taste of vomit in his mouth.

The hotel was only a few steps away when he had to stop again and heave up abundantly a second time, then a third: a mound of warm, pasty matter accumulating on the ground, tears streaming down his cheeks, his sore windpipe burning. Expectoration. A paper handkerchief.

He climbed to the third floor along a steep concrete staircase and, once in his room, persuaded himself – in a final moment of lucidity – that the solution conceived earlier for retrieving the red bundle was the only one possible: his only chance, the best. And the speed with which he rushed to the bathroom suggested that he'd have no energy left to think up anything else.

"I'm speechless," muttered Samuel. Still decked out with tubes (in a room whose bill was mounting exorbitantly, just as he congratulated himself for taking out insurance policies), Samuel couldn't shift his gaze from the ceiling, though his eyes actually saw something quite different. His complexion was assuming a healthier colour, a flushed pink.

"How did you think up such an absurdity?"

"Logic," replied Pac unperturbed, sitting at his side on the metal stool with which, by now, he was on first-name terms.

Samuel has remained the sole guest of that room, after the natural departure of its other in-patient, so they were able to talk in luxurious tranquillity; even of the gentle curves of a certain young nurse; of the spicy flavour of the warm meals; and of the infinite sadness they both felt each time their gaze rested on the dust-covered petals of the plastic flowers representing the only decoration provided by hospital management. Flowers placed on the faded blue bed-side table, forming – along with the bottle of mineral water – a rather bizarre still life.

"Logic, he says," whispered Samuel to the ceiling, as if it could reply – as if it could take his side.

Yes, Pac's plan was daring, but before he proposed it to Kimley it was important to obtain Samuel's consent. In fact, as the latter was to have the star role, it would be more correct to say that his consent was paramount. That triangular mediation amused Pac as nothing had for some time, and he laughed up his sleeve while observing the vast range of facial expressions on that character's face:

incredulous, bothered, irritated, conciliatory, disheartened.

Finally Samuel lowered his eyes from the ceiling to the level of the man on the stool, and accepted with a heavy heart, aware of the risks and anything other than optimistic. Flanked by stylised wings of wrinkles, his light-blue eyes transmitted fear, inducing in Pac faint misgivings, as if he were planning a spiteful trick against an old uncle: the hesitation one might feel when inducing an elderly gentlemen, especially if weak and hospital-bound, to put his safety newly at risk. Misgivings that were immediately repressed.

In view of the absence of alternatives, Pac remained almost indifferent. "So it's decided," was all he said, eliciting the other's agreement. Having obtained it he got up, gripped the top of Samuel's hand, feeling a certain roughness, and took his leave, satisfied. Personally, he had nothing to lose.

Stopping at the door, Pac turned round to catch the eye of the post- traumatic surgery patient with the pierced gut. "Are you sure?" he asked, somewhat belligerently.

Samuel was staring at the window. "Go away, be off with you!", was all he managed to respond, before he resumed his contemplation of the ceiling in search of... what? Even Samuel didn't know.

Pac didn't bother to walk far: the phone in the hospital's reception area would do, and once he'd obtained permission to make "... a quick local call on behalf of (and at the expense of) the foreign patient." He then phoned to book two Pokhara-Kathmandu flights and two Kathmandu-Delhi flights; but just as he was about to make the most important call, he was rebuked by the switchboard operator, who snatched the phone from him, and with an angry glare indicated he should leave.

Ill-mannered lout, thought Pac, walking towards the corridor in search of a secluded corner, crossing visiting relatives and medical staff and being obliged to respond to each punctually offered courteous greeting. Too much hustle and bustle for his liking: he'd do better to slip inside the first open storeroom he could find.

Was his chancing into a pantry full of well-stocked shelves some sort of test to obtain a diligence certificate – second class? If so, the blueberry tartlets that in a flash had put his jaws into action must be interpreted as Pac's refusal to acknowledge any authority other than his own: the same principle by which he now rejected any allegation, including that of helping himself to sweet consolation reserved for the hospital patients. And to hell with the diet, he thought: he needed to compensate for last night's dinner, and after the abomination he'd been through he undoubtedly deserved some comfort. Jesus Christ, I deserve it!

Having dispatched a mouthful or two, he needed to use his satellite phone to call Kimley, hoping that the mobile phone number he had was still operative.

It was.

"I see you haven't left yet," said Kimley, dispensing with any pleasantries.

Was the line tapped, or had Kimley memorised his number? Whatever: Pac would have liked to cram that arrogant tone down Kimley's throat with a shovel, if only he could. After all he'd done for him, his fee, expenses, breakfasts and all the rest. Who did he think he was dealing with?

But he had to stay cool. Cool and determined, he thought.

"I need to know how my new mascot is. You haven't forgotten, have you?"

"Doctor Raju, Siddharta Highway, fifteen minutes by taxi. For once you can do something for the local economy, instead of doing your best to ruin it."

A blow below the belt, but at least Kimley didn't know he'd already been there. One-nil, you piece of shit.

Kimley's tone was that of someone who, meanwhile, was playing video poker online, or having a crap over a squat toilet, with occasional grunts to fill gaps in the conversation.

Pac wasn't going to be intimidated, that wasn't his style; however, he needed to sugar the pill.

"I need to meet you. Don't worry, I've already seen the old part of town, the Devi falls, and I don't need to buy carpets..." he said, with an inward sneer. A brief tactical pause, then he continued: "It's about my friend, the one who – thanks to your audacity – ended up with an extra orifice. It would be a nice gesture on your part to let him have his stone back." To induce feelings of guilt, be tactful, suck up – and all of it off the cuff: that was talent for you!

Kimley, however, was equally tough.

"First of all," he replied firmly, "I saved your nosy friend from almost-certain death. Next, forget about the stone. It's too hot for either of you."

"What do you mean?" ventured Pac, in view of the scarcity of credible information, being unable to trust a source who'd proclaimed himself divine after a medically-induced coma.

"Forget it. I have other things on my agenda!" Kimley's tone suggested that he was either losing money or had missed the target and made a mess.

"Wait!" cried Pac with urgency, as Kimley was about to ring off. "One last question." He hated to beg but he only had that one chance. "Are you a believer?"

There was a pause, the length of a mouse click.

"What sort of a question is that?"

"Just a simple question," said Pac. "Which could change your life in a way no other human being has ever experienced. At least in the last few thousand years."

Meanwhile someone passed right outside the storeroom door; Pac grabbed another tartlet, stuffed it into his pocket and turned off the light, not caring whether he'd be discovered.

"You listen to me," said Kimley raising his voice to get as much attention as possible, "first of all this is none of your business, but if you think you'll manage to extort anything from me through your stupid blasphemy, I warn you: you're on the wrong track!"

He was a believer, and how! Typical reaction. Pac had to lower his voice lest someone should discover him. "Would you like to meet a god, in exchange for that silly little stone?"

The question sped along a few miles of old, twisted cables, without losing an ounce of weight, or its way, in what was probably an extremely intricate maze.

Kimley wasn't answering. After a reasonably long pause, Pac feared that he may have left his earpiece dangling in mid-air, so to speak.

Had he exaggerated?

He was about to say: "Are you still there?" when he heard a murmured "Uhm," and it was really difficult to establish whether it indicated perplexity; two pairs; or a miasma of the kind that makes you list your meals of the last two days, in search of a culprit. And he knew all about that. Anyway, Kimley was still there. And Pac was relieved when he heard him speak.

"Ok, all right!" he said, lowering his voice as if to avoid the embarrassment of being overhead as he evaluated such a proposal. "I accept, but only in order to add a bizarre anecdote to my memoirs."

That was it, then.

"Did you know I'm writing a book?", proceeded Kimley.

"Really?!"

"Yes, but you won't be in it."

Despite this, the meeting was finally arranged, and it was Pac who dictated a few conditions. In self-defence, he said. He knew perfectly well that the famous flame-red pouch wouldn't be handed over so easily; he hoped that Kimley would at least bring it along, show it to him.

Once the call was terminated, he replaced his satellite phone in one pocket, and took out his snack from the other: he might as well celebrate. He paused in the act of tearing open the plastic wrapping, hesitating at the sound it produced in his hands (a noise that the pitch darkness amplified, adding a certain allure), then turned on the light and put the tartlet back into its padded recess, which he zipped closed, grabbing another from the shelf behind his back; he turned the light off again and immersed himself once more in caressing darkness.

The rest of the job, the really dirty work, was up to his new colleague. If he was really a fallen ex-divinity, this was the time to prove it. That should teach him to talk such utter crap. It was he who'd insisted on laying his hands on that stone ever since they were on that hilltop shack, right? So it was up to him.

Another bite: the chocolate ones were even better. But

this would be his last – no more.

In any case he felt he should remind himself that he'd never even remotely believed Samuel's theory. On the contrary, he was convinced that the poor man had suffered far more than one trauma; at the very least, he'd allowed himself to be influenced by something he'd perceived while in a coma: something processed at a subconscious level that had emerged, creating a connection between his research – dense with mystery and therefore easy prey to deviations and conjectures – and his highly unusual experience. Not to forget his eloquent wrists. He didn't actually feel sorry for him, but something of the sort. Nevertheless, Samuel was his only means to get hold of that object and verify whether it really worked – something which, again, he doubted – and could resolve the prickly issue of how to give life, hope and propulsion to the Star Pac. The countdown was ticking away fast and the grand finale approaching while he, instead of paying attention, was nursing a senile lunatic. And the vimana was still far from ready. He had to hurry. Pac knew that retrieving a stone that he hadn't even seen – and on which he was possibly setting too much store – was one of the many trials he had to overcome in order to obtain salvation – on Earth, of course.

Finished: the tartlet dispatched in less than three bites. How was it possible that these damned confectionary manufacturers couldn't come up with something a bit bigger? He passed two fingers over his lips to insert the last few crumbs.

As for the meeting, if the worst came to the worst he'd go home on his own two feet; and thinking back on what had happened there'd been no guarantee. If a better solution came up, he'd have something to celebrate.

Incidentally, Samuel was already a candidate for enrolment in the crew as non-commissioned technical officer, by virtue of his interest in the vimana; at the same time – and in light of recent events – the vacant position of airborne chaplain was definitively removed from the list. Better not run any risks.

Pac reached for the handle, trod on something on the floor, heard a faint crackle of crushed plastic. A glimmer of light: the corridor was free.

To tell the truth, Samuel had expressed himself in that divine direction only once, and so far they'd had no opportunity to go over the ins and outs of it. Samuel engaged most of his time as an in-patient resting; or striving, under supervision, to regain confidence with normal walking. And according to the medical staff his progress was surprising, given his age.

Pac's visits were quick: he too was caught up in events, including repeated visits to Dr Raju to check personally on the state of health of the young high-altitude bovid. Who was well: he ate, slept; his bowel movements were regular, and he seemed to appreciate the sugar lumps that his new friend brought him.

After the phone call he'd made a few days earlier, Pac had returned to the room whose ancient occupant he now considered his provisional partner and, finding him asleep, had woken him by kneeling at his bedside and reciting the Hinduist Hare Krishna mantra; this, within reasonable time, had produced a satisfactory "stop it, you idiot!"

Having brought Samuel up to date on their forthcoming meeting, and on the date and destination of their package tour for leaving the country, Pac had been rebuked: India was a rotten idea! He should never have pulled such a trick on him – Samuel had complained – forgetting that, until that moment, he'd never mentioned his aversion for that country. Admittedly his clinical record justified him in part: at least in Pac's presence, and when he was in a wide-awake state. What happened in his other states was none of Pac's business. As soon as he realised he'd omitted the preamble, Samuel had apologised.

"One day you'll explain why you've got it in for the world's greatest democracy," ventured Pac.

"It's a very long story, my dear fellow. But make sure you change our destination, or make Delhi a quick stopover. And I'm not joking," ranted the old man, his features assuming an expression that didn't suit him at all. Without tubes and wires, and in clean, longer-sleeved pyjamas, he definitely looked much better.

A promise had been extorted from Pac that he'd fix the matter (though he had no intention of doing so); and to retrieve Samuel's personal effects from such-and-such a hotel, and pay the bill – which again he was tempted not to do. And he'd left Samuel to his post-traumatic clinical recovery (neural, in particular), after reminding him of their appointment.

"Do prepare for it," he'd said. "We don't want to let the side down."

And this, too, had earned him a semi-concerned and hardly divine "Fuck off", which Pac had received good-humouredly, especially as the contrast between aged body and poised manner, and a vocabulary that included picturesque youthful expressions rendered Samuel more agreeable, and more fun to tease.

One last important errand had seen Pac bounce from one end of town to the other, unravelling bureaucratic, hygienic/sanitary and logistic issues; and involved in complicated negotiations with a well-known international shipping company that was particularly reluctant to transport to his home in Lebanon what Pac considered an essential local souvenir. Negotiations which – he'd understood later on – required some baksheesh which he'd provided without batting an eyelid, once he'd obtained the necessary reassurance that the parcel would be handled with the maximum care.

Samuel – discharged from hospital and now in Pac's modest hotel room – was slumped on an old faux-leather sofa (which in another context would have gone unnoticed), talking of his coma experience and of what he thought he remembered of his past.

It was late afternoon, which could be inferred from the gradual abating of the noises habitually produced by staff below, and by some of the customers; and from the first shivers on one's skin; from the opaque beams of sundown behind the drawn curtains. And shortly the sun would have gone elsewhere, behind the mountains, reminding both of them of the approaching X hour.

This was the first time the two had had an opportunity to talk at such ease. The former customer-supplier relationship had been swept away by circumstances, replaced by budding elective affinities that might perhaps mature.

Pac demanded, first and foremost, to know whom he was dealing with; and what he'd risked his life for, while drawing from his funds a considerable amount of cash – which fortunately was still with him and would soon be returned where it belonged. Why was he doing all this, including a further meeting with a dangerous, unreliable and ungrateful killer – a meeting he'd gladly have avoided?

Samuel knew he couldn't avoid these questions, and deep down he wouldn't have wanted to. He seemed quite happy to tell his story, on the implicit condition that sooner or later he'd hear Pac's: if not the whole story, at least the part regarding certain devices that he'd procured.

Samuel was an ex-astronaut. Even if his real identity were known you wouldn't find him in aerospace agencies' lists of the famous; so that revealing it would be both unnecessary and irrelevant.

As from the mid-70s the United States – or rather, NASA and the Pentagon – had developed a "separate space programme", operative to this day: a parallel project financed with top-secret funds. It was no mystery that the Pentagon controlled NASA, but evidently interests at stake were other and far greater than was made known to the public. As had been amply documented, this space programme used launch platforms of the USAF base in Vanderberg, California, along with other little-known installations in Nevada, Utah and in certain islands of the Pacific, and from the platform on the Diego Garcia atoll in the Indian Ocean. These missions – which officially never took place – made use of Saturn V rockets and of former military test pilots like Samuel for secret operations, such as that on the dark side of the Moon. On the purpose of these missions, on their implications and on the actual business purpose that a group of uniformed friends were taking into consideration, Samuel maintained the strictest confidentiality: they weren't things he could discuss, for safety reasons.

Pac had already formed an opinion, and wouldn't have

minded a confirmation. It was linked to questions such as why, since the Apollo 17 mission in December 1972, man had no longer set foot on the Moon, at least not officially; or what lurked behind the smokescreen of ufology themes still managed by a military élite, or behind functions of the HAARP project. Or why the US Space agency made such an effort to alter photos of the Martian surface showing artificial structures, possibly still in use, together with what looked like faces and ziggurats of ancient Mesopotamian tradition. Or to the mystery of the destruction (or rather, the shooting down) of the Phobos 2 in 1989, when it was in the proximity of the Martian moon by the same name; an accident that caused human exploration of planet Mars – which the frozen water on that satellite would have rendered much easier – to be set aside.

Which is why Pac wasn't particularly surprised by what the gentleman with the stern expression was telling him. If anything, the aspect that worried Pac most was the threat that an alien presence, so to speak, could pose once they were back in the atmosphere. But Pac's concern dissolved as soon as he realised, with deplorable delay, how useful Samuel could be to his plan. Where else could he find another pilot: someone who'd already been up there and therefore had that desperately needed hands-on experience? And there was still the propulsion issue to solve.

One thing at a time.

Going back to his past, Samuel recounted that he'd been

dismissed when such missions had been cut down since the 1996 space shuttle disaster. And because he was too old for flying: the way he said it seemed to imply that he saw this as a liberation.

Anticipating Pac's question, Samuel uncrossed his legs and added his personal motivations. "I always hoped that NASA, or rather the power-holding Intelligence apparatus, would decide to divulge the information in its possession, revealing to the world what I, too, had initially thought should be kept top secret for security reasons and to protect the foundations of our civilisation. But humanity is ready, my dear chap, and has been for some time. It's these people who are the problem. You see, they're not prepared to budge, to share power, to give the planet the technology they're keeping under lock and key: the technology that – overnight – would positively revolutionise our ecological and renewable potential. I waited for that moment to happen, but it never did. It's not by touching up the photographs they release that they'll manage to stop the progress of truth. Just as I understood that my personal expectations were destined to remain precisely that – personal expectations – I was dismissed. A splendid coincidence – really splendid," he said.

His words were sincere, or so they seemed to Pac who – reclining in bed against two pillows – intended to check them out; in the meantime he was nibbling a biscuit.

To Pac's question on his role in the sale of aerospace

components, Samuel, vague and appeasing, replied with a shrug: a few contacts at *Lockheed Martin*, some friends here and there. To supplement his pension, he said.

Clearly there was more to it. And it wasn't long before Samuel came clean.

"My interest in ancient chronicles, those fascinating narrations for which I'd always had a mania, was rekindled then and there. I needed to find out... to understand how much truth there was in what ancient peoples – from the Middle East to South America, from Africa to the Far East – described as genuine historical facts: the details differed but the root was the same. What I'd seen from space; the purpose of those missions; and the mysteries buried in the past: they were all part of the same thing. I sensed it... knew it – which is why I spent my time investigating. I'd never asked myself why I had this drive, which wasn't mere curiosity. I did it because I knew I had to, I somehow owed it to myself, though I ignored the reason. It had become my personal mission. On an intellectual level, I believed that by discovering something tangible and culturally mind-blowing I could embarrass NASA and appease my frustration, my smouldering desire for retaliation. You know, it's not easy to accomplish memorable gestures while remaining totally anonymous, especially if our colleagues get covered in glory for less-risky operations. But at another level... there was a background noise that I'd occasionally try to decipher, without succeeding. My coma lifted the curtain, revealing the on-going play. Because that's what it is, you know. Tragicomic, dramatic: I wouldn't know how to define it, because the foregoing acts saw me as a forcibly distracted actor; and only now am I beginning to remember; only now do I discern a reason, rooting out the identity and intention of the very theatre company, if you'll pardon the parallel. I'm beginning to understand. I know. I thank my coma, and in a sense I thank you, too. I am indebted to you for this extraordinary experience. And I don't think it's casual: nothing is casual...", he said, waving his hand in the air as if to some melody.

Samuel's coming out was taking a surprising turn, revealing itself – in Pac's vision – to be as resplendent as a treasure trove, as an erotic phantasmagoria. An ex-astronaut, who claimed he felt obliged? What more could he ask for? Too much, this was definitely too much. Was it a sign of "his" time?

"Tell me what you remember," he prompted, resolving not to laugh. He wanted another biscuit: the repeat mechanism had gone off. But he stopped it with an iron will.

"They're flash-backs, glimmers of information," replied Samuel after a long sigh that betrayed the fatigue he was suppressing. "I don't know whether it was a biochemical reaction induced by my state of unconsciousness, or by the awakening of what some people hazard to call 'junk DNA', the non-codifying part compounding a considerable portion of the overall human genome. Or simply self-delusion..."

Pac appreciated that the latter had been included among the options, and allowed him to proceed.

"The fact is..." Samuel leaned towards the edge of his armchair, elbows on his thighs, hand on his chin, gaze lowered. His expression was troubled, he seemed to be holding back: he shook his head as if that might help him process the truth. "The fact is that my memories are... incomplete: some vague, others limpid. But they're there, and they feel authentic."

"What sort of memories?"

"The sense of defeat. Of impotence in the face of someone who usurped an original project, subverting it completely," said Samuel seriously. He stopped: a pause was needed to ensure the concept would sink in.

"A scientific project," he continued hesitantly, rubbing his fingers together nervously, "with well-defined ethics, that were deliberately manipulated. The diffusion and study of intelligent life throughout the galaxy."

Pac was overcome by a certain unease, which he tried to stifle. Running his hand over his hair he turned to look at the window, at what little light filtered there. Then at the unmade bed. And resumed his listening.

"I remember the desperation, the shattering angst I felt at repudiating my fellow beings. The desire to try again, to help and to teach," continued Samuel. "And the battle, the clashes that followed."

Pac listened, straining to remain neutral, to avoid banal jokes. He didn't interrupt; not even during the long silent pauses in which Samuel took his time and seemed to be continuing the conversation inside his head.

"I had to fight my brothers... there was a war: battles, in the name of a supremacy, between two factions of 'highly evolved' beings who proved they weren't so evolved at all. And people being forced by their gods to take sides. I was shot down on that mountain, captured, imprisoned, tried by the Council of the Wise, and condemned."

"To what penalty?", asked Pac to prevent a pause which he knew might go on indefinitely.

"I know you don't believe me, and I don't care. But you mustn't laugh at me."

"By saying this you're asking for it."

Samuel's expression became even more sullen: he lifted his eyes to meet Pac's, and stared at him fixedly. "Of chemical reincarnation. A procedure I remember as complex and painful," was his reply.

"Which means?", asked Pac, impassively.

"Which means reincarnating semi-consciously an indefinite number of times, remembering nothing. Nothing sufficiently concrete, consistent and logical to create that tangible network, that clear and plausible image that transforms a series of sensations into an assumption you can ponder. Without the mental faculties – developed over millennia – that my fellow beings are endowed with. Or rather, with latent faculties, whose awakening would require assiduous dedication without even knowing the objective."

"You mean a sort of existential, evolutionary maze. A biological handicap?" prompted Pac with a straight face: he'd decided to continue with the stoic approach.

"Sort of," replied Samuel, whose troubled eyes – Pac noticed – were moist with supressed tears. "Imagine you can fly but you don't know; you have this hunch, which you force yourself to ignore as silly. Sometimes the thought – even to try flying – lurks at the back of your mind. But because you're unaware, because you don't believe, you know you'll never be able to. So you give up."

A small group of tourists passed along the corridor, arguing loudly: voices approaching, becoming clearer, more intrusive as they reached the door of the room; then moving forward, fading. The slamming of a door.

"Maybe" said Samuel, "the spell is broken. There's no other way I can explain certain notions, certain sensations…" he added pensively, bringing his head closer to Pac's. "Our mission, new civilisation and technologies; the dividing up of territories; envy; the establishment of clans, followed by the divisions and competition among ourselves; and on the fruits of our labour."

Pac couldn't help drawing a comparison between what he was hearing – a sense of failure, of disillusion, the idea of a new civilisation – and his own long-established objective.

A coincidence? The cyclic nature of events? Or was he simply paying 'too much' attention?

"Except for a few small fragments I've little or no recollection of what happened over the centuries, of these reincarnations," said Samuel, as if to conclude the conversation, leaning into the backrest of his chair. "And I honestly hope these memories won't come back. They'd be of little use and would only take up space in my brain. At my age, you know..." He smiled.

Pac stared at him, perplexed, immobile. A crazed ex-astronaut: what use could he be? Pac's own erratic mood swings between euphoria and disbelief were wearing him out, but he knew he must take advantage of the knowledge and skills offered by this acquaintance. A unique knowledge, he conceded, but tainted with insane ravings. Yet it seemed he had no alternatives.

"And did this enlightened awareness come to you before or after slitting your wrists?"

It was a mean question, he knew, but it had to be asked.

Samuel suddenly switched off: remaining immobile, his light-blue eyes cast down to the brown bed coverlet, where Pac was seated; frowning, as if rummaging in a basket of dirty laundry, picking through various crumpled odours in search of a forgotten sensation, an experience that had somehow remained impressed, ensnared in those garments.

At a certain point, biting his lip, he appeared to nod timidly, without shifting his gaze; the flush on his lined, well-shaven face; his breathing very slow.

During all that silence, Pac almost regretted the provocation. But it didn't last long. The waning sunlight that still filtered indoors – colouring the room, skimming lightly over Samuel and the white walls, Pac, the bed-side table – was refracted from a small mirror.

"It happened a long time ago," lied Samuel, finally. "I have to tell you..." he stumbled, groping for words that eluded him.

"Forget it," said Pac. He'd find a way to go into it further.

"No!" said Samuel. "I have to tell you. You must hear how it feels to be lost; to caress the stars through the porthole window; to be skewered by that darkness. Experiencing sensations of which you don't know the origin, even less the reason: not knowing whether they're really yours, my dear, loyal client," he said, establishing a distance between them that Pac sensed immediately.

"I don't give a damn about your obscure meanderings," Pac retorted, "I just want to know who I'm dealing with". And he made sure his tone was sufficiently abrasive.

"If all your little head needs is guarantees," said Samuel with a sigh, sounding relieved and smiling, "I can reassure you. I know how to use the stone, how to activate it," observing the hoped-for reaction. "And who knows what else will come to mind."

Pac looked at him askance, undecided whether to consider Samuel's optimism as a crafty diversion or pragmatic comfort.

He opted for the latter: comfort was, after all, what he mainly needed. Still harbouring some reservations Pac smiled, then lightly ruffled his non-existent mane with both hands, possibly to ward off ill-luck in a gamble where everything he had was at stake – including (though he didn't care to admit it) his very life. Yet he was sufficiently stimulated to get going, and leapt off the bed. Quite apart from space-age theories, proto-historic delusions and awakenings of inner gods, the whole point – the objective which he should tackle as soon as possible – was to verify what that stone could do. This was absolutely vital for the Star Pac.

Pac wrapped a long red woollen scarf round his neck and, indicating the nondescript mock-antique clock on the table, told Samuel he was ready to see him in action.

"You only need to demonstrate it, my dear Samuel," he said, slapping him on the shoulder, in a peaceable tone that might just be mistaken for provocative.

The night was decidedly cold. Rather as if, behind the curtain of darkness, all those self-centred mountains – the whole club of powdered drag queens – had ganged up on him to breathe, in sync, small puffs of mentholated gas refrigerant onto the back of his neck.

Come to think of it, this too was a pretty self-centred idea. Pac walked along at a pace that quickened or slowed, depending on what went on in his mind – a pace which Samuel could easily adapt to, being equally prone to – and capable of recognising – those most significant, alternating states of mind; while Pac – as we were saying – walked with a gait between confident and hesitant; and, passing tourists complacently displaying their warts, he felt the onset of that freezing-cold air as if it were reserved for him alone; a sensation that no scarf was able to dispel. He might even have made out the sinister jeering and snickering of the drag queens up there, mingled with the gusts of wind – but he had other things on his mind.

The walk, longer and more tortuous than expected, was interrupted by peddlers, obsequious market-stall traders, and carpet sellers who almost dragged him by the arm inside their multi-coloured stores. And guides, genuine or fake, whom he was tempted to tell to go to hell.

Tall and graceful, a solitary woman approached them from a distance: chestnut hair, no make-up, no ornaments, steady dark gaze. Here she was, swathed in wool and shimmering light. As she passed by, she smiled at Pac and, while lowering her eyes, an expression of delightful femininity suffused her face. She walked on and disappeared, leaving Pac to savour the moment.

The place where two out of three hoped an exchange

would take place was the *Lhasa Tibetan Restaurant*. After carefully evaluating the alternatives, Pac's choice had fallen on a known venue, usually well-frequented by potential Western witnesses, commendable for the excellent value for money of its ample home-style menu; for its fast and friendly service; but above all for its table near the fire, which he'd gone to the trouble of booking.

No, it wasn't such nonsense to return to the place he'd accused of giving him food poisoning. On the contrary: there was the added value that he could order chai (boiling water, milk, sugar and spices) and hope that the raving lunatic (the Nepalese one) would order the full menu in what was one of the best restaurants in the area – when all went well. He'd watched him eat, and knew what his stomach was capable of. If anything had gone wrong – thought Pac – he might at least get a kick out of seeing him or knowing him about to be violently sick; which would mean taking his revenge, indirectly, also against the owner of the restaurant. Not much of a hope, but there are times when a little goes a long way.

Kimley was already sitting there, vacant chairs of white plastic on either side of him.

He wore an army-green sweater under his usual leather jacket; his hair was greased and combed; his face shaven, as if sitting in a restaurant for tourists – ergo, people with money – required one to conform to clichés that tourists themselves would try to avoid.

Pac decided to check him out from a hidden corner before approaching, which rattled an already-tense Samuel. Kimley was holding a cigarette between his fingers: more in order to strike a cultural pose than because he actually needed to smoke – thought Pac – and something about that robust, thick-featured man told him he was ill at ease. In his own country, in a privileged role, yet ill at ease; and Pac couldn't help but notice that he was now consulting a metal watch.

The perfect moment to make an entrance; but from the studied look which Kimley turned on them, clumsily stubbing out his cigarette, Pac sensed that presumed ill humour would soon become arrogance and spite aimed at him. What he feared most was that Kimley might not have brought the famous flame-red pouch and – worse still – might not be alone.

Meanwhile Samuel was shaking. Not from his usual ailments, or because he was afraid: yes, he was nervous, but knew deep down there was no real risk, although the last time he'd been involved in an exchange he'd come out of it pretty badly. There was something else, something he couldn't quite understand. He'd experienced this fibrillation before, but couldn't remember when or why. With his shirt, his pullover the colour of lunar ash, the fragrance of cologne, and his totally vacant expression, he looked like the friend of a friend dragged against his will to a party of adopted children.

That evening the place wasn't too crowded. With its bright colours, to-ing and fro-ing of the waiters, the aroma of food, and the energy emitted by the ample fireplace fuelled with large logs, it was cosier than usual: an oasis for tired souls, a mud bath for sore feelings.

"So?" began Pac cockily. "What's up?"

"I'm not here to chat," said Kimley smiling placidly, his smile oozing complacency.

Meanwhile, underpaid dark-complexioned waiters in white shirts were scurrying about on winged feet, serving steaming, spicy food whose vaporous trails criss-crossed like chemtrails in a blue sky. In an excess of zeal and speed, motivated by the hope of a service tip, one of the waiters forgot the step between indoor and outdoor dining rooms. Like a would-be acrobat, he balanced his platter of chicken-and-vegetable soy noodles while tipping first forward, then sideways, desperately seeking an elusive centre of gravity, aided in this by the mute moral support of a vast audience of customers who – if truth be told – more than by the boy's predicament, were alarmed by the risk of becoming the target of a culinary coup. This fate befell a Dutch woman seated nearby, whose beige jersey became ruinously decorated in motifs of thin dark stripes, vegetal swirls and giblets.

The noodle and the damage done.

Relieved, the audience resumed where it had left off, while the waiter was assisted to his feet and accompanied to the exit by a couple of colleagues, one of whom – on being intercepted by our three diners, to order chai – merely slowed down, before rushing with the others towards the door. Leaving Pac fuming over his missed revenge.

"I hope you have that stone with you," he said, rubbing his hands before the generous flame of the fireplace, which popped and hissed in defiance of the draught outside.

"I'm not in raptures over visions of divinities!" replied Kimley with his raucous brothel-bouncer voice. "Let me know when it's time to look at the sky: I wouldn't want to miss the fun!" He'd given the mere hint of a greeting to Samuel, whose presence appeased what little curiosity he may have had regarding his state of health.

"The stone first," insisted Pac, striving not to betray signs of weakness and confiding in an immediate performance on Samuel's part. "My friend and I are clearly outnumbered, we're the away-team, and we know the referee was bribed. You'll concede this, at least," he retorted, aiming for a dodgeball strike.

Hinting at their numeric inferiority was a studied move: he looked for reactions, observing Kimley's body language. As soon as the chai arrived on the stone table, Kimley started drinking it from his teacup. Oblivious of the scalding heat and of the small handle (in which he probably couldn't insert a finger), he encircled the rim with the whole of his dark hand. Heat resistance, a dignified gaze, eyes ever vigilant, even while sipping: what did all this imply? Scanning him warily, while feigning interest in the steam rising – like vaporous prayers to the Lord of the Rain – from his own cup, Pac watched as agent Kimley nodded to himself, as if in agreement (over what, remained a mystery), took in all the people around with one glance, and put his cup back on its saucer. Then his eyes met Pac's.

What did this convey? Disgust, first of all; followed by disdain, and by something else, probably starting with the same syllable.

Samuel sat with his arms folded, still shaking, and showed no interest in his own chai, despite an unusual effort at swallowing.

The restaurant was noisy with tourists returning from or leaving for the Annapurna circuit. Visibly excited yet relaxed, they chatted mainly in English, though a discerning ear would have caught words in German or Scandinavian. The candles on the tables illuminated their faces, highlighting busy mouths. It may have been the atmosphere that softened agent K.

"I appreciate that your position is unfavourable," he said, settling in his chair. "Which is why I'll meet you halfway... I won't show you anything, but you have my word that the stone is right here," he said, tapping his black jacket at chest height.

"Your word... are you serious?", asked Pac crossly. "The word of a spy, unreliable by definition? Of a fanatic and a scrounge?"

"You don't seem to me best qualified to take that line," replied Kimley, unperturbed and even amused by Pac's outburst, and exhibiting a better command of English than so far manifested. The two started to snipe at each other, about who was to blame for what had happened with the kidnappers, about Pac's dirty work in Kathmandu: details that didn't surprise the interested party who, on the contrary, retorted by accusing Kimley of causing far more harm through his fan-club of fanatics, who promoted their interests – just like everyone else, whatever their background – in the name of an anachronistic protection of their country, and ended up damaging it. Not to mention his murderous methods, the capacity to emerge always with a clean conscience being the most evident of his aberrations. Present and past – Pac said, seeking to generalise the conversation towards vague, ample, three-dimensional themes, to give Samuel the time he needed. So, raising his voice and holding tightly onto his mental steering wheel, he went as far as accusing Kimley of being the pimped version of an inquisitor; a backward mountaineer; as for being a tourist guide – he added – he was untrained, unable to meet his customer's demands, inexperienced, and completely out of date (this seemed to hit home, judging by the embarrassment that fleetingly swept over those Nepalese features); and finally suggesting that he change brand of toothpaste, if ever he used one.

Apart from the aforementioned flinching, Kimley remained calm inside his muscular physique, chewing over his two sole arguments: that he was dealing with a hopeless sinner and infidel. In lousy shape, moreover, judging by his blubber (he went as far as calling him 'fatso', and it was only the object of that meeting that kept Pac from answering with insinuations of a family character, so to speak); and sketching a realistic perspective of what would soon happen to *Children's Haven*, using as an example an approaching child, scruffy and dejected, who – as fate would have it – went from table to table, hand in hand with his small, blind sister, begging from the restaurant's satiated customers.

A blow below the belt: damned unsporting, even supposing he really cared; and how that third-world barbarian ever knew of his affairs was something Pac couldn't begin to understand.

Meanwhile the fire had burned down to mounds of orange embers that glowed calmly; the drop in temperature was tangible.

Samuel, on the contrary, was increasingly agitated and now shaken by tremors in the shoulders and one arm, almost as if he had little control over a nervous system whose coloured buttons – unbeknown to him – were being fiddled around with by someone else; and he'd come out in a cold sweat. The other two, who were having a dig at each other, lacing every word in sarcasm and seemingly getting a big kick out of it, were too busy to notice.

"Oh, cut it out!" exclaimed Samuel suddenly, banging his fists on the table.

It was this, rather than his words, that stopped the squabbling between the two who, eyeing each other as if they'd just got off a merry-go-round, erased with ill-concealed regret the sneer they'd been displaying all along.

"Right then: I am the God," stated Samuel, immobile, his tone aloof, his light-blue eyes fixed on Kimley, the lines on his face emphasised by his quietly authoritative expression; distinctly pronouncing words of which (one can rightly note with pride) there is no literary precedent – errors and omissions excepted.

Unable to help himself, Kimley burst out laughing with gusto, relishing the new anecdote to include in his memoirs. He shook his head and sipped some more chai, feeling somehow appeased, enjoying his evening of leisure. After all, he deserved it.

Pac heaved a sigh of relief and was, metaphorically speaking, rubbing his hands together, not having the least idea what to expect. A blinding flash of light? A sense of mystical, tingling dampness at the base of his root chakra? Shri Krishna in person, his skin the colour of rain-filled clouds? The instant incineration of an infidel, hence his own death, too? A winged seraph precariously balanced on the backrest of the only vacant chair at their table? Or should he order a round of beer to cover his embarrassment while telling Kimley that it was all just a joke, a silly prank; that they'd tried it on, and failed?

While posing himself these legitimate questions he'd momentarily lost touch with the present, or so it seemed. And now, vigilant once more, he found the two intent on whispering: talking in an undertone, side by side, so close that their two faces were almost touching. Murmuring sentences, nodding and bowing to each other.

Actually, on further and closer examination, this looked like anything other than a conversation: Samuel, his glance relaxed, was holding Kimley's hand under the table and muttering unintelligible words that didn't sound at all like sentences. They sounded like some sort of chanting, a mantra, the mumbled rosary of some unknown religion. It took Pac several minutes to ascertain that it was a long, repeated sequence, but this didn't help him understand any better. But it was when shifting his gaze on Kimley that he felt the urge to escape, to find refuge from some unknown threat: from the potential scourge that was striking the Nepalese now; and nothing, no-one could guarantee that he wouldn't be struck in turn. The poor wretch (for that was the terrifying impression Kimley made), sat with head bowed, hazelnut eyes half-closed as if observing a beam of sunlight reflected from an inclined mirror and enlarged by a magnifying glass. The tiny tears coursing down his cheeks did not bode well, though his expression was not so much one of pain or torment, but rather that of someone who finds a vein of pure regret in a mine of paralysing ecstasy. This, within the limits of the narrator's current capacity, is what the face of agent K. transmitted to an equally absorbed Pac; as the minutes went quietly by, however, Pac grew less alarmed and more intrigued; less perplexed and more amused; on the verge of breaking into one of his best smiles, and a spontaneous chortle of mindless mirth. Especially when Kimley, with his free hand, drew from his jacket's inner pocket the famous flame-red pouch, hypnotically tracing the slowest of circular movements, guided by something beyond a magnetic glance or a state of trance: a language evoking tax codes in rhyming couplets.

Without hesitation, Pac picked up the coveted object, causing it to disappear with an equally circular movement, lest he spoil the harmony of such a propitious gesture; rising slowly from his chair, he finished his cup of spicy tea, noted the general indifference of those in the room to what was going on and finally – without mentioning the bill – tapped Samuel on the shoulder. Extremely gently.

"We can go. The rabbit's in the hole!" he whispered from a certain distance.

Samuel released the hand of a Kimley elsewhere engrossed, gradually turning down the volume of the broadcast to complete fade-out. He stood up, staggered dangerously and had to lean on Pac; then, exhausted, he made for the exit with heavy, uncertain steps. The taxi journey back to the hotel seemed that much faster.

If the member of that sect (as Pac defined him, somewhat maliciously), had been escorted by his pals, there was no sign of them; unless they'd seen no reason to intervene. But had any look-outs been around, what they'd have found on approaching the mythical Mr. K. – apart from a cold, despondent hearth – would have been far from edifying for their ilk – whatever that was.

How do starfish mate?

According to the village chief of Tavarua island, Indonesia, during the so-called 'stellar' mating season – at nightfall, unseen even by the Moon – starfish are said to surface from the marine depths and float upside-down, in placid anticipation. And from the opposite direction, from outer space – or so the story has it – dozens and dozens of miniscule globes of light with long flaming tails hurtle down, streaking the darkness like tears of wonder as the sky and sea unite through the starfish. Once these are fertilised – shortly before dawn, we hear – they return to their seabed, where clumps of multi-coloured seaweed and branches of coral spread themselves out to protect the future offspring of these stellar waters.

Not knowing the answer, Pac kept wondering about how starfish mated, imagining himself on board a submarine and studying the darkness through a porthole. Samuel slouched sideways, asleep. Hair dishevelled as usual, features slackened yet seemingly capable of snapping to alert incinerating mode at any moment. Not even the dinner ritual, awaited with liturgical patience as the main function within an airplane, had distracted him from his sleep. Disturbed, if not downright irritated, at having had to tread on Indian ground (albeit for a brief stopover), he seemed in need of recovering his strength after a sacrifice that, judging by his silence, had totally drained him. A silence as meaningful as the belligerent glare he shot at every symbol, inhabitant and artefact he'd laid eyes on at the duty-free in New Delhi airport. Though avoiding movements of the head, he'd aimed at numerous targets, his body rigid as an ivory toothpick, his gait cadenced; his uncontrollable growl inducing Pac to follow at a safe distance.

On the reasons for this resentment Pac had not reverted, in respect of an impassable limit he now perceived as devoid of provocative intention, whose violation might disrupt or even compromise a relationship which he intimately hoped would remain sound beyond the planet's natural boundaries.

At this point one might easily be inclined to insinuate that Pac's aforementioned considerations stemmed from genuine remorse: remorse for having got a kick from observing Samuel's reactions in a hostile context (the stopover in India being not only avoidable but also more expensive than a direct flight); for proposing – for his own wicked amusement – that Samuel change his remaining

Nepalese rupees to shop for gifts and souvenirs in order to fill in time; and, last but not least, for watching – first with delight, then with ecstasy – as Samuel's choice not to use the toilets of that "dreadful, filthy gate", and to withhold his too-noble urine rather than letting undeserving Indian sewers have it: an unwise decision that had caused him first to stage a tragi-comic dance of the urgently needed pissoir; and secondly, when the aforementioned fluid had got the better of his aged bladder, obliging him to buy new, clean clothes. Mere insinuations, as we were saying, which will go unheeded.

Pac was beaming, in his own way, though the fatigue of his latest feats had taken its toll. The toll of heroes, of those who knew they'd achieved the extraordinary – and more than once. The stiffness of those who'd fought on hostile ground, had planned and dared; of those whose mission was obscure and secret, whose appointment transcended today's comprehension, stretching like a bow-string to a future time when all would be revealed. And though destined to perish under the debris of destruction, he who happened to hear of our hero's predestined scheme, he who had listened to the when and how, to the few details, could not but say: "I heard, but did not understand."

Which is why there was no reason or logic in divulging his plan. Secrecy safeguarded successful outcome, because from this depended the future renaissance: the future civilisation.

"Some hot tea, Sir?" asked a flight attendant squeezed in a too-tight dark uniform, handing him a white Styrofoam cup.

"My father used to piss in the sink," said Pac with a bitter, shocked expression, watching as she backed away, not knowing whether she'd fully appreciated his state of mind. Totally overcome by his aforementioned sensation he abandoned himself to the supple padded backrest, lapping up a last wave of complacency: knowing that he'd taken perhaps more than one concrete step towards crowning his epic of salvation.

Pac was carried away by the flow of slumber, ignoring the disappointed fluttering of fate's finger tips.

Signs of the end of the world as we knew it?

What was causing the global warming that interested not only the Earth, but also Jupiter, Mars, Uranus, Neptune, Pluto? And why was this last changing colour, from orangey-yellow to red, as stated by astronomers? What phenomenon could influence the temperature of the entire solar system? Was it the anomalous activity of the Sun and of its spots, registered by scientists? Were we nearing the end of a solar cycle? Or was it something to do with variations in the Earth's magnetic field: variations indicating a possible inversion of its polarity? And what would happen as a result of all this?

Could it be due to the approaching mysterious Planet X,

'Nibiru' for the Sumerians, that had slowed down space probes Pioneer and Voyager as they left the solar system, deviating their trajectory? The same that was causing disturbances in the orbits of Uranus and Neptune? The very planet monitored by the Vatican's radio telescope managed by Jesuits in Alaska, as well as by the secret probe, Siloe?

Were biblical prophecies being manipulated by the New World Order, by the Illuminated – ever behind the staging of events and of the course of history – to induce men to accept a sole global religion, as part of the scheme that included a sole currency, a sole Central Bank; and a sole World Government, in the form of a dictatorship reached by degrees of slow, programmed acceptance, using the Old Testament's conflict surrounding the Earth as the initial arena of the escalation?

A society that had delivered its most important social and scientific achievements into the hands of an oligopoly, through the pretence of a proxy, of inactive participation. More specifically, of an ignoble political class faking an alternation; of pharmaceutical companies and private universities in control of pseudo-scientific research (when in fact any trace of pure and free research had been lost for decades).

A society that had watched as its legacy of Oriental cultures and disciplines was diluted, belittled and sold off in exchange for a sloppy, miserable standardisation called globalisation, whose only purpose was better control, better management, better exploitation. A world that accepted control and power mechanisms such as fractional reserve, enabling banks to create virtual currency ex novo, which was then certified by a Central Bank, multiplying the meagre immediate liquidity actually held, giving rise to the relentless creation of debt, overproduction and inflation.

Wasn't it right to work towards the accelerated destruction of a world of this kind?

Not to mention recent climate-related experiments for making rain fall in the middle of the desert; or attempts to recreate sub-atomic conditions subsequent to the Big Bang theory; or CERN's research of hypothetical boson particles through the development of uncontrollable underground energy. In the name of whom were these gentlemen putting everyone's life at risk? Whoever asked them to? Who gave them the authority, the responsibility to manipulate, experiment, attempt? Where were the control, the restrictions, the necessary scientific information: the must-haves that transformed citizens into aware and critical people? Supposing a subatomic particle reacted badly? Irked, unrestrained as it was by the common laws of physics, who would convince it to be good, to backpedal, and respond to the researcher's questions, influencing with its presence the outcome of the experiment?

Man's statement and expression of magnificence had almost always been rejected, amputated or forbidden by a social model cast by religion and economy. Only the latter seemed to be still operative, through enslavement to 'seigniorage banking', for example: the exorbitant difference between embedded value, production cost, and nominal value of a currency no longer backed by gold, no longer convertible, that granted Central Banks (privately owned, and managed by the usual suspects) uncontrollable powers, such as the possibility to blackmail or influence nations, and even the economy of the whole world. Consciously delivering into those hands the monetary sovereignty of entire nations had been an unmistakable sign of the relentless decline and deterioration in lifestyle of unsuspecting, anesthetised or merely moronic citizens.

How much longer could such a society resist, before it collapsed?

The symbolism of messages contained in crop circles materialising overnight for the joy of farmers: was this another countdown?

Establishing something concrete was an arduous operation, requiring a painstakingly acquired mixture of intuition, pessimism, distrust, and knowledge of historical and contemporary mechanisms.

Only one thing is certain, dear reader:
The Apocalypse Will Not Be Televised.

THREE

Fernanda wasn't at all thrilled to lend her services to two people for the price of one. She had repeatedly mentioned the matter to her employer, but he'd always managed to procrastinate, placating her with words that somehow regularly succeeded in taking her in. But things would have to change soon, she told herself. Very soon. The new guest, the elderly (polite, but weird) gentleman whom, quite frankly, she didn't like at all – changed twice a day – and she had to do his laundry! He had three meals a day, substantial meals, which she prepared whenever on duty, also for the days when she wouldn't be there. And where he put all that food, scrawny as he was, she really couldn't figure. Sure, he was elegant, though a little too precious and finicky for her liking, but she shouldn't have to be responsible for his stylish dressing. Everyone knew that guests stink after three days. But his Lordship had been taking advantage of the amenities of the house for over a week: he was always either relaxing in the veranda, or somewhere else on the property, doing who-knew-what.

A distant relative? An old friend, partner, lover? She couldn't care less. She'd get things straight, and quick. She was nobody's dogsbody, no way! They could bet their arses: the fat one and the scrawny one.

Obviously Pac was well aware of what went on in Fernanda's mind. He also knew that flattery and ever-weaker excuses couldn't work much longer. He needed to hold out and be patient, however, at least until the time (soon) when all this would no longer matter: when priorities would be different, more urgent. Or until her inevitable dismissal. He certainly wasn't prepared to overlook her eating habits, or the way she took advantage of other people' generosity, obliging him, moreover, to infringe the rules of his diet and suffer the annoying consequences: guilt, paranoid feelings, distractions he couldn't afford. After all, if he couldn't lose weight – if the mirror reflected a deformed, soft, flabby image; if the bulge he squeezed with growing frustration never decreased in volume; if it still hadn't disappeared despite his enormous sacrifices – it was largely Fernanda's responsibility, or rather her fault. Her senselessly overblown figure and her implicit disregard for the implications of disorderly eating were a lousy example, a negative influence that could lead to deviations, exceptions, self-indulgence. We shouldn't underestimate the importance of the people we surround ourselves with; and of a larder full of junk food, the fridge permanently kept at a precarious level of subsistence.

No, they couldn't go on like this. She was certainly a good cook, and prepared what he ordered the way he liked it, which is why he'd kept her on. But he knew that she pilfered money from the shopping: he was no fool, and to steal in the house of thieves... To put it bluntly (and to avoid any misunderstandings), he was no longer prepared to fork out for someone who wasn't even on his list, so to speak. He needed the money. And he'd need more and more.

For this reason, too, they had to busy themselves like ants before those grey clouds up there unleashed their vehemence, rather than sing away like grasshoppers before getting cheerfully drenched.

And in all this, Samuel's role was anything other than negligible. In fact, after offering him a brief period of cushy convalescence, and making him generously welcome within his domestic walls, it was time he introduced his guest to the whole palaver. Needless to say, his skills, his background were a godsend, things that hardly needed commenting. Quite apart from his ravings, his belief that he was a god, his two horizontal scars, and heaps of explanations still pending. Mere details, Pac tried to persuade himself (somewhat unsuccessfully).

Would he be prepared to join in, to collaborate? This was the point. He'd soon find out.

It happened that very evening, in the ample veranda at the foot of the lawn, when – out of Fernanda's sight – they relaxed on wicker chairs, al fresco, surrounded by hills and mountains, cedar trees, and woods; when a scattering of stars twinkled in the sky, and the air was sweet and fragrant. When their words floated gently, sailing from one to the other, and all was quiet, except for harmless rustlings in the near distance: the regular song and muffled collective buzz of night-time creatures. Long-eared owls, crickets, owlets; not a trace of frogs or moths. When the lights indoors were low and a few books lay around open; while there, outside, the terracotta floor of the veranda still felt warm underfoot. When Pac, who normally wore only coloured boxers in the evening hours, had taken to slipping into long Cambodian trousers made of cotton, and ample T-shirts with attractive graphics of rave parties he'd dreamed of attending.

Samuel seemed to have long understood that Pac's interest in him was no longer limited to the provision of contraband aerospace components. Clearly there must be more to it. Despite his head-aches, he was comforted by a speedy recovery, and was putting an enormous effort into evoking and deciphering lost (and occasionally absurd) memories which wreaked havoc in his mind: a whirl of emotions and perceptions that at times made him feel quite lost; yet, despite all this, he was curious to see where the sequence of coincidences would lead him, he told himself: first, undercover space operator, orbit jockey, witness of unspeakable presences; then, researcher of the mysteries of man's origins; some profitable trekking on a suspicious mountain; an enlightening coma; and now the truth on his own origin. And the above-mentioned sequence suddenly lighting up in the night of his existence, showing him the entire course of his past. Wasn't this extraordinary, and pitiful as well? And what would the curious ex-customer sitting next to him want? He knew a question was about to be posed. A question preceded by a long story, a premise which, he sensed, would seem quite unusual.

And it was then – when Pac started to confide his most exclusive thoughts, from the earliest signs of the approaching end of time to his vimana projects; when he opened up in a way he'd never imagined he'd do with anyone, passionately highlighting the most important passages – that Samuel understood fate was offering him a portal, a passage hitherto concealed to the human eye, that would lead him where he knew he must go. And his past, his awakening, his memories, his newly acquired awareness – though still somewhat confused – assumed greater clarity, a meaning that would otherwise have been incomplete. As he listened, he learned more and more details regarding his role, his future duties – his Calling.

Which was another reason for knowing, deep down, that he could never refuse this request for help: Pac's signs were also his signs; Samuel too perceived the threat of those imminent dangers; just as constructing what used to belong to him by right – his celestial abode – was his exclusive prerogative. The vehicle that had once seen the conclusion of his story, before his unlawful destitution, would now afford him new hopes of salvation: a salvation that could only be achieved at that moment and in that manner.

Was this – he found himself paraphrasing – yet another sign?

He listened, silently absorbed, until invited to talk. Complying, he opened a button of his white linen shirt and dictated his conditions.

"Well, what can I say? I'll help you: I know that I must. But when it's all over (and I have no way of telling how and when this will be), I'll leave you to your project, or whatever you have in mind. I'll board the vimana and leave. Where to I don't know, but I'll go away."

"Where the hell do you think you'll go?" retorted Pac, irked at the thought of having to part with a Star Pac that was still in the pipeline.

"Sorry, but that's none of your business: it's my condition. That's our agreement. If you accept, we'll have the opportunity to save our lives," said Samuel, craning his neck to glance at the nocturnal sky.

Pac knew this request was unacceptable but – rather than give vent to his mounting resistance –rubbed his chin and forced himself to remain calm and rational. He was thoroughly sickened at having to negotiate with a guy he'd brought here after saving him and who – instead of thanking him and expressing his gratitude – was speaking gibberish, dictating conditions. He behaved like a taxi driver towards a client to whom he'd agreed to give a lift even though he was off duty. When the taxi wasn't even his!

Samuel must have noticed Pac's irritation. The graceful, almost feminine way he settled into his chair and uncrossed his legs seemed to indicate a wish to be less peremptory.

"You're right," he said. "Maybe I'm being over-demanding. You mustn't think I'm ungrateful for what you did. On the contrary. So I'll fulfil your request."

Pac hushed his inner voices and listened more attentively.

"You yourself will look after the stone," said Samuel. "Which is... and will remain in your hands. This would all be meaningless without that stone which – my new and dear friend – will be your guarantee!"

"I accept! I'll be the custodian of the magic stone. But I reserve the right to request your assistance for the renaissance plan, and it will be your duty to take my requests into consideration". Democratic, concise, realistic. "Some more iced tea?"

"Yes please. Very kind of you."

It was also thanks to this speedy exchange that the agreement undersigned enabled them to move on to the next stage. Without wasting time, without waiting for a new dawn, Pac immediately opened all of his hard-copy and multimedia archives. What he was piling in front of them he called The Theory: years of labour, research, expert advice, nights spent piecing together technology, separated by centuries of progress, that had to be adapted and implemented; ufology theories, snippets of specialised literature, articles ranging from cutting-edge physics to paleo-SETI (Search for ExtraTerrestrial Intelligence). It should be noted that none of this implied adequate and unexceptionable expertise on his part. His life, his purpose: the Star Pac. All this now lay before Samuel, at his complete disposal.

And Samuel could not but remain enthralled: he threw himself onto these records like a lunatic diving off a bridge to which he was tied with a thin elastic band. Turning the pages, reading, muttering and nodding: rationing what he'd soon find irresistible, a mouth-watering pleasure of which he would partake to the last drop. Invested of such heavy responsibility, and certain that this would absorb the best part of his energy, he decided not to commit himself yet but to postpone any comments to the days to come. It wasn't until late at night that he finally closed the files.

While all around the darkness of the wood sounded its dirge, Samuel chose to focus on a single matter: his personal sensation on The End of Time.

"In my opinion," he said in a tired, rasping voice, "Armageddon will be the final battle between man and the descendants of Ben Elohim, born of the union between terrestrial females and the Watchers, angels who chose the most beautiful women as their wives, as quoted in Genesis and in the Book of Enoch. The battle for absolute supremacy. That will be man's last occasion to emancipate himself, to free himself of his yoke and become in every respect a citizen of the galaxy. I'm pretty sure that's how things will work out!"

Pac, who'd never considered this eventuality, was even more intrigued when Samuel continued, in a worried tone:

"The battle between the stock of the half-breed demi-gods and 'ordinary mortals', if I may use this term. "The former are hybrids, who unknowingly preserve a faint trace of their origins to this day. They're usually those who distinguish themselves from others, showing a marked inclination for possession, power, supremacy, and whose features don't resemble those of animals. Have you noticed that physiognomic traits often repeat themselves among people, and how many resemble animals? The latter are the common people, the 'others': the natural progeny of primitive workers obtained by genetically upgrading the ape-man already present on the planet, and accelerating his evolution. But this is another matter...", he concluded, while using two fingers to button up his shirt. The air had become quite fresh.

There was no time to delve further into that theory; even if there had been, Pac was still reluctant to give credit to this particular source. Especially when he referred to himself as the main actor in those events; the one officially in charge of that mysterious scientific civilising mission, which in his opinion had developed into a war between two factions stemming from a twist in the original project. This wasn't the right moment, and Pac had no wish to waste time with such egocentric gibberish, which he'd privately branded as some sort of high-flying Jerusalem syndrome. There was far more to think about, he told himself, preventing any further discussion: they would need all their energy – especially their mental energy.

Which is why, somewhat brusquely, he invited Samuel to go to his bedroom and get some sleep, to which Samuel complied after lifting his eyes to the sky for a last farewell. And to put an end to all the bullshit. Pac didn't actually say so, but hoped it was implicit.

Pale, engrossed in contemplation. In the season when gardens, redolent of herbs and flowers, serenaded the Spring; when the afternoons were embraced by the sun whose light was like peace descending from the sky.

When life was to be savoured with all one's senses, and the end was like some timorous creature begging for a morsel. Not a human being in sight, to distract you, to remind you that this was once the primeval Eden, abode of the righteous; the origin of time, of purity, of hope, in which all good things could and should be invented or discovered. The zero hour on the calendar of consciousness and comprehension: the time when – if ever gods existed – they were sources of light, arms outstretched: they were love. The ideal space in which modern man continued to presage his past – the forgotten experience, the founding principle, so complete and harmonious, whose renunciation, whose preclusion troubled the human soul, inducing wrath, battle, and ruin.

The beginning of the end? Of a cycle? The era in which the supposed Lords – in the flesh, and with their limits and emotions – trod with winged sandals on that very soil?

He who believed himself to be one of them was now approaching meditatively, his long-limbed body faltering, appearing and disappearing among the trees; his gaze unfocused, his expression fixed, glancing at sheets of paper full of scribbling that seemed to be causing him some concern. He walked barefoot on the grass, soundlessly, one hand trying to shield his eyes from the harsh sunlight. On close examination he could have stood a good chance of being selected for a TV commercials on a denture adhesive: he had the sort of face that, in front of a video camera, would exude confidence while biting an apple.

Pac watched Samuel's progress from a shady spot beneath his favourite cedar tree, asking himself who this man really was. And smiled at how those bare feet appeared crazed and unpredictable – perfectly appropriate, he mused.

"You know," said Samuel reaching the shade – using two fingers to open small gaps between the sweaty skin on his chest and the fabric of his cotton shirt; fingers moving, plucking, airing; lilac shirt, its long sleeves buttoned up – "these projects of yours are really fantastic! And the more I study them, the more I remember what should be done, and how. All this is extraordinary!", he said, nodding confidently, making Pac suspect there was more to come.

"However, we need to make some changes," he added, confirming Pac's impression of cautious optimism. Samuel nodded, stared at him for a while, then seemed to hesitate. He resumed what resembled the outcome of an admission test only after he'd settled on the grass alongside him, paying great attention to his movements, to his wound – still not perfectly healed – and finally sighing. As if that position made everything much easier: as if the view of the woods, the fresh air, and the pervasive fragrance of grass made it easier to think. Which might explain why he immediately turned over and lay down until his chin almost touched the ground.

As if he wanted to dive into that sea of green.

Pac didn't say a word: he was getting used to Samuel's eccentricities, and watched as he resumed what is conventionally considered an appropriate sitting position and turned towards him with a broad smile: so broad, he feared, that the skin – revealing the full array of those white (and artificial) teeth – might crack under the strain.

"This grass!" he said, "can you smell it? How delightful it is – dare I say sublime?"

Did he want to eat it? Pac wondered.

"We should be thankful for every vegetal manifestation of grass. Grass is life itself, so full of purpose and potential that it escapes the boundaries of its sadly banal definition," said Samuel, seemingly intent on starting a monologue; and even if a dialogue developed – as it obviously might – it would distract them from the papers he still held in his hand, whose content screamed to be revealed. Why, why?

"Couldn't we talk about something else? Do you mind?", asked Pac, searching Samuel's eyes – beautiful as they undoubtedly were – for a glimmer of coherence. He merely wished to listen, now his mind had freed itself of any apprehension. At that point all he wanted was a technical consultation as to whether the entire escape plan – the one and only plan – was feasible or not.

"You're right of course," said Samuel, his tone betraying a twinge of regret for a whole series of themes to which, he knew, he'd revert anyway. He gathered his papers, glanced around, and cleared his voice.

"It's too large," he said. "It should be smaller, suitable for only three or four people at the most. With just one stone that's the maximum electromagnetic capacity we can achieve... even if we adapt the various complementary devices you've planned."

He paused, to ensure that Pac had fully understood.

The energy issue was complicated, Samuel had certain theories on how to integrate various experimental production and stocking systems; they needed time and study, but they could discuss this later.

"Then there are tests to do," he resumed. "I'm sorry but

they must be done. I know it's risky but they're absolutely essential. We could use a chaff for the test run. I don't know if you're familiar with it: it's an air-force device that releases a cloud of reflecting material that swamps radar screens with multiple returns, creating a safety corridor. Is that clear? Good. Although in these papers, under the Vymaanika Shastra chapter, I found some very interesting details that I'd overlooked."

To Pac this felt like a thrashing. He knew there was no escaping what he'd heard, he couldn't hide and protect his face with his hands. He'd have to endure and accept: this is what had to be done to go ahead, to make progress in the real world. He confided in Samuel's training: he had no alternatives; and if what he claimed was of vital importance, then he must be heeded and enabled to operate. This was the difference between an idea and its implementation.

What stressed Pac was the passing of time: the way it had accelerated to an astonishing speed, especially since he'd come home, and despite Samuel getting to work immediately on the project he'd introduced him to. He sensed the urge to fine-tune their work on the Star Pac. They needed to get hold of certain materials, certain devices which only Samuel knew and was able to find. This joint-venture would have to become more effective. But not before discussing another matter: something he'd deliberately kept on the back burner, and which had come to him just like that, when it was anything but timely, and far from top priority.

"Let's talk about the devices you ordered," resumed Samuel. "Or rather, that I procured. They're all of fundamental importance... like the Elektron system that generates oxygen through the electrolysis of water, collects drainage, recycles fluids, condenses steam. It's a perfect system for the International Space Station, though it's obsolete. That system must be modified: I hope you have the tools we need. And then..."

"How did you do it?", interrupted Pac.

Samuel paused. Furrowing his brow he lifted his eyes from the papers, which he laid on his lap.

"How the hell did you do it?", repeated Pac, looking him straight in the eye. "You know what I'm talking about."

Samuel went quiet, turning his gaze elsewhere, his dentures chewing his lower lip.

The intensity of that wordless time span was such that only a sudden breeze, stirring the large leafy branches overhead, was able to restore the suspended supply of oxygen to his lungs.

Samuel's loquacity seemed to have suddenly vanished. Pity, because the question was inescapable. Finally they were making progress, but Pac knew that until they'd unravelled this matter he'd find it difficult to trust him (granted, the 'trust' ingredient was as abundant in his psyche as the percentage of real fruit was in packaged fruit juice). Above all, he needed to know who he was dealing with, and not only in terms of practical knowledge. If things ever worked out – which of course was what he hoped – he would find himself entrusting his fate in the hands of that man, the very same individual who was again bestowing flirtatious glances onto blades of grass; this aspect was the prerequisite for each phase of the development, assembly, and whatever else had to do with the vimana. This could wait, he caught himself thinking.

Reciprocal trust and transparency would be fundamental from a certain date onwards. And that date was now approaching.

"You have lots of things to tell me, haven't you, my dear moon-walking astronaut?", said Pac, rubbing in Samuel's lingering reticence.

Immobile, Samuel sat upright and silent, his gaze fixed on the vast carpet of vegetation, his mind on a circumstance which he knew he could no longer avoid.

How strange: he'd seemed so keen to involve him in his newly-found roots.

But suddenly, just as Samuel was about to take a deep breath, a loud jingling came to the rescue: an acute metallic sound recalling ancestral memories that instantly induced in Pac an accelerated, copious production of gastric juices and a whirl of highly evocative thoughts and images. Then, from a distance, a voice called out their names – somewhat hysterically, one might say – tearing at the silence once again with its grotesquely jarring tone.

It was Fernanda: from the house, she was letting them know that dinner was ready, and – more important, as far as she was concerned – that she was going home and wouldn't be back until the following morning. From the way she was abusing her vocal cords she was clearly in a hurry.

Pac nimbly bounced to his feet and extended a hand to help Samuel up.

"Don't worry," he said. "You'll answer me in due time."

Samuel smiled awkwardly, relieved that he'd managed to avoid a subject which he didn't feel ready to broach. But he had no choice.

"I've nothing to tell you, sorry," he replied, his tone bordering on the ironic, hoping that his reticence might earn him some extra time.

Which it did, but not as much as he'd hoped for.

At that time of day, dawn was becoming a faded memory. The morning light was growing stronger, and the sun no longer tickled the PV panels, but beat down resolutely.

The vivid, diaphanous colours of the woods: irregular acres of yellowing, twisted shrubs and foliage; the colours of shadows of the birds' breast-feathers; of the teeth of fox cubs; the shades of tree bark; the aged red of tiny ants, and the opaque orange of the larger ones; the yellow of petals, the milky white of pistils; and the fuzzy green stalks; the hazy, faded blue of the patches of sky that the eye could discern through the oscillating vault of interwoven branches. That day, an absent-minded wind had forgotten to pass by.

Somewhere in the midst of all that, an odd-looking, docile quadruped with thick brown pelt and a white patch on its muzzle – an immigrant mammal with a still-fresh entry stamp on its visa – was limping placidly around the uneven grounds, munching, snoozing, and causing a certain alarm among the local fauna, unaccustomed to foreigners. There was no trace around its neck, where its shaggy fur was of lighter colour and rougher texture, of rusty bells or jewellery pouches. Only a tether: somewhat frayed here and there, no tighter than necessary, and long enough for the creature to exercise its indisputable right to explore the surrounding habitat; to smell aromas infused with freedom; and to satisfy its quest for food (albeit of less than excellent flavour), for shade and relaxation; yet short enough to retrieve it without difficulty, untie it from the tree-trunk, and lead it back to the house – provided it hadn't chewed the rope and taken to the bushes, or perceived some analogy between the rope itself and an umbilical cord, with all the associated mammal symbolism.

Did yaks eat rope? Were they driven by such an urge for independence? This was hard to establish, considering the arduous and solitary natural environment they belonged to, and their tame nature.

Pac was enjoying the cool shade of the same cedar tree. That morning he was wearing his favourite t-shirt, the acid-green one from the most important rave party in history: an unrepeatable, experimental musical event – the most dazzling, best-organised and publicised happening of its kind. Dazzling in every sense: as was its queen, Music, with her decibel-encrusted crown; as were its lights, atmosphere, and all-pervasive energy. As were the graphics of his t-shirt: no celebrative writings, mottos or dates: just a medium-sized, fluorescent drawing, a family – father, mother, older son, younger daughter – holding hands, outlined in yellow, heads exploding; brains splattering in an unequivocal flight of red butterflies.

That rave party had been on 21 December 2012, and he'd missed it. Organised in the largest capital cities the world over, and in hundreds and hundreds of lesser towns, and transmitted online non-stop by a network created for the occasion, from midnight of the first eastern time-zone until midnight of the last western time-zone. All sponsored, of course. A spectacle to celebrate the end of a cycle, according to the Maya calendar; and to other presumed prophesies whose discussion would be pointless, as nothing had happened anyway. For Pac this had merely been the confirmation – if ever he needed one – of his far-sightedness, of the strength of his intuition, of his greatness: of his being one step ahead.

Of course nothing special could happen on that date –

even less so, anything definitive. Only the gullible could fall for this gibberish: dimwits skilfully manipulated by the usual mainstream media, disguised for the occasion as pseudo hipsters, conspiracy theorists, ufologists, etc. etc. The event had been out of this world, so unbelievably adrenaline-charged as to compel millions to dance and thrash about to the intense throbbing sound of the best DJs.

Alas, as we were saying, Pac had missed the fun. And so, instead of having the time of his life in the cave, with the sort of technology that would enable him to make the most of the event (and if Oscar hadn't woken up on that occasion – Pac thought – he must surely be dead, and he hadn't noticed); instead of staging that dancing burlesque and take the piss out of dupes of all kinds, he'd had to go on a business mission to Cambodia, to some remote village whose name he refused to recall, and trick some local chief – who was destabilising their differently prearranged psycho-socio-economic development plan – into signing something or other. The usual story. And Pac didn't even need to ask himself the reason for what was – in every respect – an admonishment, one of a series issued by his employers in their own language. There is no need to repeat the motifs. And though I may be digressing excessively, it must be noted that Pac – while awaiting Samuel's clarifications in a shady shelter surrounded by this vast and private natural Eden – was suffering from flash-backs of non-participation; of a physical and mental exclusion that his slightly faded, but still acid green t-shirt recalled: ah, the power of objects! This vague ill-humour of his was transforming the sugary remains of his breakfast – fruit milkshake and peach soya yogurt – into something whose flavour he hadn't quite determined, but which evoked the colour of the above-mentioned garment. Which is why you've heard this story. (Ed. note: that time in Cambodia, while the whole planet was bopping rhythmically – convinced that was a farewell party – the only explosion reported involved two farm labourers: an elderly woman and a young, pregnant girl, who'd stepped out of their furrow, so to speak, and had been blown to pieces by an American mine. Just for the record.)

But here was Samuel. Though his tall and slightly stooping figure was noticeable enough, and despite his oversize purple-striped Ralph Lauren shirt (buttoned at the cuffs to cover his wrists, thus closing out any air), Pac hadn't even registered his approach.

Samuel could only sit on the fresh grass next to Pac, lean his back against the rough tree trunk and sigh, focusing his glance on the same point, or a neighbouring one, in the endless space ahead of them.

No need for preambles: the matter had hunkered in the doghouse all night, waiting for this outing.

"I don't know," said Samuel, picking up the lead. "Maybe..."

"I once knew a man," Pac cut in, in a business-like

manner. "He could hypnotise anyone in a few seconds, as you do." He turned towards Samuel, noting that he'd obtained the hoped-for reaction. "He asked me round to dinner once, along with two girls. I can't tell you what he got up to after our dessert."

Pac glanced at the view of the valley ahead, part arid and part luxuriant, pausing briefly before resuming his speech.

"After that I never saw him again: I made sure I didn't. I thought that if he'd wanted to, on a whim, he could have done the same to me, and I didn't fancy that at all."

"Great story. Really," said Samuel. "But as I said, I'm not going to tell you anything."

"So it's not true that you don't know."

Samuel shook his head – a grimace creasing the clean-shaven skin of his face, still redolent of after-shave – preparing to build a wall of silence around himself.

Pac, however, was determined to get things straight. "If we're going into this together, if we are to live on the Star Pac side by side for an indefinite period, I need to know," he said in the resolute tone which he knew would do the trick. "Not to mention the office as Viceroy," he added, just loud enough to be heard.

Samuel gave a start: "You mean to say...", he stammered. But didn't finish his sentence.

"Or Councillor of the New Humanity," said Pac, deliberately hinting at a vast range of desirable appointments which he hoped would convince him not to abandon the planet once their mission was accomplished.

Samuel sighed, laughing between his dentures at such foolishness and stroking the blades of grass with his fingertips – he certainly had a thing about grass! – then took a deep breath and declared he was ready to give voice to his thoughts: amorphous states of mind that would become clearer, therapeutic, once expressed.

"I imagine you've heard about the Tower of Babel."

Pac nodded. "Both the Sumerian original and the Bible's version," he answered, wondering where Samuel was heading.

"In those days," said Samuel, his gaze lost in the distance, "man only knew one language. Common to all cities, villages, settlements," he continued, as if seeing in his mind's eye an epoch in which he'd been present. "Try to use your imagination... think: one language, few words, few, clear, basic concepts, to understand and explain life, nature, laws, the cosmos, our origins. Everything: *omniscientia*."

"I'm listening, but I don't get it," said Pac, preparing for what he knew would follow.

"You will," replied Samuel almost mockingly, suddenly shooting him a lively, wide-eyed glance that transcended anxiety. "One language, before it became confused and differentiated – as did the minds of those who would use it, of course. A word expresses a thought that materialises into action. Word, therefore, is a pillar of existence, of progress, of evolution itself. The Word."

Pac nodded rapidly, inviting Samuel to continue, and possibly not to digress.

"Who do you think taught that first language to those creatures, to the first civilisation, the new people? Along with other forms of knowledge, such as writing, astronomy, architecture, to mention but a few?"

"You?!", blurted Pac, in the tone of a mine crushed by ridicule, imploring that the pressure trigger be pulled so it may explode.

Instead, it was Samuel who burst into uproarious laughter, his hand over his mouth: laughter that echoed and dispersed across the surrounding fields. "I'm not saying that at all: don't even think about it! Though we could go into this further."

"Not now. More pistachios?", Pac enquired.

"Yes please."

"I'll speak in the plural," said Samuel, as if this lent authority to his words. "Let me tell you something: those who did this, those who taught man the arts, carefully impressed these data into a corner of his mind. To answer your question, that ancient etymology, the primordial language common to all human beings, is still there in its place, along with everything else. I just happen to have remembered – but don't ask me how, or why. And in the case of Kimley I dug up that language and verified what I suspected. Speaking to that man in simple terms, repeating them over and over as often as I believed necessary, I re-awoke – shall we say – that part, never eliminated or replaced, but rather 'overdubbed'; he was petrified, inhibited in the face of something which he himself recognised as ..."

"Divine?", whispered Pac, stroking his chin and wishing he had a beard.

"I prefer the term ancestral, primal. That part of man that preserves memories of his origins, of his starting point as a conscious being."

"So in theory this could work with anyone. Including me."

"I'd never do it. You can rest assured," said Samuel, patting his arm affectionately. But, apart from Pac's pronounced shudder at this contact – its potential implications more disturbing than the actual gesture – that wrinkled, well-manicured hand was clad in its buttoned-up cuff: and how could Pac forget what was underneath?

"It wouldn't work with me, anyway," he said. "First of all I don't belong to the believers' club."

Samuel smiled, seemingly amused by their conversation and their separate roles which he considered ridiculous.

"You really want to believe this is all about faith, don't you? When in fact the answer is in your genes, my profane friend...."

His high-pitched cackle sailed up to lose itself amid the branches overhead.

Pac didn't feel like embarking on an interminable sequence of objections, yet that conversation was taking a truly hilarious twist.

"Man was born a slave... this should be clear to you by now," said Samuel. "Genetic imprinting, image and likeness: that's what they were designed for. Only when man evolves by undergoing a mitochondrial DNA mutation – forsaking these beliefs in favour of a new spirituality, at once free and scientific – will he break free of this chain."

"You reckon?"

"Actually, I must confess I'm fairly pessimistic in this respect."

"That's why we must get away, before it's too late," said Pac, steering towards firmer grounds.

Overhead, a flock of birds traversed the sky in perfectly harmonious formation.

"We can't be sure whether what we've discussed will actually happen," said Samuel, skimming the blades of grass with the palm of his hand. "But I'll help you as long as I can. Then I'll be on my way."

Those last words, breathed softly, dampened any irony. The white-haired, blue-eyed gentleman at his side emitted disquieting vibes with exasperating ease. If one believed him. Pac scratched his temple and paused in his mastication. "And why would all this happen, according to your theory? I mean, confusing the languages and all the rest." He offered him more pistachios.

Samuel didn't know whether Pac's interest was genuine. But he knew that talking would do him good, so he decided to reply.

"It was a penance... or rather, a punishment. One of the many 'corrections' inflicted on man to ensure he trod the straight and narrow. Man was approaching awareness with unexpected speed. And we, the members of my group, were helping him in this. As part of our original project, as one of our aims. As I told you, when the two factions formed, with opposite interests, we became a rebel minority and disobeyed, continuing our work in secret: a sort of underground operation. We were discovered, and a harsh dispute over competencies ensued, which led to a war. Our work was destroyed and terrestrial labourers punished, as had already happened earlier because of the so-called original sin. The opposing faction, the victorious one, saw in man's evolution a serious threat to their immense power. This is a game that has also repeated itself among men throughout history, continuing to this very day: nothing other than a replica of the teachings imparted. Different cults and creeds were created to confuse, divide, oppress humanity and divert it from progress. What I remember is that not all our teachings were lost, not all of them perished. In the latter period, aware of the awful things that were about to happen, we managed to warn faithful individuals and groups of people, who passed down the secret of our teachings. It was these men, later known as the seers, who carried on our mission."

"Uhm..."

Samuel stopped talking. Yes, that would do. It was in their mutual interest to have a break, through for different reasons.

The ensuing silence was so magnificent, so fragile, barely ruffled by distant woodland melodies. Samuel allowed his words to sink in: words that stung Pac's pride while striking unwittingly receptive cords. Such as sharing, despite what he thought, a common destiny with his fellow beings.

Samuel was unexpectedly surprised and confused by what he had just said. He smiled to himself as if he'd finally located the irreplaceable button of a precious garment, once buried and now ready to be worn. Having grown aware of the importance of acknowledging these sketchy memories, he was now savouring the resulting lightness, the rewarding sensation of knowing and of being. He didn't want to discuss it, reluctant to share what he perceived as private, as unsuitable for others – especially with tastes unlike his own. He certainly had no intention of highlighting anachronistic or speciesist differences. Although – and of this he was increasingly convinced – there was some kind of difference, potential or expressed, whose nature, magnitude or quality eluded him.

And this is what sealed his reserve.

Immobile, he observed the valleys stretching as far as his

eye could see; stimulated by transient shivers induced by the fresh air; and savouring the thrill of on-going processes which, right then, he couldn't quite identify – and chose to render inoffensive. He could have wept from the vibrations he felt in his fingertips, and from the back of his neck straight to his forehead. What was going on? Could he accept it? And why was that dragonfly moving so erratically? Why did he feel like asking it how it viewed its existence? Was it full, insipid, happy, dull? And the breathing of the tree he was leaning against: was it the same as his? God, how he would have liked to embrace it that very moment; to turn around and embrace it, tightly. Yes, to weep. But not with this one beside him. He couldn't, he couldn't, he couldn't...

For Pac, the man was clearly mad, though possibly not a threat to society. Any psychiatry student would unhesitatingly prescribe massive doses of psychoactive drugs, just to keep him quiet. Of course, Pac was prepared to consider the neurological and psychological effects of a comatose trauma; to accept as amusing and intriguing this conjecture (though he'd rather call it delusion) on the language of our origins. And he didn't even mind the implicit idea of an initial human brotherhood, bonded by idiomatic adhesive as well as by geographic adjacency. This 'theory' had caught his fancy, transporting him into another, more mysterious and inspiring reality. He had no intention of heeding it, however: no way was he going to accept it. And the more he thought about it, the more he told himself he was convinced of its unacceptability. The more he was sure of this, the more he worried, asking himself all along whether it was right to rule out – without appeal – an absurd yet coherent hypothesis. After all, he himself was strenuously critical of so-called revealed truths and of all those social control institutions that had gagged the human brain since the dawn of time. One thing was to study unofficial truths: quite another was to declare oneself a direct witness and even a protagonist of events.

The point is that an open mind can be fooled by plausibility: a critical sense heightens a can-be/can-do attitude to the extreme. This extreme contains an alarming element which, if carefully sifted, can reveal itself as credible, and therefore threatening: this is the history of rational progress.

After an adequate pause, Pac turned to look Samuel in the eye: what he saw was a distinguished, elderly person, in need of support; a competent partner thanks to whom, he conceded, his escape and renaissance plan would benefit from an unpredicted acceleration (was this a sign of the times?); and, last but not least, the second-in-command on the Star Pac whom, Pac told himself, merited respectful indulgence.

This last reason prompted him to receive Samuel's explanation with diplomacy.

"I don't believe you," he said, placing his hand on

Samuel's bony shoulder (while making a mental note of a question that sooner or later he'd have to ask him). "I think neurology still has a lot to explain regarding near-death experiences. However, as far as I'm concerned you're perfectly entitled to believe what you like. I have no intention of interfering."

The hint of a smile on Samuel's face enhanced his impressive assortment of differently-angled, stylishly-worn wrinkles. Somehow Pac's opinion comforted him: he enjoyed such consistent dissidence.

"You think you're a divinity punished by your peers in bygone times?", Pac asked him. "Good. Feel free, you're only accountable to yourself. You say you're a god? Bravo. So long as you don't expect me to grovel at your feet, to say you're right and make a fuss of you – or, worse still, to kill in your name – we should get on. Don't you think?", he concluded, giving Samuel's shoulder a firmer shake, at which the latter broke into an amused smile.

"Rest easy, my friend. I'll never demand anything of the sort: neither of you nor, even less so, of the people to be."

At that mention of the new people, of the new, soon-to-be-founded post-apocalyptic civilisation, Pac started in surprise at such explicitly converging intentions.

"That's my boy," he said. "But should you be right, I mean, should it be true, and should you remember one day, and have supreme faculties... well, don't forget your friends."

Samuel chuckled. "If I'm here it's because of you, in some ways. In fact, in more ways than you think. At this point, therefore, I can happily declare that I'm grateful to be here. Alive."

"And where might your colleagues be, right now?", Pac asked him abruptly.

Samuel's features displayed distinct muscular activities that signal the passage from relaxed to muddled to embarrassed. His casual "I wouldn't know," accompanied by a slight shrug, sounded vaguely insulting – Samuel realised – and before Pac could pursue him further he came up with a more articulate response. "I could reply that the owner of a factory rarely walks with the workers."

"Interesting jargon: old-fashioned trade union. Do you feel that's you?"

"But it is true, in a sense."

"So they're up there, somewhere."

"Maybe. Or down here. Don't think I know more than you do. Mine are mere sensations."

"You want me to believe that during your space missions you saw nothing? That NASA – whatever they might say to the public – are in the dark?"

Samuel knew he had little to hide in this sense. And why should he, after all?

"All I know is there's a lot of traffic up there – and elsewhere. That's an indisputable fact. Anyone who's seriously investigating these themes will confirm what you and I have already learned from our own studies. As far as my missions are concerned, they're top secret. But I'm unable to make any connections with my story, if we can call it that."

"You mean they threw you out or, worse still, allowed you to leave the Space Agency in exchange for your submissive silence?" Cool nail-spitting bastards, thought Pac.

Samuel exhaled noisily. Somewhat agitated, frowning, his gaze alert, he started to unbutton his shirt-sleeves, his slender fingers struggling with a particularly troublesome buttonhole. "OK, my dear friend: if what you want is this, let's get a few things straight. Point one: I wasn't thrown out... I left of my own accord or, to be precise, I resigned. Point two: I threatened to divulge certain information and documents in my possession: I'm talking about material that is indisputable, and very difficult to cover up. Point three: of course I got them to pay me, and how! You've no idea how much they profited from my services, over the years, and not only in financial terms: do you think they give a fuck about money, those dickheads?! No, we're talking about something different, goddammit, something entirely different!"

He really is fired up! – thought Pac, bending backwards to avoid being struck by Samuel's arms, whose ample and jerky gesticulating underscored his words with uncharacteristic ardour, his expression stubborn, his voice a little too loud.

"I made them pay me, and well! Leaving indemnity, maximum pension, bonus and extra bonus! Which is why I can afford to go around doing nothing. Do you think I'm still working for them? Is that what you think, that I'm a fucking spy?"

Cool it Pac, don't react, don't say a word, don't move a muscle... breathe. He'll calm down in a moment – hopefully.

"Point four: this is none of your business, you understand? You have no right to ask questions. There are rules and protocols of confidentiality, discipline, respect. That's how one keeps things from falling apart. You don't know, you can't imagine...", continued Samuel patting himself on the head and staring wild-eyed at Pac.

"I keep quiet, I don't say a word... one doesn't. And they leave me in peace. I have everything I need. That's our agreement. And no, I won't let you get me killed. Because they do that, you know? You know, don't you? Directly or indirectly." His tone became deflated, his voice now issued in a whisper, at a shorter distance from Pac's ear. "Yes, they can't do anything... except kill me. Do you see now?"

What could he say? Pac had little to retort. Acting half regretful, half consoled, he simply let that rant blow over.

Until Samuel said: "Any tortoises around here?"

"Tortoises?"

"Yes. It's been ages since I last saw one," he added. "Do

you know what a tortoise represents, in Chinese symbolism?"

"No. And I don't care to know, either."

It was time to restore the balance, to get things in their proper perspective again. Pac became serious, switching his artillery fire towards his main target. There were many unresolved questions, variables that might jeopardise the whole enterprise, and they'd have to be dealt with. "Do you think we'll have any problems once we're out in space?" he asked, nodding at the clear sky.

"Let's concentrate on getting there first," replied Samuel, retrieving the sheets of paper he'd had on his arrival. "I came to tell you that there are some problems."

"More problems?", blurted Pac. "Solvable?"

"I hope so."

"Such as?" Finally they were getting down to practical matters.

"As I told you, the spaceship is too large. We can only make room for three, possibly four people, plus food. I'm sorry, but your list will be unnecessary."

Pac banged his head against the tree trunk. "Fuck!", he murmured, banging hard. That slight pain was nothing compared to what he'd just been told. All that work, the selections, contacts; years of evaluations, the joy of discovering brilliant, capable people: hotbeds of hope, veritable assets for humanity. It was a real pity, he had to admit.

But they'd manage, somehow or other. "Go on."

"We won't be able to orbit the planet for very long. I can't predict how long, but we'll have to get back quickly. What worries me are primary cosmic rays, and I don't even know how efficient our screening will be. In addition, I'm not sure how to activate the stone, or control its energy," he said. "Speaking of which, are we sure that..."

"Don't worry, it's in safe hands."

And it really was. The clause in the agreement establishing that he would keep it himself in a secret place had been applied to the letter. For security reasons. If it really was so precious for Samuel, and until it had proved to be equally precious for him, he needed some guarantee. He certainly couldn't run any risks.

"Last point, I'm hungry," said Samuel, opening his arms wide and stretching nimbly, emitting an almost animal-like sound. On this they would find an agreement, at any hour of day or night, and Pac could not but agree, relieved to hear that the bad news was over.

Yet the matter of the crew was hard to swallow, and he couldn't help brood over it a little longer. He knew that Samuel was right: vimanas had widely been described as small vehicles. It was also true that the chances for a successful outcome of this plan were inversely proportionate to the number of people involved; despite this, his precious notebook was suddenly useless. Time wasted collecting uniquely qualified subjects: they'd all have to die. Too bad. He'd buy a multimedia encyclopaedia. They'd be able to take off faster. Someone, somewhere, would survive and take their place. Maybe. This, he thought, would be decided by the implacable laws of fate.

He was already agonising over the intolerable doom that awaited the whole animal population: a truly atrocious, merciless ill-fate for those innocent, impotent beings, mere victims of inhuman folly, whose suffering he had no way of alleviating. Damn it: Noah's ark my foot! As if being abused and devoured by humans; as if being subjected to pointless and cruel experiments weren't bad enough! How could anyone fail to recognise vivisection as the most evil and horrific concept ever produced by the human mind? Didn't this mind, along with the concrete, bloody and surgical ends on which it was bent, justify total destruction, extermination, annihilation? As did other unspeakable aberrations worthy of such an insensitive civilisation, destined to perish along with its futile purposes? Yet, adding insult to injury, these victims would die by those very hands.

Enough, better not think about it. He'd only upset himself, and what was the point? Better let that emotional surge subside.

As for his appetite, he agreed to go home and check out what the 'sweet', soon-to-be-sacked Fernanda had prepared. And had it turned out to be greasy, spicy food –

he swore to himself – he'd get rid of her once and for all: she'd be out on her arse, without a salary, even if it meant learning to cook himself. Even if he had to become acquainted with every delivery boy in the nearest village.

So he got to his feet and walked across grounds where, at that time of day, one could still be warmed and tanned by the sunlight; and disappeared among the trees to the tune of his interior *Radio75* soundtrack, whose signal became more and more persuasive as his approaching terrestrial abode – two hundred and twenty-six square metres of net floor area, square rooms in rustic taste, revealed itself in finer detail: warm and protective, white, comfortable, and safe as a well-kept secret.

Samuel had lingered there with his own thoughts, of which he seemed to have his fair share. He'd leant against the tree trunk in that pool of shade, breathing in the fragrance of warm grass, imagining currents of photosynthesis, letting himself be lulled by that tranquillity, and hoping it might soothe the growing chaos in his dreadfully aching head.

He felt as if coming to after a collapse – another coma, forcefully sedated. Opening wide his eyes didn't help, even if he sometimes had to. Better to close them, take a step back, avoid adding other thoughts to those already milling around in his head. He knew what he should do: keep still, unwind, slowly, gently, and wait for the initial pain, the discomfort, to be replaced by soft oblivion. By the same enveloping silence that was gradually seeping into his mind, like water when it finds a narrow fissure in a rock: first trickling, then daring and pushing, pushing, digging, expanding, winning more space, micro-inching ahead, front line advancing, taking up position, softening, splitting. And destroying. This, he felt, was needed: to split and destroy, to break down the sediment that over time had encrusted his being, his thinking and understanding; to rethink and to challenge what he'd been told, and what he intimately knew not to be the only truth, the only version.

And something else was surfacing from deep down, from a murky darkness whose tangible presence he was just beginning to perceive. Something out of the ordinary had emerged and, cutting through the fog, had appeared as a notion, an experience: a snippet of conversation; a friend's affection; a gesture proffered, manifesting itself like an unexpressed idea, distinct and luminous. And so he knew, re-opening old text books, revising what used to be his reality – experienced and experimented – his mirrored daily life. And he wept, as if his tears were poison, drawn out and spewed: serum neutralised by an antidote.

He distinctly felt the vertigo of a statelessness, of an ill-defined melancholy, compensated by the presence of a material body, proof of earthly veracity; of lost generations of his being human.

Here was a thought, accompanying the punishment he'd

suffered. The phrase, that phrase pronounced while, with eyes closed, he was strapped on a table. "We instilled our imprinting on the earthling, on the new creature, and this made for wonderful progress. And now I suffer the involution of the Fall of Man, for ever. And I shall never be able to judge myself."

But was it true? Was this really happening? He felt his brow: it was burning. Was he really recalling a tragic past, resuscitating his authentic nature and personality, buried by a genetic detention ruled by the Council of the Wise for having defended the creatures, for having opposed their new plans for dominating and subjugating? Or was it as Pac suspected? Was he being led astray by his trauma, by the allure of revisionist theories, by the very project of an escape and of a vimana? Was he suffering from a delusory Astronaut Syndrome? And hadn't this fixation started since he'd left NASA? Schizophrenia? Should he worry? How else could he explain recent events? Was he a victim of his own fantasies, perhaps? Yes, his trauma had certainly triggered some changes: in his extrasensory capacities? In part of that ninety-percent unexpressed potential of our brain that science as yet ignores?

He should slow down, stop. Too many questions: like tiny, bothersome insects. With an irritable gesture, he tried to brush them off – knowing all too well that they'd merely circle around his head and close in again. But it did the trick. He moved away from the trunk of that majestic cedar tree, quickly removed his shirt and lay down, stretching as far as his limbs consented. Open, passive, his naked back prickled by the grass, his skin warmed by the sun; the sky was of a peaceful blue; the air, stirred by a light breeze, of an inebriating freshness. Among the branches overhead, important proclamations competed in birdsong, the most sublime form of communication. An extra grade of awareness, and even the conversations of insects could be intercepted, as they reverberated from every direction amidst the vegetation. And the leaves that stirred and teased and rustled among themselves.

What sublime peace!

True, the end would come, one way or another, and the only certainty was that this vegetal and animal life would remain, or return. All that he was savouring around him would return to a new life, would make itself heard once again – with or without him, and despite all of them. Such was the magic of this thing called life.

Enough with questions. Yes, at this point – he thought – it doesn't matter whether these sensations (what I persist in defining as memories), are true or not. One will collect one's thoughts, apply what one believes is feasible to the construction of the flying machine; and verify with tests. This way the project will go ahead. If it works, if the vimana takes off and leaves the atmosphere, the origin of all this information will be of little consequence. We'll judge by the result. But if it does work, if we succeed, I'll also know deep down that everything else is right, and finally (oh my God, I hardly dare think about it!) I'll be able to return up there. After all these endless sufferings, to be once again enveloped in intimate, unfathomable darkness, lit by a myriad shining stars and galaxies. Good God! To be floating, contemplating from within a dream: the dream of all dreams. No, I mustn't weep any more. To be in orbit, home at last, after my long journey down here. Different, aware, and fulfilled. To die with the stars. Buried in the Milky Way. Yes, to belong. This civilisation will soon perish for the umpteenth time. But we'll reach safety; the signs were evident, that weirdo Pac was right: the countdown had already begun.

Thus he listened to himself, convinced himself. Until the setting sun washed everything in a peach colour, as a signal to anyone on the look-out. A peach that gradually grew more mature, softer, liquidised. Then brown, darker, opaque; then black. That's when the night set free its swarms of excited midges.

Brief run-up, temporal leap, backward glance.

In the foregoing weeks (during which Samuel had acquired what one might describe as a splendid form, if one weren't negatively influenced by knowing his advanced age), the two had agreed to use Pac's house as their headquarters and mission control. In fact there was little to agree, as this was already home to all their documents, materials and devices. As well as a small and well-equipped semi-subterranean hangar where the family jewel was kept: an advanced prototype of the Star Pac, of whose existence Samuel had been kept in the dark.

He'd been granted free access to projects, sketches and simulations that seemed to have been stolen from the Space Agency to which Samuel had given his honoured service for many years, and was scarcely finding time for his morning meditation. At least, that's what he told Pac, when before dawn he ventured out, torch in hand, to light his way along a tree-lined lane that flanked a half dried-up stream. This he left to climb to the top of a promontory, where he sat and waited to salute the Sun. Pac didn't altogether believe Samuel's story, considering that, on his return, it took him some time to recover from something seemingly exhausting; that put him to a test which he clearly didn't intend to discuss. In any case, if those were really the effects of his saluting the Sun, Pac certainly wasn't interested in exchanging a greeting of his own.

The irrefutable fact was that Samuel was on the mend. As the weeks went by he was increasingly fit, and devoting all his energy to concluding the preliminary phases of the Vimana Project. Even before seeing the prototype – whose material existence he ignored – Samuel had realised that Pac's youthful ideas (though 'childish dreams' might be a more appropriate definition), manifested extreme ingenuity, applied consistently in his work. It was astonishing: those tests, those calculations could have been his own work. What they were doing in Pac's hands was a mystery. Which could only be explained with one word: theft.

But Pac – who'd been watching him, hands in pockets of jeans still a little tight in the waist, but which (oh joy!) he could finally button up and wear – had to be given credit for one great achievement: that of having adapted modern scientific knowledge to millenary texts. A mixture of an extraordinary calibre.

That evening – following Fernanda's somewhat abrupt dismissal – had been taken up with extensive discussions on theoretical aspects of the entire project, starting from signs of an imminent planetary, socio-economical, environmental, nuclear, and geo-magnetic collapse, whose principal but not exclusive responsibility could be attributed to the doings of so-called Human Civilisation. From agreeing in principle, Pac had moved on to discussing remedies which, given the limited choice, didn't take very long: so he proposed what he considered the one and only solution – viable, exclusive, and above all far-seeing: an escape, with the promise of a return.

While alternating evening theory and day-time practice, evangelisation and liturgy, four noble truths and an eightfold path, Samuel was beginning to suspect that their operative profile resembled that of one of those apocalyptic sects occasionally covered by the news, usually to report some abomination. And in a sense, he'd told himself (and one can see his point), that's the way it was. Wasn't the biblical overtone of this apocalyptic vigour, combined with the awakening of the divine in him, a touching communion of eastern and western – an extraordinary Kantian synthesis? Wasn't this another sign of the times, he'd consequently asked of a Pac satisfied with his first successful conversion?

Actually, Pac had refrained from voicing his doubts on the presence of the divine in his interlocutor; and had abstained from indicating, as a clue to the truth, Samuel's wrists: despite the heat, these were constantly covered by shirt-sleeves which – as he'd repeated on more than one occasion – Samuel could have dispensed with serenely. No-one around here would have minded; yet he'd obtained an embarrassed refusal from Samuel, motivated by aesthetic implications. Pac had seen these as heavily psychological (some on-going conflict, possibly?), and had looked forward to the effects on his partner of a none-too-spiritual manifestation, which he was soon to enjoy. The moment was here and now.

Because, although he didn't know it, this was the great day for Samuel. The perfect day to put aside the graphics and simulations that coloured the screens of various tablets and old laptops scattered around the ample living room, enlivening the ambience like kaleidoscopic floral arrangements: geometric creations that seemed to be conversing, bouncing – when nobody watched – from one liquid crystal to the next, leaving behind them trails of intermittent pixels.

Fernanda wouldn't be back until the following day; it was a sunny morning, and through wide-open windows blew a warm, scented breeze that ruffled the long linen curtains. Few clouds, harmless and insignificant, were murmuring together on the edge of the horizon.

"Let's go," said Pac, wiping with two fingers some bagel crumbs that had stuck to the corners of his mouth and making for the small hall that led to the rear of the house.

Samuel didn't ask himself where they were going: he was still in that post-meditative phase where he seemingly took everything in his stride. Careful of each step, he dragged his long legs sideways down the stairs. As they went past the oak-panelled basement room which he'd visited only once, he asked himself why they should remain cooped up in that cramped and windowless space.

Then Pac halted. He lingered like an evolved cat before a mirror; then, placing himself in a corner of the room he started to feel the panelled wall with the palm of his hand, pressed one of the wooden panels at the height of his head, as if feeling its rough texture with delicate, discerning fingertips; once he'd reached a precise, invisible point he paused, hesitated a moment, then tapped forcefully on a spiral-shaped knot on the surface.

A metallic click, and the board opened slowly, like the

cover of an ancient manuscript, to reveal the secret it preserved: an advanced biometric-recognition device, of the type Samuel remembered seeing in some underground military bases. An ingenious safe, though a little too fancy, Samuel thought. But when he saw Pac move towards it with the tip of his left-side index finger, then with his whole head in order to have his retina scrutinised, he became suspicious.

This was nothing compared to what he felt when the whole wall in front of him emitted a juddering screech (like teeth drilled mechanically by a sadistic dentist), then another and another; or when he saw a gap on the right, opening, widening, and revealing more and more depth which, thanks to the immediate activation of an automatic lighting system, gave an idea of what lay hidden there: an underground bunker which, for size (around a hundred square metres, he estimated), equipment and particular collocation, would better be described as a hangar. Especially in view of what it housed.

On the thick walls of reinforced concrete were affixed wide metal shelves used as work counters, which ran around the room's entire perimeter, lending it a grey, aseptic appearance appropriate for any serious workshop.

Electronic equipment, machinery and tools were arranged in orderly rows, some hanging, others laid down hurriedly, still soiled, testifying constant use, hard work and a certain discipline; as did the pungent reek of soldering and grease.

In the centre, a large white sheet covered a mass that took up most of the floor space: something ceiling-high, which under that draped fabric resembled a monument, pending inauguration.

Pac turned around, seemingly impatient to see Samuel's reaction, and pleased to be able to show off his treasure: that small, well-hidden and protected world that would soon ensure his escape to safety. He descended the four marble steps that separated them from the unfinished floor, and advanced a few paces to welcome his guest, just as the last light went on, at the end of the room, contributing with its brightness to confer an unnatural, translucent luminosity refracted from every surface.

Samuel broke into prolonged helpless laughter, eyes moist, hands holding his sides. The spasm finally subsided; he stared around him at the hangar, while shaking his head and muttering indistinctly to himself.

"Congratulations," he said advancing, studying the most intriguing details. "Very ingenious work."

"Welcome to my workshop. You've no idea how long it took to get it properly equipped. But as you can see it's sufficiently operative," said Pac, hands enfolded behind him.

Samuel was enthralled: he felt as if he'd wandered into an amusement arcade, with unlimited credit for the slot machines. He seemed on the verge of breaking into a little dance; fortunately he refrained.

"What's underneath? May I see?", he asked, taking a half-step forward, then pausing in eager anticipation.

"A surprise for you. Uncover it!", replied Pac quietly. His arm gestured an invitation.

Needing no further encouragement, Samuel leapt forward, grabbed the hem of the large sheet, his eyes searching for Pac who – equally excited, but feigning indifference as usual – was observing him attentively from a corner, a tranquil smile denying his inner turmoil.

Having obtained the required go-ahead, Samuel tugged at the white fabric repeatedly and energetically until, with a thrill, he felt it pile up at his feet, felt its weight. As the unveiled object took form, its nature and detail revealed before his eyes, his expression changed, knitting his brows as if to counterbalance such euphoria.

And there it was: wondrous, imposing, ash-coloured. It reminded him of a fossilised shell; a special saucepan, tempered by dragonfire; a cosmic baked egg, its extremities flattened both ends. Here was God's throne; the burning beam; the chariot of the gods; the wind of the Lord; the celestial vessel. The avian arrow whose technology had been shot who-knew where or when, and had streaked across the Earth's civilisations to arrive at the present day.

The Star Pac, the vimana.

Rounded, shiny and smooth, it lay on an undercarriage set a few dozen centimetres above ground. Compact, solid, it appeared just as mystifying as it had done, millennia ago, to unenlightened eyes, incapable of establishing whether it would punish, abandon, incinerate, or accompany their fate. Its intrinsic, secret power made it alluring, exciting. Familiar in form but of unknown faculties.

With a single leap, Samuel traversed the sheet and slowly circled around the vimana, craning his neck to observe particularities higher up. It seemed like a joke, a simple, rounded, monochrome figure on a pedestal. But they both knew otherwise. Having studied the texts, posthumous illustrations, rough sketches, and all available data, they knew that what their eyes beheld was the faithful reproduction of a type of warfaring vimana; of the type that, centuries earlier, had taken part in airborne clashes and duels, deploying weapons that remain a mystery to this day.

The aircraft seemed to be able to house up to five people; to be fit for action at any moment, despite its lack of motors, lights, portholes, signal devices; an imposing, reflecting, metallised jewel in stand-by. The lines descending from its top traced regular segments that lent it a fairy-tale charm, like a large pumpkin transformed by the touch of a magic wand. Equally magic was the tangible aura surrounding that inert, crude form. Of what manoeuvers was that silhouette capable: what was its potential? Could it move through the air? Could it take off, glide, traverse the oceans, then stop and start up again?

Could it leave the atmosphere, reach those necessary eight kilometres per second, and return?

Would it have anything like the extraordinary air-flight faculties which ancient chronicles of different origins had narrated in such detail? Would it still inspire terror, like a divine punishment? More to the point: would it be noted?

An aura of intriguing awe surrounded that naked, alien-looking object: a suggestion of lost history captured the eye, evoking dreams and enforcing contemplation.

As usual, Pac fell under its spell and was pervaded with optimism, while Samuel stood immobile, upright, hands at his sides.

"So? What do you think of it?", asked Pac, eyes twinkling, fishing for compliments – proper compliments. He waited. After all, Samuel's reaction was only to be expected. Pac tried shaking him, but he continued to stare fixedly at the vimana, riveted. He seemed on the verge of grasping some enlightening insight, which he sensed but had yet to fully understand; his brow knitted, his eyes tense, his lips firmly closed – sullen. Pac moved alongside, closely studying his face (short hairs on the end of his nose). But Samuel remained immobile. Pac poked him with one finger, gave him a light push, but he was clearly elsewhere. Literally spirited away?

Pac huffed, sat on the floor. Stood up again, waited a little longer. Nothing. What should he do, try kicking him? Maybe his brain had closed down. He decided to leave him there, and went off to find something to eat. An hour later Samuel hadn't moved. Towards evening he found him sitting, cushioned on the pile of sheeting. Pac had a vision: a veritable metaphoric flash in which Samuel sat cross-legged – as if on a cloud – floating alongside a space clam; a vision immediately banished from the temple. Samuel was still staring at the same point on the space ship's grey surface, his parched lips half-open.

Moving a few steps closer, Pac noticed small tears streaming down a face wracked with pain. Not wishing to intrude, Pac left him there. He had other things to do.

When the following morning Pac went downstairs, he found Samuel sleeping on his side, his body partially enveloped in the white sheet; the lights were still on. This had to stop, it was time to wake him. He crouched down and shook him violently, twice, until eventually he managed to rouse him.

In the absence of windows or air-conditioning, the only relief from the accumulated heat was provided by two fans on opposite corners of the ceiling, which Pac immediately activated from a switch on the wall. With an uncertain hand, Samuel stroked his chin, and then struggled, groaning, to his feet, leaning on Pac's shoulder for support. He seemed tired, and decidedly stunned.

"You're a real party pooper, you know that?" said Pac, gathering up the sheeting. He was dragging it by one crumpled end towards the stairs in a corner of the hangar when Samuel grabbed him by the arm.

"No, wait. Please don't."

"I knew the Star Pac was beautiful, but not to this point," said Pac, his foot on the first step. "What came over you?"

"It was a shock, believe me, I was bowled over. I'm not sure I can describe it. Wow..." he said, gulping.

In his (unchallengeable) opinion, Samuel explained, the sight of the vimana had accelerated the surfacing of buried memories, forcing him to acknowledge – without a shadow of a doubt – the believability of those events, the truthfulness of this entire story. Touching that object, that symbolic relic, feeling its texture, had been the decisive step towards full awareness: substantiating reminiscences that continued to emerge, released from their hibernation; enabling him to re-embrace a long-lost part of himself.

"And what is it that you remember, exactly?" He might as well surrender, dive into that pile of fabric and make himself comfortable, thought Pac. A new episode of his friend's soap opera was about to begin.

"Everything: I remember my whole story, and not only mine. This is the best gift I could receive; the memories I'd been waiting for – centuries and centuries of oblivion, of repressed sensations, doubts removed, questions buried under conjectures, under historic conventions. The bonds are broken, the bars of my prison are melted... liquefied, powerless. I'm free, free! I remember, I'm aware of my knowledge, and of being what I merely suspected I was;

what I couldn't entirely accept, out of fear and false modesty. Freedom is magnificent: it's the will and the capacity to be powerful: you must learn, you too must acquire the ability. Everyone should. This is what you could be, what all of you could have experienced if I hadn't been overthrown, defeated, reduced to a minority by those who have subjected you, us, to these rules of existence, of hierarchic enslavement. Servants of masters manifest and magnanimous one moment, covert and sadistic the next. What a fate, my God..." He made to sit next to Pac, shaking his sweated head. "To what fate have we been subjected?", he growled, clutching his fists.

Pac conceded that he was affected by an odd form of embarrassment, an estrangement that didn't belong to him, diluted by sympathy: it wasn't like him, something was amiss. Yet he couldn't but agree with Samuel's statements. Though in different accents, they expressed his own impressions, what anyone might understand. But how could he accept these otherwordly delusions? Was Samuel really ill and, if so, was he, Pac, failing to take adequate measures? Was there a risk of his becoming dangerous, if he'd proceeded along what seemed to be a journey of no return? Should he intervene? And how? Worse still: could he sabotage his plan? The chronometer left no doubts: he couldn't afford to make mistakes. He certainly wasn't going to die because of that lunatic. And he wasn't a fucking nurse, Pac thought.

"And so? Go on, I'll give you another couple of minutes," he resumed, to see how far Samuel's delirious ramblings would go.

"So, yes. I'm the one...", Samuel replied, fixing on him a hard, impassive look. Those eyes, of an inebriating blue in which you could drown, seemed to want to penetrate his own. Steady, proud eyes. Pac couldn't help but notice the change. On closer inspection, they looked strange – inhuman. They glittered: not in the romantic sense, as would tears reflected in poignant sunlight; or as would a veneer of pathos on a snippet of venerable metaphysical apparition. Nothing like that. They shone, and there was nothing metaphoric or evocative in that. To put it bluntly, they emitted photons. Meaning real light: whitish, intermittently opaque, pulsing, like the weak beam of a lighthouse near a harbour in thick night-time fog.

Pac moved closer, intrigued and suspicious. The other man was still wearing an anachronistic smile: the sort you see in old photographs capturing vivid expressions of ecstatic joy, and inspiring admiration, or revulsion. He was undecided, Pac: totally incapable of expressing a sensible opinion. Samuel really was emitting light, he'd verified it; so much so that his irises disappeared, as if cloaked in a luminous expanding membrane that modified the contours of his eyeballs, dispersing on the tips of his eyelashes. It was a soft, suave luminosity; and Pac – despite himself – noticed how difficult it was not to appreciate it: to resist contemplating it as one does an unknown delicacy which – once savoured – gently urges one to take a second taste, then a third, compelled by its immediate effect. Temptation: the real thing.

Pac struggled to turn away, closing his eyes tightly before re-opening them to view the ceiling, the grey concrete walls. Feeling dizzy, he abruptly lowered his head, while screwing his eyes up as if to rid himself of a troublesome sensation that left him with a strange aftertaste.

Suddenly, Samuel also freed himself of that sensation; he batted his eyelids quickly, and in those instants of silence and readjustment they both felt the stinging sensation that a surreal phenomenon had taken place, having somehow escaped the boundaries of normality. And the retrieved ability to think, to discern the contours and subtleties of forms – along with an undeniable lightening of a part of their head, like the easing of pressure – did nothing but underline the difference between the two states: what they'd just experienced, and present realities. Further evidence of a certain embarrassment.

Pac only fully appreciated his return to normality when he was about to give voice to a comment (in that wonderful moment that follows a thought and precedes the vibration): some remark – to lighten the atmosphere – about Samuel's prodigious eye-drops. But his remark remained unspoken, as Samuel cut in to deliver another blow in a contest for which Pac was ill-prepared.

"Yes, I'm the one", he said calmly. Even benevolently, which made this all the more irritating. "The serpent, the leader of the rebels, the fallen vigilant, dismissed and demonised in order to gain unfair advantage. Depicted in legends as the epitome of evil, the one to be shunned. This is what I've unwittingly been subjected to. And my image as the bearer of light and knowledge, of self-determination, has been manipulated to promote a different version of right and wrong, of truth, of sin; this, you'll agree, has been more than effective in controlling the masses.

"I understand, Samuel, but..." Pac began.

"Yes, I'm the one," interrupted Samuel. Whom he might be addressing remained unclear.

"Should I cross myself?", asked Pac, somewhat concerned for his own safety.

As for his interlocutor, he now felt he understood his condition, and even found it amusing. Avoiding Samuel's gaze he addressed him, trying to turn the hands of the clock back to the present, and forcing himself not to make any comments. "Listen, Horus, as you know I have very little to do with religious matters. I concluded my investigations in that sphere some time ago. My conclusions were clear: evaluate the effects. Just to make this clear, my concerns focus on a constellation light-years closer than yours; which, in all honesty, my radio telescope indicates as a slowly-forming gaseous mass, so to speak. Dig my astronomic analogy? Not bad, eh? Good, and now let's look ahead...", he said, one arm outstretched to indicate the Star Pac. "You have your reasons, I have mine. Our new civilisation will be free, autonomous and progressive. And we'll establish it without expecting anyone to prostrate themselves at our feet. Is that clear?"

Finding it easier with his head averted, Pac waited for a response which he hoped would be as rational as possible.

"My dear boy, of course I agree. But you can't deny me some satisfaction, and I have no urge for revenge," said Samuel, his blue eyes still irradiating a fair amount of light. "Merely being here, lucid and present, reminiscing and conscious before this magnificent flying machine," pointing towards it, "gives me compensation, strength and conviction for all the work that lies ahead. And believe me, that's a lot."

"Strength and conviction," rant over, it seemed. But was he back to normal, or worse, wondered Pac. "Good. If you have powers, go ahead and use them," he said, restricting himself to a harmless hint. "But not against me. And next time, wear some fucking shades!"

Pac couldn't understand Samuel's freaky eye trick, and there were two or three other things he couldn't figure out, but he didn't care to know. There were plenty of weirdos in the world, and Samuel was probably one of them. Enough.

If anything, the words of that nutcase had inspired a hunch requiring urgent verification: if he remembered correctly, the awakening of the opponent, the symbolism of the serpent (incidentally, unless it was associated with the structure of DNA, why was the cute little reptile persecuted throughout history?); and the theme of resuscitated antagonisms, especially between good and evil, as respectively defined by convention: these were further indicators, stages in the inevitable countdown. Not that he intended to heed the ravings of a traumatised mind, of course. Yet such a sensitive matter merited further investigation.

He left the Enlightened to his business in the workshop, where the fans merely circulated the smell of stale air and sweat; there was a lot to do, in light of the tangible parameters he was faced with.

Pac ran to the door to consult St. John's Apocalyptic Chronometer, then stopped abruptly, returning rapidly on his tracks. He said, placing a hand on the shoulder of a startled Samuel: "Ermm... I almost forgot".

"Forgot what?"

"This thing is of coated plasterboard. A model, obviously. Of course you knew that, didn't you?"

As he raised his eyes to the craft, Samuel's lop-sided expression went through varying shades of disbelief, from cautious to flabbergasted.

"So you didn't know! In any case, all calculations must be perfect before dispatching orders to the steel works, as you know. Originally I'd considered a scale prototype," said Pac – observing Samuel's eyes and, above all, his body language.

Samuel leaned towards the disc-shaped vessel, whose skilfully-crafted translucent coating – be it polymer or glossy plaster – had somehow fooled him, he conceded. But of course, how stupid of him to be taken in... for a moment or so. Then he reached out cautiously, and with four fingertips skimmed its surface, polished yet wrinkled. And registered a feeling of shock, reverberating from between his ribs down to his stomach. He knocked on it twice with a clutched fist and put his ear against it, hearing the object respond in its own language: a dull sonic boom, which he listened to until he arrested its vibration.

"Of course I knew...", said Samuel at last, adjusting the tone of his voice. "I'd worked it out," he added with a smirk.

Brazenly lacking any credibility, and hugely amusing to Pac, who turned around to leave, looking decidedly smug.

"But don't confuse form with substance," Samuel tried to admonish, shouting after him when he'd already disappeared. "My reaction was induced by a symbol, a real image that coincided with a mental one that worked for me, unleashing dormant memories and awareness. Don't underestimate this process." He enunciated distinctly, self-assuredly. Yet an enigmatic expression of joy accompanied his every word, almost as if he was the first not to want to take himself too seriously; or the first to get a taste of some hoped-for revenge.

"Anyway, it's a fake!", Pac shouted back through the doorway, thereby closing the match in his favour, and left so they could get on with their respective business.

As far as his own was concerned – the aforementioned Apocalyptic Chronometer of St. John – online sources spewed out news to which average consumer-viewers had long since become immune, indifferent, impassive; on rare occasions they might be seized by the uncontrolled urge to lift a single eyebrow: presumably this was connected to some kind of reaction – something lost and forgotten which can't have been of any consequence. Remote-controlled drones bombard Iran. Israel ready to attack Syria and Lebanon (relax, no risk for old Pac!). Italy devastated by earthquake of magnitude 7; another hits Western America. Floods in Bangladesh, Burma, Vietnam and Laos. Wall Street closes with heavy losses. More power to Federal Reserve. Public demonstrations in China, Russia, Morocco and Australia. A coup d'état in a country in southern Africa; compulsory vaccinations; subcutaneous microchip implant gain popularity thanks to outstanding spokesperson. Etcetera.

"Pac, I was thinking...", Samuel mused, "we should start introducing iron supplements into our diet. When you're in space, your blood loses part of its red corpuscles, so there's a risk of becoming anaemic; there's the classic nausea, and all other aspects related to the absence of gravity. We'll have to sit down and make a detailed list of food, paying special attention to iron and to food combinations that will enable it to be properly assimilated."

"Aren't you sleepy?"

"Yes but... I thought this was important. Did you know that, when you're in a low orbit around the Earth, the Sun rises and sets every ninety minutes? That's a total of sixteen dawns a day."

"Oh for Chrissake! Go to bed, it's late."

"It's just that..."

"It's late!"

"Did I ever tell you that in one of my many previous lives I was a Druid?"

"You too? I thought I'd seen your face before."

"You mustn't make fun of me. If I say I was a Druid it means I was a Druid."

"All right, fine. Now let me sleep, or I won't let you into my room again."

"My room is too warm. So is yours. Aren't you hot?"

"No. Take your camp bed out into the garden. Or go lie down in the grass. Goodnight."

"Pac?"

"What is it now?"

"I love you."

"You're joking, aren't you?"

"No, really. I love you."
"Oh, bugger off."

The revelation of what was hitherto concealed (namely the vimana prototype, though undeniably there were other presences – ectoplasms and concepts – perceived exclusively by the psychic) had effects ranging from one to three, depending on how much relevance you might ascribe to them.

The first of these effects was weather-related, and consisted in the formation of a cloud-like patina insinuated between the sky and good humour: a film the colour of freshly mixed concrete, inducing accentuated perspiration and causing the atmospheric pressure to drop. And slowing everything down: from the speed of wild boars, to the voices of protest in the remote capital Beirut; and even to Pac's appetite, who'd lost another kilo but couldn't rejoice, owing to his abysmal rapport with weighing scales. This first category of effects may well be described as seemingly fortuitous. The second, more relevant effect, was the sudden acceleration of their work: almost as if, by unveiling the scale model, the two had suddenly envisaged their final objective, along with an awareness of the residual distance from its accomplishment.

Above all, they had to start afresh. In the light of the limitations identified, the urgent need to reinterpret the vimana's components had become apparent. The *Vimana*

Vitthu, the *Samarangana Sutradhara*, the *Vymaanika Shastra*, along with other Vedic texts, were consulted anew in order to find possible preparatory indications; to search for Rosetta Stones that could translate an ancient technique into contemporary and viable coordinates, that might supply the key to recompiling the long series of references to other works, to partial descriptions. Theoretical retro-engineering to be translated into words, concepts and technical solutions.

No big deal.

Finally persuaded to roll up his shirt-sleeves, Samuel claimed he could easily integrate the frequently mentioned mercury with stone. He highlighted how the use of this metal was introduced in a later epoch, when the construction of vimanas exceeded the number of stones available. Of inferior performance, according to Samuel, vimanas running on mercury vortex propulsion were destined for demigod rulers interfacing between the people and the gods, while the original vimanas adopted the stones as their far more formidable sources of energy. Considering the limited time and resources at their disposal, Samuel and Pac intended to create a hybrid system, but had yet to establish from whom it would be stolen.

Pac's interest was focused exclusively on testing the small stone's properties. He disregarded anything else, though he had to concede that to be dealing hands-on with the project's implementation enhanced his cerebral membrane's capacity to filter out, especially Samuel's ravings, which he now regarded as petty chit-chat.

He never asked himself whether this was induced by excitement or by a fear of failing.

While enthusiasm alone seemed to be driving Samuel, who claimed he could remember more and more through studying those texts, which he now consulted with different eyes. And the more he knew the more he applied his knowledge, and – conceded Pac – the more he resolved; through calculations and simulations, and fruitful solitary walks in the woods – from which he regularly returned with a special flower or medicinal herb which he introduced to Pac as he might some distant relation. With these flowers and herbs, not to mention with trees and shrubs of all sizes and shapes, and even with cicadas, crickets, lizards, dragonflies, praying mantises, ants and worms, Samuel discoursed quietly, with gentle tone and expression, and with the respect and attention of a guest in another's house. Lest we prolong this digression, we cannot say if any answers were forthcoming – except, apparently, in Samuel's head.

And so, in a brief, and increasingly cloudy period of time, the theoretical part was completed: Pac's studies were integrated, enough for them to wish to further precipitate the end of the world in order to exploit all the forecasts, graphics and other documents regularly saved in the file "Star Pac" in various hard disks and flash drives. In the evenings – the air being decidedly muggy – they would celebrate on the veranda with green tea sweetened with fructose. Conversing, smiling; their bared chests proud with exclusive optimisms; the crickets; the song and buzz of creatures whom Samuel lent an inattentive ear. The sky no longer inspired dreams, so they made do with the reality that they themselves were constructing.

However, strictly technical matters had forced them to review aspects initially considered indispensable.

First of all, as anticipated, the vessel's size would be only slightly larger than that of the coated plasterboard model: 3.40 metres in height; 6.50 metres in diameter. As already established, there was not enough space – including in the cargo hold – for a crew of more than three or four persons. And the hold itself had had to be down-sized: having made room for food, machinery and equipment, and everything that was needed to set an acceptable technological threshold for the inauguration of the new civilisation (fortunately they lived in an era when all knowledge from encyclopaedias and manuals could be stored in an external memory device, provided there was energy to power a computer), there was little space left for the Things of the Heart: an essential sample of that vast artistic expression that, over time, had produced paintings, artefacts, music, films, literary works and essays – a heritage from which anyone with enough sensitivity to call himself a personage would never have parted. Things of the

Heart, also intended as everyday objects, especially when their function was to dispatch duties or accelerate their execution. Of the Heart was also the irrational attachment to something lacking a practical function, such as a printed photograph, a toy, a scent, a knick-knack. Was scent mentioned? Uninteresting as this may be, Pac had gone to the trouble of stocking up with mosquito repellent, at least until its sell-by date. Things of the Heart, we were saying, to which innately subjective attachments developed in the course of a lifetime; possibly diminutive things.

What would you take with you, if you had to escape from the planet knowing that everything else might be destroyed?

Samuel was content with binoculars, and possibly a telescope. The ability to enlarge objects, to immerse himself in a magnified dimension, observing what the naked eye couldn't see: this was something he'd always found fascinating – and which would prove useful.

The rest, he said, would soon lose quality and meaning.

Unlike Pac who, from then on, was tormented by the very thought of making a selection and of having possible future regrets. He'd already had to renounce the creation of an ark to host all the Earth's animal species – which, he'd had to admit, was over-ambitious. And to give up mattresses, duvets and ice-makers. Not to mention chocolate: how long would it take to return to the production of something similar to the current bar of, say, milk-chocolate with hazelnuts? Or even without hazelnuts: just plain milk chocolate. Damn, even dark chocolate. How long? Or traditional Italian ice cream? Or frying oil? Nutella; and jam? And now hardcopy books, and most of his clothes; and the aforementioned crew, including one or more future Eve-queens, symptomless carriers of the feminine principle. With whom would he mate and reproduce? A silver birch? Why must he give up every pleasure, stimulus and entertainment that would have lightened an onerous task? Why must he part with everything he knew: habits, gastronomic delicacies, modern conveniences? Through the faults and evils of the few who were about to wipe out the resources of many? Through the planet's criminal and exploitative management on the part of self-appointed bureaucratic bodies, who proclaimed themselves its rulers by virtue of stolen and self-legitimised wealth? It was calculated default: the world was a fucking bankruptcy fraud! And to answer our question: no, he still hadn't decided which piece of Heart to take with him. Samuel was right: so few things were exempt from the natural decline of affection; and those few would be wiped out immediately: they weren't renewable, but they were fattening, perishable and, worse still, they'd perpetuate the memory of this epoch, of its folly. Better to move on and leave it all behind, when the time came.

Furthermore, it seemed that everything was now in Samuel's hands. He was the chief aerospace engineer, of course, but Pac still hadn't grown used to the breadth of his freedom. Until not so long ago, Pac had filled the leading role as sole creator of the planet's renaissance plan: the others had walk-on parts. While the reality that was taking shape stole his scene, reduced and influenced his wishes; and admittedly deflated his ego, when he compared himself with this self-proclaimed fallen deity, whose unchallenged capacities assumed a dominant role in the whole matter.

He had no choice but trust in Samuel: trust in his skills, which would prove themselves only on take-off, when their attempt to escape from destruction would mark an appreciable difference between life and death. Admittedly this wasn't much fun, but it was the price to pay to do things properly.

The evening was still cloudy and muggy. Samuel – barefoot, his light shirt unbuttoned – had never been so excited as in the last few days (rejuvenated, he liked to think). The voluptuous fragrance of wild flowers carried by a sporadic breeze mingled with the scent from a scattering of incense sticks. The whole living room behind their backs was illuminated, as was the veranda, where they were sitting at a small wicker table with a screen, on which – between glasses of lemonade garnished with mint – they were studying projected slides, colourful diagrams, lists and notes in block letters. Samuel was reeling off his technical notes, pointing here and there with a wrinkled but well-manicured finger. Sitting tête-à-tête, they conversed in undertones, their expressions apprehensive.

The Star Pac would be made of a special iron alloy with exact proportions of copper, mercury, aluminium, lithium, silicon and magnesium, lending the flying machine lightness, conductivity and resistance, as prescribed in ancient texts. The alloy, appropriately worked with methods that shan't be described (not for incompetence, but for reasons of confidentiality) would be enriched with sand of purified crystals, such as pink quartz, and forged in a single uniform mould; or alternatively consisting of two parts subsequently welded by a solid-state process much used in aerospace industry. Other pure crystals, supplied by Samuel, would coat the inner surface of the craft.

In the lower part of the dual convex lens-shaped disc, a system with three directional gyroscopes powered with liquid mercury (whose heavy protons would ensure a certain stability) would constitute the core of electromagnetic energy produced via the anti-gravitational effect of a rotating electromagnetic field, the form of which would be shaped by serpentine elements of decreasing size. According to the mechanics of gravitational vortexes, this would confer lightness to the craft. Beyond the power threshold, the inverter-generator system would lose momentum, producing more energy than in the ingress phase, and the effects of the ionised air would also create a kind of vacuum all around the vehicle.

"Also," continued Samuel with a self-important air, "I'm

considering a particular procedure I first heard about years ago, in Tibet. They know all about these things over there. Though perhaps I should say they *knew*, in the past," he said, assuming Pac understood what he was talking about. "It's a special method for insulating metals from the Earth's magnetic force, to lend them unique, extraordinary properties: their surface is tapped with special little hammers so that they emit sounds that are supposed to operate these transformations. Yes, quite so."

Wearing only orange boxer shorts, Pac had nodded at all this with the almost-bored expression that listening to what was tediously obvious induced; though, at the mention of this mechanism, Samuel had clearly noticed Pac crossing his fingers under the wicker table.

Their energy production and storage sources would be diversified and divided into primary, auxiliary, emergency, and imponderable categories. As well as the stone, whose power was yet to be proven – but which, Samuel assured, would guarantee a formidable performance in terms of accumulating, catalysing and multiplying the necessary electro-gravitational energy – they had lithium batteries; the battery of a truck (Pac had imposed this as an unchallengeable clause); a unipolar dynamo, evolved from Bruce de Palma's N-machine originally conceived by Nikola Tesla, which Samuel described as follows: "Instead of having a rotor and a stator, like conventional two-piece generators, the N-machine only has a rotor. Each half of the flywheel represents a pole: one electrical contact is put on the axle, another is placed on the outer edge of the gyroscope, and electricity is taken from the magnet itself. The system draws energy from the space around it: it's a generator in which electricity, once started, may then be sufficient to maintain itself even when resistance increases. This machine can continue to produce electricity after being unplugged from an external supply source, and has an output of five-hundred percent, i.e. it produces five times the energy it absorbs."

"Really..."

"Believe me," Samuel added at last, observing Pac's perplexed expression as he imagined the vindictive snicker of the Lord of Gravity who, from his throne at the centre of the Earth, yanked at an invisible thread in the sky, causing them to plunge free-fall into his presence to be suitably punished.

"Also," resumed Samuel, "this flying machine will be able to exploit the photovoltaic effect of its particular alloy, producing, while in orbit, renewable energy to integrate other sources: energy that will be stored in separate batteries," he said, indicating the brightly-coloured flow diagram, assuming Pac would find it reassuring. "Don't worry, my dear fellow; your partner here is just as concerned about his safety as you are!". Colliding clumsily against the table, he then invited Pac to move closer, as if to put him through a test, or to reveal a secret. He touched two or three keys on the touchscreen, momentarily threatened by spillage from mounting waves of lemonade in the juddering glasses. An energy diagram appeared: intricate, captivating, it was an unusual kaleidoscopic shape transmitting at once riveting complexity and harmonious simplicity.

An upside-down jellyfish, that's what Pac saw: an original version of a Rorschach test – which is what they called it from then on. The large head corresponded to the heart, which generated and distributed energy through tentacles joining up to form a dome, and through crystals, which in the diagram were represented as joints. Its affinity with a familiar figure somehow contributed to generate in Pac enough confidence to uplift him from the superstitious to the unsteadily fatalistic. Because, much as he tried to trust someone who claimed he knew far more than himself in that particular field (which wasn't saying much), the man's uncovered wrists were constantly before his eyes. Even when they weren't, they were etched in his mind, their stylised smiles hallooing, one a little more crooked and sinister than the other: that's how he saw them.

Samuel explained that those tentacles were, in a way, like catalysts, transformers – and something else that eluded Pac's comprehension. He couldn't really object to the jellyfish: he was out of his depth, and his ignorance made him all the more uneasy. The only thing he understood, he said, was that this wasn't the diagram of a normal electrical system, and that it would probably give his electrician a hard time.

Somehow, for Samuel, the craft was the actual diagram, every component and function, down to the last centimetre. The Star Pac would be energy in movement: a piloted star, an inhabited electron.

Pac refrained from mentioning that he hadn't fully understood this either: the recent succession of events had been so fast and so full of excitement that his inability to understand merely seemed to oil the wheels of time.

"And now, let's look at the devices," said Samuel, opening other files. "In addition to a suitably adapted Elektron system, we'll have oxygen tanks; lithium hydroxide cartridges to recycle the air inside the vimana and remove carbon dioxide; dosimeters to measure the intensity of cosmic radiation; tanks of drinking water; sheets of Nomex and Mylar for lining and insulating the inside of the space ship, and anything else we can protect. They're the only insulating materials on the market that can shield us from heat and cosmic radiation; and I think we should get ourselves some complete suits. As I've said over and over, we don't know how long we'll be in orbit, and I'm particularly concerned about cosmic radiation."

"I've always dreamed of dressing as an astronaut," said Pac, his tone suddenly romantic. "For fancy-dress parties my mother would dress me up as an eighteenth-century farmer," he said, gazing at the pitch darkness, lurking at a stone's throw all around and allowing neither form nor intention to filter – only intermittent signs of life.

"Sorry, I think you'll have to renounce that again. Department stores don't sell space suits. We don't need them, anyway: it's not as if we'll be going for walks in space. Also, they're uncomfortable and itch like crazy," replied Samuel with a cackle, his whole face crumpling. He loved his own jokes, which always put him in a good mood.

Taking a sip from his glass, Pac realised he was hungry.

"I'll find something through my providers," concluded Samuel, jotting down a note. "As for your dream, you'll have to content yourself with being an astronaut minus the regulation space suit."

"I'll make do with that…", said Pac. As he got to his feet to fetch some cashew nuts from the kitchen, he felt on his arm the gentle yet resolute touch of a restraining hand. He couldn't be sure, but he thought he'd perceived a sense of heat, a fleeting, circumscribed candent flush in the very place that Samuel's hand had merely brushed – like a warm cloth procuring a shiver of refined pleasure to his naked skin. But he might have been mistaken. Ignoring the sensation, he turned around, only to be faced by a suddenly serious Samuel, seemingly about to report some disaster.

"What's the matter?"

"I have something to tell you and I don't think you'll like it, knowing you. I deliberately kept this matter for last, though it's probably the most important", he said, his light-blue eyes impassive.

"Give me a second."

Pac ran off, soft spare tyre wobbling, and returned with an open can of salted cashew nuts.

"Tell me."

"It's to do with trust, with the stone, with the actual operation of the vimana, and therefore with the successful outcome of our programme... with our survival, in fact. It can't wait any longer." Samuel's words merely succeeded in increasing the irritation of Pac, whose palate was relishing the contrast of bitter, sweet and savoury flavours, rapidly diluted by copious salivation.

"Listen carefully," proceeded Samuel, while gesturing a refusal to partake in this feast. "The stone doesn't activate itself: there's no switch. It needs a particular kind of energy to work – a sort of essential, complementary element. A force that has more to do with spirituality than with physics."

"I haven't the faintest idea what you're talking about. Sure you don't want some?", replied Pac, proffering the cashew nuts again.

"I'm talking about *Laghima Siddhi*, one of the eight psychic skills: supernatural powers obtained by practicing specific mystical disciplines, in certain mental conditions."

"Is that why you spend so much time meditating lately? Watch out or I'll finish these..."

"Yes, it's a personal matter. What you need to know is that, without these faculties, there would be no levitation, the stone's full potential wouldn't be exploited, and the whole thing would be less feasible. This is the vimana's paranormal side, if you like. Indissoluble and unfathomable, without one of its halves... the overall view necessary to transcend the dualistic, phenomenal reality of nature as we know it."

"OK, got it. Come to the point: do you have this faculty?"

"It's not so simple, you know. As I was saying, it's not as if there were a switch, On or Off: often the in-between phases are more effective, crucial."

"And so? Yes or no?"

"I see you've understood."

"I was talking about the nuts. Only six-hundred and three calories per hundred grams."

"Ok, give me one."

"Only one? Are you afraid of putting on weight? Here, help yourself".

"I don't want them. I said one!"

"Shut up and eat. Relax. I'll tell you what: give me a brief summary of what this is about. Then tell me where I come into it: because that's where you're getting, isn't it?"

"Precisely. Bravo! So: we're talking about a principle that, through time, has been given a number of names: the sacred fire of the Zoroastrians; the blazing torch of Apollo;

the flame on Pan's altar; Pluto's fiery helmet; Mercury's caduceus; the sidereal light of the Rosicrucian Order; and many more. Over the millennia, all these concepts have become symbols, removed from the original concept and protected by esotericism. Its meaning can be traced to the sacred vibration OM, the Omnipresent Word: that manageable universal force constituting a magnetic grid of vibrating waves interweaving to form universes."

"And so..."

"This power is latent in every being: if awoken and adequately developed, if synchronised for perfect resonance with the Cosmic Wave, it enables us to come into magnetic relation with the living nature of matter, breaking free from the space-time bonds of physical laws. This is the sacred flame, this is the power, the vehicle I was talking about. The ability to change frequency and use one's psychic powers – to make a long story short."

"More lemonade?"

"Thank you. Without that, the stone is ineffective."

"Again... what's all this got to do with me? Why should I worry? Whether I believe you or not, what difference does it make?"

"A big difference, my friend. I can't ask you to help me: even if you wanted to, you couldn't. And it wouldn't make sense to introduce you to disciplines you don't believe in."

"And so?"

"What I'm saying is, don't interfere. Have a supportive

attitude, or at least neutral. But not hostile. I'm talking about your thoughts."

"I should avoid negative thinking, is that what you mean?"

"Exactly. You've no idea what influence adverse thinking can have on a certain process, idea, or mere wish. It's the old story of opposites, of contrary forces: creative awareness versus sceptical conviction. Although you might think this foolish – and all the more if you do – what I'm asking isn't that you believe, or pretend to believe, but just that you keep a neutral attitude; control your mind and prevent it from expressing thoughts against that which I will strive to achieve. Which I assure you won't be easy."

"Sounds reasonable enough. Nothing surprises me anymore. Have the last one? Go on, I'm feeling generous."

"In particular, try to refrain from unplugging the power supply during take-off, for example."

"That sounds even more reasonable. Listen, you know what I think: you're free to believe and to do whatever you like, as long as you get us out of here. I'll be as good as gold, believe me. And you have my word that I'll keep my thoughts in check. Nothing could be easier."

"I'm glad you think so. Have you ever tried?"

"To keep my head in check? Sure."

"Ok. Do it now."

"What?"

"If it's so easy for you, try for five minutes. What's the

problem?"

A challenge, how exciting! Samuel couldn't possibly know about Pac's bygone training in Rangoon jail, about Ashin's advice, about the willpower he himself could deploy.

It must have been a pleasure to see Pac close his eye and keep quiet for a few seconds. The ceiling lamp overhead illuminated the vestiges of his hair. An Indian psychologist had once explained to him that the cause of his hyperactivity could be traced to his mother's conduct. Like many Western mothers, she'd wasted no time getting back into what conventional canons consider an acceptable shape. Immediately after giving birth she'd started taking plenty of outdoor exercise – jogging, in particular – and involving her new-born baby, suitably strapped to her chest so that he faced outwards, towards the new world. For an infant, this was tantamount to being chained to the first car of a train running at full speed, facing windward. Not to mention a typical daily routine of going to shopping centres, taking strolls and so on. Her hyperactivity was inevitably transmitted to the child, whose nervous system, overstimulated from a tender age, was already sketching the traits of his future personality – and his choices. This, the psychologist had claimed, explained many other things. What things, she hadn't said.

The fact is that, even before we reached the end of this short anecdote, Samuel had caught Pac off guard, twice.

"You did it!", he said, pointing to him accusingly.

"Did what?"

"You thought."

"But it was only..."

"Only?"

"OK, go to hell," said Pac with an incinerating glare, before giving it another try.

Silence.

"There you go again!"

"It's not true! No. You can't read my non-thoughts."

"You reckon?"

Pac hesitated, but soon capitulated in the face of something that was... what? Anything but evidence. For some obscure reason he was unable to lie or circumvent: he couldn't use the insolence, the shamelessness that formed the base of his character.

"Go to hell, again," he murmured, finishing his lemonade.

"Listen, please. You must practice," said Samuel, getting to his feet. "Unless you want to hurtle into a void."

From this perspective, and in view of the usual tendency of plausibility to gnaw at even the most ingrained scepticism, Pac accepted. After all, it wouldn't do him any harm. On the contrary, keeping silent could have its attraction.

He certainly didn't make any major changes to his rigid daily routine. He merely designated this as a morning exercise, scheduled between visiting the yak (who still had a slight limp), and letting him out of his pen to graze as far as his tether allowed; until sunset, when he'd retrieve him before wishing him goodnight.

Samuel genuinely appreciated Pac's occasional disappearances. At heart he was convinced that their chances of success would now soar, given the sort of kick in the backside that only a constructive turnaround could minister.

Fernanda was in a particularly bad mood: it showed in her jerky movements; in the belligerent expression etched on her pudgy, flaccid features; in the way she rubbed her hands on her grimy extra-large but amply filled knee-length apron. And in her cold fury with the fresh green beans, which she was decapitating on the chopping board with a meat cleaver.

It was now evening, a time unconcerned with people's troubles: these were the daytime's lot. Evenings were designed for other things, but at that precise moment Fernanda seemed unaffected by rotational dynamics, almost as if she were conspiring with the stars to opt out of the game, preserving her biorhythm for something better. After the green beans she attacked the carrots, whose lymph-bleeding remains now floated in a common saucepan among vegetables of inferior classes, while wondering why.

Fernanda glanced at the plastic watch on her wrist then

quickly double-checked with the clock on the kitchen wall, and her huffing and puffing clearly indicated that what she'd seen – twice – was not to her liking.

Samuel was busy in the hangar, but Fernanda reckoned that he was lazing around under some tree, distant enough not to disprove her theory.

Pac took great care not to mention their project – not even in passing. She must be kept in the dark, and anyway she wasn't on the list – although, as we know, the latter had ceased to exist. She mustn't know: full stop.

But clearly she did know. Something: details gleaned from all-too-easy intuitions.

Throughout Fernanda's time in his service, Pac had considered the possibility that she might suspect those anonymous parcels – delivered by unlikely-looking couriers – of being indicative of some shady activity; of some scheme – certainly illegal, but not necessarily immoral – which her employer wanted to keep to himself.

As curiosity, women's in particular, was a wild beast that needed occasional concessions, Pac had proffered a tempting morsel: an innovative patent commissioned by a government agency. He hoped that the mere mention of such a client (deliberately vague, ambiguity lending extra flexibility) would have the matter wrapped and sealed. And it was entirely consistent with his real cover as a consultant for a large multinational.

Of course, one might easily object that the word 'cover'

was inappropriate, as Pac did in fact work as a consultant (though with other means and purposes); also, inappropriate because his client, indeed a multinational, had long been playing musical chairs in institutions that some still insisted on calling Sovereign States, an obsolete and meaningless term except for the usual brainless masses – who'd soon be wiped out.

Anyway, the trick seemed to have worked, but this was a long time ago, before the events of our story took place.

But going back to the present, Fernanda was preparing dinner with unusual energy; Pac was watching the world news, to check where the arms of the Countdown clock were pointing (they seemed to be turning at a worryingly accelerated pace); and Samuel was struggling to solve a particularly challenging problem: how to be sure (as sure as possible, under the circumstances) of returning into the atmosphere without burning to a frazzle, or smashing to the ground. Yes, the Star Pac would be energy in movement, but the craft's energy level would mark the boundaries of their survival, like musk sprayed in an overcrowded maturation chamber. The forthcoming test-run would be the ideal occasion to verify the matter. Data in his possession proved that the vimana had all the characteristics to qualify as disposable. This was making him dread that, at the end of it all, the craft might not manage to leave that god-forsaken planet and sail towards more fortunate, far-away shores; furthermore, it risked compromising their lives even before the successful conclusion of their space mission. The thermal insulation material was, in fact, of good quality; yet he could safely say, based on his experience, that no Martini on the rocks or mint-flavoured ice lolly would do much to alleviate the dreadful heat they'd suffer in there.

He'd been working on it for days, but until that moment he'd concluded nothing much, apart from grunting raucously, or lapsing into sullen silences fuelled by puzzled concern. Which is why he, too, was feeling irritable and touchy, and why Pac had let him stew in his own juice. Apart from the morning when Samuel had blurted that the house was complicating matters ever further. Not the house itself, Samuel had specified, but its location, which was totally off-axis, according to the principles of Feng Shui and of geomagnetic ley lines, not to mention knots.

"Knots?", Pac had asked, before realising that his question would lend wind to Samuel's sails.

"Of course, my dear fellow, the knots forming the Earth's energy grid," Samuel had explained testily, as if growing tired of having to teach him everything. "Those are the Earth's most powerful energy points, the vortexes of cosmic connection."

Pac had tried, unsuccessfully, to make an escape.

"Imagine a telephone booth, of the kind still occasionally found in small villages. Think of the possibilities it offers to communicate with someone at the other end of the world. Think about it."

Listening to that anachronistic example, imparted as one would to a twelve-year-old, Pac had been tempted to drop his trousers and extinguish that evil, that maddening source of irritation with a potent jet of urine. And he would have done, gladly, if they hadn't needed someone wise and sensible around the house, and it had to be him. What a grand fellow he was, he congratulated himself.

"I'm dreadfully sorry about this inconvenience, Samuel," Pac had said as evenly as he could manage, "but Stonehenge would have drawn too much attention; I couldn't obtain the necessary authorisations for Giza; and Bron-Yr-Aur was teaming with pilgrims. Other sites, such as Angkor Wat, posed serious logistics problems. My only remaining option was this modest plot of farmland." And this had as conclusive an effect as that of particles of matter and antimatter chancing to meet in the same night club.

A sombre sky blew on the embers of irritation. All day, a fresh wind had been heralding platoons of menacing clouds that rumbled in the distance, boding no good, projecting dark, grey shadows; and hinting, with increasing insistence, that the next few hours would witness the whirling and thrashing of a violent storm; a bittersweet prelude, a-flutter with forebodings of inevitable damages to be accepted with perverse stoicism.

The yak had remained in his bed in the den, and Pac was

wondering whether he might be frightened, and what to do about it. Had the young bovine ever been exposed to thunder and lightning, to strong winds and all the rest? Did such storms ever occur in the giddy altitudes of his native country?

He'd absent-mindedly left his doubts on the back burner, having decided that it would be cool to leave all the windows open (all of them, including the large French window opening onto the garden), when Fernanda had communicated – or rather, had shouted – her unchallengeable decision to lend her services for a half-day only, offering no justification: the very absence of an explanation seemingly being her underlying motif for this announcement. And Pac had found himself faced with a provocation, an unconscious plea to be dismissed – or a more challenging strategy – he really wasn't interested. So much so that when Fernanda left, banging the door – and crushing so horribly her moped's shock-absorbers that those of the pick-up in the garage winced sympathetically – when this had happened, smiles had spread all around; the lights had gone on, and the clouds amassed overhead had observed her tortuous progress, discussing the opportunity to try out their new electrical aiming aid.

Pac peeled off his shorts and t-shirt, and stretched out on the sofa. There wasn't much he could do that night, apart from hoping not to receive any last-minute assignments from his employers. He wanted to stay right there: to lounge on his sofa, in his own home, breathing in the silence and minding his own business. Pac smiled, thinking how lucky he was; knowing that he needn't even remotely dream of leaving his job – important as this was in the grand scheme of things: this would simply be a natural consequence of events that would unfold, he was sure, according to his general plan. When the right time came, he would cast off his moorings, starting from his job, and sail away. What was left to do now, quickly and resolutely, even if it meant burning his residual forces, was lay the table.

Fernanda hadn't done it: may Thor incinerate her for this!

Samuel shuffled in slowly, looking shattered. He greeted Pac with a grimace reflecting a partly-absent/about-to-return state of mind, reached the kitchen table and sat down. Meanwhile the wind had subsided almost entirely, and through the windows filtered the sweetish scent of soil that precedes rain. An odour that Pac didn't notice, as his nostrils – and all his other senses – were already otherwise engaged.

"Isn't it rather hot?" asked Samuel.

"A little."

"Why don't you wait? You'll ruin your stomach."

"What..."

"I'm going to let mine cool down."

"Look, I'm going to help myself to some more. You'd

better get a move on."

"It's good. It's really good this time."

"Last time it tasted of rust. I can't imagine what the hell she puts in her soups: they're either disgusting, or superb."

"Well, this time we're lucky."

"Bah... she's lucky she's still got a job. By the way, have you made any headway with that problem, my friend?"

"Still up in the air. I have to check out a few ideas, but I know they're weak. If only I had the right tools!"

"Would you like to pop over to Florida, tomorrow? I'll take you to NASA's outlet. We might find what we're looking for."

"Very funny. Hey! Don't overdo it: that's your third helping."

"Relax, it's only vegetable soup: I can have as much as I like. And it's better than biting you in the calf. You were saying?"

"Forget it. I need to work on it, at leisure. Maybe after dinner. Don't ask me anything, please! Until I'm ready. I'm already overloaded. For Heaven's sake, leave me alone at least when I'm eating!"

"All right, all right. Don't get excited."

"Everyone's always grilling me, asking me questions, there are numberless vital details to think about: you've no idea. And I'm always cooped up in there, working."

"OK. I'm the only one who's asking any questions, so don't make such a big thing of it, please."

"At least when I'm eating."

"Calm down, point taken. It's all right. Enjoy your fucking soup! Would you like some more?"

"No, thanks, I'm full."

"So much the better. Go on, get back downstairs, we have work to do."

Once the food had been polished off, Pac stacked the dishes in the sink for Fernanda while Samuel, arms folded, made for the open French window.

The lights in the garden illuminated a large square of lawn, and he remained immobile, as if undecided whether to venture into the conventionally designated 'outdoors'. He took one look, seeing nothing but clouds, a flash of lightning in the distance, an eerie silence. He turned towards Pac, illuminated in turn by the light of the refrigerator, inside which he was peering. On feeling himself observed, Pac closed the fridge with studied nonchalance, as if its handle and his hand had come into contact by chance, irrespective of his innocent intentions, while on his way to quite another place.

Samuel looked outside again. There was something in the air that night, and it wasn't just the impending rain. A heightened tranquillity, an unnatural immobility. He scratched his bare foot where Sister Mosquito had supped, and was about to turn his back on the wood when a sudden gust of wind put him back a step, ruffling into life a long wisp of his white hair, making him squeeze his eyes half-shut, breathe in deeply and exhale noisily. The tree-tops were tossed by an unusually chill wind that lifted eddies of dust and leaves, pollen and aromas, invading the living room and demolishing the concept of outdoors. Its force whipped over the pages of a magazine on the floor; a window banged shut. There was a blinding bolt of lightning; a fluttering of papers; curtains billowing in the icy breeze; the table-cloth fluttered; a vase was knocked over, the Tunisian pottery smashing loudly to the floor. A loud crash of thunder seemed to crack the window panes; leaves and dust grazed the naked skin; shivers of a furious poltergeist, seeking revenge for not being invited to the wake. Disorienting, the wind howled, blowing dust in their eyes, in their face. Samuel was smiling, amused. Thunder approached, at first dull and faint, then rumbling, before exploding violently.

"Should we close the windows?" shouted Pac to Samuel, who was still grinning fixedly, immobile.

"I got it."

"Then let's get moving!", he said, half-naked body shivering, nipples erect, as he started shutting the windows against the blast. First the small kitchen window, then the large folding French window whose tall wooden-framed glass panels drew the confines of reciprocal jurisdictions.

"I got it," repeated Samuel, hands deep in his trouser pockets, staring at Pac fixedly, his hair mobile and dishevelled. A dried leaf blew against his chest, tilted and slid to the floor, only to be wafted elsewhere.

In that old man, and in a drop of rain the size of a radish crashing to the floor nearby, Pac perceived a clear threat to his mental and physical balance. Being unable to contrast the elements, however, he pushed Samuel out of the way; postponed hurling abuse at him, and proceeded with closing the windows, while the same sentence, "I got it," issued again from Samuel, still getting in his way. Meanwhile the storm raged – more outside than indoors – with thunder and lightning, rain pelting down, temperature alternating between chilly and mild; and their bodies cold and damp on one side only. Pac couldn't understand why Samuel kept on smiling; and the less he understood, and the more he got soaked, the more he was pissed off. "What the fuck is it that you got?" he asked mutely. Water was coming in. To hell with it, he decided, first of all he must know. He turned his back on the downpour – a defiant gesture in which, for a moment, he saw something of the heroic – and addressed a limp and stock-still Samuel, to give him a piece of his mind. He searched the sunken face for an answer that – in theory – shouldn't need a question, or take up so much time. Drops of rain tapped on his bare shoulders as if to draw attention, provoking, inviting him to play. He ignored them. And the more he ignored them, the more he realised he should close the shutters; and not having done so – shit, water was pouring in! – his fury was mounting above danger level.

More thunder erupted overhead: everything shook.

"If you don't tell me what it is that you got I'll kick your balls in! I promise you," he said, so close to those light-blue eyes that he was virtually breaking in and bashing them.

Samuel's smile faded, an arched lock of wet hair, glued to his flushed forehead, leaving a bald patch uncovered.

"I got it. I know how to get round our problem, at last!" he said in a half tone, his gaze unwavering.

"How?", asked Pac, rain dripping from his shoulders to his feet.

"Yes, how?", asked Kimley.

Kimley?!

The two had hardly had time to sense something in the air, or to recognise that off-stage voice, than they had an M9 handgun pointing towards their heads. Suddenly the infernal metallic shriek of an airborne blender broke out, while from a corner of the sky it traced a narrow curve: like a die-hard bluebottle, growing bolder rather than intimidated by the storm. It landed on the lawn's dishevelled grass, while a stronger gust of wind shifted its trajectory. Then from its interior emerged two other figures, and started running in all directions. More lightning, and pouring rain: and a black-eyed armed man, his gun pointing at Samuel; Kimley's smile. A bewildered Pac being shoved along; a crash; a laser sighting tool; a voice in an incomprehensible language, shouting something; a gust of wind. Kimley replying with a gesture, weapon firmly in hand; more thunder, diminished. The noise of a door being forced open; a voice, now in English, the words unintelligible. The French window finally closed, shutting out the storm; the black helicopter immobile; the living room invaded, taken by force.

In a last burst of audacity, Pac –face to the wall – whispered something while his wrists were being tied behind his back: "Borrowing the power of..." but was prevented from finishing by a sharp blow delivered to the back of his head with the butt of Kimley's gun, which made him buckle over; this called for the intervention of strong-armed volunteers, who calmly dragged him away along the floor.

"Time for a snooze, fatso" were the last faint words he heard, followed by something which his muddled head was unable to distinguish from the rain's incessant pelting on the roof and windows.

Shit, my head. What the fuck... Kimley, that son of a bitch... Ouch, shit, that hurts. Calm down, think. Don't open your eyes, that's the most important thing. I must think, work things out. Go on Pac, concentrate, keep still. Let them think you're still unconscious, play for time. Breathe slowly. How the hell did he find me? Should have been impossible for anyone: this is my hide-away, and I'm in no telephone directory, land register or tax database. They'll pay for this, I'll show them... Hold it, concentrate. No point asking yourself how he got here: the point is, he's here now. But why, what the fuck does he want from me, an honest citizen? The stone, obviously. Jesus, it hurts! What an idiot I was to go to Samuel's rescue. Should have left him to rot in Nepal, changed my number and found someone else... look what happened! Ok, stop digressing. Kimley's here. He wants the stone: is that all, or is it revenge he's after? Maybe he's touchy, how the hell do I know? Wasn't he a religious fanatic? Aren't they supposed to forgive and forget? Why all the drama? Cool it, Pac, you'll pull out of this alive and kicking, as usual. I won't be intimidated by a couple of ignorant mountain goats. Not me. And the yak? Is he ok? Sure he is, he's in his shelter, poor pet.

What can I do? If only I could rub my head. They've tied me to a chair, and tightly: shit, I can't feel my fingers. Yes I can, I can move them – slowly, they mustn't notice. Great. I'll have an enormous bump on my head. Bastards, I'll kill you all: you've no idea what kind of shit is about to go down. I swear I'll destroy you. This is outrageous, offensive, disgusting. How dare they? What law, what principle entitles them to trample on my rights, my dignity as a human being?

Ok now: resolute, determined, lucid. I'm sitting on a wooden chair. It could be one of mine. Not a sound: if I'm at home it's stopped raining. Yes, the air is fresh. I recognise this smell, this should be home. Strange it's so quiet: am I alone? No, that's impossible, absurd. Although... Shit, my head!

Hold on, I hear steps. Coming this way? Keep still, hold your breath.

He's turned away, but... that was my fridge: whoever it was has just closed it. Shit, I should know! I recognise the sound it makes when it closes, the glass bottles rattling. So I'm at home.

Need confirmation, must open my eyes. Only one, just a fraction: there. Yes, I'm at home. Christ, that's good news! Everything will be ok, I know it will. It's night time, I'm in the living room: there's the sofa in front of me. With two bastards sleeping on it: on my sofa! You'll pay for this. What sort of people are they? All dressed in black from head to foot, like undertakers... No, more like Indians being trendy, Western style – except they're twenty years out of date. Boots, combat trousers, sweater... all black. A uniform? To recognise one another in a crowd, perhaps. But no, dickheads always stand out: they don't need weird outfits. They're both young, dark-skinned, thirty at the most, clean-shaven, casual-chic. These guys are wearing a uniform, they've been recruited... even in what they aren't wearing, they're too alike for it to be a coincidence. Shit, in hospital Kimley had talked in the plural; an organisation, a brotherhood or something: that's it. That explains those two.

Right, here we go. One of them is moving, but... no, it can't be possible... he's nicked a can of iced tea from my fridge: I'd better close my eye. You... you miserable scumbag, you come to my house and steal, you nick iced tea from my fridge, that's my fucking can! Oh, you've no idea what you did: your tiny brain can't begin to understand what a crime you've committed. You'll pay for this, my revenge will be ferocious, you son of a bitch. You don't steal in other people's houses; didn't that slut of a mother teach you anything? You're finished, finished, all of you.

And Samuel? Oh fuck: Samuel. Where is he? I can't re-open my eye, too risky. Shit, I don't know what to think of him. Whether to feel sorry for him – is he a poor, needy lunatic, a lonely, unhappy old man? – or whether there's some truth in his ravings. Well, he has competence – even skill, I have to say. And on the whole he's a good person: he deserves respect. That I can't deny. Is he alive? Well, if I'm alive, he must be too. Where have they put him? Have they tied him up? Have they hurt him? No, how could they hurt such a kind, frail old gentleman? Knowing they'd shot him in the past, what's more. No. And why hadn't he used his primeval language to stop them all? Stupid of me to even think of that. I'll ask him as soon as I see him: take the mickey to distract myself. It'd do me good. So would a sip of iced tea – my throat's dry – a sip of *my* iced tea. Oh, you'll pay for this....

So my head fucking hurts. Must concentrate. They were lucky, just because I didn't manage to complete my sentence, my activation. But now, just you wait till I get going. Determination, here I come. "Borrowing the Power of the Sun... the Deadly Sun Attack!" Yes, it's me, here I am, here's my strength: I can do anything, here and now, I have no limits! There's my objective, I can see it, I can hear it clearly: I'll get there, victorious, unharmed, awesome – as ever. Not an obstacle in my way: target in focus. Here I go, I'm ready, I'm mighty, I'm fearless. I know no fear. Bring it on, now! You're in deep shit. I'll tear you to pieces, I'll...

Perfect. I can breathe: take a deep breath.

Open my eyes.

From the kitchen behind him came a smell that was too familiar to be real: it couldn't be. And a sound like a classic symphony: something stir-fried, simmering. The fragrance of a sauce.

When Pac opened his eyes, they glowed almost as much as Samuel's had on that particular occasion; but his own could easily incinerate, disintegrate or liquidize – he thought.

First he saw the two on the sofa – coarse expressions, ape-like movements – passing the can of iced tea back and forth. They didn't notice him.

To his left, the garden with the helicopter: it had stopped raining; on the window panes, a disorderly spattering of droplets raced down friction-less vertical tracks to the bottom, leaving future marks that would have to be cleaned.

Turning his neck with extreme caution, measured effort and unspeakable suffocated pain, he saw to his right a third thug in funereal attire, intent on leafing through one of his glossy soft-porn magazines. Though absorbed, he occasionally shot quick, furtive glances to the kitchen and to the sofa, bypassing Pac, before re-immersing himself in his cultural pastime; at his feet lay all Pac's books, manuals, magazines and leaflets from the now-empty, meaningless bookcase: an assembly of wooden planks forming rectangles, thickness and dusty depths.

From his chair, Pac perceived the top of that heap of paper, half-hidden by the sofa and table, and discerned its height and meaning. Mountains didn't bring him luck, he decided: another reason why his ideal habitat was tropical.

He was sorry, briefly, that he hadn't been noticed, given that he could be none other than the centre of attention, however benevolent or malevolent that might be. And that fragrance, behind his back: a simmering mixture of garlic, onion, celery and carrot; a pinch of salt; the unmistakable aroma of olive oil. Any moment now they would add canned tomatoes, the right amount of herbs and spices – all of this pilfered from his larder. Ah! There was *Radio75*'s

Masked Speaker, broadcasting official bulletins (all punctually ignored), and announcing a playlist of supercool artists, of slick evergreen rockers... before the intruder was grabbed, squeezed and devastated by a supreme fisted hand materialising out of nowhere (no use struggling), its clothes torn to shreds, its cape in tatters. Then the assault: the radio station bludgeoned to smithereens by the Brain Liberation Brigade, letting all hell loose inside Pac's skull and transmitting – yes! – a stream of uncorked effervescent emotions. How long had he dreamed of such an ally intervention? Too long! A cathartic *Fuck You*, for domestic use only. A moment's bliss, then back to reality: he was tied.

Kimley appeared. Pac was gratified by the frowning attention reserved to him, while the two men on the sofa jumped to their feet and the third dropped the magazine, his gesture implying disgust for such materialistic propaganda; the three nodded martially to Kimley, who didn't bother to acknowledge them while scanning the room approvingly.

He was clearly the boss, but of what? And what where his exclusive faculties? No point discoursing on the colour of his outfit; suffice it to note his chunky gold ring and bracelet, imposing physique, deliberately slow gait, hair greased and back-combed, jutting chest and straight backbone: all indicative of his walking onto the stage of what he seemingly considered his favourite scene. The script demanded that Kimley stop in front of Pac; stood still

– arms akimbo to emphasise his role – and held him in a withering stare, while counting up to ten without batting an eyelid. And that's exactly what he did. Pac was inevitably cheered by his antagonist's pathetic and predictable behaviour. To the emotional charge that was assailing him he responded with the hint of a sophisticated, enigmatic transcendental smile, while inwardly revving up his engine.

Then a thought assaulted him, followed by a tingling sensation that he managed to disguise while holding on to his chair: he was still in his boxer shorts, the close-fitting compression sanitary underwear he wore to enhance his battle against the unsightly effects of a surplus of calories. He clamped his jaw: he certainly wasn't going to let this embarrass him – though at that moment he'd gladly have avoided comparisons and differences, and the aforementioned tingling sensation associated with his increased vulnerability. Behind his back resounded pots and lids, and the fan of the ventilation hood going full blast.

With the three thugs lined up behind their boss like bowling pins on a track, Pac couldn't but symbolise the ball that would knock down all three of them in one go: strike! That was the only possible outcome. And he found himself swallowing as slowly as possible.

Kimley began pacing wordlessly to and fro along a horizontal line of barely two metres, hands now locked behind his back, chewing the inside of his cheeks, licking his upper teeth, seemingly engrossed in some complicated speculation. To and fro.

Pac couldn't help but remember, for the umpteenth time, the breakfast bills he'd footed in Kathmandu and Pokhara for this guy, while the latter impersonated the smiling, needy tourist guide – so much for faith in one's fellow beings! He watched Kimley stop, while his three underlings returned to the comfort of the sofa.

No-one broke the ice with introductions, presentations, formalities, etiquette, bon ton. What had happened to good old-fashioned manners, Pac wondered, fuelling his war machine. At a certain point he thought he was in for a boring, endless questioning which he really didn't fancy. But the blow, sudden, sharp and mean, that hit him full on, obliterated his thinking capacities and almost knocked him unconscious: almost being the operative word.

It was only the cord securing him to the chair that kept him from crashing miserably to the floor. The pain arrived a fraction later, preceded by the vision of a blinding flash of lightning; followed by minor stars, and by a piercing buzz that penetrated his brain, imposing a pervading dizziness, before subsiding to give place to a hot numbing of his face. This was quickly followed by a cruel, pulsing ache, impeding his ability to breathe.

Kimley was touchy and, characteristically, vindictive.

He had his back to Pac and was massaging his hand, when he turned around suddenly and lashed out again, straight to the jaw. Pac, still dazed from the first blow, felt himself thrown in the opposite direction to the dull and too-evocative sound of crushed bone, or tooth, while he witnessed the birth of a supernova on the side of the impact. Unable to investigate, he felt liquid escape from his now half-open mouth. Saliva, blood. Blood which, now he'd recovered an upright posture, he tried to swallow, to hide from their sight, though this proved more complicated and painful that he'd hoped.

It was some time since he'd last been beaten: he'd forgotten how damned painful it was. His cheeks started to throb; his whole head was humming loudly; he held his head up as best he could – which wasn't much; very little air in his lungs; heart pounding in his throat. But that was fine, that was how it should be. Indeed, he could take more: or were they already tired? His physical pain was like chlorophyll in the sunlight: it was the fireball that was about to hit them. Soon they would be begging for mercy before the gun that would waste them, in the garden; before he dragged them into the wood, still conscious, to feed ravenous beasts; right up their street, wasn't it? Come on then, have your fun while it lasts, miserable bastards!

His gun, the one in the trapdoor in the kitchen. After he'd freed his wrists and found a suitable pretext. That was his plan. It was all clear, that was how it would have to end.

"Hey, chief. Spaghetti or rigatoni?", boomed a voice behind them.

Leaning half a buttock on the armchair next to the sofa,

Kimley had exchanged vacuous glances with his mates in a communication that, judging by their expressions, had been fruitful.

"Spaghetti."

What the fuck was this? Why did they speak English when they had an unintelligible idiom all to themselves? And why were they cooking? Wait, but of course! Psychological torture: that must be it. He'd have to make sure he didn't fall for it, he had to keep his cool. But were they really so clever, these grave diggers? To tell the truth – thought Pac, swallowing more foul-tasting blood – he should no longer be surprised. Kimley had turned out to be a chameleon, skilfully taking the piss from the very start: ergo, Pac should expect, and be prepared for, anything. This added an unforeseen variable to the whole matter; how capable were they, the sods? They were far too sure of themselves to be beginners; too well-organised to reach Lebanon from Nepal; and well-funded. So? The way they disoriented him, the way they provoked him with their implicit knowledge of his weak points; their knowledge of English. Shit.

"Chief. Some wine? Red or white?"

"Both. Open everything."

Educated people, resumed Pac, investing part of his energies in pretending he hadn't heard; telling himself there was no problem: he'd buy more of everything; he'd eat, drink, crap and piss on their graves. Educated people, feigning ignorance to avoid attention. Part of what Kimley had told him was true. Alternating truth and well-disguised lies: confusing yet reassuring. For a long, bone-chilling moment, Pac nourished the unspeakable suspicion that this presumed brotherhood could be a viscid, burning tentacle of the monster that controlled the agency he himself worked for: the tentacle of which he was but a miniscule sucker. Colleagues, distant relations? No, impossible.

"I know everything," said Kimley, breaking the silence with his botched-laryngectomy voice.

Heirs of the nobility removed by the Maoist movement? Was this why they had it in so much for those people? Nobility, hierarchy, absolute Hinduist monarchy, divinity, religion, fanaticism, orthodoxy, xenophobia. Interesting plausibility, Pac convened, but how could he use it in his favour?

He hadn't even heard the words uttered by Kimley, who was forced to repeat them, much to his annoyance.

"I know everything."

Pac said nothing.

"I care little about your work: your life is insignificant."

Silence.

"Did you really think you'd get off so lightly? You naïve fool. Not a leaf stirs in our country without leaving a trace. And where there are traces, there you'll find us."

"Who's "we"?" mumbled Pac, making the pain seem even worse than it actually was, which was awful enough.

"Aren't we all on the same side?"

Kimley rose slowly, shaking his head. Snorting, he suddenly leaped closer, responding with another punch aimed at Pac's abdomen: a light, precise blow, which paralysed his breathing, turning his lungs to stone. Turning purple, Pac slumped forward, stunned: no air was penetrating, he couldn't breathe: he knew this wouldn't last, but in those panic-filled seconds he feared he'd never be able to breathe again despite his desperate efforts; a tear rolled down his cheek; he felt himself waver.

"You're not the one that's asking the questions. Learn to save your breath."

Air seemed to begin to filter into his lungs again. Rather too slowly, damn it.

"Hey chief. *Al dente*?"

"No, well done. And drain it well. I don't like it watery."

Pac took hold of himself: he wouldn't allow them an inch of satisfaction. He'd force himself to recover, banishing all weakness, swallowing more blood, repressing any lament. And while his air intake was gradually re-established, he realised that it was raining again, lightly: a soft pitter-patter in the depth of the night.

"Where's the stone?", asked Kimley, his voice growing bored and impatient – and boding no good. And that exceedingly arrogant countenance, the physical and emotional overbearing that oozed from his dark, well-shaven face, contrasted with the smile initially described as benevolent: a smile that Pac could still remember. The contradiction between reality and memory left a bitter aftertaste almost resembling disappointment: this inflicted sensation shed new light on his inability to grasp things, to sense danger and treachery, to smell a rat. It was all a matter of trust, Pac found himself thinking as he swallowed more bloody saliva. He felt a faint stinging reaction at the nape of his neck, where the blow that had knocked him out had landed; that's what it was.

Kimley resumed his to-ing and fro-ing along the same horizontal line (dangerously close to Pac's face), arms hanging at his sides, like a shaven orang-utan wondering where he's left his house keys, his expression that of someone waiting for an answer: straight out of the interrogation manual, or whatever.

One of the three rose from the sofa: the pock-faced intellectual whose tyre-coloured boots were covered in partly-dried mud, Pac noticed fleetingly as the man tramped towards the kitchen, unheeded by the others. Sounds of a rummaging among cooking utensils; the sudden crash of a plate being thrown to the ground, followed by a glass being smashed to smithereens, its pieces skidding along the parquet floor; finally, in rapid succession, a second and a third plate, thrown methodically.

"Where's the stone?"

The metallic din of falling saucepans; followed by

dishes, lids, more plates and pans: a hellish, deafening clatter a few steps behind the back of Pac, who was initially alarmed, then merely irritated; now concentrating, impassive.

To and fro. "Where's the stone, fatso?"

The thug in the kitchen started kicking shards around violently, scattering them in every direction, etching long screeching tracks into the floor with pieces of glass and ceramic trampled into the muddy soles of his boots; using his whole weight, he finished underfoot a glass already cracked and shapeless: he pounded and ground, the friction making it shriek until it was powdered to silence.

"We're not in a hurry. You know that, don't you?"

Pac forced himself to remain silent.

"Think anyone will worry about your absence?"

Rooting around shelves, fittings, cabinets; the sauce boiling; a bottle of soy sauce suddenly flying across, fast, in a descending trajectory, and crashing against the window, then ricocheting to the floor: both intact. Here came a larger one, vinegar this time, tracing the same arc in the air, landing roughly in the same place, with the same effect: a dull sound immediately replaced by that of a bottle of hot ketchup landing in the same place – excellent aim – followed by tabasco, smaller and therefore faster: same result. Finally something he didn't recognise. Then no more. The oil was needed in the kitchen.

Presumably infuriated by his failure, the thug

approached with a short run-up and kicked the pile of books, launching a few into orbit, scattering some sheets of paper that subsequently floated down gracefully, until Kimley with a glance dispatched him to the other rooms. Whether in reward or punishment wasn't clear, but the noise reaching them from the bedroom, the studio, from every corner of the house, seemed to indicate that the Nepalese scoundrel was finding ways to give vent to his juvenile frustration.

"Where's the stone?"

Pac sighed. Time to put an end to all this: here was his chance, worth enjoying despite the pain. "It was confiscated at the airport, before boarding. They found it with the metal detector: I believe it was on the list of prohibited items. Actually, it never left your lovely country. Sorry."

For Kimley, the first six words (It-was-confiscated-at-the-airport) were enough to realise he was wasting his time. Actually, he didn't mind being offered so many excuses to indulge in some healthy exercise, and his hands were itching for action.

In preparation for the imminent onslaught Pac, backbone upright, eyes half closed (wanting to see, yet endeavouring to protect himself), noticed that Kimley had his back to him and was gesticulating to the two still sitting on the sofa, who observed him attentively, as if receiving instructions. Which didn't encourage optimism. Craning his neck towards them Pac tried to capture fragments of information, but all he gathered was that they were speaking Nepalese; this, again, was not a good sign; nor was the sudden furious barrage of blows delivered full in Pac's face by Kimley, who'd turned around abruptly with a twisting, lurching movement: a crude battering, right-left-right-left; eye, jaw, cheek bone, temple, eye, lip – as in a workout: instantly proving that Pac's prediction was correct, Kimley beat him nearly unconscious, almost breaking his determination by inflicting open wounds, visions of stars and black-outs, blood and vulnerability. A growling, wild-haired Kimley pounded and punched, again and again, on Pac's chest, neck and face.

When he'd finished he massaged his hands, smoothed back his hair, dried his forehead, and disappeared to the kitchen, leaving his two brothers-in-arms, partners, accomplices or whatever, fresh and rested, to carry on the persuasion campaign.

Upstairs, the crash of furniture being overturned and dragged, of glass being smashed, presumably with gusto, of hammering thuds resounding at regular intervals.

Judging by the steamy fragrance wafting into the living room, the sauce was now ready.

Kimley, too, had some red on a corner of his mouth, but it wasn't blood. This was the first thing Pac saw when he came to; when – following an effort of which he wouldn't have thought he was capable – he finally managed to clear the bleariness from his eye, and focus.

Kimley sat in front of him, within arm's reach.

It wasn't easy for Pac to sit up straight: there was something, some force that tried to make him hang his head. But he mustn't. God knows he would have liked to, but he couldn't: he mustn't give in. No, never! The pain was such that, once he's finished dividing the pie chart into perceptions, it was practically absent: present because inevitable, yet absent by dint of sole-agent efficiency. This was strange, really strange, but knowing it was only a matter of time he decided not to think about it until he had to. He had to stay concentrated, lucid; but he was battered, exhausted, near the point of no return. He clearly couldn't withstand another beating, especially not like the last one; he'd have surrendered much sooner, to hell with it all. But he couldn't let it show. No, not now. He didn't even have the strength to swallow any more blood: he simply let it dribble out of its own accord; when he really couldn't help it he half-spat. Lucid. Yeah, great to think he was lucid – fucking brilliant. Who was he trying to fool? He could barely understand what Kimley said, and often resorted to guessing. Anyway, it was always the same question. Fuck the stone, he thought. Enough was enough.

Kimley, we're told, was the first thing he saw. The second, when Kimley stepped aside deliberately and nodded towards it with a smirk, was just behind him: it was the yak.

The three on the sofa – two of them familiar, plus a third whom we might, at this point, refer to as the cook (in the absence of the scoundrel whose traces were lost) – were tinkering with their hunting knives, pretending to clean them on the fur of the unaware, defenceless, placid-looking animal. Held still, Pac noticed subsequently.

Pac was too stunned to hear what Kimley was telling him, but merely saw his lips moving. His ears felt bunged up; his head at times would spin, forcing him to keep his one functioning eye closed to try and stop the dizziness. Which worked, but when his head cleared he'd realise that he'd missed something, that things had gone on without him. How could he possibly communicate, negotiate in these conditions? He opened his eye with unspeakable effort and as he saw Kimley smirking, and the three threatening the young bovine, he felt a dense liquid oscillating inside his brain, blurring his sight, enforcing a pause.

However, that first image had been enough: there was nothing more he could do at that point. Resist out of pride and leave his yak in the hands of those... those what? He'd run out of words, he'd used them all up; and it wasn't even worth it, for Chrissake. If that was how things were meant to be, all right then, fuck it all. He'd sort out the rest. Later – if at all.

"Again, where the fuck is the stone?"

"It's in front of you," said Pac in a hoarse whisper.

Kimley's face all but lit up with glee, if we can call it that.

"But it's nothing to do with the yak, leave him alone. Don't be a jerk."

Hard to say 'jerk'. Whole sentence an effort, a huge effort.

Kimley addressed the three, and they all started enthusiastically groping the yak, concentrating respectively on his belly, thighs, hind quarters. And while the latter were circumspectly inspected by a bewildered cook, for a few incomparable moments the shaggy young yak seemingly appreciated and wagged his tail.

At the first sign of impatience, Pac – who was observing the scene with all the attention he could humanly muster – indicated where to look, knowing all too well that the consequences of any further delay would be inflicted on the poor animal.

Kimley took over and, having ensured that the others held the animal still, started to feel him, locating and piercing with the tip of his knife a spot at the base of the yak's neck, where his Himalayan DNA had foreseen a thick layer of subcutaneous fat. And from among that thick hair a miniscule flame-red bundle appeared, like an Aztec ruby discovered in a slab of roast beef retrieved from the freezer.

Kimley's nod immediately certified its authenticity, and in the dwindling hours of the night his eyes shone with emotion and tears of ineffable joy, while the others were busy stitching up the biological safe, and dispensing to the treasurer the honourable treatment he deserved. After all, in a sense, a precious fragment of sacred Nepalese land had been transferred inside a member of the family, a native. Seen from that specific angle, the stone had never left its place, temporal and spatial logics apart. And this was the extraordinary revelation of a superior design, such as to earn the animal due respect for his role in the matter. An animal that – one could safely claim – had been in touch with the Divine, and therefore merited to live, to remain where he was, his investiture being over and there being no possibility of transporting him.

Which is why they made him comfortable; and why they called back the fourth man, just as he was wielding the jack from the pic-up, preparatory to the destruction of the vehicle. By virtue of this blessed outcome Pac's life was saved, and the four climbed onto the helicopter.

While from the open French window wafted a dark, pungent breeze, Kimley lowered his head level with Pac's, which was bowed, dripping and, at times, absent.

"There's one thing I can't understand."

"Only one?", said Pac, the devastating pain in his lip reminding him that any energy expenditure would lower his chances of survival.

Kimley merely sneered. "How did you manage to put dope in my chai, in that restaurant?"

Pac wasn't sure he'd understood correctly, for a number of reasons; but if what he'd heard was true, he was in for a new barrage of blows.

Not knowing what to say, he answered with a shrug (in an abortive attempt to seem cool), peering up at that Asiatic face with his one operative eye.

"It was your friend, wasn't it? I confess I can't remember anything," said Kimley, emanating long-nurtured resentment.

It there was a positive side to all this, it consisted in the additional support to his own rational explanation of Samuel's post-traumatic ravings. Until that moment he hadn't had a chance to consider this possibility; but when Kimley claimed that, once analysed, his chai had been found to contain a potent anaesthetic, Pac was barely able to control a surge of indignation.

"This would be reason enough to break your legs," said Mr. K. into his bleeding ear, but Pac had already stopped listening.

Instead, he was concentrating on the satisfaction of knowing that he'd been right, if ever he'd had any doubts on the ravings of senile dementia. This in itself wasn't particularly surprising. What he did find infuriating was that he'd had to listen to all that bullshit from that nutter. Because that's what he was and, right now, he'd gladly have given him a good bashing and had him locked up somewhere. All those ridiculous stories, the time wasted listening to him conjure up that aura of insufferable divinity...

And what for? What was the point, at the end of it all? If only he could have laid his hands on him just then. But no, he couldn't have done a thing: all that was left was a rhetoric satisfaction.

"Well fatso, thanks for everything. And be grateful to the gods who, in their infinite mercy, have granted a common infidel the grace of salvation. Temporarily...", said Kimley with a glance intended to be benign, gently patting him on the shoulder. "Also, be grateful to this, their servant, endowed with the supreme faculty of reading and interpreting the will of the highest."

"Sure, to the sound of your fists," Pac managed to mumble, surprising himself.

"I'll be forgiven by those who discern the virtue of necessity. Goodbye fatso," he concluded ceremoniously, regaining an upright position.

Say fatso to that bitch of a sister of yours, thought Pac with a huge effort. He hadn't the energy to speak, or even to raise his head to look him in the eye, while trying to force his own open – at least one of them. Far too exhausting: he'd leave it at that. After all, some implicit abuse still hung in the air: that would have to do.

And rightly so, with hindsight, when with a slit-eyed side

glance he perceived Kimley moving behind his back and drawing his gun. From the garden resounded the whirr of the helicopter ready for take-off, while a blast of air reached his naked skin; and the blow he received on the back of his head was abrupt and strangely painless.

He was lying on the sofa. This was good news: unfortunately, the only good news.

Long moments of benumbed oblivion went by before a total, paralysing pain took hold of him: a pain in every way definitive, arresting even his will to think; digging a moat filled with crocodiles between his imagining to lift one finger and getting the designated muscles to comply. One attempt was more than enough for him to surrender, lay down the weapons of his intellect and bow to the supremacy of the new sovereign invader.

He would have liked to open both eyes: add some information to this special-edition news bulletin; but of the two, only one responded; fortunately it was his right eye, commanding a better view. Dark blotches, halos, shadows moving in a milky whiteness. Might as well close it.

At the second attempt, the white-washing was almost completed, except for a few opaque outlines, especially around the edges. A figure in the foreground was peering closely at him.

Sitting on a chair, his legs crossed, his short-sleeved shirt pink. It was Samuel, holding something white which he was trying to slip into his mouth.

Pac gave a start: instantly a hollow scream escaped him, while a galaxy of lights exploded, shimmering vividly behind his closed eyes, dancing erratically to a thin hissing sound that rose to the threshold of nausea. The accumulation of acid saliva in his throat augured danger and impeded his breathing. Downtime. Slow pulse, knocking insistently on the door of his chest.

"Keep calm, you must keep calm."

Pac couldn't believe he was in such poor shape, when he could think at all. He gulped, as Samuel skilfully disinfected his most urgent wounds with what turned out to be imbued cotton wool: upper lip, eyebrow, cut on cheekbone, closed eye. Practically his whole face. Swabbing gently, discreetly, imbuing again, throwing soiled cotton wool into a waste-paper basket he'd brought along.

Samuel was frowning, his expression exceedingly serious, as if believing that words would add little to such an eloquent picture. He was busying himself with a bag of cotton-wool swabs in his lap and a bottle of hydrogen peroxide on an occasional table beside him; and Pac wouldn't have been surprised if he'd seen him devote part of his antibacterial treatment to the scarred skin bracelets conspicuous on his wrists.

Thus the fresh morning proceeded in burnished silence; the windows that weren't damaged were wide open. An amber light verging on orange illuminated the living room with bright reflections, embellishing that devastated battlefield with faded embroidery and ornaments; illuminating a painting that hung lop-sided on the white wall, an orphaned book-cover on the floor; shattering on a spiky crest of broken glass, irradiating in shards and bearing warmth to abraded surfaces. Birdsong steadily broke forth from the trees: a balm lightly flowing over the scene of the crime, over the baseness of those wounds, soothing, healing, then abruptly bursting like a bubble. Gusts of crisp breeze caressed their brows, refreshing and stimulating their lungs, recharging their blood cells; and left, exhaled.

Samuel medicated with slender fingers and a lifeless gaze, reaching out, withdrawing. Pac refused to think, didn't want to know: about the damage, about the how and why, about anything. He'd find out, there was no escape. And his rescuer would certainly not be exempted. But all in good time. All he need do now was hold on, resist and decipher an…

"Sweet Mother of Jesus! What on earth happened here?" Fernanda.
"Good morning." Samuel.
"Oh, Mother of God. What a disaster. Look at the... the mess!"
"Be careful there, you might trip over." Samuel again.
"Fennanna…" Pac, in case you were wondering.

"Are you all crazy in this house? Are you out of your mind? And who's going to clear this up now? Good Heavens! Help me Lord, I can't believe what I'm seeing!"

"No, hold on, don't come in. There's broken glass everywhere."

"But what have you done? And what about him? Who did that to him?", she asked, indicating Pac.

The latter made to answer, but merely shook his head.

"And now you expect me to clear up this mess? Listen, you two; do you really think I'll stay and clean up? Holy Virgin, look at the kitchen! I see you've also been eating, eh? Well done!"

"Look, it's not like that. You see, you must understand..." Samuel tried to explain.

"I must understand, eh?"

"Fennanna, listen."

"Right, so you two have your orgies, Christ knows what you've been up to, smashing everything... your little games. Just look at all this!"

"What little games, Madam! We were assaulted, can't you see? By burglars!"

"Yes, yes..." dribbled Pac.

"Do you wise guys think I'll fall for your bullshit? You really think I'm so stupid? Eh? Am I stupid? Oh no! My potted hot chili beans... look! Dirty dishes in the sink: well well. Didn't have time to wash up, did you? Or did the burglars take the sponges?"

She was spinning like a top. She seemed possessed.

"Really Madam, believe me. They broke in, it was..."

"Martians, no doubt."

"But can't you see the state this poor man is in?"

"That poor man, as you call him, is lying in his boxer shorts, half naked, beside you; looks like you're cuddling."

What the fuck is she on about, wondered Pac. Even thinking was painful.

"Excuse me?"

"Bravo. You take me for a fool? You think I didn't know? Disgusting. You keep to yourselves, always at home, you disappear during the day, leaving me alone. God alone knows what you get up to at night. So that's it! Your dirty little games! And I should clean up? You'll be lucky!"

"I'm afraid you're definitely mistaken. You are mistaken Madam. How dare you?"

"Disgusting."

I'll kill her. Here I am suffering like a dog, and she dares...

"I repeat, Madam, we were assaulted by burglars."

"Oh yeah? And if you were burgled, where's the police? Did you call them? I bet you didn't."

"We didn't, in fact. The thing is... it's not so simple, you see, in these precise circumstances we are unable to manifest to the authorities a situation that might be... shall we say, misunderstood!"

"I thought so. Shame on you! At your age, what's more.

Disgusting. What a mess, Holy Mother of God: what scum. I thought I knew, but not to this point."

Fernanda fuck off, you're fired, thought Pac. But all he managed was a strangled groan.

"You know what? I'm fed up, I've had it, I can't go on like this. Carry on with your dirty little games. I'll never set foot in here again. I'm off. Find yourselves another slave, I'm nobody's servant, you hear?"

"Fennanna..."

"And don't you try fooling me with your mumbo-jumbo. It won't work this time. I've been to the trade unions: I'm no fool, you know? I know my rights. They told me that under the new labour laws you'll have to pay me a leaving indemnity, holidays not taken, Christmas bonus, subsistence. And a seniority increase, because I've been working here over eighteen months, even if it was off the books: and you might have to pay dearly for this. I could take you to court, if I wanted to. But I'm not mean and stingy like you, so I'll be content with, yes, say, six months' salary, as a bonus. There, call it a golden handshake."

Pac exhaled noisily, shook his head. He squinted at her, in disbelief. With one eye only, of course.

"I'll send my husband over with the bill. Goodbye."

"Goodbye Madam."

"And you should be ashamed, at your age. Disgusting!"

No stone.

Pac moved slowly. Each movement of his legs – right, left – cost him inches of life. He trod on tufts of grass and daisies, from the garden to the patriarchal cedar on the hill; the grass was redolent of sweet fragrances that low gusts of wind swept away and deposited at the edge of the wood. It was summer, one of the warmest in living memory, if his own was anything to go by.

Wearing only a t-shirt and boxer shorts (his burgundy ones, so shabby as to be fit only for the dustbin), he lazed around, strolling in the open air. More than laziness, his was a lack of motivation. He meandered senselessly, absorbed in a void. A void consisting of precise absences, linked like warm ash-grey pearls spewed by wandering oysters. These pearls lay on his mind as if set in a crown, and each one had a name. Today's was called 'stone'. Light, fragile as the eggshell of an unknown, off-the-grid species, it transmitted an ambiguous sensation, as effective as it was incomplete. After all, what did he ever know about that stone? He hadn't even looked at it: not even in those few instants before slipping it inside the yak's subcutaneous fat (he hadn't made the mistake of entrusting the operation to Dr Raju, a friend of Kimley's; though his shrewdness had hardly been rewarded). Not even when, completely alone, he could have opened the famous flame-red bundle and admired first-hand the real reason for his absurd commitment in flying to Nepal to save Samuel. Oh, so long ago: so much had happened since then. What juicy times those had been, with their manifestations and interlinked events... He couldn't even imagine how the hell that stone was made, not to mention its never-tested applications. All bullshit? Judging by Samuel and Kimley's conduct, it wasn't. One sure finality he had to concede: the damned thing had ruined his life – which was no negligible matter. In any case it was gone, vanished, he would never know: an irreversible *never* projecting beyond the boundaries of his very being, contaminating what he touched; what his eyes lingered on; the air he exhaled, corrupted, from his nostrils.

Never, ever, ever. Forget about the stone, and the possibility of ever flying a vimana.

No Fernanda.

The smallest, most opaque of those pearls, the ones used as fillers, compensating their negligible value by increasing the composition's overall selling price. When this was on his mind he wasn't sure whether to be pleased or sorry: so he'd simply stroll along, sometimes barefoot, refusing to think; raising his glance to the implacable sun, shielding his eyes with his hands; loitering self-indulgently He could have died as he stood there, and there were times when he wished he would; but with the cooling shadows of sunset, even these yearnings would be left to rot.

Fernanda's luck, in short, was anticipating his move: at a time when he was being well and truly buggered, with coarse sand as a lubricant, she was but a hiccup: an insignificant bother in circumstances far more taxing, far more vital than her hysteria. That was her fucking good fortune. At any other, more lucid time, he'd have destroyed her, cut her down with all the ammunition at his disposal: and what with personal and occupational motives, he could have counted on a satisfactory number. If he'd dismissed her without undue hesitation, it wasn't so much for the heft of her Lebanese husband, or the fact that he'd showed up with three mates – all four of them acting as if their greatest pleasure in life were bashing the likes of him. No, it wasn't this cowardly intimidation, no way: the ultimate meaning of his existence had evaporated, like the pharaoh exhaling his last breath upon the opening of his sarcophagus. Nothing. There was nothing left in him that could be described as a purpose, except to wait for the end; and with it, the victory of others. So let them have all that bloody money. And fuck off, starting with Fernanda: may her left foot be incinerated by lightning! He no longer needed money, anyway: as an instrument it had outlived its millennial purpose. What was the point, when he was about to be annihilated? Only retrospective consolation: she wouldn't enjoy it either. But in the present circumstances, wasn't ignorance of the imminent end a blessing? So much for his consolation!

Samuel had replaced her. Samuel, who'd refused to leave, after he'd been violently thrown out, the day after ministering to Pac's medication. He'd been accused of exploiting his need of surviving Armageddon; accused of fraud, of double crossing him. He'd become dispensable.

"If what you claim is true, how come you didn't use the ancient idiom with Kimley and his moronic, pilfering ilk? See what they've done to my face. Could you have stopped them? Then why didn't you? And with Fernanda? Why have you always refused to teach me a few words, even one, so that I might at least get rid of her without being ripped off?"

"No. I'm not leaving."

"Oh yes you are. And fast."

"No."

"Go back to what you were doing before. Stealing from NASA warehouses, talking to flowers, collecting minerals... Bugger off! Do what you like but leave me in peace! All you've done is get me into trouble, you've aborted my plan, you've..."

"It was our plan, don't forget. I wouldn't know where to go, anyway. I don't have much, you know."

"I have even less, for that matter."

"You need help. I'll stay and look after you. It's got to be done, and I'll do it. Sorry, but I'm not leaving."

They hadn't hurt a hair on Samuel's head; they'd lifted

him bodily and locked him up in the bathroom. He'd somehow managed to break free as soon as he'd realised they'd cleared off. This, again, was extremely unfair – but Pac had already got over it.

Samuel had stayed on. He'd cleaned up the debris and put things straight, all on his own, without asking for the help he wouldn't have obtained. He'd drive the pick-up to town, do the shopping; cook healthy, tasty meals (needless to say, Pac's palate was no longer influenced by his target weight). The sensible use Samuel made of the washing machine and dishwasher bespoke his solitary, autonomous past; and he didn't expect to be paid. Moving like a shadow, he spent his days in the woods; Pac saw him whispering to the tree trunks, and gathering wild herbs. And in the evenings, when Pac withdrew to weep in the privacy of his bedroom, Samuel would lie in the garden observing the vault of the sky, and counting falling stars – knowing perfectly well they were meteors. His eyes glued to the Moon's every phase, he would murmur softly, awaiting a response, enthralled as if this were the only spring that could quench his thirst: as if from the depth of his heart he really yearned to return there, to alight softly on its surface, and hop around, knowing he could do no harm. The man, Pac had decided, must have left a part of himself on that dusty bogey, a long time ago. And this explained numberless things.

Pac eventually accepted the other's presence with

ungrateful resignation: they kept each other company in a way that some would have found dismaying.

No work.

There was an impalpable lightness in his voluntary, temporary unemployment. Pac could have sat down, hugging his knees, meditating on the intrinsic and relative meaning of that much-abused word. Unemployment: he could have sat in the shade, sipping iced tea, probing the depths of that concept. But he didn't.

On leave of absence (which would be followed, in sequence, by unused holidays and by sick leave, ad interim, substantiated by a succession of counterfeited medical certificates), his application had been accepted in record time, although he knew that his Agency was snowed under with work, and even obliged to turn down contracts and consulting work; almost as if, in these circumstances, he'd won a marathon he didn't even know he'd entered.

Money, as we were saying, was now virtually unnecessary, except for the provision of an adequate food supply and not much else.

No Star Pac, no future, no time, no salvation: death, encroaching at the hands of others. While not knowing and not having to stay alert was the best state to be in, more rewarding still was looking after the young bovine, taking him for walks, feeding him, washing and brushing him, observing his quiet, lumbering gait; imagining he could share that state of grace, harbouring harmless envy and a sense of unspeakable relief. As well as finding, in the care of this spark of nature, a sense of belonging, of an intimate commonality between living beings, albeit for a short time. From early morning to late evening, a proactive part of himself was busy keeping company to the no-longer lame yak, along paths filled with flowers and delightful shade, pic-nicks and games and laughter.

The other part of Pac's being revolved entirely around two formerly evocative words: Star Pac. No way, he simply couldn't get over it. Kimley had ordered that everything be destroyed, and his orders had been carried out with the customary impressive efficiency.

Samuel had tried to dissuade Pac from going into the workshop, in what had been the hangar of their hopes, but his words had fallen on deaf ears. The Star Pac (the fact that it was a plasterboard prototype clearly didn't make the least bit of difference) had been totally destroyed, with maniac precision: like a chocolate sculpture assaulted by an iconoclast diabetic, it had been smashed to smithereens, leaving grey dust and rubble on the floor, the stench of urine. Pac couldn't bring himself to cross the doorway.

He'd stood there, flabbergasted, gulping, leaning for support against something more solid than he felt. And what he'd felt then – and had continued to feel every moment, especially when in denial – was a pre-packaged sensation: as if wrapped in layer upon layer of cling-film. Familiar-looking yet capable of suffocating, of restraining, of sealing in one's purpose, one's very capacity to express the merest exhalation: a traumatic separation which, via a largely unknown shortcut, had bypassed the hold-up phases of acceptance and aimed straight for the heart, to what specialists define as velvet-lined despair.

He'd remained stunned for some time – almost long enough to be clinically relevant – before being roused and induced by carer-Samuel to get out of bed; to be force-fed with spoonsful of millet in vegetable stock; and then being led to a seat in the veranda, where he contemplated his inner void; and finally taken back to his own room. Until, step by step, he'd gradually regained control of his own will.

The destruction of the vimana was surpassed only by his learning that every single device, piece of machinery or tool purchased over years of commitment and sacrifices – all the equipment smuggled at risk by Samuel (also shaken and indignant, needless to say), and delivered with great effort and caution to his address; everything: from navigation radars to range finders, aerospace software, Elektron system, oxygen tanks, storage batteries, dosimeters, as-yet-incomplete directional gyroscopes, and even his brand-new screwdrivers and electric drill – was all gone. Vanished – stolen.

They'd taken everything: there wasn't even a trace of the

pick-up's two snow tyres and of a bicycle that he hadn't got round to returning to the garage since last winter. The affront: the greed, the abject motivation for such conduct were overshadowed on the one hand by the impossibility of a healthy revenge, and on the other by the awareness that he and Samuel were potentially vulnerable to a second assault, which neither of the two felt they could exclude.

Vulnerability and looting, weakness and control: this seemed to be the gist of Kimley's temporary farewell note. Temporary.

Added to this Queen of all pearls, ablaze with sinister splendour, was the absence of a future, of salvation, of a renaissance. Overhead, the end of time performed a complex ceremonial dance that would culminate in the inevitable human sacrifice – he being the victim. While he, defenceless, could do nothing but take stock and die, his life already over, losing substance in ways too obvious or ambiguous to describe.

Looking after the yak, letting himself be crushed by the weight of inevitability, suffocated by the fumes of a sweet desperation.

Which is why he ambled so slowly, his thoughts lame and livid, allowing the unusual summer heat to burn his skin, when every other creature had taken refuge in the shade. And why there was no point in drying his tears, or desiring a death that had already come, or counting the hours that might separate him from the end, whatever form that may take. Because he, Pac, would no longer leave, escape, orbit round the planet, rejoice in the stars and in his redemption, savour rebirth and new civilisations. He would neither witness nor participate. He would end like the others: the irresponsible, the morons, like everybody else – including the cowardly, the culpable, the slayers. He, the deserving, would perish without distinction. More absences.

So, what prevented him from laying down and leaning his cheek on the warm soil, moving the grass aside so he could perceive the rhythmic breathing of the earth, the tranquillity of abandon, the marching of ants in their tunnels, the writhing progress of worms? Oh my God: was he following in Samuel's steps? Was he losing it? Prone, awaiting his execution.

Is there a remedy for death? There used to be, but not anymore.

Was there life in the universe? He could have gone for a stroll out there: could have had a good look round, checked out some of those theories. Mars; the Moon itself (in view of Samuel's reticence); Jupiter's satellites.

He could have.

Who would found the new humanity, after the upcoming collapse?

Not him. Someone else, maybe, how should he know? Whoever it was, they'd certainly not have his charisma.

Pac, how do you feel? Is there anything you'd like to say, live, to our audience?

Whatever could he say?

You were within inches of saving yourself from the crack of doom. Do you see any religious implications in this, more specifically in bringing your body and soul back to a dimension of equality, aligned with the rest of us, with common mortals?

Ahem...

Do you feel closer to God, at this moment?

Please. My client has already been through enough.

Yes but the public wants to know. They have a right to know whether...

Excuse us.

Pac. What are your comments on the full acquittal of the offence you were charged with? Everyone believed you had killed Samuel. But the judge validated your thesis that – in view of the precedents of the deceased – it was involuntary suicide.

Precisely.

What will you do now, Pac?

Yes, what will you do? Will you wait for the end, with the rest of us?

Do keep us company. Honour us with your presence!

Hey, hold on.

Come on, we need someone like you to make our vigil

complete.

Calm down, get a grip. Let go of my jacket!
Do you feel defeated?
It's all the system's fault, right?
Oh fuck.

That morning was identical to all the others. The photocopy of a morning. Same heat, same almost imperceptible breeze, incapable of performing the only function it was accountable for. Usual colours: of the terse sky, of the trees' foliage, of the plants, of the entire valley, swaddled in a maddening, monotonous silence. Everything within sight immobile.

Pac scratched his knee.

Alone. While everyone else, he was sure, was having a good time. Little did it matter what they were up to; he knew that out there – beyond the boundaries of what used to be his precious, indispensable and now meaningless privacy – the inhabitants of the entire planet were busy dealing with things they found interesting, amusing, entertaining. Alone; or with their mates, with kindred spirits. Television, the Internet, cinema; games, music, shows, drugs. They were having a ball. They were making important, cultivated conversation. Maybe they were practicing sports, sweating, then showering with gentle, pH-neutral gels, respectful of their skin.

A long draught of fresh water, and the glass bottle went

back where it belonged.

Synthetically evergreen women were buying Ayurvedic, organic products, having massages. Some, he was sure, were doing yoga and even claiming they were more in touch with their inner selves.

And they were right, all of them.

That was the point. Even those who sent their children to Sunday school, or wherever it was that children got brainwashed. They were right. Even Samuel was right. Not so much for what he said or did, but for the how and why, for the intensity and quality of what he did.

The rest was waffle. He was the rest.

Looking up, he saw two small birds darting from one tree to another, chirping loudly before flying off.

He couldn't go on like this. Not anymore.

He wound a thick tuft of grass, rough-textured as nautilus tentacles, in a slow anticlockwise spiral; the grass held tightly in his fist, possessed. Then liberated, tousled, smoothed vertically, blade by blade, the abrasion on his fingertips procuring an unlooked-for, gratuitous pleasure, which he allowed himself – moderately – to enjoy.

He couldn't go back and start all over again. He was a speeding train, diverted to a siding. He lay down, arms and legs spread-eagled. Before his eyes, scraps of sky, branches and bark, a vertical depth. Vertical, as in take-off, for example. Suddenly, boredom.

He couldn't go on like this. As he'd been thinking: it was

like... a photocopy. Repeated, day in, day out, week after week; at first unaware, insensitive; but then.

A sigh, a sniffling, an ache in his backside, and behold! He forced his lifeless flesh to sit up, moistened his parched lips, nibbled the lower one.

Crouching in the shade of the cedar, he watched the dying sun, aware that he wouldn't be granted a stellar rebirth; listening to the sudden noises, the chirping in the wood; observing the yak as, tied to a nearby tree, he rested from his efforts. Then, on perceiving a deep, kitchen-sink gurgle resounding suddenly from his no-longer ample stomach, Pac had an intuition. Of something as yet undefined. A pod, narrow and protected, as between crossed, shaven legs: a dormant urge – the colour of that sunset, a vivid orange – something to be cherished and nurtured. A budding idea that might just be. Why not? After all, what had he to lose, apart from his biological life? And why not lose oneself precisely in that way?

Signs lighting up in rapid succession along the dark, deserted driveway, which he could fill with special people. That's what he should do: something so relevant that he had to return home – the yak trotting along with a questioning air – and shut himself in the bathroom to force the conclusion of a chapter. And start a brand-new one, ad hoc.

FOUR

He'd thought it over all night. From every point of view, this final solution seemed the only possible one, reverberating with a burnished brilliance.

The decision was made, the new day had broken, graceful photons were tapping on the broken window, then on his shuttered eyelids, as he reluctantly surrendered to the inevitable.

The day was glorious, of the kind that caused an itch inside his yellow-snail patterned boxer shorts, while, bare-chested, he ate his breakfast. Now that the threshold of aesthetic acceptance was framed in a solid doorway. Optimism. And rusks, spread with organic honey; warm soy milk and seasonal fruit; sweet surrender and papaya juice, extra-rich in anti-oxidants.

On seeing him so radiant, his hair combed, sitting upright at the kitchen table, Samuel – who'd already eaten, as usual – nevertheless helped himself to a rusk, placed it on a paper napkin, before crunching away with his false teeth. He'd got up before dawn, as always, and made his way with a torch to his sanctuary in the wood: there, he'd abandoned himself to the intimate connection that he'd perceived to be activated, and which activated him. He'd retraced his steps as the sunlight tinged the dawn concert with wonder; had caressed a purple-crowned flower and the dew drops: nectar for wayfaring insects. After his ablutions and breakfast he'd asked himself, as he did every day, which of the two was really the guest; what he should expect of Pac. And he'd prayed that their roles – along with projects and horizons that he himself struggled to imagine – would soon be readjusted. And while he opened the French windows onto the garden, on that splendid and already-warm summer morning, Pac had come downstairs, light-footed, and had approached him with an unusual twinkle in his eye, smiling. Samuel hadn't made the mistake of spoiling the positivity of the moment with commonplace questions. No. He'd let Pac have his breakfast, eyeing him sidelong, studiously, and had come to the conclusion that his conduct was as likely to conceal good intentions as it was some alarming decree. Hence, while passing him on his way to the sofa, he'd let Pac know where he was heading, in case he wanted to talk, and in doing so had perceived something unfathomable in the air: something that induced in him a compulsion to pluck tiny hairballs off his black tracksuit trousers. One by one, plucked from his right, crossed leg, pills of white fabric of unknown origin floated to the parquet floor: a departure proclaiming to be definitive but acknowledged deep-down as impermanent.

There were hundreds of those hairballs, on his right leg alone.

"Kindly explain all that bullshit on what happened at the restaurant, with Kimley."

Samuel averted his attention and started rolling a ball of fuzz between thumb and first finger. "Good morning to you too. Did you sleep well?"

Wielding his knife, Pac scooped up as much honey as was technically possible, a thin dribble of it falling along the way to his rusk.

"If you want to come with me you'd better answer."

"Come? Where to?"

"I haven't heard your answer yet. Why, with all the crap I had to endure, did you have to come up with the pre-Babel idiom and all the rest? Why did you need to lie to me?"

As the vice around it relented, the ball of fluff landed with surreal slowness, while Samuel's fingers resumed their meticulously useless removal operations. During these he was sure he recognised a white cat's hair. This posed extraordinarily relevant questions, as there was an irrefutable lack of felines in the house: or so he'd always thought. But that hair, that single, pointed white hair – discovered almost by chance – had implications whose complex repercussions he was unable to assess at that moment.

"Ok, too bad. I'm leaving today. Don't know if I'll ever come back. In fact, I don't think I will. It's been good to know you, Samuel. As they say."

"Oh hell... all right. I was scared, you see." Samuel, keeping his eyes cast down.

Pac bit into a honey-laden rusk, which broke in two, shedding crumbs. "I'm listening."

"I wasn't sure I could do it... I'd just risked my life, was just out of hospital. I still hadn't acquired the necessary self-awareness. And, well, deep down I was afraid you might be right: that I might merely be suffering from post-traumatic delusions."

"Is that why you used anaesthetic, probably stolen in hospital? The same that should have relieved the far more urgent pain of bed-ridden invalids?" Pac had no doubts: a pinch of moralistic sarcasm had rendered his rusk scrumptious beyond anything.

"Right," admitted Samuel quietly. "But I also used the ancient idiom I told you about. You're free not to believe me, if you like, but that's the way it went."

Pac shook his head.

"I don't know what did the trick... but one thing's for sure: I wanted that stone too. I really did, damn it!" At this, his fist pounded ranks of variously assorted hairballs.

This time, Pac sketched a hint of acknowledgement, a sort of extended sigh, though it might have been mere appreciation for the honey, savoured almost ecstatically. Momentarily satisfied, he brushed the crumbs from his boxer shorts and from his naked, hairy thighs, and stood up.

Yes, it was a special day. Luminous, redolent of the

essential oils of a renewed will. Pac stretched luxuriously, his gaze scanning the entire living room, the garden, and beyond. The sun set fire to golden, treacly forms, shafts of light revealing the specks of dust suspended in the air; a shower of light, colour; a deep silence, disturbed solely by the metallic buzz of the refrigerator behind him.

Which brought him back to his plan, the latest.

"Time to go," he said to Samuel, who was still waiting interrogatively on the sofa; his gaze somewhat lost; the air of someone who – for reasons that Pac would never be able to fathom – suddenly reminded him of fragile, abandoned souls. And those eyes, that auspicious blue gaze – the same gaze he's always seen blazing with a vitality that he'd summed up as unique – now appeared dulled by a precariousness, a solitude for which he, Pac, was responsible. No, he'd never do it. He'd already decided to continue and to conclude his journey, so to speak, in Samuel's company.

"Yes, it's time to go..." repeated Pac with a meaningful nod, inviting Samuel to move. "We can't stay here any longer: we're vulnerable. Kimley and his lot could be back at any moment, if only to have fun... I don't feel safe."

"And where would you like to go?", asked Samuel, paper napkin screwed up in the hand that wasn't pill-picking.

"You'll soon find out. Now get the van ready, load it with all the food we have in the house. As if for a long camping holiday. Then get your things, if you have any. I'll get mine; and I have to see to something else."

The colour of Samuel's complexion, already ruddy from having been exposed to gamma rays, deepened so significantly that Pac suspected embarrassment might be the cause – though his arched white eyebrows seemed to indicate the contrary. In any case, Samuel didn't move from the sofa but, head bowed, resumed the random plucking of hair-balls and dust particles from his tracksuit – paying particular attention to what looked like specks of dirt.

If this was a case of senile dementia, thought Pac, he might have to rethink his decision to take Samuel with him.

"Problems?"

Deafening silence.

"I'm offering you a chance to save yourself. The only one left, to be precise."

He saw Samuel inhale slowly, at length, to his lungs' full capacity; holding his breath long enough to induce a sense of dizziness, then exhaling noisily. "You wouldn't understand," he said.

"Well, give it a try."

Prized off his knee, a pill of fuzz dragged in its wake some hardy filaments, to the muted sound of tearing.

"I'm tired. All this is too much for me. I don't think I can bear it."

"Yeah. It must be frustrating to be a god without

believers." Pac waited for a long moment, but got no reaction. "There's a place, in Asia Minor," he continued "Pergamum, I believe. Here, moved to pity, the ancients dedicated a stele to unknown or forgotten gods. Just think of those divinities, waiting for someone to invoke, to implore, to supplicate them with sacrifices. So sad!"

Not a stir.

"Now: I was thinking you could buy a space, even a small one. Have a couple of lines etched with your name: bequeath to posterity your hard-won and – may I add – more than merited testimony, at once earthly and divine. Come to think of it, this combination of earthly and divine reminds me of someone. Do you know him, by any chance?"

How could he fail to react to such a good joke?

When Pac moved closer to peer at him, he noticed that Samuel's eyes were closed; he was immobile. Was he asleep? Old age did play such tricks. He moved closer still, within inches of his face. A scent of aftershave. He shook him by the shoulder, which felt particularly bony. A light slap and a pinch established that he'd passed out there and then. But was breathing.

Supposing he was about to die? Was it better to try and revive him, or to let Samuel's singular brain sort it out of its own accord?

Leaning into the back of the sofa, Pac observed Samuel. He couldn't help thinking that a gentleman of his kind, so elegant and well-mannered, would probably have been happier in a farm house, recounting tales of his adventures to a team of boisterous grandchildren. He could just see him, pretending to lick the moon, eyes dewy with nostalgia, like a lovelorn butcher's boy evoking the lucky day, the celestial, albeit fleeting moment he'd caught a glimpse of his beloved princess.

"Cut the crap." Samuel had re-opened his eyes, and Pac prepared to shoot the remaining bullets willing to be struck by the hammer. S&M ballistics.

"I don't think I can do it," interjected Samuel.

"What do you mean?"

"Listen, I shan't bore you with my considerations on how difficult it's been (and still is) to accept what happened to me, though I'm not ungrateful for your part in it. Which is one of the reasons why I'm still here. My memories, my awareness: I assure you it's a painful and truly dramatic process, even physically. But you wouldn't be able to understand, so I shan't waste time trying to explain."

Pac slumped on the sofa, stretched out his legs and, with his feet propped up on the coffee table, was trying with the tip of his tongue to dislodge some remains of rusk that he felt stuck between his teeth.

Samuel was looking at the floor. "I'm merely depressed because now that I know who I am, that I know the story, I remember a remote past that no longer belongs to anyone.

I'm an exhumed relic. At the end of it all, your sarcasm, Pac, is justified. I have a genuine past that I can't even... and all of it is – how shall I say? – overlaid by dozens of other lives, births, deaths, and rebirths, that I'm unable to appraise. Whether useless or necessary; wonderful, as is each existence, or depressing – as is every form of detention. And I see no future, because I don't have any. This could actually be my happy ending, my grand finale! In which case, yes, I might see the sense of it: a logical, balanced reason. The revelation and accomplishment of harmony."

Racing towards them was a mass of rain-laden clouds, auguring hostilities against the mild weather hitherto enjoyed. The warning went unnoticed.

Pac did see clouds amassing on the horizon, but of a different type.

"What are you trying to tell me?"

"That my journey ends right here. I already feel saved, in my damnation. I've expiated sins that weren't even my own, but it doesn't matter. We'll be coming full cycle soon, I'm sure you know that."

The topic of cyclic events – whether micro or macro – would have made for fascinating discussion, especially those of calamities, astronomic events, the evolution, philosophical aspects and lots more. Unfortunately this was out of the question, and acting psychoanalyst to a despondent divinity was something Pac really couldn't fit into his busy schedule.

"I'm free, and I want to put an end to this cycle of rebirths," said Samuel somewhat haughtily. "I want to die for what I've been and what I haven't been, over too many lives. I want to re-embrace the universal mother, lose myself in her arms and become immaterial spirit, without emotions, or the desires of the psyche. I want to ascend to the level where I belong, whence I can take the plunge, and see what happens. Conscious choices, you understand?"

"What? Right now? Please, Samuel, *I beg you.*"

Jesus wept! This was too much. When he realised what he'd just said – and to Samuel, of all people – Pac cringed, feeling pretty cheesed off with himself. Of course, his 'I beg you' was just a figure of speech. "You don't even know where I want to take you. Come on Samuel, stop playing hard to get. Go and get changed, it's time to go!", he concluded, gesturing towards some vague destination beyond the window. Where the late-morning hours exuded invigorating warmth and light; and the fragrance of flowers, hyperactive in their apparent stillness; where life – devoid of human meddling – was sparkling, ambrosial: all to be explored, enjoyed, rediscovered.

Samuel couldn't resist its allure. He turned, his eyes immediately captivated by the garden bathed in light, beyond the deck chairs, while retracing in his mind the paths he'd learned to love and to contemplate.

Pac observed Samuel: he would give in, eventually, but

Pac was in a hurry. Though no longer keeping an eye on signs of the End – because of some vague, self-imposed disappointment, a corollary of his general mood – Pac was well aware of what time was generating; and, at least for this last project, he hoped to be up to the great event. He couldn't ask for anything more, though to whom he might address this request shall remain a mystery.

In all this, it was imperative to convince Samuel, who was bound to enjoy himself: that same Samuel who was now returning his attention to Pac, though reluctant to leave the invocations of nature.

"No, this is too much. I don't want another move. I'm fine here, and in this house – with your permission – I want to lay myself down to rest," he'd resumed his painful whispering.

"Permission denied."

"I have no reason to follow you, wherever it is you want to take me. I'm free now, don't you see?"

"I'm still trying to understand whether you're depressed, or else hoping you'll have me begging."

Samuel smiled, covering his mouth with a very crumpled paper napkin. "You know what the truth is?", he said, shaking his head in a gesture that invoked an irritated sigh from Pac. "The truth is," continued Samuel, "that the end is approaching. You're perfectly right. We might not even reach the end of the driveway before 'puff', we vanish in thin air. So I think you'd better sit down too. Yes indeed."

He laughed.

"But that's what I'm trying to..."

"Truth is, time is against us, the first signs of the upcoming End are already manifesting themselves all over the world. From that precise direction, for instance," Samuel said, his tone sombre, pointing southward. "Already, beyond those mountains, there are clear signs of what will develop into a local war. One of the many, possibly waged against some evil oppressor with whom they've been in business for decades; or in order to export Democracy and protect the defenceless – as will be reported initially, in order not to alarm the public. But destined to spread like a spot of oil, until most nations are involved. As was written, and as is. Not as will be, but as is now, in this precise moment. You haven't been keeping up to date for some time, have you, Pac? People don't realise, but when they do, it'll be too late. That's why so many prophesies, even biblical ones, are so incomprehensible. Because they're useless. When the time comes, they'll be busy with other things – ephemeral matters, considered important, interesting, yet ephemeral and stupid nonetheless – and no-one will notice. Because of this, and because it's not possible to deviate the course of fate, it was necessary to render certain prophesies unintelligible, indecipherable. Even if they weren't, it wouldn't change a thing. A time, the times, half a time..." He laughed again.

"Apart from the two of us and our mascot: we could get

out of here, if you get a move on."

"You don't really mean to take him along?"

"Do you think I'd leave him here to die ?"

"But he stinks!"

"So do you, for that matter."

"Sure. Anyway, I know it's not true," said Samuel shrugging. "Go ahead. I've run out of will: I've paid, suffered, remembered. Now I know, and I am – that's enough for me. My cycle is concluded."

Samuel rose from the sofa and in two steps was out in the garden, in the open air, where he sat facing the sun.

Heaving what he hoped would be a last heavy sigh, Pac ran his hand through his hair: longer than he remembered. And greasy.

Then he, too, took a couple of steps into the outdoors, where he assumed a more comfortable position, relaxing his shoulders. Soon the sun was gently warming his entire body: a tingling pleasure he'd have liked to prolong by remaining there, motionless, his eyes closed. He would have liked to, but his objective was another. So he crouched slowly alongside Samuel; doing, instead, what he'd rather have avoided.

Certain that the matter was resolved, Samuel was busy savouring the delightfully energising sunlight when, on turning around, he was confronted with a desperately sombre face; and with its damp, pungent breath. So close that it seemed about to overpower him. A breath exhaled by a mask of controlled anguish that was now staring at him – a moist, tremulous glance that ensnared him immediately: brown eyes swimming in tears as yet held back, which Samuel immediately felt his duty to arrest.

Pac's face had assumed the outlines of a remote, unspeakable wretchedness – of which he himself seemed unaware – such as to render explanation impossible; such as to evoke the same monsters of the soul that Samuel – now assisted by the sun suddenly reflecting on the surface of the eyes in that drawn face – was sure he perceived.

"I..." he said.

"I don't want to die alone, Samuel."

"Of course not."

"It's my last wish... the last wish on Earth of a poor man like me. To abandon this violated retreat and re-embrace my only son," said Pac, releasing a small, transparent drop that coursed down his cheek, hesitated at the corner of his fleshy mouth, then resumed its descent, down to his chin, whence it was wiped off with the back of his hand.

A tear that hadn't in the least impinged on the composure of Pac's intensity.

Samuel, overcome by a sense of impotence and by a vague, empathic sorrow, felt the urgent need to compensate.

"I... I didn't know you had a son!"

"I'm sorry, I should have told you. It's a long and complicated story, but I can't bring myself to talk about it.

Forgive me, I just can't."

"You needn't apologise. Seriously. My dear friend, this throws an entire new light onto the matter. Of course I'll help you, how could I refuse? Good Heavens, a son is a son!" said Samuel, smiling, watching for a reaction which finally came about, healing Pac's anguish and drawing forth sighs of relief.

"I'm really grateful to you," said Pac weakly, nodding, the lines on his face relaxing as he gazed up at the clear sky, at the boundless horizon.

Thus offering Samuel his best profile.

The pick-up was parked in the garden, and the afternoon was about to start its shift, taking over where the morning had left off. In the veranda, boxes filled with food and camping equipment.

Samuel was collecting the last few things from the living room, unsure whether he was convinced or resigned, especially as he ignored their destination.

Pac arrived from the back of the house, dragging a very long wooden plank which must have been sturdy, judging by the grimace on his sweated face.

"I can't see the use of that," said Samuel, peering out.

Pac propped one end of it on the back of the van, like an inclined ramp for wheelbarrows, toy cars – or whatever. He dusted off his hands, slapping them several times against his cargo trousers, while eyeing Samuel smugly. "I need you. Come on!" he said, before disappearing again behind the house.

Samuel approached the pick-up and started kicking out at the tyres with his gym shoes; he went round the van kicking them, one by one, emitting small grunts of approval after each inspection. Oil and fuel had already been checked, as had the various liquids, the lights and indicators; a new, citrus fruit-scented deodorant was in place, and the windscreen had been cleaned inside and out. He'd already made his farewells; from all those within reach, obviously: especially his favourite plants and trees, his path into the wood (only the entrance to it); and he'd raised his hands skyward in a pantheistic embrace that included every biological form inhabiting that small Eden. With ill-disguised bitterness, of course; but after all, he'd concluded, this was the best solution.

Pac reappeared from the same direction; or rather, his head appeared from round the corner; he glanced across, disappeared, then was back again. There seemed nothing unusual about him, as he eyed Samuel sneakily while fiddling with one arm behind his back. Not until a few moments later – five steps at a normal pace, to be precise: that's when the silhouette of a horned bovine appeared at the end of what had just revealed itself to be a rope.

The young animal had grown. As well as emitting an unmistakable odour, his cappuccino-coloured woolly coat enhanced his dimensions: almost as if he were wearing the very blankets and garments that greedy shearers could have made out of him. His mottled face was grumpy: he seemed to have guessed that this wasn't his usual – albeit belated – daily grazing.

The two trotted towards the parked van, but when they got to the ramp the animal rebelled, anchoring his legs to the ground in sign of protest, and displaying a strength that his size and weight rendered altogether justified.

To tell the truth, the yak wasn't the only one opposing the plan, Samuel being visibly displeased about Pac's admittedly noble intentions. "Where do you think you're taking that flea-ball? This isn't Noah's Ark, you know!", he yelled, arms akimbo like an old housewife.

"He's coming with us, he's part of the team," said Pac, knowing perfectly well that convincing Samuel would be far from easy.

When the confrontation started, each used the most effective rhetoric devices to bend the other to his will. Samuel accused the animal of being a potential murderer, there being a significant precedent in the speaker's recent past that saw him as the victim of gunshot; he further accused the animal of infesting, soiling, of being a vehicle of bacteria, viruses and parasites, of diseases that he could well do without. If historically the yak had never risen to the rank of domestic pet – he concluded – there must be a good reason.

Not in the least intimidated, Pac replied with a barrage of

spiritual and holistic arguments: but having got on his soapbox – and being, in fact, somewhat out of his depth – his reasoning was lame and full of flaws; though, to his own deep embarrassment, he was holding his own. His point of view embraced the idea that the goat (no mention of the fact that the yak, being a bovid, wasn't a goat at all, but merely resembled one – vaguely) was an ancestral symbol for the expiation of sins, as proved by the term "scapegoat", originally referring to a Jewish rite in which a he-goat was sacrificed for Yom Kippur. In addition, the yak represented a metaphor of change. Ever at man's side, he was an ally: not only did he alleviate man's physical hardships – which was undeniable – but also, cyclically, he provided his precious wool, at forbidding altitudes, in the season of nee. He was a faithful companion, as well as a token – like an engagement ring – of the bond between man and nature. His being present right from the outset of recent developments, therefore, couldn't be casual: he was a card played by destiny.

Around his neck, the yak carried the damned stone in its famous flame-red pouch. True, he'd shot Samuel but – as a result of that fortuitous combination of scuffle and ballistics – he had, as Samuel himself conceded, awoken the divine side of Samuel's Inner Self, or whatever. Which could be interpreted in end-of-time terms, or even as a leg in a journey of initiation. And again, thanks to the young Tibetan yak, the stone had flown from the heights of Nepal into their hands. At this, Pac paused, allowing the memory of Kimley's raid to provide the reason for the stone's disappearance; which, he knew, hurt Samuel even more than it did him.

These were all signs, not coincidences (Pac's words, again): obvious and unchallengeable evidence that the humble young animal, an unwitting actor in this story at the edge of the Apocalypse, had a precise role, had earned their company, and had a free pass backstage to the show.

As for the interested party, he would have liked to produce a number of excuses to avoid boarding that van, but he wasn't offered the chance: his defender had turned his back on him, and seemed to have crossed to the prosecution side. So he simply took one hoofed step backwards, turning his black gaze towards the nearby woods and the lush hills, which he seemed to be missing already.

Surprised and perplexed by those words and by their speaker, Samuel remained immobile, speechless, his hand on the van like a bus conductor about to comment on the validity of a bus ticket. It's hard to say which part of Pac's address had opened a breach in his position: the fact was that when he found himself pushing the animal from behind, bothered by the brushing of that hairy tail against his cheek; while Pac struggled to pull him aboard by his flea collar; when the yak emitted a desperate noise like the lament of a rusty grass-cutter trying to trim concrete; and when the animal finally released a sonorous, oily fart that burst like an intestinal bubble dangerously near his face: at that precise moment, Samuel – we were saying – had quite forgotten why he'd given way.

Finally, despite everything, they managed to accommodate the yak inside the van within a circle of cardboard boxes; and while Samuel, disgusted, ran indoors to wash himself thoroughly, Pac, ever more considerate, patted the animal reassuringly. And, but for the young bovine's further farting and lamenting (his sole indication of disappointment), the journey could have been smoother.

Their destination was announced when the door of the van was drawn to. The house grew smaller, until it disappeared from view. And to Samuel's pressing requests for more details Pac, eyes glued to the road, the sun at its zenith, merely proffered a meek "Trust me," meeting a lukewarm reception.

Indispensable ingredients for the preparation of a fine-tuned and satisfying gestation:

1 – Food

Ignoring the quantity factor – index-linked to an almost insignificant time span (days, possibly hours) – it was wise to focus on quality. More specifically, on quality that disregarded calorie, health, or nutrition-related implications; quality for taste-buds, for a hedonistic, self-indulgent suspension of self-critical willpower. To this end, regardless of provisions already hoarded, the pick-up made a stop for a single, specific circumstance: when approaching the neon sign of a small, well-stocked supermarket which – for a surprisingly short time – swallowed up Pac and his bad intentions: easily forestalled, if only one remembered not to shop for food on an empty stomach, especially after a spell of particular ill-humour.

When the cubic monster spewed out Pac and his purchases, he held, perfectly balanced, an overflowing carrier bag in each hand, immediately deposited behind their seats in the van's cabin, to the deafening screech of crushed plastic: an acute disturbance subsiding only when the packages had achieved a precarious balance, though continuing to emit the occasional isolated crackling noise. Scrumptious crisps, creamy chocolates, tantalising tea-cakes, snazzy snacks – the classic waffle of viral marketing for spruced-up over-flavoured junk food in variously-sized packaging whose total calorie count could have caused *Radio75* to burn by spontaneous combustion, if it hadn't already been clubbed to extinction. Now the hold could be declared well-stocked.

Why waste energy on sacrifices, when their physical aspect, including a natural layer of fat, would soon melt like a candle in a furnace, leaving naked the wick of their essence (provided they had one, which Pac strongly doubted)? They might as well eat, entrusting carbs with the arduous task of relieving the tension.

Needless to say he hadn't forgotten the yak, whom Pac – before returning to the driver's seat – delighted by proffering from the palm of his hand a fruit drop; this was studied and immediately lapped up by an enormous, rough, sticky tongue, while Pac's hand was brushed by the bovine's hirsute chin.

Empty car-park, clear roads, an old dog lying in the shade of a tin roof; the air hot and muggy. The world might as well be already dead.

2 – Semi-automatic *Smith & Wesson* revolver, loaded, full cylinder, and a second, fully-loaded cartridge. Plus a new box of ammunition, unopened.

The future was uncertain. If a fortuitous, unhoped-for aligning of the stars should ever determine his post-apocalyptic survival, then a weapon – for self-defence or even for attack – would be vital, more than ever. If he found it hard to open up to strangers in times of peace...

Pac's holding that weapon would imply one of two things, depending on what he aimed at: an external target, in the first case; an internal one, so to speak, in the second.

He was prepared to give up everything – Pac told himself in the silence of the cabin, negotiating an uphill hairpin bend flanked by towering trees – except the control of his own life. He was a free, evolved and intelligent being; he was responsible and independent. And his independence and responsibility placed him first and foremost in command of his own will. No-one had the moral authority to forbid or, worse still, manoeuver this control: no pope, imam, prophet, burning bush, reverend or allegedly enlightened being. Far less some poor sod with public duties: some bureaucrat or functionary. Let alone philosophers, scientists or shamans. The inestimable value of his own existence was grasped firmly inside his sweaty hands; as was the steering wheel at that precise moment, while he steered his life, his pick-up and what little future he had left. So long as he safeguarded his lucidity, his determination and free will, this essential asset would remain within his own unchallengeable jurisdiction. Life was too important, special and magical to allow others to defile it; to grant undeserved faculties to systems of social control, who were themselves the very cause of the approaching epilogue.

Let others do as they liked: let them delude themselves that they'd reached joint or commonly accepted conclusions; let them even adapt unreservedly. He wasn't the 'others'.

The road was now straight, narrow, monotonous. Gravel and stones had tumbled from the rocky heights, piling up dangerously on the edge of the road. Some, small and round, had rolled to the middle, and were crushed and scattered by the van's large tyres. It was late. The sun had started its decline, and the air that blew in through the windows was growing fresh, tousling wisps of white hair around Samuel's pensive, absent face, and drying beads of sweat on Pac's brow. The passenger crouching in the back, watching with curious eyes the panorama as it unfolded, tree after tree, bend after bend, was delighted, finding in the ever-cooler temperature incomparable relief.

The possession of a gun at the right moment – assuming Pac had the hoped-for chance to be aware of what was happening – would enable him to choose whether to die by his own hand and considered intention; a moment before becoming a victim, before undergoing an altogether premature, unjustified, unreasonable and unavoidable death. The mere thought caused Pac to jerk the steering-wheel abruptly, almost rendering these cogitations superfluous. He'd have liked… he'd worked so hard – years of efforts and sacrifices – the solution had been within his hand's reach; but on balance, and through no fault of his own, he'd failed. Driving onwards, he resumed his fantasies.

The moment before he pulled the trigger. The moment that all hell broke loose: fire, thunder, the ground quaking underfoot; cries in the distance, possibly; visions of Jesus and the apostles in period garb; bomber formations, explosions, giant flying saucers. That precise, hard-fought, most intense of moments: when the dense, muggy air impeded breathing; when sulphur stung the eyes; when every human being on Earth shared an unequivocal sense of guilt and defeat, and the single, mind-numbing perception of being about to be dismembered, to die atrociously, to have their brains reset to non-thinking mode, to be traversed from ear-drums to soul by the sole harrowing truth of damnation.

That was the single, delimited instant, Pac was sure, when he would love with all his heart, as he'd never been able to in his whole life: a sentiment of such compassionate pity, empathy and intensity – so overflowing and explosive as to be uncontainable – as to kill him. Kneeling down on a rock of ember warmth, the barrel of his gun at his temple or, better still, in his mouth (the metal cool against his tongue in that last farewell); while everything succumbed to a higher force, be it the nature of the Universe, a colonising power, or Nothingness (which after all was another supreme element). There, right there, in the sudden, all-enveloping silence, as he pulled the trigger with a sudden start of his finger, he would savour his individuality, his power, his determination in choosing to be the master of his own destiny: fuck fate! When and how he left the scene was up to him to decide. Yes, his *Smith & Wesson* was probably the key ingredient.

3 – Bag of sweets, previously emptied and filled with pills (another must, after food and a gun).

The pills that activated Pac Man's super-powers: flashing, intermittent, not-yet stroboscopic. Various amphetamines, tranquillisers (to be on the safe side); and especially LSD. Difficult to combine with a gun, but he'd see about that when the time came.

The upside of a bullet in his throat was the poetry, the extreme freedom and joy of irrationality; at least, that was how he planned it. He'd choose between gun and pill. The former, rational and dramatic: the latter a little less so, but decidedly more fun. What a riot it would be, at the first signs of the end of time, to down a pill and start seeing and perceiving things in a manner that was, shall we say, 'different'? The best farewell in history. Laughing, jumping about, turning up to mind-boggling levels the volume of all his senses – hearing, smell, eyesight (oh, eyesight!): these would suffice. And possibly garnering further insight, receiving information, amplifying the spectrum of his learning. And who knows: maybe, in the process of abandoning one's body, one could gain access to channels otherwise precluded and denied, tunnels of escape towards dimensions in which a different salvation was plausible.

At which point, anything could be possible, and welcome.

Another hairpin bend, the engine of the pick-up going full-throttle; the scent of resin, the waft of a warm breeze.

Dissolving in a barrel of boiling perceptions: bathing in the sultry waters of a colourful river alive with splendid scaly creatures. Oh, what a fine way to go! He'd suggest sharing this final experience with his companions, all together – and how could they refuse! At which point any reflection would be vain, as would any sense of bitterness, danger or fear, wiped out and redefined by the translucent, four-dimensional spectacle unfolding before their spellbound eyes; until their death which, at that point, would hail not in the form of the grim reaper, but in the more engaging guise of, say, a harlequin; or maybe an astronaut. They wouldn't even notice its appearance, much less their own passing away, as they side-stepped in kaleidoscopic abstraction, with a smile and a tear in their eye, what would have been – for everyone else – unspeakable suffering.

Was there a more intriguing prospect than kicking open the doors of perception just as they were about to close, locked and chained?

"Nearly there. Not long to go now," Pac said. Stealing a glance at the rear-view mirrors, he slowed down gently and steered into a dirt track.

Samuel nodded, closed his window and fastened the top button of his tartan shirt. Looking tired and lost, he reclined against his headrest.

4 – Music. A must, and Pac had brought his entire rave collection; plus chill-out and rock classics for moments of relaxation.

5 – Rechargeable batteries and solar-powered battery charger.

6 – A bag of grass.

No, not for the yak. He'd have plenty, where they were heading.

Grass for smoking, to ease rough come-downs.

Would Samuel like that, seeing as he had a thing about

plants? Or would he find his proposal indecent and be offended? Bah.

7 – Bottled water galore. Blankets. Lighters. Sleeping bags. Camping stove and a small saucepan. Other stuff, of little relevance.

Pac drew the handbrake and turned off the engine in the middle of nowhere, right where the shrubbery concealed a footpath.

"Here we are. We'll have to proceed on foot."

The ascent was steep, and more arduous than Pac remembered. Only the jagged rocks, shrubs, long-leafed plants – and twigs, scattered on the ground as if by a cyclops with a passion for Pick-up Sticks – seemed at ease here. And the yak.

Pac was short of breath. Once the sun had dispelled the memory of the breeze blowing through the van windows, his backpack was weighing him down. Stumbling, straining his legs and swearing, he battled on, animated by the burning desire to play the last chip of this gamble, the one that would result in his being ushered out of the main entrance of the casino with a cartload of banknotes, or out of the rear exit, with a kick in the backside.

Samuel, walking ahead to set the pace, was already blue in the face and wondering what on earth he was doing there, beyond a none-too-clear involvement in a family reunion. On this, Pac had maintained the strictest reserve, but had mentioned something about a surprise, some uncertainties, and the hope to find his son at his latest known address. And as they proceeded further along that out-of-the-way path in the wood – which in other circumstances Samuel would have been glad to contemplate – Samuel couldn't help asking himself where the hell the young man lived.

Their enforced halts had become frequent, and poor Samuel (who'd already unbuttoned his shirt) was so drenched with sweat that his handkerchief was useless; he volunteered to wait for Pac on the spot, insisting that it was wiser for one of them to remain near the van, since it was risky to leave it unattended. After all – he reasoned – it wasn't so long since he'd been discharged from hospital – despite his glorious past as a healthy astronaut. He was getting on, and didn't feel up to such vigorous exertion (avoiding any mention of his excursions on certain forbidden mountains in Nepal). He'd slip off his rucksack, placing his weight on his thighs and arching his back, to give his lungs some respite; but each time, Pac would help him up and, encouraging him, place him again at the head of their convoy.

He was well aware of the limitations of old age. But they had almost arrived at their destination. One step at a time, huffing and puffing, gritting their teeth, gaining more ground.

Light and shadow alternated, the difference in

temperature immediately perceived where their skin was exposed. The shade emitted the pungent aromas of the soil, of the crushed moss, undergrowth, mushrooms: a fragrance that teased the nostrils, wafting up from the carpet of grass and recently-fallen leaves, and spreading around as boots and hooves left their tracks behind them. The caramel quality of the light; the pollen of flowers; bark; aromas of warmed rocks and dried compost. The cocktail of fragrant molecules circulated and mingled in the drift of low gusts of wind; the same that the yak sniffed and discerned as, step after step, he was gently led by his tether. Odours new and rediscovered: of predators, of water, of droppings; of the two men ahead of him; of food that he'd have liked to consume.

The sun was setting behind the tall trees when Samuel collapsed, exhausted, feeling dirty and unkempt. He'd made his decision: he wouldn't move a single inch. He took the bottle of water proffered and emptied it in long draughts; he poured some into the palm of his hand and rubbed his face. Then he lay down on that small grassy clearing whence a charming view could be enjoyed: they'd risen in altitude, and now commanded valleys and peaks, infinite open spaces.

He didn't even have enough breath or strength to announce his decision, when Pac said: "We're here."

This, and a fifteen minutes' break, had partly recharged Samuel's moribund batteries, so he staggered to his feet, his sweat now dried by a gentle, refreshing breeze.

Having tied the yak to the trunk of an old tree, Pac headed towards the mouth of the small cave. For a moment he felt anguished, as if a ball of thorns were rolling inside his belly, tracing ample concentric rings. A long moment's silence, a shiver of cold sweat as he stood mid-way between Samuel, the yak and the cave – and the sky. There was a lump in his throat of something he struggled to swallow, perhaps the very nature of the fear that hung in the air he was obliged to breathe.

A sense of the End: that feeling of evanescent guilt, of inexorable doom?

Somehow he managed to shake off the sensation.

"You don't mean to say your son lives here?"

"Sorry?"

"You want me to believe that your son, your flesh and blood, lives in there? In that dirty hole in a mountain in the middle of nowhere? What is he, a hermit?"

"Listen, I must tell you something."

"I hope for your sake that... What sort of a parent would leave a child in a place like this? How old is he, for God's sake?"

"I've no idea, Samuel. The fact is..."

"You don't know how old your son is?"

"He's not my son."

"What? What do you mean? You expressly declared – I remember perfectly well – your indisputable (and quite touching), desire to re-embrace your son. You implored me to accompany you, not to let you die alone. So what is it now?"

"I meant that I love him like a son. It's the same thing."

"Not at all! It's not even remotely the same bloody thing, damn it!"

"Calm down. Listen, it makes no difference any more, we're here. Just forget it."

"What do you mean, forget it? You dragged me all the way up here!"

"But we're perfectly well organised, as you know. We have everything we need. And when I tell you why we came to this particular place, you'll be grateful. Trust me."

"But..."

"Look where I brought you, look at the view. Look over there, my dear Samuel, precisely in that direction."

"And what's so interesting, over there? Apart from thin air, and a few distant ridges?"

"You'll soon find out. Now I'll introduce you to a friend. Someone I'm very fond of, in a way."

"In a way."

"Exactly. Come with me."

"And who the hell is he, this friend of yours?"

"I don't know exactly who he is. All I know is that he spends all his time here."

"I'm speechless."

"The thing is, nothing seems to disturb him. Nothing at

all, believe me."

"I..."

"Come on. The important thing is, we're here – and the show hasn't started yet."

Before entering, Pac turned around, savouring a landscape in which your gaze could roam in any direction, unhindered. *He* was there, as usual. It took Pac's eyes a moment to adjust to the semi-darkness and see him clearly. A weak light filtered through the rock, revealing the irregular geometry of the space, redolent of damp and moss.

Placid, immobile, sitting cross-legged on a straw mat.

The first thing Pac noticed was that, oddly, there was no sign of the orange tunic he used to wear, and the effect was remarkably different. He was even thinner than last time: his bones could have been catalogued during an exposition on anatomy; he only wore a red loin cloth, the rest of his body resembled a hairy mass on an assembly of sticks. Against his hairy chest he wore the same chain, with the same lock – like some sacred golden medal. A thick, black beard and astonishingly long hair partially obscured his features, which evoked some delightful Peruvian hamlet abandoned, for some mysterious motive, centuries ago. What little of his face was visible, however, was perfectly eloquent: sunken eye-sockets surrounded by thin lines, perceptible only on closer examination; those eye-sockets held eyes never seen before, and which were now open – very wide open.

This was the second thing Pac noticed.

He stood frozen on the spot, mouth agape, his breathing arrested. This was nothing compared to how he felt inside: stunned, unable to decide what to do, not daring to move at all. This was the first time he'd seen those eyes open; two deep-set hazelnuts, scrutinising him with such magnetic attention that he felt naked, wretched, as if scanned by an imperceptible radar that penetrated his skin and flesh, searching, noting emotions and reactions. He had the disturbing sensation that the man was somehow exploring his mind: like a creature so evolved that it had learned to discern by sense of smell whether something was edible, harmless or threatening. Not a pleasant sensation, yet Pac was in no condition to do anything about it, especially as he was a guest. Moreover, he didn't know whether that fixed, impassive gaze – half-disturbing, half-hypnotic – harboured any trace of resentment for Pac's past 'antics': those wild, regenerating parties of ecstatic rebirth. Outrageous trespassing, one might be inclined to call them.

The third thing he noticed should more logically have been the first, if Pac's brain hadn't refused to register it at a conscious level. Possibly through a self-defence mechanism – though your guess is as good as mine – it was only in that disturbing moment that he realised that Oscar was holding close against his chest a small rectangular blackboard. On which he'd written something.

From where he stood Pac, seized with anxiety, tried to decipher the totally illegible writing, which became intelligible only after he'd recognised its style: that of primary school children. So rounded, orderly and ornate as to look outdated these days, when no-one any longer wrote by hand.

And when he'd finally read the message, and understood what it implied, Pac felt – as if he'd been hit by a vertical thunderbolt of urgency – the immediate need to escape.

"*I was waiting for you,*" it said.

There was something momentous in the dense atmosphere of that cave, something seemingly capable of arresting time while accelerating his breathing and heart-beat. The semi-darkness that enveloped the figure of Oscar, revealing few but eloquent details of his face, was what made Pac hesitant. Afraid of disrupting that inertia to which he was just beginning to become accustomed – and wondering whether he should expect to be attacked with a sudden feline pounce, to be bitten in the neck or whatever – he found the courage to take one step backwards and, moving with surreal slowness, turned to Samuel and pushed him forward.

"Hello," said Samuel smiling, "pleased to meet you."

Oscar picked up a rag which he kept within hand's reach on the ground, near his knee, and wiped the blackboard clean. Moving with a calm and grace seemingly alien to the human race, he let tumble to one side his mass of black hair, the ends twisted into dreadlocks.

Pac and Samuel watched in silence, even when Oscar took a white chalk from the side opposite to the rag and started to write, inducing Pac to cut short the list of things he hadn't noticed.

"*I was waiting for you as well*," announced the blackboard, now clutched against Oscar's chest – his words traced in that same childish handwriting, evoking distant memories – as he looked across at Samuel with a peaceful expression.

Samuel and Pac looked at one another at length, as if searching for something magical to explain that which eluded them, and which at heart they couldn't believe existed. But Oscar's stick fingers were already busy erasing that message and replacing it with another, evidently addressed to Samuel, who stood there transfixed.

"*You are the god I was waiting for*," it said.

Pac froze.

In a silence, as if within padded-walls, Samuel – who was seen to be weeping like some Balkan Madonna – risked a hesitant step towards the now smiling Oscar. Samuel's was a silent, spellbound weeping, releasing bright tears. With lips half open, he seemed to be in the throes of an emotion that had taken him unawares, and which rendered his body momentarily absent and meaningless. His red face had relaxed, his tears were of a rare joy that perhaps he'd never expected to feel: an enraptured happiness irradiated from his eyes to meet others, equally moist, returning a message of ineffable love, of grace; an echo of fulfilment, of symmetry achieved, of electrifying, unleashed exhilaration.

The two seemed to be spiralling around one another like new-born butterflies after a for-ever promise exchanged while still inside contiguous cocoons. They wept and they smiled.

Pac thought he might go and pet the yak, who'd been left outside, all alone. But just as he'd quietly lifted one foot from the ground, hoping not to be noticed; just as he was gulping down an uneasy sensation that tightened his throat, and was shifting his trunk – with movements slowed to the limits of perception – towards the safety exit: at that precise moment something happened that would alter his mental equilibrium for ever.

Oscar, from sitting immobile as Pac had known him (and as his mind willed him to remain), leaned forward, arms outstretched, until he touched the ground first with his forehead, then with the palms of his hands with their extraordinary nails; there was a clang as the metal lock hit the rock floor.

At this, Samuel traversed with wavering steps the short distance separating them; then, crouching, he took Oscar's hand and caressed his head. Oscar straightened up and their eyes met again. Samuel broke out in a deep, sonorous laugh that boomed in the depth of the cave, deafening Pac; and was joined by Oscar's equally loud laughter, which spread all around him tears of mirth.

One of these landed on Pac's hand, just as he was calculating the distance and the speed necessary to make his escape, because all of this was simply too much. He was sufficiently terrified to consider taking to his heels immediately, without a thought of how heavy and stiff he felt; of how much tar coursed through his veins. Or how inefficient the antifreeze in his head was, considering that his brain was trying to tell him that this wasn't for real: that it must be a joke (a bad one), or that he was dreaming. And that he could wake up, if only he'd realise that he had to get out of there, to save himself. Forget the end of time: hop on the yak's back. Spend the rest of your life trying to forget it all.

Having exhaled to the best of his momentarily-impaired ability, he was forced to breathe in a bare minimum: enough to ensure his survival, while endeavouring to prevent his chest movements from disturbing the telepathic idyll of the other two.

It was noticed, however, by both.

As Oscar started writing: *"Stop! Where are you going?"*, Samuel ran to Pac.

"My dear, my special friend. This is the best gift I could ever receive. Seriously. You can't imagine how happy I was... Oh, this was such a surprise!"

Pac looked at him, mystified.

"Stay, please. You were right. Oh, you were so right. Now we really can wait for the end. The end of it all. The cycle is concluded, you see? The truth has been revealed. This is the end!"

"I..." Pac was about to speak, but Samuel intervened.

"Thank you... thank you... thank you," repeated Samuel, embracing him. Pac, in a daze, would have liked to remain enfolded indefinitely.

When he managed to regain lucidity, he was determined to ignore – to ignore everything. That was the best thing to do: mind his own business, somehow or other. While the other two were still inside, immersed in their confab, he was stroking the yak, unable to remember how he'd ever got there; or how long ago.

Time, time! Fuck.

It made no sense to remain bogged down with things he couldn't explain, about which he couldn't care less. He was there for a precise reason. Rooting in the side pocket of his trousers he fished out a herbal sweet, then noticed the mottled-faced yak observing him with what he saw as endearing fondness; so he placed the sweet on a stone and covered it with the palm of his hand. The animal immediately nudged it gently with its moist, hairy muzzle, eyeing him sidelong: it was their little game. Pac's hand lingered briefly over the sweet, until an oversized, dribbling tongue licked it; and so it was appropriated.

Pac straightened up again and observed the immensity extended before his eyes: more specifically, he focused his attention on a strategic cardinal point. A whiff of fresh air on his face, his thoughts swept away, an all-pervasive silence. Then a sense of power, a shudder; and a sigh, as he felt a pang in his stomach. He must hurry.

He ran to the entrance of the cave, took a deep breath and walked in. He was ready.

The two were sitting facing one another. Oscar hadn't moved from his position.

"Here you are!" exclaimed Samuel.

"We must get ready," responded Pac, his tone never more serious. "Or rather, I don't know about you – I don't even want to know – but I must get ready. I didn't come here for nothing."

Oscar took up his blackboard. "*I know*," he wrote. The twinkle in his eyes reflecting the smile beneath his beard.

For Pac (and for all we know), this was and should remain a great way to await the end of the world as we know it. Pending the first signs that would soon be manifesting themselves out there, in the sky, in the direction of Mount Megiddo.

Har Megiddo.

Armageddon.

That, Pac told himself, was the last sign of the times.

EPILOGUE

Dawn was near. Birdsong could be heard from the fading darkness all around; or the flurry of early flights, flitting quickly between the branches of the trees: melodious songs and sounds arousing the day after its night's slumber – or other occupations. And had that orchestra of miniscule praises not been able to make itself heard, that soft shade of purple would have served to announce something new, something different, from its position obliquely opposite to where Pac sat cross-legged. Rising slowly, the incandescent plum set the whole, vast and gloriously visible horizon on fire. A light that, from timid and opaque, grew clean and distinct, transmitting brilliance to the periphery of its field of action as it widened, flaring like an immense ring of burning petrol on a floating platform.

Pac's eyes were open. He was smoking a joint and was near the cardboard filter. A box of assorted chocolates lay casually open at his side, its shiny golden surface now becoming alabastrine, as were the tin-foil wrappers of the few remaining chocolates: red, green, blue, silver. The chessboard of a game already ended.

Pac took a drag – ember heat on his fingers – and held it in. Then, without turning, he picked up a rectangular chocolate draughtsman. It was green, reminding him of those insects that stink when you tread on them. Unfortunate comparison, he thought. His gaze fixed on the brightness, on the dissipating haze, the hint of a smile suggesting an all-embracing gratification.

The music persisted at his back, spewed from the mouth of the cave and only recently turned down to a less overpowering volume. Empire of House, volume 5.

Nothing had happened yet; no warning signs of the Apocalypse, no destruction, no implosion. Nothing yet. He might as well continue his vigil, his exclusive party, his bittersweet celebration. And Pac Man needed a new flashing pill; too many ghosts, too many hollow-eyed sheets floating around, aloof, silent: for all he knew they might come after him, surround him, entrap him.

Fuck, no!

From the side pocket of his trousers he fished out a bag of sweets, impatience compelling him to take one, squeeze it between two fingers and gobble it down, without even looking. A bitter taste, a draught of water, a chocolate, another drag. Perfect sequence.

And light invaded the air, expanding, irradiating an intimate testimony, a lucid perception of being there, at that precise moment: of being alive.

Pac remained still, occasionally moistening his lips, savouring the warmth on his skin.

When suddenly a sensation in his throat induced him to gulp repeatedly: he was starting, he was ready, he nodded to himself. Then he saw Oscar and Samuel: they were at his side. They too were sitting on the grass; one held his blackboard et cetera; the other, Pac was surprised to notice, had brought the yak with him and (Pac now realised) was holding him securely by a tether. They all crouched there, in a half-circle, observing the rising sun, music at their back. A family reunited, a heterogeneous complicity, that's how Pac saw it. And he smiled: and they all smiled.

Oscar wrote something, with never-ending slowness.

Pac had never seen Oscar outside that cave and – for reasons he'd rather not investigate – found it hard even to accept that he was capable of leaving it. Yet his presence out there was of a beauty difficult to fathom, to define in thought. He was. Full stop. And in the early sunlight the golden lock hanging from his neck was (oh my God!) an Incas talisman activated by the spring equinox on the walls of that temple-body. Filthy, of an outward filth devoid of any relevance; oblivious of the unnecessary; candid and immaculate in secluded regions which others perceived as important throughout their lives, though they didn't pause to investigate.

"*That music isn't bad, thank you,*" it read.

Pac knew he should answer, one way or another. So he smiled, offering everything he had: chocolates, sweets, water. Should he roll another joint? But all his offers were turned down with a startling and very white smile, illuminating that hirsute face, with the dry skin and the frizzy black hair.

"I know a good blacksmith," Pac said, indicating the shiny chain.

While waiting for an answer he gulped again. He had to drink, so he sipped water from the bottle from which Samuel had just drunk.

"How far have we got?" Pac asked him.

Samuel, unshaven, said nothing but looked up towards the sky; then towards the lateral light of the rising sun.

"I can't answer that," he replied at last drowsily.

They'd been up all night, busy with multiple activities, all to the throbbing of electronic music pumped up full blast.

Pac turned towards Oscar, who seemed to have finished writing.

"*I need it when I open my eyes, to remind me of my existential condition,*" announced the blackboard, in handwriting reduced to fit the space.

Pac felt the beginnings of a genuine smile. It was so good to be there with these people! He'd have liked to ask them some questions, go inside and change the CD, then resume where they'd left off.

He would investigate, satisfy his curiosity, use up the chalks; he would run around and find pebbles with which to write, if necessary: he'd start up discussions, provoke; he might even tease, gently – for hours or for a whole day, between a joint and a snack, why not?

That's what he would have liked: but suddenly he saw lightning streaking across overhead, cleaving a cloud in two, and shooting off in a flash, like a rocket (perhaps it was a rocket?) Then he heard a distant rumble, growing ever nearer: a sound like a giant percolator with a hole in it, dull and powerful, that shook the ground and seemed to be racing beneath him. The noise became a piercing whistle that obliged him to block his ears, inducing his heart to pound and arresting his breathing. Next, a devastating light exploded in the depth of his head (that he was now holding between his hands): instant dizziness, a sense of nausea, a momentary loss of consciousness; disorientation; all of this overpowered him, finding him defenceless.

Then it vanished.

"Jesus Christ! What was that?"

"What?"

Silence.

"This is it, then? Eh, this is it?"

Pac gulped again, his heart drumming violently; a bitter taste in his mouth, his brow burning; he was drenched in sweat all over; a fever had seeped into his eyes, which now burned, producing tears as yet restrained, a presage of some imminent disaster.

But why were the others so indifferent: why weren't they reacting? He saw them, immobile, as he turned around – everything moving jerkily, each vision sketched, each perception delayed. He frowned.

"Oh shit."

Even as he sat still, his gaze fixed straight ahead, there was something missing. His ears were muffled, noises and sounds reached him as through a funnel; and there, once again, that nauseous sensation.

The sky was tinged with orange, at first nuanced, then gradually more intense; and red, of a bright, fiery red. A burning sky, traversed by too-fast objects: two or three flashes and they were gone. Before his eyes, a mushroom sprouted in the valley far below. It grew taller and taller until it skimmed the incandescent vault, turning to ashes in the eerie silence (imputable to these events, or to his own helplessness? Pac couldn't tell).

This was it, then: the signs! Palpitations. But why only him?

"Oh fuck."

He turned: they were all immobile, smiling, staring at him.

"Oh, shit."

Oscar: very thin, half-naked.

On his other side, Samuel: white, old. What was he saying? Pac couldn't hear. And next to Samuel, the yak: was he looking at him, too? And why was he smiling?

"Oh, fuck."

From the direction of Mount Megiddo rose a column of crystal. Winged creatures flew overhead, their reflexive light-blue skin contrasting with the red sky. Holding strange objects, they sped towards the column in the distance, and were sucked into it.

What the hell was going on? Was this the End? Should he run and get his gun from his backpack? Why had the music stopped playing? Why was he the only one who...

"Oh, shit."

"Thank you for saving me," said Samuel. His azure gaze back-lit, penetrating, his eyebrows white and bushy; Pac immersed himself in those eyes, letting himself be cradled for an instant of consciousness.

On his other side, a gentle tapping on his shoulder summoned his attention. Pac turned. It was Oscar. *"Thank you for saving me,"* said the blackboard.

And Pac went out of his mind, or so he thought, unable to control, to understand; to distinguish what should be separated.

"I deserve to be the first to die." That was his own shaking voice he heard, as he turned his head, overflowing with some condensed liquid. And Pac watched as his voice poured out of his mouth: flattened, horizontal capital letters, moving away lightly and gradually crumbling into fragments that spun in the air then settled gently on the ground.

"Oh no, fuck."

The yak? Not him! The young animal raised his head – pointed horns, long muzzle, fuzzy beard – and opened his mouth:

"Thank you for saving me," Pac heard, as the bovine addressed these very words to him, in a voice that came from unfathomed depths. Reclining his head on his legs again, ears alert, he turned to gaze towards the column of crystal.

All this was impossible: it couldn't be, it wasn't as he'd imagined. Pac could neither stand nor move a muscle: his whole body was pervaded by a stifling fear, his head almost exploding with panic. He realised he was weeping; he would have liked to run, to hurl himself into the void: this couldn't be his end. Safe in some kind of hell? Was this how he'd die?

"Unless... oh fuck. No!"

"Aren't you happy?"

"Eh?"

Silence.

"No! Please say I didn't..."

"Didn't what?"

"Don't tell me I took the wrong pill!"

www.fabiocasto.it

Printed in Germany
by Amazon Distribution
GmbH, Leipzig